Dragon Lan

KESH

Glacier Lake

Marissa

Old Keep

Mtn Meadow

Mtn Pass

Terrell's

VLATHA

Blackthorn
Forest

Rope Ford

Border
Mountains

Horace Rock
(Refugee Camp)

Hunting Blind

Kesh Camp

Korvell

Elister's Abode

<-- To The Western Sea

Cree

To Fornz
|
V

CLAIRE-AGON

DIAMOND STAR
PUBLISHING

RANGER RISING

Published by Diamond Star Publishing
For information contact; Salvador@salvadormercer.com
www.salvadormercer.com

Edited by: Courtney Umphress
Book and Cover design by Christine Savoie aka 'Cagnes' c2015
Art and Stock Photo Credits:
Rodrigo Gonzalez Toledo
Interior Icons: Svetlana Shirokova | Dreamstime.com
Book Design & Typesetting by Write Dream Repeat LLC

ISBN: 1514323540

ISBN 13: 978-1514323540

First Edition: May 2015
Second Edition May 2016
10 9 8 7 6 5 4 3 2

Claire-Agon Ranger
Book One

RANGER RISING

SALVADOR MERCER

other books by
SALVADOR MERCER

CLAIRE-AGON RANGER SERIES:

Dead Druid: Claire-Agon Ranger Book 2

CLAIRE-AGON DRAGON SERIES:

The Black Dragon: A Claire-Agon Dragon Book 1
The Blue Dragon: A Claire-Agon Dragon Book 2
The Green Dragon: A Claire-Agon Dragon Book 3

SCI-FI-TECHNOTHRILLER:

Lunar Discovery

For:
Masha

CHAPTER 1

TERRELS

"Run, Targon, run!" his grandfather yelled at him.

Targon Terrel was running, and had been, for the past few hours, but the snorting of horses behind him and his family, as well as the barking of dogs, caused him to stop and turn to see what was chasing them.

"Keep up with Father," his brother, Malik, said, as a hand propelled Targon forward from the middle of his back.

"This way, quick!" his father said, leading the family back into the woods from the nearby river, which was now crawling with Kesh brigands, intent on plundering, pillaging, and killing this night.

Targon felt his bow chafing across his back as he ran. He could just see his father ahead, leading his family into the Blackthorn Forest again as they sought escape from the death that pursued them.

His mother was carrying his baby sister, Ann, in a sling across her chest, and he saw the hem of her dress sway rhythmically as she ran across the rough ground. His grandmother was helping her keep up with his father while his grandfather and brother brought up the rear.

The shouts of pursuit became louder, and the braying of dogs continued to permeate the cool air of this fall night. The family's path was sure, despite the darkness. This was the forest near their home, and they knew the area well. Tira and Sara were high overhead, peeking through the canopy of trees and casting a slight illumination upon the ground where their rays could penetrate the leaves of the forest.

"We will never make it," his grandmother, Julia, said.

"Go on now, my love, keep your wits and your bearings and stay with Dareen," his grandfather replied from behind.

Targon slowed, allowing his grandpa to catch up to him. "Will we die tonight?" Targon asked, his tone serious as he breathed heavily from the run.

"Not tonight, Tar," his grandfather said, a rare smile now crossing his face. "Your father is the best woodsman in all of Ulatha. Those Kesh scum won't stand a chance, but keep running. Go on, keep up with your mother. Malik and I will bring up the rear."

Despite the smile and calm words, Targon felt uneasy. The tenseness in his mother's voice when she woke him that night and the stern look he saw on his grandparents' faces were enough to fill him with a sense of urgency.

They ran on in silence now. The ground they covered was smooth with no tree roots or half buried rocks to slow them, despite the forest being so close to the Border Mountains. After some time, their path veered back to the west, and Targon caught sight of the old game trail and heard the roar of the Rapid River as it became louder.

"We are almost there," he heard his father say as he ran by him. His mother and grandmother now knew the way and they ran on, south along the trail near the river, with his mother still clutching his baby sister tightly. Either by luck or chance, they were fortunate that she did not cry nor utter a word. Targon could see her big blue eyes open, looking

back over his mother's shoulder as she bobbed up and down with her mother's gait.

Malik quickly overtook them and ran in front, now leading the way. There seemed to be some sort of argument between his father and his grandfather behind him as they ran, but they spoke in such hushed tones, Targon couldn't hear them clearly.

Finally they reached their goal: the roped ford. The Rapid River ran from north to south, cutting across the realm of Ulatha as it was fed from the cold, icy waters of the Border Mountains that enclosed half the valley. The river was all but impassable except for a bridge to their north a half day's journey or more. Only here, where the Terrels had put up two large braided ropes from bank to bank, could they cross safely, and only then when the river was at its lowest.

The ropes hung somewhat tautly, one at waist level and the other at shoulder level set slightly off on one side. Where the ropes crossed the river, there was a series of boulders and rocks that lay strewn across the water as it fell into a series of rapids dropping over thirty feet in a very short span. Falling into the river meant almost certain death in the rocks below.

"Watch out!" he heard his grandfather yell. A black bolt suddenly appeared in a small tree near the riverbank, just missing his mother's head.

Quickly, an arrow from his brother returned back along the game trail and hit a shadowy figure that was kneeling near a bush in an attempt to minimize its silhouette. It didn't matter against the expert eyes of a Terrel. The man uttered some sort of death cry before dropping silently onto the moist ground.

"They have crossbows," his grandmother said with a tone of defeat in her voice.

"It doesn't matter. Cross now!" his father commanded, unslinging his own bow and nocking an arrow.

"They will kill us while we cross," his grandfather said. There was a moment of silence as his parents looked at each other, and then Targon saw a frown come across his mother's face.

"No, Baldric. You can't do this alone," his mother said, approaching his father and grabbing his arms.

"You must trust me, Dareen. Take the children and get to Korwell. Alert the town. Now go, before it's too late." There was a second more of hesitation before his father turned to his grandfather. "Take them, Luc, get them across now!"

Luc turned to the family. "You heard him. Let's go . . . now!"

Malik grabbed Targon by the arm and tugged him into the icy cold water, which nearly swept Targon off his feet till he could grab the topmost rope and then sling his own bow in order to use both hands for the crossing.

His grandfather led the way, followed by his grandmother, Julia, and then his own mother with his sister, Ann, strapped to her chest so she could use both hands to cross. His older brother, Malik, brought up the rear, and as Targon crossed, he could see his father still standing guard at the large rock along the river's edge with his bow nocked with a large arrow.

A couple of crossbow bolts whizzed by their heads, and Targon could hear the zipping of the air as they passed despite the rushing noise of the water around his legs. The crossbowmen were quickly silenced by his father's bow as it answered in return but with a more accurate aim.

"Are we going to die?" Targon asked again, practically shouting to be heard above the rushing water.

"Maybe," his brother answered, perhaps a bit too honestly for Targon's taste, "but not while Father stands guard."

The crossing was just over one hundred and fifty feet, and with great relief, the Terrel family reached the western bank of the shore just in

time to hear the barking of dogs and the shouts of brigands on the opposite bank.

"Why isn't he crossing?" Targon asked.

"Draw your bow, little brother," Malik said, unslinging his own bow, nocking an arrow, and then aiming it across the river.

There was a scuffle behind him as Targon unslung his bow, mimicking the same moves his brother had just done. He could see his father move toward the ropes at the river's edge when several dogs jumped over an old log and down the riverbank to attack him.

"No!" he heard his mother scream from behind.

"Shoot, little brother!" Malik said, unleashing his first arrow into a leaping dog that appeared more like a wolf than one of Ulatha's domesticated species. The arrow ran true, and its impact hurled the dog down onto the ground as the force of the arrow arrested the dog's momentum in midair.

Targon saw another wolf-like dog coming up from farther down the river, and he shot, leading the animal a good few feet to account for its speed as well as the distance involved, just as his father had taught him. The arrow struck home, and the animal fell dead instantly.

Targon saw his mother, but without his sister, slosh back into the river as she grabbed the ropes and tried to return to the east bank. He looked back as he removed another arrow from his quiver and saw his grandmother holding Ann, who was hidden beneath a small blanket. Only her feet stuck out to indicate she was even there.

His grandfather, Luc, lunged after his mother and grabbed her before she could get more than a few feet, wrapping his large arms around her small waist and holding her tightly. He heard the familiar twang of his brother's bow as another arrow was dispatched to the far bank of the river. "Again, brother, protect Father!" Malik yelled as he reached for another

arrow, never taking his eyes off his father, either oblivious to or simply disregarding their mother's own actions.

Targon nocked another arrow and watched fascinated as his father dropped his own bow and removed his large axe from his belt.

He swung the heavy weapon effortlessly and dispatched the last of the two wolf dogs that attacked him. Several brigands suddenly appeared at the top of the small bank silhouetted against the pale dark sky. They would not make that mistake again as two of the brigands dropped dead from arrows by the Terrel brothers.

Several more suddenly ran down the small embankment and, with weapons drawn, engaged Targon's father. "Let me go, Father," his mother exclaimed as she struggled to cross the river.

His baby sister must have decided that this was enough as she started to cry a high-pitched squeal that could be heard above the sounds of combat and death and the roaring of the water. "Come back, Dareen," his grandmother pleaded.

His mother started to cry, not a loud cry of self pity but a softer sound of oncoming despair as his father, Baldric, engaged the brigands. Instantly three of them fell along the bank as two died from arrows and the third was almost cleaved in half from the large wood axe that his father wielded as if it were a light branch.

Several more brigands breached the bank top and streamed down to the shore while a few more aimed crossbows across the river. Soon the air was filled with the whizzing of missiles as arrows flew from the west and bolts flew from the east. One such bolt struck his grandfather in the leg as he turned to use his body to protect Dareen, his own daughter. Luckily the bolt dropped in flight due to the distance it had traveled, but Targon was sure they would adjust their aim higher for their next volley.

The attack lulled for just a second when the crossbow-wielding bandits turned their attention to Baldric instead of his family across the riverbank. Baldric had lightning-quick reflexes as he knocked two bolts

down from midair, but the third and fourth struck home. One bolt hit him in his left arm, and the other penetrated his leather tunic, embedding itself deep into his chest.

Dareen screamed as she and her father shook the ropes. "Cross now, Baldric, cross now!" Targon heard his mother yelling.

There was a renewed attack when the brigands saw that the ferocious woodsman was seriously wounded. This was a serious mistake. Three more fell to his axe, and Malik was relentless as he nocked another arrow and took a crossbowman out that was standing on top of the bank aiming down at his father. The bolt released errantly and wounded an attacking brigand down at the river's shore.

"Throw me an arrow, quick!" Malik ordered, apparently out of his own arrows as he nocked his last missile.

Before Targon could comply, there was an eerie silence. Only the roaring of the river and the muffled cry of his little sister could be heard. Targon looked for another target but then focused on his father. What was he doing?

Baldric had stepped back into the water, still facing the brigands, who had also paused when their last attack failed. With a slow determination, Targon watched as his father turned his back on them and faced his family across the river. Targon locked eyes with his father for only a split second before his gaze was released, and he knew his parents were looking at each other.

His axe came up high overhead and, swinging a full half circle, Baldric brought the metal weapon down with such force upon the stanchions that were lodged into the large boulder holding the ropes taut. The blow was so fierce that not only did it sever the ropes at their base but the axe lodged into the large boulder as sparks flew in all directions.

Several bolts tore into Baldric's body as a couple of brigands also lunged forward, stabbing him in his chest. With powerful arms, Baldric

yanked both brigands clean off their feet and pulled back as all three of them fell into the dark, raging river.

Targon attempted to scream in horror, but he couldn't hear himself over the piercing cry of his mother as he slowly watched his father's body, accompanied by two flailing brigands, plunge down the rapids and out of sight.

Then a pale green mist like an eerie fog floated from the forest and down to the river's edge as the brigands suddenly started to scream in terror and pain. The sound of trees falling and leaves being pulled from their branches by the thousands permeated the air above the roar of the water and the scream of Targon's mother.

Soon the entire eastern bank was enveloped in a sickly green fog and nothing could be seen, but the cries of terror from the brigands were replaced by screams of death and pain from the far shore. Targon stood in both fascination and shock as he listened to the breaking of tree trunks, the sounds of death, and an ungodly roar before he felt a strong arm grasp him by his collar.

"Time to go, little brother," Malik said.

"But Father . . ." Targon said.

"Father is gone. He saved us from the Kesh brigands, but we can't stay here. Time to go," Malik said.

Targon loosened his iron grip on his bow and slung it across his back again, re-quivering his arrow. Pulled by his brother, he saw his mother sobbing as his grandfather limped at her side, supporting her despite having a crossbow bolt sticking from his leg. His grandmother led the way with Ann along the small river trail they rarely used. They crested the bank, and with one last look, Targon saw the fog across the river dissipating in the moonlight. He turned his back, and as the river was lost from sight, he heard one last roar of defiance come from the forest across the river, a roar he would never forget.

CHAPTER 2

KESH

Seven Years Later

The air was crisp in the morning as dawn slowly approached at their backs. The three men stood on the edge of a cliff in the Felsic Mountains, which the locals simply referred to as the Border Mountains. They were aptly named as they cut across two realms of Agon. To the east was Kesh, a semiarid, chaotic land of lawlessness and danger. It was once a land of a great civilization based on a highly intelligent and functioning but benevolent Magocracy, or "rule by the wisest wizard."

Of course, there were not supposed to be any wizards left in Agon, not after the Great Dragon War a millennium ago. The war devastated Kesh, which was once a large, bustling realm of artisans, educators, philosophers, and, of course, magicians who lived in relative peace and harmony with their fellow man.

Until one particular wizard, the High Arch-Mage of Kesh, Am-Torra, who was proud, greedy, and more than a bit haughty, changed all that. *It was said* it was he who wanted not only the gold of the great dragon

drakes of the North but their many plunders as well, including books, scrolls, and other artifacts with powerful spells and magics entombed within them. *It was said* he undertook a great journey to the North, where they plundered and killed several large drakes before returning with their spoils. The remaining dragons, angered by this heinous act, took to the skies and, in an unprecedented act of war, took out the entire kingdom of Kesh, burning it into utter ruin, and, in this event, destroyed the High Arch-Mage of Kesh, Ke-Torra himself, or, at least, that was what the stories said.

There were many collateral actions as well, where most of the remaining realms, in an attempt to assist Kesh and protect themselves, perished in the dragon wars to follow. Blinded by rage, the dragons destroyed all in their path, but this same rage also brought about their doom as it appeared all of the dragons also perished by the hands of great wizards and elite warriors.

The phrase *it was said* was often used because right after the great Dragon-Wizard War, the transit event of Dor Akun occurred in its two hundred year cycle. Great tidal waves and earthquakes quickly finished what little was left of the many great civilizations of Claire Agon. Thus, for the last thousand years, most, if not all, of the great achievements of the civilized realms of Agon were lost to mankind, and a sort of barbaric Dark Age encompassed the land. Centers of learning and lore, great libraries and universities were utterly destroyed between the two events, and while written records either ceased to exist or became very rare indeed, facts were passed on from father to son and from mother to daughter. Facts became legends, and in time, some legends became myths, and so the dangerously reduced population of Agon started anew, settling in ruined strongholds and cities, repairing what they could, yet failing to build much of anything new.

Farming and hunting, the old ways of Agon before the great civilizations formed now, returned to take over as hunters and gatherers

rebuilt. Each time the "Death World" approached, the myths and legends would become real once again, but with each passing of Dor Akun, the inhabitants of Claire Agon adapted and became a bit stronger, not just to survive the event, but the rush of charged particles *changed* them. The event was marked over and over again, and in time, some prepared for it. Some even welcomed it.

And so it was that on a certain morning, high above the world on a cliff of the Border Mountains, stood three men. They were dressed differently from the many men below them along the ancient trade road. They wore cloaks of red, gold, and black, and each man had a staff with some sort of stone or gem set in the top of it. The staves were metallic, and oddly enough, the men wore pointed hats with some small tassels around the edges: however, each man was clearly of a different age. One was elderly, the other mature, and the third a young adult.

The other men below them wore black leather boots, burlap trousers, and cloth tunics. Most had cloaks, also black, with hoods covering their swarthy faces. They stood taller than most other inhabitants of Agon and more slender, with wicked curved blades, crossbows, slings, and spears. They marched westward from Kesh over the ancient mountain pass, which was once blocked completely due to earthquakes and tidal forces of the last transit event, but recently had been cleared and, in many places, augmented to allow for large lock carts to be brought by horses and oxen. The lock carts all had iron bars welded together to form an iron cage with a lone gate at the rear. They were all empty now, but they had not yet fulfilled their purpose.

Upon crossing the high mountain pass, the supply train continued its slow but steady approach into the next realm, the realm of Ulatha, and there was to be no warning of their arrival.

At the pass itself, many of the black-clothed men worked on erecting a wooden wall twelve feet high with wooden square towers at either end of a double wooden gate. The wall ended on either side by reaching the

mountain cliffs of the pass so that the only way through the wall was the main gate, sandwiched between the two towers. Each tower had a square vaulted roof attached to it for shelter and shade, though the weather was cool and crisp as spring had just arrived and winter was quickly retreating. The tower roofs and the main gate were not quite finished yet, but the main wall spanning nearly two hundred feet was complete. Several other black-clothed men stood at either end of the wall and gate and looked around intently.

"Is everything in order?" asked the oldest looking of the three men as he leaned on his staff and looked at the other two, his bushy white eyebrows slightly raised.

"Yes, Am-Ohkre," said the mature man, moving his own staff to his other hand. "Hork is preparing the troops for an assault at dawn tomorrow. We should be in position by then."

Am-Ohkre looked at the mature man who just answered him, taking a moment to lower his eyebrows but never blinking. "Careful, Ke-Tor, that the Ulathans do not detect our presence before then. We do not have enough resources for our attack if they are prepared. Manpower is in short supply," he said, nodding to the many brigands working below them.

"We will camp by day at the old keep at the base of the trade road," Ke-Tor said, motioning far below at the valley floor with a quick move of his staff in his right hand. "By sundown today, we will be ready to move out and set the ambush before dawn tomorrow. Ulatha will be ours."

"I hope so," replied the elder man. "Is your apprentice Khan ready for the task? He looked at the young man standing beside Ke-Tor.

Ke-Tor stepped back to allow Khan to see Am-Ohkre. "Well?" Ke-Tor asked, arching his own brow.

"Yes, Master, I look forward to my duty," Khan said in deference to his mentor, continuing to fondle his necklace. "Do you want me to lead the assault on the Ulathan capital?"

"No, stay with the train and make sure no one raises an alarm," Am-Ohkre responded, interrupting Ke-Tor before he could respond. "The fools built homesteads east of their capital. There are farmers and other peasants spread out all along the Gregus River on the west bank. We must slip through them first during the night. In fact, one fool built their hovel east of the river near the Earlstyne Forest. The entire area is infested with them. See to it that members of your company take care of them first."

"I will, Master," Khan said, looking down at the valley floor, unable to see the offending homestead but wondering exactly who would dare to live any place near the Earlstyne Forest, east of the Gregus. Kesh occasionally sent raiding parties that way, though it had been seven years since the last major incursion, and many Kesh brigands died while transiting the forest. It now had a bad reputation in Kesh as a haunted forest, a forest of death. *Who indeed would dare live there?* he thought.

Another man, clad in black, approached the trio from the rock wall stairs behind them. He was different from the other men working below. Despite his hood, his face wasn't swarthy but pale, and his stature was much like someone from Ulatha, not as tall, but stockier than the men from Kesh. *He walks differently*, thought Khan, who hadn't even heard him approach, though Am-Ohkre turned to face the man before he reached them. *I thought one's hearing was supposed to worsen as one aged?* Khan thought to himself, pondering just how the old man managed to hear the newcomer who was as silent as a cat.

"Kendral," the Arch-Mage said, facing the darkly clad man. "Are you and your people ready?"

Better to call them assassins, thought Khan sourly.

The other man was silent, and whether or not he expected them to hear him, he showed no outward signs of surprise, unlike Ke-Tor, who seemed flummoxed at this man's arrival. "Yes, Am-Ohkre, my people

are in position and the so-called 'King of Ulatha' will be dead as soon as you order it."

Khan hated the man and his kind. It was bad enough they had to attack Ulatha, through no fault of its own, but to murder someone in their sleep: and sleep it would be as Khan was privy to their details, which called for a predawn attack.

"Good," Am-Ohkre said with a mild grin and twinkle in his eye.

Khan thought the Arch-Mage was enjoying the prospect of the Ulathan king's demise too much. They didn't need to be here, despite what High-Mage Am-Sultain thought. Khan knew that Kesh was suffering from a serious lack of resources, and even after a millennium, the wizard ranks were just starting to grow enough for any kind of action. There were only three Arch-Mages in all of Kesh, and not more than a dozen wizards, like his master, who could perform the arts of magic and the arcane. Even apprentices like himself were rare as too many of the noble Kesh bloodlines had perished and what was left from the commoners' class had degenerated into thieves and cutthroats, raiders and brigands. Khan thought to himself, *we are nothing more than that.*

"You're sure the stones will work properly?" Kendral asked.

"Yes. Have no worries: the magic of the stones will alert you and yours when the time is right. Keep them safe and keep them close. After many years, we are down to just a few more days, and I will not tolerate failure," Am-Ohkre said, his twinkle quickly gone, replaced with a scowl.

"Very well. I go now to take care of some last minute affairs." The assassin turned and walked back to the small staircase that was carved into the rock, and descended into the mountain pass.

"He did that on purpose!" Ke-Tor said.

"Do not blame him for your inattentiveness. One day you may find a knife stuck in your back," Am-Ohkre responded, turning back to review the work being done below on the gate and wall.

Khan inwardly chuckled at the exchange, taking some small measure of comfort at his mentor's discomfort. For too many years, he felt he was always on the receiving end of his mentor's verbal barbs and constant criticisms, so it felt redeeming for a change to see a measure of karma meted out to his mentor.

"We have no need for them!" Ke-Tor exclaimed, seemingly more flustered now at the thought of a dagger being stuck into his back. "Waste of gold and effort, something any Kesh warrior could do easily enough."

Am-Ohkre turned to look at the middle-aged wizard before speaking. "Perhaps, but the only Ulathans that could rally any kind of resistance against us will be the king and his cousin. Consider the payment as a form of . . . insurance," the elder mage said with a less stinging tone in his voice.

"I still disapprove. I do not trust the Balarians for that exact reason. Too many thieves and backstabbers. I would torch their lands if the decision was mine."

"And that is why you are not leading this attack," Am-Ohkre said. "You need to learn to mind your temper, perhaps even your tongue. You could take a lesson from your own apprentice on this matter." Am-Ohkre then nodded to Khan.

Khan's contentment at his mentor's discomfort quickly left once the attention of both wizard and Arch-Mage were on him, but in keeping with Am-Ohkre's observations, Khan decided to simply bow his head just a tad, showing respect and deference, tucking his healing necklace under his tunic and hoping the conversation would not focus on him further.

Ke-Tor looked at Khan and then back at the Arch-Mage, deciding to drop the matter. "Fine, but why did Am-Sultain decide to make the attacks this year? I thought we all agreed on a ten-year master plan. We should have three more years to prepare. None of the apprentices are ready. If I did not know better, I would say he is holding something back from us."

Now Khan was starting to feel very uncomfortable. *Whose fault is that,* he thought to himself. He should have been initiated last year, but Ke-Tor held him back. Jealousy and a hunger for power were two of the traits that marked a wizard from Kesh, and especially a wizard as ambitious as Ke-Tor. Even his name was a self-indulging reference of the greatest Arch-Mage ever, Ke-Torra.

"Sultain has his reasons," Am-Ohkre said, and Khan noted the familiar use of the High-Mage's name without the proper Kesh title to show respect. It was no secret Am-Ohkre thought he should be the High-Mage. He was only one of three Arch-Mages. The third Arch-Mage, Am-Shee, was leading the other Kesh assault on the realm of Rockton.

"He should have finished the Ulathans off seven years ago when they entered Kesh!" Ke-Tor said, obvious disgust in his voice. "They took serious losses then."

"Yes, but so did we, and although they routed the garrison at Ulsthor, they retreated without coming closer to Keshtor. Thinking themselves victorious was a tool to be exploited and an advantage to be pressed. As I said, Sultain has his reasons."

"I am sure he does, but as you said, our manpower is low and we are attacking not one realm but two. This is not wise to split our forces."

"Very observant of you, Ke-Tor, but Sultain has the Eye of Seeing, and our own scroll lore has confirmed the approach of Dor Akun. If we do not move now, there will be no slaves to capture. The peasants of Ulatha and Rockton are not aware of Dor Akun's approach, and no doubt many of them will perish if we do not intervene and . . ."—there was a long pause as Am-Ohkre chose his words for effect—"assist them in preserving their precious but miserable lives. Once preserved, they will have no choice but to serve Kesh. If you still disagree, I could arrange a meeting between you and Sultain to discuss the matter."

Ke-Tor understood the implications of what the Arch-Mage was saying. While all of them were arrogant, Am-Sultain was perhaps the least

agreeable of the three, unlike Am-Ohkre, and any *discussion* between him and the High-Mage would, no doubt, be most unpleasant, if not fatal. "No need for that," Ke-Tor finally responded. "We should proceed according to plan. The border gate will be finished by sundown, and then we can move to the old keep in the valley."

"Any reports from the North?" Am-Ohkre asked.

"None. The northern scouts returned late last night and reported that there are no barbarian contacts near Ulatha." This was significant because, while the Kesh were known for their raids and brigand activities, the desolate dragon lands to the north were inhabited by wild Agonians referred to as barbarians, and they were literally the only other race on Agon that actually raided the Kesh.

"Then our plans are set. We attack in two days, just before dawn. Is the Horn of Isla ready?" Am-Ohkre asked.

"Yes, Hork has made arrangements and the horn should be here by nightfall." Ke-Tor nodded.

Khan knew the large horn required an entire wagon to transport and it was enchanted. It was too large for a Kesh to sound, but it was perfect for one of the stone trolls that occasionally served the wizards. Of course, there was no mention of this. His mentor, Ke-Tor, was not thorough in his answer, and Am-Ohkre seemed too distracted to notice. If a stone troll wasn't with the horn, then it was useless to serve as the signal. "I assume there is a troll accompanying the horn?" Khan said, finally deciding to add his voice to the conversation.

"Do not be an idiot, Khan, of course there is," said Ke-Tor, now mildly annoyed by his apprentice asking the obvious. "I said the horn would be here tonight."

"It would be a shame if the horn arrived but not the troll," Khan replied, holding his ground.

Ke-Tor seemed to think this over for a second and then turned back to Am-Ohkre. "We are finished here, then?"

"Yes, I think I will retire to my tent until we move out tomorrow. You will see to the horn?"

More than mildly annoyed now, Ke-Tor looked at Khan for a moment and then back to the Arch-Mage. "Yes, I will take care of it." And then he turned and headed down to the brigand camp below.

Am-Ohkre looked at Khan for a moment, waiting to see if Khan would say something, and then he nodded and left Khan standing alone along the small cliff overlooking Ulatha.

Khan didn't like attacking anyone. Perhaps he wasn't cut out for the life that was chosen for him. In Kesh society, many of the brigands simply took slaves for wives, and the women bore children who were either slaved if female or raised as raiders, fighters, and thieves if male. A few noble-born Kesh were different. If their bloodline was pure, their offspring would follow the father and become wizards, or at least apprentice wizards like Khan was now.

From what Khan knew, his father was a wizard and his mother was a slave. Both died when he was young, and he could barely remember them. Ke-Tor took Khan in as his apprentice, which most likely saved the young man's life, but it was not an altruistic gesture. Ke-Tor gained an apprentice who was treated much as a slave, albeit a gifted slave, as any other. Khan had conflicted feelings for his mentor, both hating him for his cruel treatment and grateful he had sheltered him. Sheltered him for what, the life of an apprentice wizard?

More apprentices were killed than became wizards, as magic wasn't as safe as one would think. Spells backfired and potions and scrolls weren't always exact. Also, considering the base nature of the Kesh, oftentimes an ambitious and greedy apprentice would see to it that a "magic accident" occurred, oftentimes killing a rival apprentice. Finally, add the paranoia that accompanied someone from Kesh naturally, and the end result was actually a pretty short lifespan for brigand or wizard. It was precisely

these elements that kept Kesh society down the last millennia and was forcing them to take action now.

Khan didn't want to think on the matter anymore. He was unhappy but forced to do what he had to do. For the moment, he savored his time alone, without the oppressiveness of his master and mentor, Ke-Tor, or the pretentious and arrogant company of the Arch-Mage. He felt free, freer than he had ever felt before, and while he wasn't happy with his current lot in life, at least he took some comfort in the fact that it could be much worse. He could have been born an Ulathan.

Am-Ohkre went to one of his chests inside his tent upon his return and pulled out a glass orb. He set the orb on a shallowly indented plate to hold it in place, and then walked over to his tent entrance and closed the curtains, ignoring the two guards outside. This made it dark inside, but he could still see well enough. Pulling up a chair, he sat at the table, closed his eyes, placed his hand on the orb, and started to mutter indecipherable words while slightly rubbing the orb with his left hand.

The orb started to glow and then very quickly lit up bright enough to illuminate the entire tent, large that is was. Am-Ohkre opened his eyes and looked into the orb, seeing a familiar face. "Am-Sultain."

"You are early," the figure in the orb responded. "What news?"

"Ke-Tor suspects," Am-Ohkre said simply.

The figure in the orb leaned back, showing more of his upper body and not just his face. He took a moment to contemplate the news before responding. "The information remains with just the Arch-Mages. Some of the wizards are bound to be suspicious, if they are half intelligent, so we should expect this from them. Did you say anything to him about it?"

"No, I said nothing other than you have your reasons, but why not let them know about the Alore Staff? What harm could come from that?"

Am-Sultain leaned back further, stroking his long grey beard. "Perhaps you are too trusting. It was difficult enough to share this knowledge with you and Am-Shee, but what do you think would happen if over a dozen wizards learned that we may have located the ancient artifact of Alore?"

Am-Ohkre now leaned in, making a show of doing the exact opposite of his leader, the High-Mage Am-Sultain. "One or more of them could pose a risk, but I think the risk would be to you."

"Yes, only one of us can wield the first staff of magic, but we will need all of our powers combined to obtain it, and there is not much time left remaining to us. I do not think you will want to sleep for two hundred years in order to have another chance at obtaining it, do you?" Am-Sultain replied.

Am-Ohkre thought about this for a moment and unconsciously stroked his beard. Sleeping for two hundred years was magically possible. It had been discovered thousands of years ago by the first mages of Agon, but he knew what the High-Mage was referring to. When asleep, a mage was very vulnerable and had to spend considerable energy and effort to protect himself or something unwarranted or even fatal could befall him. *Sleep isn't actually a good word to use,* he thought to himself. Hibernate would be more accurate, but no matter, Sultain was using this as a veiled threat to keep him in agreement with the course of action that the Arch-Mages of Kesh had all agreed upon beforehand

Finally, he spoke. "No, you are correct. The time to act is now, before the passing of Dor Akun, and perhaps you are correct in not telling the wizards. They will simply have to accept our decision."

"I am pleased to hear this, Am-Ohkre." We first, however, must determine if the information in the Balarian scroll is correct, and it refers to writings done nearly a thousand years ago by the Ulathan historian Diamedes. If any of the writing from Diamedes survived the war or any of Akun's passings, it would reside in Utandra, the capital, so we must take Ulatha and secure anything that survived the great war."

"I take it you mean the town of Korwell when you refer to it by its original name," Am-Ohkre stated more than asked.

The High-Mage leaned back into the orb, looming larger. "I will not honor the Ulathan usurper by calling it anything other than its rightful name. The ignorant, petty, arrogant fool has no clue to the land's history or heritage," Am-Sultain said, anger in his voice, but then he took a moment to lean back and take a deep breath before continuing. "He can call himself *king* or anything else that he wants to, much as the prior six rulers of Ulatha have done since its fall, but in two days, I expect you to fulfill your mission and take Ulatha for Kesh. Secure the castle and town. Am I clear?" he said, the last three words almost inaudible.

"Understood, Am-Sultain." The globe quickly went dim, plunging Am-Ohkre's tent into darkness again. The old man stood and walked over to the curtains, pulling them open and letting in the morning light. His two guards barely made any movement or notice of the act, but he could tell they were jumpy. They always were when they had to pull sentry duty for the wizards.

Am-Ohkre looked around at the edge of the small flat plateau that served as the wizards' base camp. It was just large enough for three fairly large tents, one for each wizard, with enough space at either end to congregate or meet with their subordinates. Although technically every Kesh was of the same race, the wizards did their utmost not to consort or fraternize with the common class, and so while the main brigand camp was right below them, the thirty-foot cliff wall served as a barrier between the two castes. It had taken several days for over a dozen stonemasons to carve the crude stairs into the cliff face for no other purpose than to isolate the wizard caste from the brigand caste, and Am-Ohkre felt the effort was most worthwhile.

He noticed the young apprentice Khan standing where he had left him, cloak pulled around him closely with only the top of his staff sticking above his hooded head. There was something strange about the

young man, almost as if he was more Ulathan than Kesh, though Am-Ohkre knew this to be folly. One look at him and his tall, lean stature, despite his lighter, pale complexion, could only indicate he was from Kesh blood. It was more in his attitude, however, and lack of ambition that set him apart from the other apprentices, and even wizards, for that matter. It was almost as if the young man had a set of morals that differed from those from his homeland. *Too bad,* Am-Ohkre thought to himself. More than likely, any morals he had would be a liability to him and not an asset. More than likely, this apprentice would die sooner rather than later. *Such a pity, too. He showed so much promise.*

The Arch-Mage returned to his table and sat while taking a moment to reflect on his conversation with the High-Mage. *Indeed,* he thought, *if Ke-Tor knew the truth, then maybe a knife was waiting to be plunged into his own back, though that would not help the wizard obtain the one staff of Alore, the first staff of magic.* No, only he and the other two Arch-Mages knew the truth. The powerful artifact of Alore was not on Agon at all, but soon, one day soon, it would be very close to Agon again, and with it, the Kesh would reclaim their proper place amongst Agon's people. A place of world domination.

CHAPTER 3

FAMILY

Targon was born an Ulathan. He had just returned the prior day from the family's hunting blind, just over half a day's walk from his home near the large and powerful Rapid River that roared nearby. The blind was not far from the crossing where their family had lost its patriarch. He had to skirt the Blackthorn Forest where his home was located just at the north end of it. He had hoped to land a deer or even a buck, but with no luck and his time running out, he returned home to see if he could at least scrounge up something for the family. For some reason, the animals nearby seemed to have literally disappeared. There were no birds chirping and hardly anything larger than rabbits around.

He could feel the warmth of the sun rising at his back. It was still cool enough that he could see his breath as he breathed. Despite the cold and the dawn of an early spring day, he stayed focused on the wild hare that was just now peeking its head out of its warm warren hole. Targon was determined his mother would have a nice rack of conies to cook for her birthday today, and it would start with this particular rabbit.

The animal slowly poked its head farther and farther out of the hole, smelling the air for any telltale sign of danger. Slowly, Targon pulled

back on the bow he had always carried ever since he could remember. A deep breath and a slight rise to clear the mound on which he had been hiding behind, he let loose the arrow with a twang, and it flew quickly to its mark, but not quick enough. With a start, the wild rabbit must have sensed or heard him as he pulled himself up to let loose his arrow, and the rabbit ducked back down its hole to safety just as the missile arrived to lodge into the back wall of dirt.

Failure, Targon thought. He had been so careful, too, and waited patiently for the rabbit to appear. Turning to sit on the rocky mound, he mulled over the events of his morning. He had the sun at his back. The wind was blowing from side to side, and he had arrived early enough to settle in and not give the wild animal a cause to his location. He felt sure that his preparations were satisfactory, but obviously, his execution was lacking. He made too much noise either when rising or when pulling back on his bow. Just a half second quicker and he would have scored his first kill of the day. "Hmm," he muttered aloud to himself.

Before he could decide on whether it was his movement or the movement of the bow, he heard his little sister, Ann, come splashing through the water of the small brook, and thence upon the twigs and dry grasses of the small hillock on which he was sitting.

"Hoi, little brother," she cried as she spotted him on his rocky mound. He could see her clearly now coming up over the berm by the water with her dark brown skirt flowing in the morning breeze and a light tunic made of wool tied over her shoulders and chest.

"Little?" he responded with a chuckle. "I am nearly twice your size and height, little sister, and triple your age, so it is you who are the 'little' one. Come, let us return home together. It would not be good if Mother caught you wandering so far from home."

"So why do you always get to wander so far from home," Ann asked in a whining "why me" sounding voice.

"Because, as I said, little sister, I am twice your size and twice your age. I can take care of myself out here on the edge of the forest, but if you strayed too close, there is no telling what would come out for you." Ann looked up at him as he finished with just a tinge of fear in her eyes. She clasped his large hand in hers tightly and started back down the small rise toward the brook.

She was only eight years old, and Targon that summer would be twenty, having completed his second decade time of Adulting, in which many cultures referred to as "coming of age" or "becoming a man" or part of a tribe or clan. Here in the world of Claire Agon, or just Agon as most of the locals called their world, the time of Adulting was the time of change from childhood into adulthood. This was a time of celebration and of responsibility, but Targon knew scant little of the rites of passage for his world. He lived pretty much alone with his mother, older brother, and little sister, far from the closest town on the edge of the wild.

His older brother, Malik, had finished his own Adulting several years ago and was conscripted to serve in the king's army for five years. Well, king if one can call himself a king. In most lands, the king may have been called a baron, if that, but for the lack of knowledge that Targon had coupled with the grandiose perception of himself, the good *King Korwell* oversaw the Realm of Ulatha, consisting of the capital (now named Korwell, of course), a few small, poor towns, and one or two small squalor-filled villages along the main trade routes that the "good king" saw fit to tax and tariff. And if a good citizen of Korwell could not pay taxes, they had to send a family member instead to serve the king and make good on the family's obligations. So it was that having almost no coinage with which to pay taxes, the Terrels sent instead their firstborn son, Malik.

It was a sad time when they had said their good-byes and Malik had left the family homestead, leaving Targon alone with his mother and sister. Up till that time, Malik had taken care of the heavy lifting around

the homestead, having been a great hunter and strong enough to move rocks and small tree stumps from the small plot of land they used as a garden during days of no snow. Targon didn't fully realize how much he loved and would miss his brother until he was gone. Of course, there was no real thought of Malik staying. The penalty for refusing the service of the king was harsh, and all able-bodied young men in their first year after Adulting were to serve in their king's service and protect the realm from its enemies, unless the family was rich enough to pay proper taxes instead. Targon mulled over the idea of his obligation to serve when he completed his Adulting. In fact, around the same time that he himself would have to serve, his brother, Malik, would be released and able to return home. It was, of course, for this reason that many families decided to either space the birth of their children apart by more than five years or to simply have many children in general.

The walk back was quick enough. His mother was already up laying out the wet clothes she had washed on the large granite rocks to dry in the rising sun. Ann had run up to hug her and tell her about finding her "little" brother so easily near the forest. Ann's face conveyed a smile, but Mother was frowning just a tad at the corners of her mouth at hearing just how far out her daughter had meandered by herself. It wasn't that she wanted to live so near to the wild with her precious children, but rather, after many years of wandering and travels, she and her husband had decided to retire to the family home after her parents were ill, and well, this was their home. The wild just seemed to get wilder and to have kept creeping closer and closer to their homestead.

"Good morning, Mother, and happy birthday to you!" Targon said, and then smiled as he walked up to the rustic wooden cabin they called home.

"Good morning, my sweet!" his mother replied. "Up early you are on this fine morning, my young gentleman. Did you find what you were looking for?"

Targon frowned a bit and looked down at his worn leather boots as he shuffled them and kicked a small rock over twice while thinking how best to respond to his mother's probing question. "Well, I found it well enough, but catching it is another matter," he said.

"Well, my, my," she said, "perhaps another try before lunch, my little hunter?"

He hated it when she called him "little," and it was no doubt a good reason why his little sister enjoyed using the word as a taunt herself, despite the fact that he was the tallest and largest Ulathan in the entire valley. "Yes, Mother, another go to be sure, but this time a different outcome!" With that, he sprang back down the path toward the brook. This time in a roundabout way, he headed downwind of the rabbit warren so as to try to catch them unawares. If nothing else, Targon was persistent if not stubborn.

The family homestead had stood for centuries enduring the many transits of Dor Akun and remembering in history a time of much greater civilization. Passed on from one member of the Terrel family to another, the homestead had belonged to Targon Terrel's grandparents, Luc and Julia. Targon and his family had moved there not long before the death of his father in the Kesh bandit raids more than seven years ago. His grandparents were ill and getting older, and with a family to take care of, his mother, Dareen, thought it best to return to her ancestral home. The Terrel family lived there in relative peace and happiness through the passing of both Luc five years ago and his grandmother, Julia, three years ago. Malik had left just after the passing of his grandfather and was not home for the burial of his grandmother. Targon had done his best to fill in for his missing brother, who was effectively filling in for both their father and grandfather, as the man of the family.

Many centuries ago, there was a small keep not far from their house on the ancient trade road leading out of the realm from Ulatha to Kesh in the East. After the Great War and the transit of Dor Akun, what was left of the inhabitants found themselves in a nasty skirmish with lawless Kesh brigands and even small bands of northern barbarians. That had seen to it that the nobleman and his troops were driven out and the keep abandoned, and not long thereafter, the small town around the keep as well was given to nature and now stood as a remnant of what civilization was like in that part of the world. Still, the Terrel homestead endured where most all else faltered.

The initial cabin was only one room with a door in the front and a small porch as well as a door to the rear. Later, two more rooms were added, making the square home a rectangle with each added room of equal size. When the Terrels moved there, Luc and Julia took one room while giving the other to Targon's parents and baby sister, Ann. Malik and Targon slept in the main room upstairs on a flat wooden loft built in the small rafters of the cabin. The boys and Luc had made it themselves, and Targon slept there still, preferring the perch above the main room to one of the backrooms that were now available since Ann still slept with her mother.

At the other end of the cabin, directly opposite the two rooms, was a stone fireplace and mantle. There was only one window in the entire cabin facing the front, so it was often dark inside, and Targon spent as much time outdoors as he could. The family lived too close to the forest to allow for a window in either bedroom. It would not do to allow any wild things access to their sleeping quarters.

The family had a small garden plot directly to the rear of the cabin and a small barn barely as high as a man could stand and just enough room inside to shelter their dairy cow and a few chickens that provided eggs for the family.

The homestead was once right on the northern edge of Blackthorn Forest, but decades of chopping wood and clearing land for gardening had made the entire area around the homestead devoid of anything larger than tall grasses and small bushes. Many granite rocks and boulders were strewn across the landscape, most being too large and heavy for any sort of removal, and they resisted the encroachment of man into the wild.

The small stream that Targon and Ann crossed was just inside the forest's northern edge and linked up with the Rapid River about two miles to the west. There was a particularly large boulder near the river that Targon used to rest on when he went spearfishing with his grandfather or brother.

A small trackway led from the homestead north, parallel to the river, eventually reaching the ancient trade road that led from Ulatha in the West to the Kesh pass in the Border Mountains, about a day's journey to the east. Targon had used this road several times in the preceding years.

A couple of miles to the west was the only bridge over the Rapid River for several days' journey south, and the capital lay southwest of the bridge. For this reason, the Terrel homestead was the only homestead east of the Rapid River. Several other homesteads were located to the west of the river. The Blackthorn Forest also reached only as far as the river, and so the locals stayed on its western banks and shores, keeping the deep, cold, and fast running river as a buffer between them and the forest. All except the Terrels, of course, who were often thought of as reckless for living so close to the forest and mountains.

The Terrels didn't always use the ancient trade road to reach Korwell. It took nearly an extra day to travel that route. Instead, near the hunting blind, there was an interesting place in the river. Large mountain boulders lay across the river to create a sort of ford where the water rushed quicker than normal over the rocks and plunged into a series of white water rapids. At the top, the Terrels had strung a long length of rope between two large boulders along each bank, and when they had to trade

in the capital, they would oftentimes use the ford to cross the river and the wild badlands to the west to cut cross country and reach the capital in less time than using the north road. Of course, if they had a need to trade a lot, or as was the case when they traded for their dairy cow, the road was necessary.

Unfortunately, the rope was lost two years prior in a large flood after a particularly bad winter, and Targon was unable to string the rope again without the help of his older brother or grandfather. The memory of his father's death there deterred him from making the attempt. The Terrels now seldom traveled to the capital or anywhere else for that matter.

The sun had started its slow journey back to the land's end, and Targon was now smiling, somewhat happy with himself at the brace of three fresh coney kills earlier that day. *One for each of us*, he thought to himself. Some mornings he would be lucky to be able to snare one, much less three, and he had to move farther and farther from their home in his hunting. It was as if the rabbits of the warren knew of him and gave the homestead a wide berth when it settled a new warren.

Targon quickly returned the conies to his mother, who was more than happy to receive them and start dressing them for dinner. He ate some wild berries that Ann had collected the day before and started to sharpen his knife on an old cut rock they kept on the front porch for just such occasions. He knew he would have to grab his father's axe and head toward the forest yet again for more firewood. They had nearly exhausted the supply they had built up last fall as winter had been most bitter that year. Life on the frontier did not come easy: he learned a long time ago. Still, watching his mother hum a gay tune from an old nursery rhyme gave him cause to smile before he headed back out toward Blackthorn Forest.

The forest was called Blackthorn for a reason. There was a rather nice-looking but thorny alder bush that liked to grow amongst the pines,

cedars, and oaks of the forest. Its stalks and vines had thorny spines for its protection, and after dying off, they turned a hard black as the wood quickly petrified in the extreme weather. Any human, animal, or other creature without armored skin could quickly become punctured, scratched, and just overall bloodied if caught lost in the old, dead alder bushes. Some creatures, such as the conies Targon hunted, found shelter and refuge amongst the thorny spines, but for most creatures, they were best to just be avoided.

Targon found a nice old oak that had died two winters before, and he had purposely left it last year so it would dry out more during the prior summer. He learned that allowing a dead tree to sit through a summer gave the best result for firewood, and so he marked the new trees that had died to leave them for the next year and started to earnestly hack the old oak that had died two years ago. Once he had several piles, he carted the wood back toward home. It took him several trips. Did anyone mention just how difficult life on the wild frontier really was? His bow was starting to chafe across his back, and he made a mindless decision to leave it with the axe against the dead hulk of the oak tree, a decision that may have saved his life, though he did not know it at the time.

With his chores done for the day, Targon took it upon himself to put some final polishing touches on the small wooden carving he had been working on all winter. The carving was done, but he needed to sand it down and polish its rough edges before he could give it as a gift to his mother. The bird carving was of a Clairton, a small, lightly fleeting forest bird that oftentimes sang songs in the early morning and at dusk. It was his mother's favorite bird, and he fancied his carving quite a piece of artwork to be sure, though others might disagree. He used some wet sand from the bank of Bony Brook. Yes, he called it Bony Brook, because too often he found remnants of bones along the banks, mainly just small fish bones, though occasionally some bird bones and rarely bones of an unknown nature.

Using the wet sand, he scrubbed hard enough at the rough edges until the overall sheen lightened up, and then he took his carving back to the brook to rinse and left it to dry on the large granite rock his mother had used earlier that day. Later that night, he would tie it to the top of a pine-cone and present it to her to hang from the rafters near the lone window by the basin, which by all accounts acted as a sort of kitchen sink, though there was, of course, no real plumbing.

"You still working on that ugly bird, little brother?" Ann asked in her whining high-pitched voice he should have felt was annoying but instead found more adorable than the former.

With a false mocking look, he glared at her and responded, "Ugly bird? Why you little mouse, I will have my bird peck your eyes out this very moment!" And with a lunge, he ran after her, screeching bird noises as he went.

"Aye, Mommy!" she cried in mock terror. "Not the ugly bird!" And with a holler, she ran screaming into the family cabin to seek her loving mother's attention.

All in good fun, thought Targon as he hooted and hollered around his sister with an occasional bird-sounding screech. He actually wasn't quite sure if his screeches sounded like a bird or more like a cat dying a horrible death, but he was having quite a good time scaring his younger sister. Hey, what were older brothers for if not to scare younger sisters?

"Now, now, the two of you, take your bird calls and horseplay outside before you break something we can't afford to replace." As always, the soothing voice of their mother was a comfort to them, and they glee-fully ran outside.

Eventually the sun started to set, and Targon put a few finishing touches on his carving so it would be ready for gifting. He brought in a few armloads of wood for the hearth, knowing full well that once the sun set, the temperature would plummet, and it would not do to have to return outside to retrieve firewood once Uncle Frost came to visit. He

remembered his large wood axe and bow, both left unattended at the old oak tree. They would be all right, he decided, and quickly discarded the thought from his mind.

With that, the Terrel family had a festive dinner. Ann had made a crude but delicious salad of cabbage leaves, berries, and nuts, with a sweet onion vinegar dressing, and Mother had mashed and baked soft potatoes to go with the conies, of which there was no lack of meat that night. Blackthorn conies were not small in size to be sure.

After cleaning up the lone table and setting most of the wooden cutlery in the basin, Targon gave his mother the bird carving perched atop the wooden pinecone he had just recently finished. She beamed at him in delight and gave him a huge hug and, much to his chagrin, planted a large kiss on his right cheek that seemed to make Ann smile all the more. Ann, too, had spent some time picking a bouquet of wild flowers from nearby the cabin and had Targon obtain a few wilder ones from farther afield since she was not allowed to stray far from the homestead.

As was tradition in Agon, Dareen gave each of her children a small lock of her hair tied to a little stringy bow. "Just something to remember me when you're playing," she said.

Targon looked at the few blonde strands of silken hair tied in his hand and then looked at Ann with her lightly golden locks of hair. Then, almost without thinking, he touched his own head and thought of the deep brown strands of hair that ran through his fingers.

"Was Father light-haired as you, Mother?" Targon asked gently, still stroking the hair on his head.

"No," she replied. "He had a deep brown color to his hair, the same as yours. Brown and dark and smooth as a strand of earth-colored silk. Don't you remember?"

"No, I can't remember Father's hair color. Silk," he asked, "what is that?"

"Well, something you haven't really seen yet," she said. "It's a form of fabric much like your tunic but very soft to the touch."

"How soft?" he asked.

With a gentle laugh, she pulled Ann to her bosom. "As soft as Ann's skin when she was just a baby." Targon remembered touching his sister's soft skin when she was just born and before her skin was weathered by living along the wild frontier.

"Did Tar have soft skin, too, when he was a baby, Mommy?" Ann asked with a mischievous grin. She knew he didn't like being called Tar anymore than he liked being called little.

"Of course he did," his mother replied. "Our little Tar had the softest skin of all." She gave a wink and a nod. Targon could only smile and let loose a little chuckle, and he was a tad amazed at how perceptive his mother was to her children's every word. Targon couldn't help but feel a closeness to his family.

"Mother, can you tell us the story of your birth?" asked Ann after picking up the last of the wooden dinner plates and settling into a soft blanket near the hearth.

Dareen looked softly at her daughter and laughed out loud. "The story of *my* birth? Well, honey, I was much too young to remember it, but Grandma Julia told me enough to know it was a special moment in time, just the same as your birth. But I can tell you the story of the birth of Agon instead," she said.

"Yes, please do, Mommy," Ann replied.

"Oh, not again, I've heard this one far too many times," he complained, but only half-heartedly. If anyone could tell a good tale, it was his mother, and he really wasn't that perturbed to listen to her soothing voice yet one more time.

"Very well," his mother said. "But it is getting late, and after our story, we shall sleep the slumber of the spirits of the earth and prepare for the next morning. It was a wonderful day today, and I will always remember

it." She blew out the lone candle and pulled the blanket up closer to her and Ann. Targon also pulled his blanket tighter around himself where he now lay on a small wooden bench.

"Once upon a time, there lived a princess . . ." And with that, his mother went on to tell the tale of Princess Arkala and her capture by the evil wizard Dak Mul, who took the princess to a tower to be guarded by a rather large and wicked red dragon, a dragon so fierce that no sword or man could kill it. But the knight, Sir Baldwyn, came and did not slay the dragon, but instead flew a giant hawk into the wizard's keep and stole the princess back from the evil wizard. The dragon chased the pair far into the night sky where it almost caught them, but the knight was smart and wise and threw a pouch of gems at the dragon that breathed fire but was blinded by greed and turned to chase the falling gems before they could land and be lost to the ground below. It was then that the good wizard Gren cast a spell of time stopping, and the soaring dragon was frozen with the gems for all time, while the princess and her knight escaped back to her father's kingdom to live happily ever after. In the sea of gems, there was a large blue one, a sapphire called Agon, and thus their world was born. One could simply walk outside into the night and look up and see the dragon breathing his flame and see the many other gems frozen in the night sky and know of the birth of the world of Agon. And how could one find the dragon in the night sky? It was the constellation that always pointed toward the fire of the rising sun and could only be seen late at night just before dawn.

Ah yes, his mother could indeed weave a good tale. He was pleased to notice his gift set prominently on the mantle of the fireplace in a place of honor and remembrance. Targon closed his eyes and listened to his mother's soft humming while he could hear Ann's breathing slowing but getting slightly louder. He, too, started to sleep with the same soft hum in his ears, not realizing or appreciating that this would be the last night his family would fall asleep together, and with that, darkness took him.

CHAPTER 4

CAPTURED

The moon wheeled across the dark sky, and up came the Dragon Constellation from the east. Soon, the head of the dragon became visible, and for anyone in Ulatha watching, one would know that the dragon's fire was soon to be seen. What Targon could not know, and did not know, was that while the gems overhead moved through the dark night sky, several dark figures lurked near the family cabin.

Many centuries ago, the old road near the Terrel homestead was a fairly actively used trade route, but that was before the dragons of the North came to Kesh and destroyed it. The road quickly came into disrepair. Rocks fell and water weathered the road where it crossed the Border Mountains just to the east of Blackthorn Forest. The rare but constant passing of Dor Akun added to its demise every two centuries. In time, almost all trade stopped and bandits and brigands emerged, roaming the lands, risking the wrath of the dragons if ever caught in the open, until finally, the last of the dragons died at the hands of Heroes from the South. It was during that time that the old keep was overrun, but the brigands from Kesh were turned back and the old destroyed keep was abandoned.

In time, almost no traffic moved along the old road, no one ever saw a dragon anymore, and Kesh and the East were utterly forgotten.

Then, not so many years ago, a small incursion of brigands had once again crossed over the mountain pass and assaulted what was left of the surviving farms and homesteads along the river. That was seven years ago. Targon's father, Baldric, had died to save his family during this incursion. Afterward, many soldiers were enlisted by Lord Korwell, along with over a thousand other farmers, ranchers, and peasants, and they moved east over the Border Mountains and engaged the Kesh bandits for nearly a year. The Terrels received word when the army returned, only half as strong, that the bandits were destroyed. At least they did not see another brigand again for over seven years, until this very night.

Despite the history of raids and counter-raids, there was more to this group of bandits than just pillaging and plundering. For the first time in decades, they moved with a purpose. They were the fingers of an armored fist, smashing with a controlled mind against the fair people of the realm of Ulatha.

With a large crash, the front door of the Terrel cabin was kicked open, and several brigands entered. A couple of brigands busted open the back-door and entered at the same time. Targon was caught unaware, but his mother, Dareen, had already jumped to her feet and grabbed a rag and the pot of water hanging over the family hearth, and in one fluid movement, she hurled the hot water across the small room and onto the first two brigands that had entered. They yelled in pain, one kicking a chair at her, which missed easily.

"Run, Targon, run!" his mother yelled. "Take Ann with you!" She grabbed a kitchen knife, moving to place herself between the brigands and her children, but there was no other way out.

"Mother, no!" Targon yelled, jumping up and grabbing an old wooden stool, swinging it at the head of a third brigand near the doorway. The brigand smashed the stool with a large metal mace and kicked Targon

hard in his chest. Targon stumbled, trying to regain his breath, but his large legs held him steady.

Unarmed, Targon closed the distance with the mace-wielding brigand and embraced the man so that the mace could not swing. Using his powerful hands, Targon gripped the brigand's head and brought it forward to meet his own forehead as it flew forward in a bone-cracking head butt.

The brigand's nose was instantly shattered, and his eyes glazed over as he lost consciousness and fell from Targon's grasp to the floor, dropping the mace as he went.

Without warning, two small darts were sent flying into Targon's neck from the brigands who had entered at the rear door. He instantly felt the powerful pharmaceuticals as they rushed into his body, and realized the brigands had just drugged him as he felt his limbs grow heavy and fall. His last memory was watching as his mother took a glancing blow to her temple by another mace-wielding brigand as she, too, was subdued.

In a matter of seconds, it was all over. Targon didn't know for how long they had been knocked out, but soon, he was revived with a foul-smelling concoction that was placed under his nose. The revolting smell was enough to bring him to his senses, but he realized he was now thoroughly tied up, and quickly the brigands brought him to his knees.

His sister, Ann, was screaming, and what a sound it was. *A high-pitched wailing as if an animal had just died and was being sent to hell*, Targon thought. Targon noted, with some content, that at least one brigand was wounded with a slash across his arm, but he remembered the mace-wielding brigand and how he had caught his mother a glancing blow across her left temple. Had it hit full on, he was sure she would have died from the blow. He saw her being revived as well, and one brigand even mopped away a large amount of blood from the side of her face.

"No killing!" he heard someone yell through the doorway. "Get them out of that rat hole and out here in the open, and for the love of Agon,

someone stuff something in that girl's god-forsaken shriek hole and shut her up!"

A rather large, menacing-looking brigand dressed in black leathers with a wicked-looking curvish blade in his left hand grabbed Ann and covered her mouth with his right while holding her in a sort of headlock as he carried her through the front door. Two other brigands grabbed his mother and dragged her through the front door as well. It took four brigands to grab Targon off the floor where he was just catching his breath. He wondered if a rib was broken: the pain in his lower chest was excruciating as all five of them headed outside.

Another brigand, but with a plumed helm on his head and some sort of wooden stick in his right hand, pointed at the family. "Check them for weapons and especially that she-wood witch. Gag her mouth so she can't utter a spell, and check the bindings on their hands." With quick motions, they tested and tightened their hand bindings and Targon's mother was gagged, an old rag stuffed into her mouth with an oily knotted rope tied about her head to hold it in. His mother looked over at him and shook her head, warning him not to do anything foolish . . . yet.

"Blimy, I don't see nothing shiny in dis damn rat house," said a brigand, exiting the cabin with two handfuls of cheap crockery, wool linen, and wooden tableware, dropping the lot onto the ground where it made a large noise. "Not even two pieces to clink between me fingers." The brigand was dismayed.

"Shut your trap, Cutter. There ain't to be any nice clinkers about these parts. Wez here to procure us a bit of nourishments is all." And with that, the plumed and helmeted brigand looked over at the small shed the Terrels used as a barn, pointing with his wooden stick, and five brigands immediately ran toward the shed hooting and hollering and pushing one another as they went. "Get us our goods and let's be off. We must meet the others by the old keep before daybreak or there will be hell to pay."

"And what'z we to do with these here rats?" asked the larger of the brigands. "They don't hardly look worth slaving even."

"Puts them in the cage and off with you, and keep an eye on that wood-witch I tell you!"

The larger brigand put his fingers to his mouth, shrieking a shrill whistle, and in the distance, barely audible, Targon could make out the *click clack* of a horse's hooves and the creaking of wooden wheels. Just then, a large commotion came from the shed area as several chickens were being chased and bagged while Myrtle, their trusty old dairy cow, was being led to the trackway. "And what's we to do with the rest of this filth?" he asked yet again.

"You and Traps stay here till dawn. When you hear the signal, burn the place to the ground and meet us at the crossroads."

"What!" Targon cried. "You can't destroy our home. What have we done to you? Leave us alone and let my family free!" Targon was angry now but forgetful of his circumstances.

The lead brigand walked over, grabbing a dagger from his belt, tucking the wooden stick in its place as he swapped the two. Placing the blade against his mother's throat, he gave a stern look at Targon. "Or what, you oversized man-child?" The look in his mother's eyes was pleading. Fear, yes, but not fear for herself: he could see that. In fact, he could see the courage in her eyes, and yet they compelled him to be calm. He could almost hear her voice whispering to him in his head. *Not yet, little one, not yet.*

Targon said nothing. In a sign of contrition, he bowed his head, shut his mouth, and stared at the ground. "That is what I thought, little man," the lead brigand said, sheathing his dagger and walking over to meet the driver of the cart that was just arriving at the homestead. The irony of the brigand's words were obvious as Targon out-massed even the largest cutthroat by a large margin.

"Puts them chickens and other supplies on the back cart and stuff thems into the lock cell and duz its now. Cutter, gets your damn arse up here and square them aways!"

Targon felt strong arms grabbing him from under his shoulders, and several brigands half carried, half dragged him to the wagon, where the back half was enclosed in iron rods with a large locked gate on the back. Targon hit his head on the top of the gate as it only stood about three feet high. When he finally looked up, he saw his mother and sister also in the cell with him. Poor Myrtle was tied to the rear of the cart, and he could see several small burlap bags moving with, most likely, their chickens stuffed inside of them. *This is so wrong*, he thought. Why could he not have done something?

"Did you check 'em?" he heard the lead brigand ask.

"Yeah, they're clean," responded a tall, skinny-brigand, with blackish teeth and a gleaming sword in his hand as he jumped onto the back of the cart, slamming the small door shut. "She was only armed with a pan and a kitchen knife." He guffawed.

"Well, what was that racket?" asked the driver. "I could hear a damn banshee witch screaming from where I waited way back yonder."

"Ah, that was only the she-brat," answered another brigand. "I wager she's more a threat than the man-child there, louder to be sure," he mocked.

Targon could only glare at him, but a glance from his mother told him to remain silent. With a lurch, the wagon started to circle the front of the cabin and return along the old trackway toward the ancient trade road. One brigand jumped up next to the driver and started drinking from a leather canteen. The lead brigand jumped onto a horse that was brought up with the cart, and he took off, followed by at least a half dozen, if not more, brigands on foot running back north.

The Terrel homestead was off of a small, narrow, overgrown track that acted as a crude road from the ancient trade road, which was in places lined by rocks and stones. The old trackway ran parallel to the Rapid River a few miles to the west from the homestead, north several miles to the ancient trade road. The large Rapid River convened with several other smaller rivers that ran from the Border Mountains down through the Blackthorn Forest and farther down into the Ulatha Valley and began its long journey to the sea. A very old stone bridge along the ancient trade road allowed people to cross the violent river.

After several hours on the cart, Targon could see his mother was moving her chin from side to side, trying to dislodge the gag from her mouth. After about a minute of inching it this way and that, it dropped free just below her bottom lip.

"Tar, are you hurt?" his mother whispered.

"I don't think so," he replied. "Maybe just my pride. And you, Mother?" He looked saddened as he asked.

"Nothing too serious," his mother replied. "Listen carefully to me now, my son. You must find your brother, Malik, and have him warn the Lord and the people of our villages, do you understand?" she asked. Targon nodded but was still frowning. "I don't think they will hurt us. We seem too valuable to them alive. They most likely will want to sell us as slaves. That is what the Kesh do, and by their talk and look about them, I'd say they crossed the Border Mountains not long ago and are headed to the valley to pillage and plunder. The people must be warned. Someone must tell Lord Korwell before it's too late."

"Shut your traps down there!" bellowed the rider brigand next to the driver. "You'll have plenty to talk about soon enough," he said with a wicked grin, and then turned his attention back to the dark track ahead of them, seemingly either too drunk or too inattentive to notice that the "she-wood-witch" was no longer gagged.

Dareen sat motionless for a few minutes and then, turning to Ann, softly asked, "Can you free your hands?"

"I don't know," whispered Ann.

"Listen to me, Ann. Just try to wiggle one of your hands free. Can you do that for me?" Ann nodded and then started to wiggle her arms and shoulders ever so slightly. While she was doing this, Dareen leaned forward toward Targon and, in an almost inaudible whisper, said, "When I tell you to, I want you to push the cage gate open. Jump into the river once we reach the old bridge, but jump on my side, not yours, or the rocks will kill you. Then swim back south and don't look back. Can you do that for me, my son?"

Targon couldn't believe what he was hearing. He nodded his head and looked up at the guard riding at the rear of the cart, who was standing and peering around, looking at the dark reeds near the small creek along the track road. The other two brigands were engaged in some sort of nasty conversation about strangling or cutting throats, which was better or quieter when trying to dispatch some poor, unwary victim in his sleep. But what did his mother have planned? Then Ann smiled and showed her mother her free hands.

"Very good, my dear," Dareen whispered. The *clackity clack* of the horse's hooves and the squeaking of the cart provided just enough cover for them to whisper. It was more than likely the brigands heard them but didn't care so long as they weren't interrupting their jolly conversation about throat cutting and strangling. In fact, the cart was old enough and made enough noise that Targon understood why it had to be brought up last at his homestead. *It would have wakened and alerted us, for sure,* he thought.

Ann pulled her mother's cords free, and Dareen motioned down into the straw for Targon to present his hands. Without talking, Targon leaned

forward with his bound hands, and Dareen quickly freed him. "We won't have much time," she told him. "Are you ready?"

"Yes, but again, what about you and Ann?" he asked. He couldn't just leave while they stayed behind. By this time, the cart had finally reached the old trade road and they were traveling west toward Korwell. Soon, they would cross the only bridge that spanned the Rapid River.

"We have no choice, Tar. Ann and I will survive. Find Malik, warn the people, and then find us!" Targon could see the old bridge of the ancient trade road looming in the near distance. They would reach the bridge and cross it shortly.

With a pained but understanding look, Targon nodded and felt a tear crowding one of his eyes. He quickly brushed it away and moved to his feet in a squatting position. "How are you going to open the gate?" he asked. His mother paused, looking forward, waiting until the cart reached the edge of the bridge and began to cross it.

"With a bit of magic." His mother smiled and winked at him. He thought for sure she had lost her mind, but he braced himself and looked at the brigand standing at the edge of the cart blocking the cage gate. His mother reached into her hair and pulled out what he thought was something to hold her hair in a ponytail. It was a small piece of polished wood. He had seen it before but never thought much of it as it was small and not sharp and usually hidden by her golden hair looped around it.

With a fluid motion, his mother reached over to the lock and, very loudly, said, "Otkroi," touching the gate lock with the end of her hairpin. With a searing bright flash, the gate flew open, but only a foot or so to hit the standing brigand square on his knees. "Now!" she exclaimed. "Run, Tar!" Almost shocked into paralysis, Targon felt his helplessness turn to anger, and he ran, stooped over at the waist, at the gate, hitting it with all his might with his broad shoulder.

"What the . . . ?" was all the brigand could say before Targon hit the gate full force, knocking the brigand clear off the cart and onto the old

bridge where he landed on his back. Targon jumped out and down across to his mother's side, pausing at the edge of the bridge. He paused and, with a last look back, he could see the driver trying to calm the startled horses while the other brigand seated next to him sat still with a dumbfounded look on this face. Lastly, he saw Ann smiling and his mother with a serious but fleeting look on her face, reminding him of her last words: "Run!" With that, Targon leaped over the north side of the bridge and fell nearly twenty feet into the icy cold waters of the Rapid River.

The sky was getting dark, and Lady Salina looked out from atop one of the castle's crenellated towers in Korwell. She missed her husband, who was the captain of the king's guard. He had been gone a week on a personally led patrol far to the southeast in search of raiders. There had been rumors of bandits from Kesh that had crossed into Ulatha and headed south to pillage and plunder, and her husband had decided to lead the mounted patrol.

This left her with her two sons: Karz, who was three and soundly asleep at the moment, and her eighteen-year-old son, Cedric, who she was sure was in the library burning yet another candle as he perused yet another old scroll or tattered book. She closed her shawl around her even more as the cool air chilled her soft skin. Winter was gone, but summer had not yet arrived. The air was still cool in the spring night.

She looked at the small town of Korwell surrounding the ancient castle. Lord Korwell had claimed it for his own, and it served as the capital for the small villages and towns dotting the realm of Ulatha. She placed her hand down atop one of the large pieces of mountain granite the castle was composed of. No doubt it was carted here from some quarry in the Border Mountains many years ago, but the ability of the Ulathans to replicate the feat was nonexistent. Perhaps much smaller blocks of stone could be pulled at great cost and effort, but not the ones

that were used to construct this castle. They were massive and beyond the scale of anything currently capable. *So much lost,* she thought, feeling the rounded edge beneath her hand. So many centuries of weathering and use had the huge slab feel almost smooth to her touch.

"Missing your man, my lady?" an older woman asked, approaching from the stairwell onto the tower top.

"Ah, Agatha, you startled me. I didn't hear you approaching. Is Karz still sleeping?" Salina asked, turning to face the newcomer.

"Yes, been asleep ever since you put him in bed, and yes, before you ask me again as you do most every night, Cedric is burning a candle in the old library as usual."

"Well, he doesn't seem to be following in his father's footsteps. That's for sure," Salina said.

"You know the rumor in the court is your husband wants a second son to take up his sword when he is no longer capable."

Salina's face frowned. "You should know better than to listen to idle gossip in the kitchens. Karz was a gift. He just happened, and I am happy for it."

Agatha approached the tower's edge and looked down at the town, dimly lit with sooty oil lamps and glows from crude windows showing candle and fire light coming from within the simple dwellings of Korwell. "I meant you no offense, my lady. You know as well as I do I am fond of both your boys, though your older boy spends far too much time in his books and not enough time in the training yard. You know Lord Moross sees it the same way as I do," Agatha stated.

Salina noticed her use of the formal title for her husband. "Bran loves both his sons equally. Cedric is just . . . different, and if he doesn't fancy using a sword, then I'll be happy for him to learn something of the ancient ways. We've forgotten far too much, and few enough of us can even read. Let him find his own way, Agatha."

"Well, the way you baby them boys . . . it's no wonder Cedric turned to the book instead of the sword like his father. Karz will be different. You mark my words, my lady."

Salina looked away and gazed far to the north where she could just make out the line of mountains that practically encircled the realm, from the north over to the east and back again to the west. *Ulatha is one immense valley, and not so much a realm,* she thought to herself. The women stood in silence for a few moments more. "You may be right, Agatha, but either way, I support Cedric's work."

"Well, it's mighty strange with us common folk to see him this way, especially considering his lineage. It's been a while since you wielded the metal, but with warrior parents, it is confounding to understand how you have a bookworm for a child."

Salina thought deeply at Agatha's remarks. She and her husband had met when she was a warrior as well, and she could wield a sword still. Agatha did not take note of the yard sessions Salina partook of with the weapon's master. "Well, thank you for looking in on the boys for me before you retired for the night. You've been a good friend, Agatha."

Agatha shook her head, returning to the stairwell. "Good night, my lady, I look forward to seeing you happy again."

With Agatha gone, Salina focused her attention back to the town. It was getting late and she would retire soon, but she had a feeling of dread coming over her. The feeling wasn't overwhelming, nor did it happen upon her suddenly, but more it felt like it grew slowly this last day as if something bad was going to happen to her. She tried to shake the feeling off. She would head to the kitchen and pack a few provisions for a picnic, and first thing in the morning, she would take her boys out to their favorite spot near a small stream west of the town. It would do them good to get some fresh air, and for her to get her mind off of her husband's absence and the feeling of dread that pervaded her mind.

She walked away from the inner edge of the huge granite blocks that crenelated the tower, oblivious to the darkly dressed figures sprayed out in a three-point hold onto the tower wall with wicked looking daggers in their hands.

Craylyn breathed a sigh of relief as the Ulathans left the tower. He and his companion were Balarian assassins and had spent the better part of two hours laboriously free-climbing the northernmost tower of the king's castle. Just when they were about to finish their climb, the damn Ulathan woman appeared and interrupted their ascent. They had both pulled their daggers and were ready to kill her instantly if she looked over the outer edge of the crenelated tower, but the cold wind and stone must have kept her away from the edge. Then that chatty old hag had showed up, complicating things further, before, finally, they both left.

Normally, he would have preferred to make the ascent during the middle of the night, but they had orders to find the library and look for a specific book. Their instructions indicated it would be easy to find by its color, blood red. So they needed to make the ascent and find the time to look for the book first and then proceed with the primary mission when the signal sounded.

Both climbers stayed motionless for several minutes, listening to any sounds coming from above, but there were none. *The security of this place is a joke*, Craylyn thought to himself. Not even a sentry posted here. Most likely, the lord of this place thought the castle unassailable. Eventually, he placed the dagger in between his teeth, careful to keep the edge away from his lips, and with a quick motion of his fingers, signaled to his companion to finish the climb. Within moments, they had made it to the top and crouched low near the open stairwell entrance, which had no door. It looked like there was once a large wooden one there, a few small rotten timbers visible on three massive, rusty hinges.

Craylyn sheathed his dagger, feeling his back to make sure his sword had not shifted, and then quickly patted his inner tunic pockets to make sure his darts and poison vials were still there. He noted his companion had done the same, and the other assassin signaled him with his fingers to his eyes and then pointed to the door. Craylyn nodded his head, and his colleague took up a lookout position at the stairwell, guarding against anyone coming from above.

His wizard clients paid well but were harsh and strict in their expectations. Although the Balarian had never been to Ulatha before, he had a crudely drawn map and information from his leader, Kendral, who had met them at a tavern below earlier that evening, providing the necessary information to complete their mission. When the twin sisters rose on the horizon, they would move into the castle and start looking for the distinct red book.

Our second mission is going to be most delightful, he thought, looking forward to taking care of yet another pompous man who had set himself up to be king. *There are far too many fools in Agon,* he thought to himself, pleased at the idea of meting out some Balarian justice. The foolish king probably had no idea of the traitor in his midst. They would find the wizard's book, meet with the traitor, and then kill the king. Now it was just a matter of time.

CHAPTER 5

ESCAPE

Targon felt the icy cold water hit him and take his breath away. He was not sure if the lack of ability to breath was from the twenty-foot fall or the icy coldness of the Rapid River. At either rate, he jumped to the north side of the bridge and the water flowed from north to south, so the icy, fast moving water instantly swept him under the bridge and out past some rocks and a rather nasty five-foot fall into deeper water.

With a powerful lunge of his arms, Targon stroked hard to break the surface of the water. All he could hear were rather profane expressions of where the "little rat" disappeared to. The water of the Rapid River swept Targon quickly downstream, and the yelling and profanity soon faded into the distance. He did not know it, but his head had just missed a large boulder under the water during his fall that would have killed him. He was lucky in that regard.

With his mind reeling from the shock of the cold water, it was all he could do to keep his head above the river's surface as his entire focus right now was on just breathing. He couldn't say for just how long he struggled to maintain his ability to breath, but after some time, the river

finally relented its powerful grip on his body, and he could finally start to swim toward the east riverbank, the side his family home was on. Targon pulled himself out onto a large, flat rock that jutted out into a bend of the river, and just laid there, taking in deep breaths of air to replenish his stock of oxygen.

After a short period of time, he felt the urge to move before some of the brigands decided to run downstream after him. He was still shivering from the cold of the water. He wasn't sure which way to run at first, but then the thought of his house burning was enough to anger him, and he set out toward his homestead. The cold water had started to kill him, and his limbs ached and burned as he tried to run along the shore's bank. He veered cross country toward his homestead.

It took a few hours before he arrived, sore and half frozen, wet clothes dripping still from his body. He was close enough to sense danger, so he crept around the back of the shed that doubled for a barn, looking for cover to see if there was anyone about. He saw no one and was just about to leave toward the old oak tree where his bow and small axe were at when he could hear noises coming from along the trackway. Quickly, he ducked back behind the old shed and peered around the corner.

"Look, lively mates," said a brigand, entering the area from the trackway.

"What'z all dis aboutz?" asked the brigand called Traps.

"Seems dat one of dem damn rats has slipped the cage, he has," said the just arriving brigand as he looked around the homestead. "Have you seen him?"

"Notz at all," replied Traps. "Oi, Skinner, you hearz anything about dis little ratz?"

The brigand Skinner appeared from the cabin doorway shadow and looked about. Targon feared he would be spotted as for one moment the brigand appeared to look directly at the shed. "Ain't seen nothing at all, but if the little bugger comes home, I'll give him a rightful greeting

indeed." The brigand guffawed, taking a swill of drink from a flask at his side.

This seemed to relax the first brigand who brought the news, and he chuckled slightly as he headed back along the trackway. "The chief seems to think he will head back here, so stay alert, mates," he replied, sauntering back up the trackway.

Targon pondered this for a moment as a plan formulated in his mind. Behind the shed, he had laid in some old dry straw that was used for their cow, Myrtle. This helped Targon warm up a bit, and he took off his wet cloak and tunic and grabbed a dry burlap sack that he wrapped around himself to try to get warm.

It was two on one for now, and, despite what his mother told him, he was not going to let them be sold as slaves anywhere if he could help it. Targon was younger but just as tall and much heavier than these Kesh brigands. He had been raised his entire life on the frontier in and around the Blackthorn Forest. He was smart enough to know he could do scant little unarmed against these ruffians, and so he slowly crept back behind the shed until he was out of sight and sound of his home, and then he headed to the old oak tree.

The tree had stood for half a century before dying and then later succumbing to Targon's axe the day before, but it silently stood guard over Targon's bow and axe tonight. Targon let out a sigh of relief as he secretly worried that someone, or something, had taken his weapons. Weapons, indeed, now, though before he always thought of them as tools to chop wood and hunt for food in and around the forest.

Tonight, however, as he hefted both items, he realized the severity of what had happened, and he thought not only of his family, his mother and sister being held in a dirty cart cage and his brother unwarned and vulnerable somewhere on a parapet wall or manning a murder hole in the capital, but he thought fondly of his deceased father and how he sacrificed himself seven years ago to save the family from these same brig-

ands. An emotional fire of feelings, could he call it *hate,* welled up within him, and he quickly headed back to the homestead, a glint of determination flashing in his eyes.

"Doz you thinks the little rat willz return here?" asked Traps, looking north along the trackway near the homestead as if expecting the little "rat" to come strolling along merrily on his way.

"Nah, I don't think he is that stupid even if he thinks as young as he looks," replied the other brigand.

"What didz you—" But the rest of the sentence was cut off midstream as instantly the shaft of an arrow appeared, protruding from the brigand's throat where his vocal cords were. The other brigand gasped for a moment, half spitting out the wine he had just started to swallow and dropping his flask as he ducked and pulled a wicked-looking curved blade from its sheath, but the action proved to be too slow.

Targon was miffed his first shot fell short. He wasn't used to shooting from such a distance and was actually aiming for the first brigand's head, but the arrow lost some altitude in the cool night air and hit the man's neck instead. Probably a good thing, as the arrow would have hit a hard skull, and from that range, there was no telling if it would penetrate or just make the brigand angry. Targon didn't have to worry, though. The bow was made by his father using the finest and strongest oak wood and a slight but strong string his mother had crafted especially for it.

The second arrow ended that debate as Targon was now aiming for dead center mass and hoping to hit the gut of his enemy. The enemy, however, ducked just as the arrow arrived, and the shaft buried itself into the brigand's skull with such force that it pinned the brigand's head to the doorjamb as the curved blade dropped to the ground.

Targon took a moment to assimilate what he had just done. His entire life, he had only been in a situation once, seven years ago, that required him to take the life of another human being. He trained for it as any frontiersman did, but usually wolves, bears, deer, and, of course, rabbits were the most he ever expected to have to slay. Today, however, he understood the meaning of family, freedom, and honor. He did what he had to do. They started this, and by all the gods of Agon, he was going to finish it . . . again.

Well, first a change of clothes, he thought as he shivered and let fall the loosely tied burlap sack. He was a hunter, after all, and knew that running off after the Kesh was a bad idea with his skin shining in the sister's moonlight and his teeth clattering from the cold. Normally, he had a nice dark brown leather tunic and a lighter brown cloak, but those were soaking wet, as were his trousers.

He ran over to the front porch where the brigands were and, taking a quick look to make sure they were indeed deceased, he entered the cabin and began to change his clothes. He took his old black cloak that was tattered, as his newer, cleaner one was stolen by those filthy thieves. He grabbed the darkest trousers he could find as well as a black tunic left behind, as it was too large to fit any brigand, and besides, as their leader had said, they were mainly there to rob and steal provisions. Targon was pretty sure they had cleaned out the shed and barn area, as it was too quiet on the homestead. He could not hear any animals making any kind of noise at all.

Finally, he grabbed his pack that he always used to carry provisions in and a large coil of rope that was stored in the upper rafters where he would normally sleep and where the brigands had luckily overlooked during their thievery. There were only a few apples and some jerky in the small pantry underneath the basin they used as a sink, and again, he was glad for the inattentiveness of his enemies. He made sure he took everything he could and placed the rope, apples, and jerky in his pack and hoisted it onto his back.

He was about to leave when he spotted his carving of the Clairton bird he had gifted to his mother. It was knocked off the pinecone where he had set it, and it was just near the hearth, lying in the corner. It was

hard to see, but Targon had excellent eyesight, especially at night. With a quick reach, he grabbed the carving and stuffed it into his right tunic pocket, determined to return this gift when he freed his mother. Newly dried from head to toe . . . well, at least down to his knees, as his socks were dry but the boots still squished when he walked, wet with cold water. He only had one pair of boots, anyway, and wet or dry, that was what he had to wear. With a squishing sound of each step, Targon took off, leaving his homestead, and headed north along the trackway after his mother and sister.

Hork was not happy. He could see the old, partially destroyed keep tower from the road as he approached it on horseback, riding quickly with his lieutenants. *Amazing,* he thought when he had crossed the only bridge north over the Gregus River, *that the large but old structure remained intact after so many centuries, and yet, the old keep is crumbling and half destroyed.* It did not appear that the same builders had built the two. The differences were obvious.

Hork didn't have time to dwell much on the finer points of ancient engineering and architecture as he approached, and could just barely make out the figures of his three Kesh masters. They weren't as forgiving as he would have liked them to be, and Kesh brigand captains had fairly short lifespans, so when he was "promoted" to lead this raid on Ulatha, he pretty much felt as if he had received a death sentence.

There were successes and the entire Kesh army, if one could call a loose consortium of brigand bands an army, was ready to strike, and he was about to report that news to his masters. The other news wasn't so good. He had talked to one of their spies who had reported a fully mounted patrol had left the capital and rode south in search of raiders and pillagers. No doubt one or more of their Kesh patrols had disobeyed orders and started to have a little early fun. This could jeopardize the

entire mission. The wizards wanted to trap the entire armed contingent inside the capital and not have an armed patrol running around the realm at will. Hork understood this, and that was most likely one of the main reasons for his "promotion."

Hork arrived at the base of the keep and saw the sentries at the base of the ruined tower stairs. He handed the reins of his horse to a handler and started for the broken stairs to ascend to the top, mindful not to step on a crack or gash in the staircase and break a leg or sprain an ankle. Informing them that several peasants and children had also escaped from the many farms and homesteads that dotted the surrounding countryside didn't look good. It made him look incompetent.

Hork arrived at the top of the tower followed by his two lieutenants, Arkhale and Kritor. He saw the group of mages standing silently, looking out from the ruined tower west toward the heart of Ulatha. This was just the opening of a grand offensive the Kesh wizards had planned for many years. There were not supposed to be wizards left in Agon after the great Dragon-Wizard war a millennium ago, so the sight of the three wizards was indeed out of place in Ulatha. Hork approached them. "All good so far, Masters." He bowed his head a tad in deference to them, yet peeked out with his left eye to see their reaction.

"Good," said the tallest of the mages, Am-Ohkre, as he turned from the parapet to face Hork and his henchmen. Though it pained the wizards to admit it, the brigands were Kesh just the same as they were, though they clearly thought themselves the superior class, as their fellow countrymen had devolved into lowly thieves and cutthroats, uneducated and uncultured. "Has the main army reached Korwell yet?" he asked.

"Yes, Master, the city will soon be under siege, and the outlying farms and villages have been cleared of all resistance," Hork replied as he swept his arms open, demonstrating the sweeping actions he just described, yet a tinge of hesitancy was apparent in his voice.

"And . . ." the tall wizard said with an arching of his white bushy eyebrows.

With a look at either side to his lieutenants, and seeing no help or aid forthcoming there, he stood erect from his bow, declaring, "Our spies reported a few horsemen from the city rode to the south about a week ago . . . and tonight there is the possibility that a farmer or two, children really, nothing to concern ourselves with, may have escaped our locks."

There was an uncomfortable pause until, finally, the elder wizard exploded. "The insolence!" he exclaimed. "Not to mention your incompetence. Those riders will alert those in the South before we can implement our plan. I ordered no raiding before the attack." The wizard starting shouting, and his face turned a bright shade of red. "There can be no failure, Hork!" And with that, the wizard lifted his staff from his right hand and a light began to glow at the end of it.

Hork was sure he was dead. There was no standing up to the power of a wizard. Hork grimaced as he closed his eyes and waited for the inevitable. There was a large, blinding flash of white and the crackle of a sonic boom as the sky was lit for several leagues, and the lieutenant standing to his right suddenly vanished in a puff of light and the only thing remaining was a quickly dissipating cloud of ash.

"That was excessive, no?" said the youngest-looking wizard as he stepped over to wave his hand around the ash cloud, stifling a cough with the sleeve of his other arm.

"Mind your tongue, Khan," replied the second wizard as he, too, stepped over to see the Arch-Mage's handiwork.

"Oh, please, Ke-Tor," Khan replied as he rolled his eyes. "Any secrecy probably just went out the window with Am-Ohkre's fireworks display. Most likely they could see this from Korwell."

Hork froze in place, not wanting in the least to get in between squabbling wizards, and somewhat elated he was not a pile of ash right now,

but Kritor was a good lieutenant and Hork would miss him as they had much work to do. Am-Ohkre was not in the mood to deal with a wizard apprentice, much less this one. Khan was notorious for his insolent mouth, and Am-Ohkre was just as suited to allow his one-time apprentice, Ke-Tor, to handle the situation.

"Khan, take Hork and track down any survivors from around the countryside. I will personally take care of the contingent of riders from Korwell. Do you understand me . . . wizard?" Ke-Tor asked with a mocking emphasis on his last word. Khan understood clearly the sarcasm sent his way as he himself didn't even warrant nor deserve the prefix title any Kesh wizard would add to his name. Once a true wizard, Khan would take the Kesh prefix for a standard wizard and add Ke to his name, becoming "Ke-Khan," but not yet and not today. Today, he would simply remain Khan, the wizard apprentice, though Hork and any other brigand didn't really distinguish between them, as even an apprentice was more dangerous than most brigands, and any true wizard would wreak havoc with an entire company of Kesh fighters.

"Fine, I'll start now, then," Khan replied, looking over at the tall wizard Am-Ohkre as he gathered his personal belongings and headed to the top of the partially destroyed stairwell. "Come on, Hork, show me where these dangerous peasants were last seen so I can take care of what you should have done already," he said mockingly, and with a motion of his hand, Khan gestured for Hork to lead him down the broken staircase.

After they had left, the wizards returned to the south-facing parapet, and Ke-Tor cleared his throat. "Was that really necessary?"

"Maybe," replied the tall wizard. "The filthy thieves are plentiful enough, and besides, that should motivate old Hork properly." Then the tall wizard chuckled a bit, seeming to enjoy the events that had recently transpired.

"Understood, Am-Ohkre, but Kritor was a capable leader even for a thief."

"Yes," replied the tall wizard, "but Hork is the most capable, and, despite his failure, I was not ready to lose him yet. Had I taken any of the other brigands, they would have lost respect for our order and thought the whole incident amusing, no doubt. No, an example was set, and the right example it was. Now just keep that insolent dabbler of the black arts on his leash or I will set yet another example," Am-Ohkre replied, referring to Khan.

"I will," replied Ke-Tor.

"Good. Take the Iron Hand Company and the Red Throat Company and finish Korwell. Track down those riders who escaped and meet me at the eastern edge of Cree in three days," Am-Ohkre said in a stern voice, referring to a village near Korwell. "Oh, and see to it that the Bloody Hand Company finishes its business on the near side of these mountains. I won't stand for some sort of peasant uprising behind our lines. In fact, see to it that Khan deals with it personally." He chortled, quite pleased with himself, as he knew Khan was not a cold-blooded killer, and that was exactly what the duty called for. It would be a form of punishment to put the young apprentice in his place.

"Yes, as you command." And with that, Ke-Tor walked over to an open crack in the parapet and stepped out from the top of the keep, falling at first but then gliding as his cloak opened and he murmured the spell of floating, gliding down to the ground where the waiting brigand captains were, and then he barked orders. "Time to kill!" he commanded, and then the wizard and brigands departed the keep along the ancient trade road toward Korwell.

"Indeed," gloated the Arch-Mage Am-Ohkre as he watched Ke-Tor depart for Korwell. So far the move down into Ulatha had remained uneventful. The mountain pass was now fortified and guarded. Several companies of brigands were marched into Ulatha and had taken up strategic locations, ready to attack when he gave the command. Kesh did not have enough soldiers to hit Ulatha everywhere at once, and that was why

Am-Ohkre was so upset. The plan called for hitting the North first and taking out the "king" and his ilk so the rest of the wretched realm would be leaderless. Am-Ohkre was worried the news from Hork would bode ill for Kesh, but it was too late to change anything. They were committed.

Am-Ohkre stood alone on the top of the tower, resisting the call from the Cretir located in his tent in a field behind the old keep. He knew Am-Sultain was calling for him, and the urge to respond was growing in a part of Am-Ohkre's mind. *How insulting, to be forced to act like a lap dog to a lesser mage. Yes, lesser*, he thought. Sultain did not deserve the position of High-Mage, sitting safe in the Onyx Tower while he directed others . . . No! Not others, himself, too, the mightiest Arch-Mage to reveal himself since the last passing of Akun.

No, he would clear those thoughts from his mind. No telling what kind of mindreading sorcery Sultain commanded, or perhaps he simply exercised astute powers of observation. Either way, sooner or later, he knew he would be dragged back to the Cretir, back to the orb to answer Sultain's summoning, so he would do so with a clear mind. As soon as he finished that thought, the hair on the back of his neck stood on end, and he felt as if he was being watched, alone though that he was on the top of the ancient ruined tower. He took one look up before heading back to his tent.

Even the mages didn't notice the falcon flying high above them, circling and watching. There were stranger things than mages and dragons on Agon, and arrogance often blinded even the smartest living creatures to the natural world. After sometime, when the many troops had left and the wizards as well, the lone remaining Arch-Mage finally looked up and thought he saw the vanishing form of a bird flying south, but he couldn't tell for sure if what he saw was real or part of his imagination.

Many miles later, and just before sunup, the falcon glided slowly, circling above Blackthorn Forest. Barely noticeable was a large rock, a hilltop actually with an enormous rock capped on top of it, and standing there was an old man in a brown robe, also with a wooden staff but dressed much differently from those from Kesh. It was too dark for anyone or almost anything, except the hawk or maybe an eagle, to see the man, but slowly, the falcon landed on the outstretched arm of the brown-robed man, and the pair quickly vanished into the forest just before the dawn.

CHAPTER 6

MARISSA

The chill night air was always coldest before dawn. Dawn was still a couple of hours away, and despite his anger, Targon was starting to feel not only tired but stiff and sore from all of his exertions. Despite his attempt to run quickly and silently, it appeared he could do neither. He squished with every step in his wet boots and the weight of them kept his legs from making long strides, so he struggled to maintain any speed or momentum. Only the thought of his family kept him going.

Suddenly, there was a flash of light from the northeast. In fact, Targon was sure it came from the old keep that was abandoned not far from his homestead. So suddenly was Targon illuminated that he simply dropped to the ground and held his breath. It was impossible for someone to miss seeing him with that much light, but just as suddenly as it appeared, it vanished into darkness, and the entire area was bathed back into shadows and darkness. Then a sudden boom rolled over him, much like thunder on a stormy night. He could only shiver at the thought of whom or what was powerful enough to make a flash and roar as if from the gods above.

Finally, after several moments of silence, he found the courage to stand back up and resume his journey.

"I'm not moving fast enough," Targon muttered to himself in desperation. After dispatching the two brigands who threatened his home, he had traveled all the way back to the ancient trade road and looked west toward the bridge he saw in the far distance, indeed the very same from wince he had jumped. He didn't like the looks of the road now: it was set much higher on an embankment to either side, unlike his homestead's trackway, which was nearly invisible if one wasn't looking for it. In fact, it was mostly blocked on either side: brushes on the riverside and tall grass and weeds on the other side. Was there a brigand guard on the bridge? It looked empty, but he couldn't be sure of the far side as the old stone bridge arched somewhat from the east bank, peaking over the river and descending on the western side. That side he could not see for sure. He had to get closer, so he ran along the edge of the road over half a league before hiding on the southern side of the road, and just in time.

Just before he could think of making a run for it, he started to hear the hooves of horses rapidly approaching from the east. Quickly, Targon ducked for cover in a particularly large group of rushes near the bridge and road and waited for the riders. Not long thereafter, a large group of brigands led by an older rider with a cape and a strange pointy but crooked hat and a staff set over his saddle rode past the trackway along the road and quickly were lost to sight after crossing the bridge.

Targon suddenly realized the futility of his situation. Yes, the cart traveled down the trackway at walking speed, but once on the road and across the bridge, there was no reason for it to travel so slowly. In fact, the brigands that had left his homestead took off in a run after their brigand leader, who was horsed. He was going to have to pick up the pace. With one last listen and a deep breath, Targon stood, though still in somewhat of a crouched stance, and darted off to his left toward the bridge. He

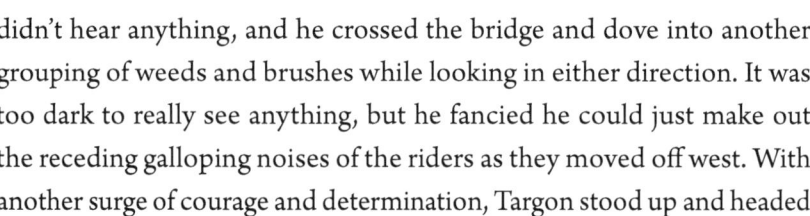
didn't hear anything, and he crossed the bridge and dove into another grouping of weeds and brushes while looking in either direction. It was too dark to really see anything, but he fancied he could just make out the receding galloping noises of the riders as they moved off west. With another surge of courage and determination, Targon stood up and headed west, staying just off the road in case more riders approached, or worse, there was a guard or sentry along the road.

After what seemed an eternity, Targon noticed the growing light in the east. Dawn would soon arrive, and he would have to make a decision then. He had traveled a couple of leagues when he noticed there was a trackway again to the south. He was familiar with it, as it headed to some other homesteads of some woodsmen and their families as well as farmers. The problem was while there were horse tracks heading down this trackway and the road, there were also several cart tracks heading in both directions as well.

He desperately wanted to continue, but which way had they gone? Despair started to set in so he took a deep breath and composed himself. He was a woodsman, and he would think this through. Targon stepped back from the old road along the little trackway, careful not to disturb the cart and horse tracks, and began to look at the tracks slowly and carefully.

Kesh was to the east, so that was the way from which they came. Those tracks were arriving ones. Targon started to think about the cart. It had uneven wheels, barely perceptible but uneven, he knew because he rode in it. Yes, the left wheel was larger, meaning it bit into the ground more when it turned. He turned his attention back to the tracks heading west. In the pale moonlight, but with his excellent eyesight, he could just make out the left track appearing deeper than the right one. *Of course!* he thought to himself, somewhat elated to have accomplished such an important task. They arrived from Kesh but continued westward toward the capital Korwell. Other cart tracks did turn down the small trackway,

but not with the same bite the left wheel of his cart had. They had for certain continued west and did not go to the South. He was just about to move out yet again when he heard a loud horn sound from the east.

Ah-Roooommm. The horn sounded, both loud and deep. It was in turn answered by several other horns sounding in the distance. One horn sounded, and it was a smaller horn but much closer and much sharper, coming from down the rutted trackway. Targon turned and again darted into some bushes and weeds and gripped his axe. He thought he could hear in the distance shouts and screams and the sound of metal on metal, but he couldn't be sure. *This must be the signal,* he thought, and indeed, not long after the first sounds of the horns began, there appeared many spots of lights throughout the valley. Targon recognized them as burning homes, cabins, and hutches. This was the fate that had awaited his own cabin had he not gotten rid of those foul brigands.

Targon was torn between wanting to run down the trackway and assist his neighbors—though they lived quite some distance from him he knew many of them by name—or to continue on his quest to free his family. It took a long while before he finally decided to head west along the road. He was not sure what, if anything, he could do for his far flung neighbors, and he had promised his mother he would find and alert his brother and it appeared he had been too late to keep his promise. Even if he had a horse, it would have taken him much longer than this to at least arrive in Korwell. Perhaps his mother did not think the Kesh had gone so far so quickly? At any rate, he took off west toward a small fire in the distance.

Targon approached the small hamlet, which was burning brightly. He could feel the heat coming from it. The roar of the flames was loud and intermingled with the occasional popping of gas pockets within the wood of the structure as it burned. It was set off the main road by only a stone's throw. He remembered seeing the farm when he had to use the road between his home and the capital. There were no signs of brigands,

though they had to be close at hand, as the fire had started not long ago. He saw no signs of life. Most likely they cleared this roadside home out earlier, much the same as they had done to his own.

He was about to continue when he noticed a set of gleaming eyes riveted upon him from a pile of old stale hay just to the side of the burning building. Targon gripped his axe tightly, leaving his bow strung across his back, and faced the set of eyes. He did not think it a brigand, as the eyes were much too low and the Kesh tended to be taller and lankier than what he was looking at. He crossed over slowly and quietly to where the eyes were, and they suddenly blinked and disappeared into the haystack. With a quick lunge, however, Targon managed to get ahold of the edge of a dress and pull on the little girl who had dove headfirst into the hay-stack. Pulling back and clearing the child's head from the straw, he was quick to shush the child, motioning for her to remain quiet.

"Shhh, what's your name, little one?" he asked, brushing some straw from her matted hair. When the child didn't answer, he prompted yet again. "Your name? Can you speak, girl?" He smiled.

The smile must have done the trick, and the girl looked over once at the burning building and then back to Targon. "My name is Marissa. Are you one of those thieves?" she asked nervously.

"Of course not. My name is Targon, and you can see from the manner of my dress that I am no ruffian from Kesh, and neither do I hurt inno-cent people. Are you okay? Are you hurt at all?" he asked while looking her over from head to toe, relieved not to see any signs of blood or injury.

"I am not hurt," she replied, "but my family . . ." Then she broke off and started to cry silently, small tears starting to stream down her cheeks.

"Shhh, I understand . . . Marissa it is, right?" he asked while holding the young girl and allowing her to cry into his tunic.

"Yes." She sobbed a bit, gaining control.

"Were they in the building?" he asked tentatively.

"Just my papi, who they killed first," she replied, new tears forming in her eyes. "But they took my mother and my brother. I ran out the back and hid in the haystack. I saw them in a cage, do you know where they are? Will they come back?"

"I don't know, but we will do what we can to reunite you with them. My family was taken as well," Targon explained, pained emotion evident across his face.

This is getting out of control, Targon thought to himself. How could so much go so wrong so fast? First, his family, then, this family, and most likely every family in the entire valley was affected. Targon felt spent. The adrenaline from earlier in the night was fading, and he was still cold and tired and now he had a little girl to deal with of all things, though in all fairness, the girl appeared to be in her younger teens and much older than his sister, Ann, was. He was just about to suggest they go and search for her family when he heard yet again the sound of approaching hooves.

"Quick, into the haystack," he said, pushing Marissa on the small of her back, shoving her deep into the base of the small haystack, following alongside of her as best he could. He wiggled near the edge so he could peek out and see who was arriving. He didn't have long to wait before two horses arrived with tall, lean brigands atop of them.

"Hoi, Crates, where are you?" the taller of the two brigands called out. Much to Targon's shock and dismay, two more brigands appeared from around the other side of the burning building. He felt so stupid this whole time talking to the girl and not more than one hundred feet away were two ruffians ready to kill them both or worse.

"Waz looking for dat girl dat ran away," Crates responded with a forlorn look into the fields north of the burning house. "She'd fetch a pretty penny on da market, for sure." He chuckled, and his companion nodded his head in agreement.

"Well, don't waste your time on just one slaver when we have plenty more around that are easier pickings than running through the brush all day. Now, gets going to the rendezvous point before dawn or there'll be hell to pay," he said sternly.

The two brigands on foot headed west just out of sight of where Targon could see, but very quickly, they were mounted on horses that must have been tied up just out of sight. Also, over the roar of the flames and fire and the cackle of wood embers and trapped gasses blowing and popping every so often, it was hard to hear anything unless one was near another or as was the case of the brigands. They were practically yelling at each other to be heard over the roar of the fire. Soon, the galloping receded into the distance as the four riders took off west and out of sight and sound.

Targon thought for a moment and felt Marissa squirming beside him. He hoped she could breathe adequately enough, and since the hay was coarse, there was room for that and more. He pulled her to the edge of the stack and made a decision. "Marissa, we need to stay here for now, all right?" he asked. "We need to stay off the road during the day, and I think we both could use some rest, eh?" He nodded his head, encouraging her to agree with him.

"All right," she said, stifling a yawn, "but wake me if my family returns?"

"Of course," he said, pulling some stray hay to cover up their heads and feet. His adrenaline had finally left him, and the near shock from meeting Marissa, followed by almost getting caught by what he felt was his sheer stupidity, left him utterly exhausted. He had no idea what to do with this young girl, and looking after someone else wasn't part of his plan, either. He couldn't just leave her here to the fate of one of those leering Kesh brigands, but neither could he just take her with him, could he?

He saw through the random straws of hay, as much as he felt it, the growing light in the east. It would be dawn soon, and he would be more

vulnerable if caught out in the open. He needed time to think. Having been up all day and most of the night, he started feeling tired, though he was more confident they were not visible to any passerby on the road, and so he closed his eyes and sleep took him quickly.

This is all wrong, thought Khan as he rode down a small trackway toward the closest hut to Kesh in this valley. Slavery, rape, pillaging, and plundering were the way of the Kesh ever since the Dragon War, but Khan never took a liking to it. He found it hard to believe even the remnants of a once proud people and race had succumbed to this as he looked around at the brigands around him. *A lonely group of degenerates if ever I saw one*, Khan thought to himself as they arrived at a clearing and a small hut where the trackway ended. He wasn't sure he would have even seen the trackway if one of the brigand trackers hadn't pointed it out to him.

The hut hardly deserves notice, he thought as he looked at such a sad structure. "And what exactly was here?" he asked Hork.

Hork motioned for one of the riders to move forward. "Tell the young master what transpired here, Bolt," he said.

"We took a wood-witch and her two children," Bolt started. "No problems at first, and we put them in the lock cart . . ."

"What did you call her?" asked Khan.

"Who, Master?" replied Bolt.

"A wood what?"

"A wood-witch, Master," replied Bolt, looking confused and unsure why he was being questioned in such a manner.

"What exactly is a wood-witch?" asked Khan, both impatient and yet curious to find out what exactly had happened here and where this "witch" was at.

"A druid," responded Hork, cutting Bolt off. "Some of the boys here refer to the wood-folk as 'witches' when they mean druid."

"Rubbish, There is no magic outside of Kesh, much less in an out-house of the frontier of the wild, but do go on," he finished mockingly with a look of disdain crossing his face.

"Well, uh, anyways, Master, we left Traps and Skinner here to torch the place and took off after the other huts along the valley, but theyz on the other side of this here river and I hadz to go all the way back to that der blasted bridge, you sees?" He looked over at Khan to gauge if he was following and possibly approving of his actions so far.

"And . . ." was all Khan said.

"Then the she-witch, er, I mean, druids lady, places a curse on me boys here and blinds them something fierce. I told them, I did, to gag her, but she somehowz got free and loosed the cart gate as well, and off jumped her little rat boy, he did, and jumped into this herez bloody river."

Khan thought for a moment more. "And what happened here?" He motioned to the two dead bodies of Traps and Skinner lying side by side in front of the little cabin where some other brigands had dragged them.

"Well, he must have come back and slain them, Master," Bolt replied, looking forlornly at the bodies of two of his soldiers.

"Some 'rat' boy he must have been, eh, Bolt, to have bested and killed two of your foot soldiers?" Khan commented in a condescending manner.

Bolt decided silence was the better choice than to try to defend the actions, or should he say inactions, of two of his troopers. Besides, he didn't want the wizard, young though he was, to pry too much, else he might find out Bolt had ridden on ahead of the cart, eager to find himself some more spoils before they were all taken.

"Let's ride," stated Hork. "Time to move out. Bolt, you stay here and torch the place when the signal comes, and see to it personally." He looked him once over to put him in his place.

"No," responded Khan simply. "Leave the place as is."

"Two of our own lay slain, Master," replied Bolt. "Surely the code demands revenge, no?"

"Yes, it does, Bolt," Khan replied, slightly rolling his eyes as if speaking to a child, "but this young 'rat' as you call him will most likely return here, back home where his cheese is, so to speak. Our forces are even now scouring across these lands, and he won't have many places to hide. No, he will return eventually, and when he does, you can capture him. But if he sees the place burned down to the ground from a distance, he will not return and we cannot afford to have an entire company out searching for him. There is work to do."

"How 'bout kill, Master?" replied Bolt with a wicked grin on his face.

"Not yet. Let us make him talk and tell us more about his escape. I want to know how they managed it from one of our sturdy lock carts. Not an easy task."

"As you command, Master," Bolt responded.

"Good, see to it personally," replied Khan, wheeling his horse around and starting off toward the ancient trade road again, Hork and company in tow, leaving Bolt and a few other brigands of the Bloody Hand Company to set an ambush for Targon.

CHAPTER 7

REFUGEES

Targon knew his family was far from where he was, and things were now far more complicated with the current situation he found himself in. He couldn't just leave Marissa to her fate, and with her, he couldn't cover near enough ground to look for his family. Still, he knew he had to warn the people of Korwell, though he felt for sure it was too late for that now, and at least look to see if he could find his brother, if not his mother and sister.

"Wake up, Marissa." He shook her in her sleep. The sun was just past high and starting its decent to the west. It would be a bad thing to travel with it in their eyes, but neither did Targon like the idea of just sitting for a few hours more to wait for the sun to set, and he had an idea.

Stifling another yawn and pulling some straw from her matted hair, she replied, "Have you seen my family?"

"Not yet," he responded, afraid to say more. "I have an idea, though. Let's go search for them. Can you do that?"

"Sure," she replied, a smile growing across her face.

Targon looked her over. Thank goodness she had shoes, though he wasn't sure when she found the time to put them on. *Probably she was*

up early before dawn to tend to the animals, he thought as he looked at her some more and saw she was dressed simply but adequately for a day's long work. "Okay, but we stay off the road and you can't speak. Just whisper like me from now on," he said, lowering his voice to a whisper. She just nodded, but the fire had died down to a smoldering heap of embers and there was nothing to be heard at all, not even the tweeting of birds.

Targon led the way from the haystack over to the trade road, peering in both directions while crouching low. Seeing nothing, he darted across the road and into some tall grass and motioned for Marissa to follow. Soon, they were working their way south away from the road and slightly west away from the cabins to the south and east along the previous track-way Targon had come across. Thus, Targon hoped to travel south, and Korwell was indeed south as well but also west, and he didn't want the sun in their eyes. He would turn west when the sun set.

When it was almost dusk, they stopped under a low-limbed tree, affording some protection from being accidently discovered, and Targon pulled out two apples. Marissa hadn't complained of hunger all day. She ate it quickly and to the core. "Good?" he asked her.

"Yes, I was hoping we'd get something to eat. We had supplies, but I saw the thieves take everything, even the eggs in the hen house," she lamented.

"They took most of our supplies as well," he responded, "but not everything. I managed to tuck away a few items from our second pantry that they missed." And he handed her a piece of jerky as well as his flask for her to take a drink.

"Thank you so much, Targon," she responded, a smile on her face.

Targon returned the smile and drank and ate. They waited maybe half an hour more when dusk turned into night before taking off, this time heading more west than south. After several hours, they both were starting to get tired. They walked over a small rise near a small running brook,

and Targon thought he saw a very slight glow of light. "Get down!" he whispered in a high tone to Marissa. Marissa laid flat beside him as he peered out into the darkness across the brook. *It isn't that deep of a stream,* he thought. There was just enough starlight to see rocks just under the running water. The glow from the far side of the brook was so faint, yet just inside a crevice on the far shore. *Brigands?* he thought to himself. Seemed odd they would be this far from the road, but he had to know.

"Stay here," he told Marissa in a low whisper. "I'm going to have me a look." She just nodded and pulled herself closer to the ground. Targon edged back over the slight rise of the small east bank, crouching low, and headed north until the glow of the light was no longer visible. He then carefully approached the brook and walked lightly, careful to step and balance himself on each rock all the while making as little noise as possible. Once safely across, he took his bow from his back and nocked an arrow, creeping toward the light, which was now once again visible.

It was a good thing he was quiet, because as he approached, he thought he could just make out slight murmuring as if someone was talking in a hushed tone. He was going to turn the corner of the rock draw when he almost stumbled on a sentry. There was a shadowy figure sitting behind a small rock, just able to see over it, but the sentry wasn't looking out. Instead, he was peering in as if trying to follow the conversation, and of all things, he appeared to have a book in his hands. Targon thought for a moment whether or not he should shoot the sentry, but something didn't look right. Besides, he was so close to the sentry that an arrow seemed like overkill. *Okay, we do it nice and quiet-like,* he thought to himself.

Slinging his bow over his back and sheathing the arrow, Targon took out his axe, twisting it in his hand so that the side of the large blade was now facing outward. Targon took four quick steps moving to the sentry, wrapping his left arm around the other man's neck, covering his mouth with his hand, and at the same time, swinging the side of his axe across

the sentry's right temple. Targon was worried that if he didn't use enough force, the sentry would cry out and send an alarm, but too hard and he could kill the man, which if this was a brigand, he didn't mind, but the sentry seemed too small for one of the tall, lanky Kesh.

With a small *humph* and a slight exhale, the sentry was down. Targon peered over toward where Marissa should be and was satisfied to see nothing. *She stayed well hid*, he thought. Another glance down and he pulled back the hood of the sentry. It appeared to be a young man, much the same age as Targon, but from the looks of the lad, he was from the city. He was not Kesh: Ulathian, for sure, one of his own people dressed in fine but dirty clothes. Well, fine from Targon's perspective, as his clothes were actually made of cloth and not burlap. What was going on here?

Targon belted his axe and grabbed his bow and nocked an arrow again. He wanted to be ready to run if he had to, but he thought he had come across some fellow people from the city and he needed to be careful that they didn't kill him before they realized he wasn't a brigand. He crept around the corner and saw the glow of a small fire mostly blocked by a large blanket hung over a section of rope tied across the small gully. He could hear voices now, and he crept slowly up to the blanket and peered around the corner with only one eye.

There were several people there huddled around the fire, dressed much the same as the sentry was: fine clothes, robes, cloaks, and some blankets and linens. There were even some bowls and utensils and a pot hanging over the fire.

". . . but we can't go back," said a lady, elegantly dressed but no less dirty than the rest as she held a small boy in her arms, facing outward so Targon could clearly see the features of her face. She had high cheekbones and light blonde hair pulled up, exposing her ears. Her build was slender but fit. The boy she was holding had the same high cheekbones and blond hair.

"Well, neither can we walk around the wilderness with half of Kesh roaming around these parts. It's just a matter of time before they find us," said a large man, his back toward Targon but facing the lady, and his clothes weren't so fine, Targon noticed. More like those of a hired hand but with a chainmail shirt, he could most likely be a soldier.

"I'm telling you this time it's different," pleaded the lady. "They came here for good, not just a raid, and I'm telling you they breached the castle. Korwell is dead!" Her face turned ashen, and she grimaced at her own words.

"Well, if your man hadn't turned tail and ran off with half the troops, we wouldn't be out here now," the tall, rough-dressed man said.

"He was going to raise the alarm in the South, Will. You know good and well there is more at stake here than just our city, and where exactly was your duty post?" she replied, putting her boy down and standing up to face the rough-dressed man known now as Will.

With a quick movement, Will stepped around the left side of the fire and came face to face with her. He easily stood a full head taller than her, but she stood her ground and met his stare. "And just what do you think you are implying, eh?" he asked, anger in his voice as he spoke louder. "I killed several of them Kesh scum before the main gate was taken. I had no choice but to run for it just the same as you!" Taking his finger and pointing it directly at the lady's face.

Targon had had enough. If the light of the fire didn't bring an assassin, then surely the two of them arguing in the middle of the night would. He stood erect and came around the blanket, drawing his bow and, in one quick, fluid movement, unleashed his arrow between the two into the back wall of dirt in the crevice.

"What the . . . ?" exclaimed Will in shock. Several people dove onto the ground, groveling and crying, while a couple of others ducked behind some small rocks in the crevice, though truth be told, there was scant room for them to hide anywhere in the tight confines they now found

themselves. The lady pulled her son back behind her cloak and pulled out a small, slender sword from her belt sheath and stood facing Targon. Will was about to reach for his sword, leaning against a rock near the fire, when Targon spoke.

"Hold! Don't do it," he said and, at the same time, stepped forward more into the light and lowered his bow in a non-threatening manner.

"You're no Kesh," Will stated, eying Targon from head to toe.

"No, he's not," said the lady, looking at first at Targon and then past him. "Where is Cedric?" she asked, looking concerned.

Targon sighed, relieved the ordeal wasn't more unpleasant for any of them. "If you mean the young man you posted as sentry, he is still there, but his head will hurt by morning."

Pushing past the others who were all now standing and regaining their composures, the lady walked past Targon, giving him a glance that could almost be felt. "I hope you didn't hurt my son seriously," she said.

Reaching Cedric was relatively quick once past the blanket, and it took a second in the darkness to find him, but the lady reached down and started to stroke the young man's dark hair and call his name. "Cedric, can you hear me? Agatha, fetch me some water and a cloth quickly. I think I see blood," she said without looking back.

"What the hell did you do to him?" asked Will, striding to stand next to Targon near the blanket as he watched the lady tend to her fallen son.

"I gave him a nasty knock on the head. Some sentry you all posted, and lighting a fire was stupid," he said, looking back at the glow of the small fire that even now seemed to be sending out a pulsating signal saying *we are here* to anyone watching. "Put it out now," he stated rather firmly for being barely a young man in his own right and a stranger to boot.

Will looked him over and grudgingly grunted in the affirmative while walking back to the fire and kicking dirt on most of it, and then he pulled out one brand that was burning. He grabbed a flask and dumped the water on the fire pit. It went dark with a hiss and a cloud of white steam rising from the fire pit. A very little light was left from the one brand, which was all that prevented them from being plummeted into pitch blackness, deep in the crevice. "Here, hold this," Will demanded as he gave the low-burning brand to another man dressed in what looked to be a sleeping robe and a small cap.

An older woman with water and a rag rushed by Targon, giving him an evil glance, and then knelt by the sentry called Cedric. "Here you go, me lady," she said while offering the water and cloth followed by another scowling look back in Targon's direction.

"Thank you, Agatha," the lady said as she dipped the cloth rag into the water and gently wiped the face and brow of Cedric, who was still lying unconscious. "What is your name, lad?" she asked while turning to give Targon a quick look, eyebrows raising just the slightest.

Who is she calling lad? thought Targon, almost scowling at her, but there was something still gentle in the way she spoke, so Targon decided to forego any confrontation over his status with the group. "My name is Targon Terrel," he said while slinging his bow over his back and securing it in place. "What is your name?"

"I am Lady Salina of house Moross," she stated, "and this here is Will Carvel of the king's guard," she motioned with a nod of her head at Will, who had walked back to the other side of the blanket covering and was looking into the darkness.

"You alone . . . Targyll?" Will asked, not quite getting his name correct.

"It's Targon, if you please, Mister Will, and no, I have one other companion," he said, striding away past the ladies and Cedric, looking toward the little brook. "Marissa," he called softly into the night, looking at the hill where he had left her a little while earlier. "Marissa, it's me, Targon. You can come out now." He took a few steps into the brook, careful to step on solid stones and not get his feet too wet.

With a slight bound, he could just make out Marissa's silhouette as she stood up on the small bank line, and lost it when she walked down to the brook. "I can't see you well," he said, looking for her and thinking he could make out her dress in the pale starlight. "Can you cross here?" He motioned with his hand for her to come over.

"Yes," she said. Taking off her shoes and lifting her dress, she skirted over to the other side with the water coming up to just above her knees at the deepest. Arriving on the other side, she opened her mouth in a large gesture of surprise and said, "Is everything all right? I could hear noises and some muffled screams. Did you kill anyone, Sir Targon?"

Targon was just getting his eyes adjusted again to the night and could see her plainly now. "Don't call me sir. I am a simple woodsman, not a knight, and no, no one killed here, but one careless sentry does have a rather nasty bump on his noggin," he said, looking back over at the others, who, much to his satisfaction, were now much harder to see without the larger fire illuminating the area. "Do try to stay quiet, and don't talk to anyone until we know more about them." He looked at the small group gathered near the entrance to the crevice, curiosity now starting to overcome their fear.

Walking back over to the ladies and Will, Targon presented Marissa to them. "This is Marissa. She lost her family to the Kesh bandits last night," he said. He noted happily that poor Cedric had come around and was leaning against his mother's side, holding his head but remaining rather quiet and docile. No doubt the bump on his head and being taken by surprise like that didn't make him any more social than he already was.

The city folk looked at her in silence for a moment, not knowing what to say. The idea that others were affected hadn't really crossed their minds yet, and seeing this young girl, also muddied from head to foot standing there with a sad countenance on her face, was a bit much for most of them. "Come here, child," Agatha said, walking over to Marissa. Agatha

took off her cloak and wrapped it around Marissa and started to guide her back to the crevice. "Are you hungry, my dear?"

"Oh yes, it's late, but apples and jerky aren't very filling," she replied, looking hopeful.

"Well, we have some stew on a pot in the back," Agatha said as they walked past the blanket and out of sight.

"Is that your sister?" asked Will, looking from Marissa as she disappeared from sight back to Targon.

"No, I found her hiding near her home on the old trade road near the Rapid River," he said, motioning north. "Her family had either been killed or taken prisoner." He looked Will up and down and thought him to be a soldier of Korwell, but without any uniform or emblems to speak of, not the way he remembered his brother, Malik, dressed a year earlier when they met in the city. "Are you from Korwell?"

"Yes, Chief Sergeant of the main gate," he said, standing a bit taller and with a bit of better posture.

"And my husband is captain of the king's guard," replied Lady Salina. "We were overrun by brigands from Kesh." A look of sadness crossing her face. "Will Carvel here and I gathered what few people we found trying to hide and fled the city before they could kill us or take us prisoner. What happened to you?"

"The same. They took my mother and my sister prisoner, and I managed to escape," he said, leaving out the part about his mother's magic. Surely she wasn't a wizard, but he still had no idea how she had opened that locked gate on the lock cart, and he didn't want them to confuse her as some sort of sorceress. "My brother is a member of the guard in Korwell. Any news on how the guard fared in the attack?" Concern now showed across Targon's face.

Lady Salina looked down and then over at Will, who was now shuffling his feet and not appearing comfortable, either. Finally, Salina looked back to Targon. "The guard was slaughtered," she said, almost whisper-

ing the last word. "Only a few of the king's personal guards and knights escaped on horseback before the city was surrounded. Any soldier was put to the sword, while women and children and some men who were not soldiers were all locked away in large carts and taken," she finished.

Targon felt as if he was punched in the stomach. It felt hard to breath, and he started to feel tears well up in his eyes. Surely, he thought, when this ordeal began, he thought he could warn his brother in time of the danger to come. Even when it was obvious Korwell was attacked, he still had hoped the worst fate his brother would face would be being taken as a prisoner or slave, much as his mother and sister were. He didn't think the Kesh would commit wholesale murder on any soldier, much less his own brother. Strong men like his brother would be prized and valued as slaves for the labor they could perform. Something didn't make sense, and Targon was determined to find out what. "I have to go see for myself," he said finally, looking at both Will and Lady Salina, as Cedric rose to his feet.

"It's too dangerous," said Will. "They might mistake you for a soldier too, dressed like you are in all black, or an assassin and kill you first and ask questions later." Lady Salina nodded in agreement.

"I'll be back by tomorrow evening. Get some rest," he stated simply, a look of determination on his face, "and look after Marissa for me as well . . . please," he added, as he felt a twang of guilt for just dumping her on these people.

"You may not like what you find," Lady Salina offered, "but go and we will look after your friend, and we will wait a second day here for you." She smiled at him. "Fact of the matter is that we aren't sure what to do either. Go and tell us of what you find."

Targon cinched up his belt and took one last look at Will, Cedric, and Lady Salina. "I should be back by tomorrow evening, but if I'm not back by sunrise of the following day, it means the area isn't safe and best if you all head south. The north is crawling with brigands."

Targon did not look back. He walked a bit south, and then, finding another draw in the west bank, he climbed up and over the edge and continued his journey for a few more hours.

Just when the sun was about to come up, he came across a ridge line he thought he recognized. Lying on the ground and crawling slowly to its edge near some brushes and a large tree, he peered over the ridge top and down into the Korwell Valley, where he could see smoke and ruin. It was soon to be dawn, and there was no sign of activity. With his keen eyesight, he could make out the castle walls, but no guards were seen moving there. Finally, he saw some motion and looked closely, straining to make out the two figures that moved near the main gate. Bandits from Kesh! Then, slowly but steadily, a long procession of lock carts left the castle courtyard and headed northeast along the old road Targon knew so well.

He could make out what looked like a driver and a rider sitting up front and a guard on the back of each cart. After counting thirty carts, he noticed a smaller group of riders approaching the castle from the opposite direction. The two groups passed each other and then, with a sad heart and hope being replaced by despair, Targon reluctantly started to crawl back from the ridge top.

Good-bye, Malik, he thought to himself as he felt sad and at the same time his will hardened into a steely resolve. The brigands of Kesh would pay for this. Indeed they would, but first he started to formulate a plan. Maybe, just maybe, if his family was in one of those carts, he could find a way to free them. Not much he could do against ninety brigands, but against three, when it was dark, all he needed was a few seconds to free them. So, as the sun started to rise, Targon headed back, a plan formulating quickly in his mind.

CHAPTER 8

BATTLE

The taking and torching of Korwell was a success, thought Khan as he looked at the smoldering ruins of the castle and town surrounding it. Of course, they hadn't burned everything to the ground, but most of the town was, and the few bandits left in the city were in the castle while the rest were scouring the countryside for prisoners. Despite the many successes of the initial raid two days earlier, there were reports that far too many Ulathans escaped into the wilds around Korwell.

Khan himself had just returned from overseeing the burning of most of the homesteads to the east and the capture of various refugees trying to flee the area. They would fetch a hefty price in the slave markets far from here. The homes were burned to prevent any type of uprising or guerrilla warfare by the Ulathans. The Arch-Mage came up with this idea to deny sanctuary and sustenance to the inhabitants of Ulatha. So far it seemed to be working, as most of their prisoners were eventually caught near the roads and burned homesteads looking for food and/or provisions.

Having done his duty, though he really loathed it, he was returning to Korwell to meet with his mentor in charge of the offensive and report on his successes. Hork was riding alongside him, none too happy to have missed the sacking of the capital city, and no doubt as punishment for some of his prior failures. *Kritor had paid the price for that*, he thought sourly to himself. The column of brigand riders passed a long line of lock carts filled with mostly women and children and a few men who were, most likely, talented in one of several trades Kesh found lacking.

After some time, they passed through the burned city and through the main gate of the castle. Khan dismounted and headed to the top of the tallest tower, certain he would find his mentor there gloating at their dirty deeds. Khan wasn't sure why, but he often found his comrades at the top of towers, overlooking, always overlooking, but never really seeing what they had just stepped on. The sun was about to rise, and Khan was looking forward to its warmth.

"Greetings, Khan," said Ke-Tor, turning from the tower top and facing Khan, who had just climbed the three hundred and thirty-three stairs to reach the top. "How were the farming raids?"

Trying hard not to breathe too deeply and let his old mentor see his exhaustion at the long climb, Khan composed himself first before replying. "We finished the job. Took plenty of provisions and made sure there were no places of refuge for any Ulathans in the entire area."

"Good, Am-Ohkre will be pleased at the news," Ke-Tor responded, a smile crossing his middle-aged face. "I have to meet with him near the southern village of Cree." He turned back to look down at the remains of the capital city.

Khan walked over to the edge and also looked down. The sun was just rising, and the smell of death and burned flesh wafted over him despite how high he was standing above the mess. "So does Am-Ohkre intend to complete the raid on the entire realm?" he asked, swatting his hand at a fly buzzing near his nose.

"Indeed, I think he will. In fact, he will most likely move on Cree next and then finish with the outlying towns and villages to the south, including Forns," he said.

"Forns is south of the great Ulatha river. It will be difficult to cross it," replied Khan, again swatting at the annoying fly buzzing around his head. *How in all of Agon does a fly get to the top of this tall tower?* Khan thought to himself, momentarily distracted by the small insect.

"Am-Ohkre will see to that. Do not doubt, Khan, the power of the Arch-Mage," Ke-Tor responded, a stern look to his eyes.

"I'm sure he will," was all Khan said in return, finally just allowing the fly to land on his nose as he absentmindedly fondled his magical necklace.

"You will stay here and oversee the capture of any survivors from the initial raid. I must meet Am-Ohkre in one day's time outside of Cree. I'll inform Hork he is back in command of the army, and take him with me. We will leave you with the Bloody Hand Company as well as part of the Black Dagger Company to secure the area. We will take the other companies with us," Ke-Tor said.

As long as I don't have to deal with the Bloody Throat Company, thought Khan. They lived up to their name and were, in his opinion, the worst of the worst, killers through and through. "Fine," he said. "Do we use the balls or the birds?" he asked, referring to the preferred forms of communication in Kesh. Every wizard had a crystal ball called a critir, though not every wizard was adept at using it, and messages often got misread or not read at all, and while many were sure this had less to do with the ball and more to do with the wizard, they also had a backup system for the brigands to use: homing birds. Birds bred and used to find their mates. They always used them in pairs, one locked, and the other as the messenger bird, instinctually returning to its mate.

"Birds for now," replied Ke-Tor. "I doubt Am-Ohkre would trust you to use your critir effectively," he said mockingly but with a faint smile on

his face as he teased his young apprentice. "And stop your compulsive fiddling with your little healing trinket. Those Talamans are a waste of time and gold," Ke-Tor finished, referring to Khan's magical necklace. Striding away and jumping onto the parapet of the tall tower facing the northern courtyard, Ke-Tor jumped off the tower.

Normally it was a sight to see, as the wizard plummeted most of the way to the ground, and despite his desire not to look, Khan leaned over in time to see his mentor, pointy hat still on his head, staff in his left hand but his cloak flapping wildly, plummet almost all the way to the ground. The man's cloak ceased is flapping and, almost like a feather, Ke-Tor floated the rest of the way, landing on his feet, with several brigands wide-mouthed, looking at him in awe.

Khan tucked his necklace into his tunic. *One day*, thought Khan, *he will not say the spell correctly and his little fall will have a different result*, and then with one fluid stroke, he swatted the fly from his nose, and it, too, began the long fall to the ground.

Targon suddenly woke up, almost hitting his head on a small tree branch. He had stumbled wearily back toward the small brook and crevice where the refugees and Marissa were hiding. About halfway back, he found a nice little place in a hollow with dried pine leaves and low-hanging branches. He only intended to lie there for an hour or so, just rest himself enough to return, but he must have slept longer, much longer. He couldn't see any shadows nor could he see the sun. He peered out, and from what he could tell, the sun was getting close to the western horizon. *Damn*, he thought to himself, *how many hours did I sleep?*

He oriented himself and just started east again when not far from where he had slept he came across a group of large tracks. Not tracks from the refugees he had found earlier, and not his own, but deep, booted tracks and at least one horse track. Targon kneeled and took a close look.

While he was only used to tracking wild game, it wasn't much different to track a human. Targon shuddered: he thought he counted at least a dozen tracks. "No, no, no . . ." he muttered to himself as he started off east at a much quicker pace.

After what seemed to be hours, Targon heard the running water of the brook. His heart chilled as he heard faintly some sort of cruel laughter and something else. *Sobbing cries?* he thought to himself. Slowly, he pulled out his bow and nocked an arrow. He only had nine arrows and worried what he would do if there were more than nine Kesh here. Creeping low, he found a small draw and started down into it and approached the running brook.

"Poke him good," Targon heard as he slid around a bush near a small tree and could now see clearly several brigands dressed in their usual black standing in a semicircle around the crevice where he had left his fellow Ulathans the night before. Targon couldn't see into the crevice, which while deep was very narrow, and it appeared the brigands could not enter it or wouldn't enter it.

"Use a pike and loose some bolts," shouted the lead brigand from atop his horse behind the others as he pointed toward the crevice with the same type wooden stick Targon had seen at his homestead the night he and his family were taken. Targon was sure it was some sort of leadership symbol or device the Kesh used.

Two brigands stepped toward the center of the group but back from the opening. Targon could see two wicked-looking crossbows in their hands as they aimed them into the crevice and let loose. Two crossbow bolts went flying out of Targon's sight, but he could hear screams as at least one of them found a mark. The crossbows changed things as any farmer, peasant, child, or even an idiot, could be transformed into a lethal soldier when a crossbow was present. It took little skill to fire and only some modest strength to reload, and that was exactly what the two brigands were just now doing.

"Die, you vermin!" yelled a voice Targon recognized as coming from Will Carvel, and then he saw Will leap forward from out of the crevice, a huge broadsword in both his hands. With a lunge and thrust, it buried itself deeply into the closest brigand, and, just as quickly, Will had pulled it out and gave a slashing cut to his right, barely missing the next brigand, who ducked and fell back at the same time the dead brigand fell.

Rocks started flying from the crevice, hitting several brigands, including one of the crossbowmen, knocking him off his feet. *This is the refugees' counterattack,* Targon thought. *They can't just stand around waiting for the crossbow bolts to slaughter them, yet stepping out into the open is almost as suicidal.*

With a quick stand, and closing his right eye, Targon drew the bow as far as he could with his first arrow ready to strike, but where? "Ulatha!" yelled Targon, not knowing for sure where the emotion came from as he loosed his first arrow and it buried itself deeply into the side of the horse-back brigand. The rider toppled over and fell lifeless to the ground, his command stick still stuck to his hand as the horse neighed wildly, suddenly bolting over the brook.

Targon reached back and grabbed another arrow, nocking it in one fluid motion. The many years of practice of missing his target and having by necessity to draw and nock a second arrow now served him well. He saw the one remaining crossbowman as well as a tall, seedy-looking brigand with a long pike he had in both his hands near the crevice entrance. With a quick bead, Targon chose the crossbowman, leaving the pikeman for Will. This was in part due to the danger of the weapon, but when the crossbowman turned and raised the freshly loaded crossbow, leveling it at Targon, he decided he wasn't about to find out just how much faster a bolt flew than an arrow.

With a whoosh, his second arrow found its mark squarely between the surprised brigand's eyes and planted itself in the brigand's head. The brigand toppled backward from the arrow's impact at the same time the

brigand loosed his bolt. The crossbow bolt flew up into the air well clear of Targon, like a missile to land who in Agon knew where. Targon was about to nock his third arrow when he heard another scream.

"Targon, watch out!" cried somebody from near the crevice entrance. Targon lowered his bow just enough to see a brigand from up on the bank trying to get above the refugees. He had not seen this brigand before, but the man threw a large spear right at him. He had little choice with his positioning but to roll forward and downward, closer to the group of brigands. With one fluid motion, Targon completed his somersault and knelt with his bow now facing more to his left and above the bank of the brook and let loose his third arrow. He could just make out the brigand either ducking or falling, and Targon was not sure if he had hit the man or not, so he nocked yet another arrow.

By now, Will had managed to down two more brigands, but one had cut him on his left arm and the heavy sword was now almost down to the ground as Will struggled to defend himself, but Will was not alone. Whether planned or simply desperate, the refugees charged single file from the brook's crevice right into the middle of the fight. Even Agatha was there charging with a large cast iron pot. The entire image was surreal to Targon.

Two more arrows he loosed and both missed. The brigands were aware of him now and the element of surprise was lost, but his actions allowed for another surprise as Lady Salina stabbed one brigand with her slender short sword and Cedric hurled knives at another. Rocks continued to pelt the remaining brigands, but the last straw for three of them was when Agatha flung hot soup from the pot, hitting two brigands near Will squarely across their faces, and a third got an armful of the soup, which now had become a newly painful projectile. While the soup was not fatal, the pain was excruciating for them, and, with a yell, they started to run toward the brook, two of them practically blinded by the scalding liquid.

Targon barely had time to react, however, as two brigands had left the main group and charged his position. Finally, another arrow hit one brigand square in the chest, stopping him in his tracks, but Targon was forced to drop his bow and pull out his axe. The other remaining brigand had a nasty sword, not as long as Will's broadsword but with a longer reach than the axe Targon carried.

Targon ducked the first swing as the lead brigand swung the sword hard, trying to cut poor Targon's head from his shoulders. *That is his first mistake*, thought Targon as he rolled again on the stony dry rocks from the riverbed, and with a swing of his own, he caught the brigand in his left calf. The brigand howled in pain and brought the sword up and around in another swing, this time just scrapping some hair off of Targon's head and drawing blood along his left scalp just above his ear. The motion of trying to wrench his axe free from the brigand's leg had just about cost Targon his life, but he managed to stand, and, with a solid blow, hit the brigand in the middle of his head.

The brigand toppled forward almost on top of Targon, and any idea of quickly pulling the axe free from its resting place was obviously impossible. Again, the act of losing his final weapon could have placed his life in jeopardy, but his actions were the last of the small battle. Targon saw Cedric's last knife imbed itself in a fleeing brigand near the brook, and the last few brigands were soon out of sight, running. Their leader was dead, they were ambushed, and the refugees weren't so docile, after all. They had lost the will to fight and had fled for their lives.

"By all the gods of Agon am I happy to see you, lad!" Will declared, falling to a sitting position and letting his sword clang on the rocks as he released it and held his left arm, where it was bleeding, with his right.

"Agatha, look after Will. I think he is hurt badly," said Lady Salina as she looked around. "Cedric, are you hurt?" she focused on her son who had just retrieved several of his small knives he had just used.

Shaking his head, Cedric answered, "I'm fine, Mother, just a little jumpy right now. How did they find us?" he looked around, wary that other brigands would be nearby and not really believing they had just won this unwinnable battle.

"They followed your tracks," said Targon. "I picked up their trail a few hours back, and they appeared to come from Korwell. Is everyone all right? Where is Marissa?"

"Here I am," called out Marissa as she appeared from the crevice and ran up to Targon, giving him a hug around his waist. "I knew you'd come back for us," she beamed. Targon hated to admit it, but despite being older, Marissa reminded him very much of his sister, Ann.

"Indeed," said Targon with a return smile. "I'd never leave you to those ruffians," he put his hand on top of her head, smiling at her gently.

The two started back toward the crevice, stepping over the scene of carnage all around them. "Don't look," Targon told Marissa as he guided her back to the sanctuary of the others.

An old lady, Celeste was her name, came out of the crevice then and informed the group a bolt had killed one of their own, another elderly man by the name of Sarson, who had stood in front of the woman and children to protect them.

"Karz, come here, little one." Lady Salina motioned for her smallest son, whom Targon remembered was on her lap the night before when they first met. Salina looked her son over for any signs of injury, and, satisfied that there were none, gave him a hug and wrapped a blanket Agatha had brought to her around him. "We need to get to safety," she stated almost desperately. "This is no place for children."

"Or for the elderly," Will said while Agatha returned to tending to him. Targon left Marissa to walk back into the crevice and assess the situation. Targon could see now that there were nine more people back there, three more children and six adults and most of the adults looked

elderly. They reminded Targon of his grandparents, Luc and Julia, before they had died. The large blanket the group had used to shield the fire the night before was now lying on the ground, covering the brave man known as Sarson where he lay. The others sat almost in a state of paralysis along the far back wall of the crevice.

Returning to the front and seeing Will's bleeding had stopped under the ministrations of Agatha, he turned to face Lady Salina. "You'll need to leave tonight: this area isn't safe anymore," he said as he watched Cedric walk from brigand corpse to brigand corpse, poking each one with a Kesh spear to either make sure they were dead or to actually help himself believe what had just happened wasn't a dream.

"We can't travel at night," she said, "and the sun will soon set." In fact, as she spoke, dusk was arriving and the eastern skies were now a dark purple, that dark purple one sees just before the black and the stars arrive.

Looking around and seeing a few looks of fear from Salina's son Karz and Agatha, Targon thought for a moment and then made a decision. "I will guide you as far as the Rapid River," he said, motioning to the east. "You'll need to cross it where you can before it links up with the great Ulatha River to the south. Otherwise, I don't think you'll be able to cross the Ulatha River, and I am pretty sure the northern shores will be crawling with Kesh brigands like these. Can you walk, Will?"

"I'll manage, boy," Will responded while starting to stand.

"This is nonsense. He's lost a lot of blood and is weak. I don't think he can walk far, and I am not sure he can use his sword again," Agatha said, not sure if she should try to stop Will from standing or if she should help him instead.

Finally getting his feet under him, Will adjusted the makeshift sling for his arm Agatha had hastily made. "I'll manage," he said. "You did well, lad," he said, stepping over to Targon and placing his good right hand on Targon's shoulder. "I thought my fate was sealed back there in that damn crevice," he stated, looking back at it.

"Will, that was one of the most heroic things I've seen any man do," said Salina, stepping towards Targon and Will, a smile evident on her face. "I don't think we would have made it without the two of you," she sheathed her small sword, embracing them both for a quick moment before looking back at her boys. "You have all our thanks."

Marissa had also come over to join them in the embrace, and just then, Agatha threw a bloody rag into the air. "Well, we don't have all night to sit here and hug one another."

"Right you are, as usual, Agatha. Get the others ready to go in thirty minutes. Tell them to take only that which they can easily carry: food and blankets and no more," Salina said, quickly looking around in the failing light.

"Make it fifteen," Targon said after Agatha as the elderly lady headed into the crevice, and Targon started to go from brigand to brigand, looking for any protruding arrows. He managed to find a couple that had missed their marks. One was buried in an old, dead tree branch that was hanging down from the bank near the crevice entrance, and he noted with some satisfaction that several brigands had died, and not only from his arrows. This group of refugees had some bite to them, or at least Will and Salina did, though he was sure Cedric and Agatha contributed, and he could only guess at which of the others had successfully hurled their rocks at the brigands.

Once finished collecting his arrows and waiting for the others, Targon walked over to Lady Salina and leaned over to whisper to her. "I didn't know you could use a sword."

"More than just use, Master Targon," she said, a smile crossing her face. "My husband is . . . well, was, captain of the king's guard, and I am not one for just pleasantries of the court."

"I can see that now," he said, leaning back and looking at her in a new light despite seeing her in a tattered cloak and dirty dress, with her small sword sheathed.

Soon, the entire group was ready and assembled. Somehow, Agatha had seen to it that a small pile of rocks was placed over the body of Sarson in respect and honor for what he had done. The brigands they left, of course, but had searched and pillaged their bodies for any drink or foodstuffs or anything else of value, though it appeared most of the drink was wine and was discarded. Targon noticed with some amusement that both Cedric and the only other old man in the group, called Horace, both had crossbows slung over their backs and crossbow bolts tucked into their packs and belts. *They look ridiculous,* he thought, *like two large porcupines with crossbow quills sticking out from every part of their torsos.* Still, he decided to say nothing about it for the moment.

"Here," Will said with his good hand extended, handing Targon a sword with a black handle and snake heads coming from each end of the hilt. "It was the nicest Kesh blade I could find. It came from the rider you first shot." Targon noticed two more swords tucked into Will's pack on his back. Again, he didn't understand why Will needed three swords, but if the man wanted to lug the blades, so be it.

Targon took the sword, and it felt awkward. It would take him some time to get used to it, if at all. Targon took the blade and scabbard and latched it around his waist. He felt a bit clumsy with it on his left side as if it unbalanced him, but he was determined to learn how to wear it and eventually use it. "Thanks, Will," he said, and then smiled at the soldier. *Sergeant of the gate, indeed,* he thought to himself. *He earned that title today, for sure.*

"Let's go," Targon said as he led the loosely knit band of refugees south along the west bank of the running brook, forcing them to cross it first. He wanted every advantage, and putting the small brook between themselves and Korwell, from wince the brigands had come, seemed like a good place to start. The brook got larger and deeper the farther south they traveled, but quickly, it turned east. At one point along the

bank where the ground was easy to navigate, he paused to count just how many Ulathans he was leading. Fifteen was his count when he counted Will Carvel bringing up the rear, oftentimes looking back behind him for any sign of pursuit. From one Marissa to fifteen Ulathans, not including himself. It was going to be a difficult night.

CHAPTER 9

FLIGHT

The group walked slowly at first, but once they became accustomed to the night's pale starlight, they picked up some speed and traveled for nearly three hours before Lady Salina asked for a break. Despite Will being a leader in the king's guard and Targon's obvious skill with the outdoors, the others looked to the lady for aid, support, and comfort.

"The children are getting tired and some are hungry," she said to Targon as they stopped briefly near a group of bushes not far from the small brook they were following. "Do we need to travel so far?"

Targon looked around. Will favored his left arm, which was bandaged and bloody from the fight they had just survived, and most of the others simply had plopped onto the ground where they stopped and had their heads down, some on their chests. *Dozing, most likely*, he thought. Only Cedric still stood with his mother as Will moved to a large stone and used it for a stool to take a rest. "I'm afraid the few killers who did get away will raise the alarm, and from what I can tell, they will be actively searching for any Ulathans," Targon said, motioning back along the way they

had come. "I know this area well enough, and if we can strike out east a ways, we will soon come to the Rapid River and Blackthorn Forest, an area I know much better, and I have an idea where we can at least cover our tracks and hide."

"How long will it take?" Salina asked, pulling a small piece of cheese from a cloth she carried in her bag and offering a small piece to Karz, who was sitting beside her. "Everyone, grab something to eat while we are resting," she said a bit louder as she turned to the others. Some started to grab foodstuffs from their bags and packs, but others just continued dozing as it was now close to midnight and they were not used to being awake at such a late hour.

Targon thought for a second, refusing the cheese Lady Salina tried to offer him. "I think if we can manage another six hours, we can reach the river before sunup," he said somewhat confidently.

"That is a long time in the dark with four children and several older folk," Salina responded, looking back at her group, a look of concern on her face.

"Well, you don't want them to face another group of brigands out here in the open, do you?" he asked.

"No, I guess you're right. Just keep your pace slow enough so we can follow you," she said, determined to make this work.

"Right," was all Targon said in response. He knew now that while the group looked to Salina for leadership, she was now looking to him and not Will, nor anyone else, for her own support. It was a great responsibility, and Targon was determined to not let them down. His mother and sister would expect that of him and understand. Finally, after ten or fifteen minutes more, Salina started to prompt everyone to stand, and the group started off yet again, heading in an easterly direction near the brook, but not too close. It could just be heard to their right, but Targon

didn't want to be too close to it. The sand along the banks and dry parts of the riverbed left tracks that even a blind man could follow.

After some time, Marissa came up to him from the middle of the group. Targon was leading, followed by Salina and then the group, and Will was bringing up the rear with Cedric. Will was instructing Cedric with a branch of leaves how to cover their tracks as best he could. "So, can we search for my family when we save the city folk?" she asked, a smile crossing her face despite the tiredness and trauma of the night's events.

"Well, yes, I think we can," he said, pondering for a moment how best to address the new situation, "but don't you think one of us should stay with the city folk and help them?" He nodded behind him and gave her a wink.

Marissa quickly lost her smile, and a small pout came across her lips as she looked back at Targon, ignoring his wink. "You mean me, most likely, Sir Targon. Besides, you don't even know what they look like," she said, her tone serious now.

"Then you can tell me their names and I will stop every lock cart I see and ask for them by name," he responded, an equally serious look on his face to match hers.

"Hmm," she said, walking and pondering the offer. "Very well, Master Targon, you must ask for Mary Thorton, and my brother's name is Marc, though I call him 'Boo-boo' because he's always hurting himself."

"Marc, Mary, and you're Marissa?" he said. "Don't tell me, your father's name is Mike?"

"Not funny, Targon," she said, dropping the formal title she had used before and now just referring to him by his common name. "His name was Alar, and he fought bravely, as brave as Sarson, and he gave me enough time to escape," she said, a tear welling in her eye.

"Right you are, Marissa," Targon said, now fully understanding the loss she felt and in turn being reminded of his brother who most likely encountered the same fate as Marissa's father and the old man Sarson. "How old is your brother?" he asked.

"Six years old, and he has blond hair and a nasty scar above his right eye," she said, motioning above her own right eye to where the scar would be located. "Fell from a tree, and a branch caught him and almost poked out his eye."

"Okay, I will look for Mary and Marc, then," Targon said matter-of-factly, "and you will help the city folk stay safe in the meantime. Do we have a deal?"

"Deal," she said, a smile returning to her face. "Do you have any more of those apples?"

Targon reached into his pouch, feeling the last apple left. "Yes, I do. I have two more left. I'll eat mine later," he said, pulling his last apple from the pouch and handing it to her.

Marissa ate as she walked and slowed her pace to return to the center of the group, leaving Targon alone up front. After another hour or so, he stopped and indicated a new direction from east to northeast, leaving the brook behind them. Targon knew the place he wanted to take them to. In fact, he thought of it himself when he first escaped but knew he had to free his family instead. On the east bank of the Rapid River, his grandfather had built a hunting blind near a place in the river where the water flowed and eddied into a calmer, slower running pool of water, and many animals, including the wild forest deer, would come to that pool to drink. The hunting blind was well hidden in some brush and trees but had good fields of vision for firing a bow, and while hidden well, it wasn't very defendable if found, as it could easily be surrounded.

After one more stop to rest and several hours later, Targon was relieved to hear the faint but distinctive sound of a large river course running, much louder than the brook they had left a few hours earlier. The main problem he had now was how to cross the quickly running, cold

and deep river with a group of old and young refugees who were tired and weak from having walked most of the night. Soon, Targon cleared some brush and stood on the west bank of the Rapid River, and he could see the Blackthorn Forest coming right up to the river on the other side.

"Impossible," was all Lady Salina could utter.

The rest of the group caught up, and finally Will and Cedric stood with them on the bank. "You intend for us to cross that!" Will asked while motioning with his good arm.

"Yes," Targon replied quickly, "but not here. If I have my bearings about me, then I came a bit too far south and we need to head upriver another mile or two where the river narrows but is faster running. There is a rocky bed where the river isn't too deep, and we can ford it there."

"I hope you know what you're doing, lad," replied Will.

"Get everyone to follow me into the water. We walk upstream just on the edge of the river where it is shallow, no tracks on the banks," he said, walking down the bank and into the river's edge only a few feet. Once he was sure everyone had followed him, he headed due north but stayed in the river. Once again, his feet were cold, and there were some complaints about walking a mile or more in cold water, but the cold was a motivator and they quickly covered the distance in just under a half hour.

Once they reached a spot where they could go no further, Targon led them the last few hundred feet back onto the bank and up a small rise where the river was now a full white water rapid. He took out a section of rope from his pack and asked for the only other rope Cedric carried in his pack and, tying the two together, he handed one end to Will. "Tie this around your waist. You can't grip it with two hands, but you are a large man: I need you to anchor yourself behind this large rock while I cross the river and secure the other end," Targon said. "Once across, I'll give you the signal and have everyone follow just above the white water using the rocks to step on."

"This looks dangerous," Salina said, looking out at the dark, brooding water. "I'm not sure we can do this."

"You'll have to trust me," Targon replied. "I'll go first. Watch where I step: you should just be able to make out the rocks underneath even in the faint starlight. They are a light brown, and the water is a darker, murkier color. Besides, as I said before, getting caught on this side of the river by the Kesh will be worse."

That seemed to motivate the entire group as they all understood they were lucky Targon happened to surprise the brigands outside the crevice. Otherwise, they all would be captives or dead by now. They lined up, one adult with a child, and Salina took Karz personally by his hand as Cedric and Agatha tied the rope around Will's waist. Will took up a position almost in the river by a large rock that stood waist-high, and planted his feet on either side of it, bracing himself.

Targon stepped out gingerly at first, and then with more confidence, and started across the river, careful not to let go of the rope he had tied to his waist and making sure his footing wasn't braced against a slippery, moss-covered rock. At one point in the middle of the crossing, the water almost came up to his waist, and he quickly moved through the area, arriving on the east bank. He had, of course, crossed here before, the memory of his father's death still too vivid in his mind. Once across, he found a small dead tree trunk to loop the rope around and secure it so the entire rope was now hanging waist-high across the river. With one last tug on the rope to make sure it was secure, he called out loudly above the roar of the river. "Ready. Start crossing."

Salina was first with Karz firmly clutching her belt, with Marissa following as they used the rope with one hand to cross the river. Agatha came next alone, followed by an elderly couple, Horace and Emelda, if Targon remembered their names correctly. Then came Yolanda with her daughter, Amy, strapped to her chest. Amy was the youngest in the

group, barely three years old, and so Yolanda, the single mother, had simply lashed her to her chest and used both hands on the rope. Targon noted that poor Karz was almost completely wet as the water reached all the way to his neck when they reached the center of the river. Salina had a firm grip on her son so the water didn't sweep him downstream and most certainly to his death. Two elderly women crossed next, Celeste and Olga, followed by the oldest child, Thomas. Thomas was twelve years old and was crossing by himself, both hands wrapped tightly around the rope. Bringing up the rear was Cedric, who held onto little Jons or Jonathan, the last of the children, a lad nine years old, as well as a young girl called Monique, who appeared to be a teenager just about the same age as Targon.

Salina reached the east side of the river, and she and Targon helped the others across and onto the bank, one by one. Once everyone was across, Targon motioned for Will to come over. Will only had the one good arm now and almost slipped twice, but finally he, too, crossed, and the wet, sorry-looking group of city refugees was laid out along the rocks, too cold and too drained to do much more than breathe. "We need to get moving!" said Targon as he looked up into the sky, which started to glow a deep reddish color in the east. *It is a beautiful sight*, thought Targon as the crenellations of the Border Mountains' silhouette could now be clearly seen with the approaching dawn as a backdrop.

"Can't we just rest here?" asked Horace, trying to warm himself and his wife, Emelda, as they leaned against a rock near the riverbank.

"It isn't far," said Targon. "In fact, we passed the river pool and the place where I intend to hide us not long ago before we crossed the river, just over five minutes, and we can rest there."

"Come on, everyone. You heard the lad. Let's finish this," Will said while still standing but offering his good hand to Horace for him to take. Not wanting to let this one-armed man outdo him, Horace took Will's hand and stood up and then helped his wife. Cedric grabbed Jons, and

the rest of them stood again on shaky legs. "Lead on, lad," Will stated, motioning for Targon to lead.

Targon took off south again, this time walking farther away from the river, which after about five hundred feet, the ground leveled out and the water eddied and slowed quite a bit and became much broader and deeper. Targon knew the ground along and near the river would leave footprints, so he walked them first into the forest and then south, skirting the river by a healthy margin.

"I thought you said five minutes?" asked Marissa, as they now had taken the long way around and were shivering in the forest with only the sound of the river, faint as it was, to their right. "It's been at least twice that now."

"There it is," stated Targon, motioning toward some brush through some trees in the direction of the river.

"I don't see anything," said Lady Salina. Targon walked a short distance, about a hundred feet. Then he walked by a tree surrounded by some vines and low bushes, disappearing from view. The rest followed and found themselves entering a crude doorway into a small, dilapidated shack, since building would be too extravagant of a word to describe the structure. It measured barely ten feet long by ten feet wide and was just high enough that Will didn't bump his head against the roof. The group huddled together inside the structure, taking off their wet cloaks and pulling blankets and dry, if not clean, clothing from their packs.

"Well I'll be a dragon's mother," exclaimed Agatha, looking around in disgust at the dirty four-walled structure. There were slots along each wall, including one in the door they had just used to enter, obviously for shooting arrows through, but vines had covered most of them. They peered out and saw the faint early morning sunshine from the sun, which had not risen yet but was quickly lighting up the area with its impending light. "All you boys out. Go on now, scoot!" she said as she went back to the door and opened it, giving Cedric a nudge out the door as he was

closest to it and had entered last. "Give us ladies ten minutes to change properly, if one can do such a thing in such a dirty room."

Will just chuckled but exited after a confused Cedric, and Targon took Karz by the hand and stepped outside. "And no peeking!" were the last words they heard Agatha screech as the door was shut rather abruptly.

"Come on, follow me," Targon said, heading to the river but back upstream where several rocks were visible. The sun finally started to rise. There was a large, flat boulder Targon knew well, and he took the ragtag group of men and boys to it. The forest blocked direct sunlight from reaching the bank that early in the morning, but there was a clearing where another pool of water had eddied into the east bank, and the forest had to maintain its distance. The rock stood right in the middle of the pool, and Targon reached it by stepping on three other rocks that were shallowly submerged. Targon sat on the large, flat piece of granite, looking east. "Soon we shall feel the dragon's warmth," he said, referring to the Agon sun.

Cedric, Will, Horace, Thomas, Jons, and Karz joined him on the rock. Targon stripped down to his leather breeches and laid his boots and other clothing items on the rock to dry. He grabbed his almost empty pouch and put it under his head and closed his eyes. Soon, the sun rose above the Border Mountains, and the first rays of light hit the river, the far west bank, and the rock they were on. Its glowing warmth felt good and, despite the cold rock beneath them, they were too tired to care much.

Cedric had taken out an odd-looking book bound in red and seemed to peruse a few pages before tucking it back into his pack and using it as a pillow beneath his head. Soon, the heavy breathing of the boys and old man Horace could be heard. Targon cocked an eye open and looked over at Will, who was sitting, holding his injured arm, looking across the river. "What happened at Korwell?" Targon asked softly, now sitting himself up, facing Will.

Stifling a yawn, Will looked over at Targon and then closed his eyes as if trying to remember. After about a minute, Targon actually thought Will had dozed off before the grizzled veteran began to speak. "It was late at night but not long before dawn," Will began, thinking back a few days to that fateful event. "I was up early as usual, preparing the gate to be opened for our usual business. I always enjoyed watching the dawn, and I was in my usual place on top of the eastern gate tower waiting for it. That was when it happened, when hell broke loose." He opened his eyes, looking at some unknown spot to his west, like a man lost in a dream.

"What happened?" Targon asked more tensely now. "What happened to the guard?" He wanted to know, thinking of his brother, Malik.

"The horn of death sounded," Will responded as he continued. "The attack came without warning. They were already in the town, and a few somehow infiltrated the castle even though the gate was still closed. They hit us first, killing almost all of my soldiers. I took three of them before being forced away from the gate. They hit us from inside and outside. I cut the clamp that held the gate shut so they couldn't raise it, but after being forced away, the gate somehow opened. I saw the chains drop, so it should have been impossible to open it. The gate weighs more than ten horses and would take a hundred men with pulleys and rope to open it, but I could hear it opening, and then I saw the Kesh scum come streaming through it. I could only think to warn the king, so I ran into the castle just in front of the oncoming horde of thieves and cutthroats. I reached the inner courtyard and started to climb the king's tower. You know the one in the center of the castle?" Will asked, suddenly looking over at Targon for confirmation.

"Yes, I think I've seen it from a distance," he said. "It would be the tallest tower, no?"

"The tallest, yes," Will responded. "But before I could start climbing, the king's cousin came down screaming the king was dead. He was

covered in blood, and, for a moment, I thought him either mad or that he had harmed the king, but then two of the assassins had followed him down the stairs and one of them finished the deed by throwing a dagger into his back."

"And the guard?" Targon asked, now fully immersed in Will's story.

"As Lady Salina said . . . slaughtered," he finished.

Targon took a moment to take this all in. He assumed the king would have escaped: surely they had secret tunnels for just such an occasion as this. This was the first time he had confirmation from anyone that the king had died in the attack. "Well then, how did you escape?" Targon asked, saddened at the news.

Will seemed to compose himself and continued with his account. "Well, I ran out the back into the rear courtyard where I came across Lady Salina and her two boys. They seemed confused but were unharmed. My captain, the lady's husband, had left days earlier to lead a patrol to the southeast, having heard that some bandits and thieves had robbed and killed a few farmers near Cree. He was already overdue by half a day, and so the castle guard was leaderless without him, the king, or the king's cousin. I didn't trust the escape tunnels in the dungeon. I thought for sure they were compromised and no longer safe. Lady Salina wanted to use them to escape as we heard the screams of death all around us. I managed to rally half a dozen soldiers around me, and we headed to the southern wall where we had a few drainage culverts. You know the ones covered by cast iron bars and gates? The culvert gates were only used for maintenance and had a sturdy lock on each of them. The culverts were few in number and very small. I barely fit in the one we used, but I used my key, as the sergeant of the gate, controlling access to the castle was one of my responsibilities, to open the small gate in the southern culvert." Will paused for a moment, thinking.

"You mean you escaped through a drainage ditch?" Targon asked incredulously.

"That's exactly what I mean," Will continued, looking back at Targon eye to eye. "We found ourselves facing a small group of pillaging thieves as soon as we got out. We surprised them and took them out, but I lost three of my six soldiers, including Hans and Kovar. We ran south then east through the town and saw several people hiding or lying wounded. The Kesh were taking no male prisoners. We could see young men and old men and even a few boys lying dead in the streets. Fires started to sprout up all around us, and we could only think of escaping. We took what little we had and grabbed anyone who was willing to flee with us, and we headed east into the tall fields of spring corn and wheat. There is no hiding to the west as those fields were just plowed and had little cover, while the Kesh came from the north, and the south also was just pastures filled with cattle and livestock."

"Is that where you found Horace and the others?" Targon asked, motioning to the sleeping man.

"They were on the east side of town, yes," replied Will. "We fled, but before we could reach the tall grass, the bandits were on us. The rest of my soldiers fell while covering the retreat of our group. I would have fallen, too, if not for Lady Salina. She took me by the arm and told me they were defenseless now without me. We ran off and on for half the day before stumbling to that crevice by late afternoon where you found us." Will started to laugh just then.

"What's so funny?" Targon asked, confused by Will's laughter in the midst of such a sad story.

"Agatha," Will said, stopping his laughter but still keeping a smile across his face. "We took whatever we could find from the town before we fled: a few carrots on a cart, some potatoes that were sitting on a window sill drying, some corn from the fields, and a few blankets that were hung out to dry. But Agatha . . . well, she had taken her cooking pot and was using it to hit any brigand we came across on his head. I swear she must have given at least a half dozen brigands headaches with that

black pot of hers." He looked away from Targon and back across the river again. "So when we arrived at the little brook and looked for a place to hide and sleep, we found that draw in the creak bank and we started a small fire. Cedric had some flint and was able to start a fire, and, well . . ." Will started chuckling again. "She set her pot on top of the fire and we all threw whatever we had into it, and she started cooking stew,"

Targon started to laugh as well at the thought of Agatha swinging her deadly pot projectile and then using it to cook with. "I see what you mean," he responded, "but what about the captain? What about Lady Salina's husband?"

"Well, we saw them from the small rise on the east side of town. We cleared the fields and started to climb as we were still in the shadows from the early morning sunlight, but far to the south we could see the patrol, nearly forty horsemen strong, trying to reach the town. The lady almost ran back down, forgetting her children and the rest of the group, but then, just as they reached the town, they ran into a large group of brigands. There was a fight and many fell, but more than half fled again to the south, including, I think, the captain, followed by thrice their number of mounted Kesh. I had to drag Lady Salina back, but when she saw her children, she gained control of herself and we fled east. So there is hope her husband and many soldiers still in Cree and Fornz may have survived. At least, one can hope."

Targon looked from Will over to the rising sun's glare, letting its warmth strike his face. He was understanding now that the events that impacted his family's lives were much greater, much more complicated now. "Well, we need to do something, and I need to find my family . . . and Marissa's family," Targon stated.

"What do you intend to do, lad?" Will asked, now looking around and yawning again.

Targon, too, yawned, and thought for a moment. "I must head north to the old trade road and see if I can get to those lock carts."

"What carts?" Will asked, confused.

"When I went to Korwell, I saw over thirty of those slave carts the Kesh use, and they all looked fully loaded. I fear anyone who survived the attack was taken prisoner and they are being taken to Kesh," Targon said.

"How is that possible?" Will asked. "The old trade road ends at the Border Mountains. I rode patrols there in my younger days, and the mountain roads into Kesh have been destroyed, crumbled into the canyons, and the bridges were all fallen."

"I don't know," replied Targon, "but the slave carts are here, and so we must assume they have found a way in."

"Well, individuals on foot, maybe horses single file, could pass, but those mountain passes are narrow and the drops are deep. I just don't see how they managed anything larger than a single horse," Will said.

"It doesn't matter. They are here, trust me. I was locked in one for hours," Targon stated, remembering his experience. "So I will go and see if I can track those carts and see where they are being taken. I fear my family has been locked inside of one for a couple of days now, at least."

"Better get some rest, then, first, laddie," Will responded a bit softer now, understanding the boy had his reasons just as good as anyone else. "What about the rest of us here?"

"You'll be as safe as you can expect here," Targon said, shrugging. "Unless they know where the ford is at, the river will cause them some pause," he continued, "and the Blackthorn Forest is practically impassable for anyone. I myself don't dare venture too far inside it. Though I live on its borders, it's not natural." Targon's voice trailed off to a whisper.

Will nodded his head in agreement. "I've heard weird tales meself, lad, about these here woods. Amazing any of you have the courage to live this close to it. Now seeing it for meself up close, I wouldn't want a tour of its innards, to be sure."

"Well, that is why we are called wood-folk," responded Targon. "We are used to living on the frontier, and we know the way of the wild woods.

Still, I must go soon, and you are right: I'll get me some sleep first, but what if the Kesh cutthroats arrive?"

"They can have me, for all I care," Will said, smiling, and finally laid his head down on a wrapped piece of dirty linen. "Do you think the women are all right?"

"They are probably already asleep and not thinking of us," Targon said, laying his head down and, in the glow of the sunshine, closing his eyes, and sleep quickly took him.

The old man watched silently from the forest as the two men on the rock finally finished their conversation and lay quietly. He wore an old brown cloak, worn but clean, tattered but well sewn at the seams, and he carried a gnarled wooden oak staff. His head was hoodless and capless, balding a bit, but other than that, unadorned. After a moment, he motioned with his left arm and laid it out horizontally bent at a ninety-degree angle like a perch. A falcon glided in from out of sight and landed on the old man's arm. "Come, Argyll, show me what you have seen," the old man whispered, and with that, he turned and headed back into the forest from which he came.

CHAPTER 10

SANCTUARY

Targon allowed the sun to dry and warm him thoroughly before rousing himself from the large granite rock. He had slept, of course, and while not wise to be lackadaisical in their actions, the simple truth of the matter was that the entire group was too exhausted from the battle the night before and the long overnight journey to care much. Besides, Targon calculated from the lumbering slow march of the lock carts he had seen in Korwell that it would take at least two days for them to pass the old keep, assuming they moved only during the day. They were heavily loaded, and when one included the logistics involved of feeding and organizing such a large caravan, he doubted they would even make that time. Nevertheless, his family, as well as Marissa's family, could be there even now, and that drove Targon into action.

He had a plan, and resting half a day was actually advantageous to it. The old family hunting blind was just over a half day's walk up the Rapid River and then slightly east by a couple of miles, and he fully intended to return there once the sun had set. From there, he could make for the trade road and see if the Kesh slave caravan had passed, in which case he would follow, or yet to pass, in which case he would lie in wait for it to

arrive. Either way, he wanted to use the dark of night as cover to find it and free his family. He was brave but not stupid. Thirty carts with nearly a hundred brigands was too much for him to take on in a fight, but now he intended to use a different tactic. Now he would utilize stealth and show these thieves what the word "sneaky" really meant.

"Hoi, Will," he said, leaning over and nudging Will's leg.

"What!" Will almost yelled, startled from his sleep, his good arm reaching for his sword.

Targon pulled back and then whispered loudly, "Quiet, you fool, you'll wake the dead with that screaming. Don't you city folk know how to lay low?"

Will looked over at him and then around and remembered his current situation. "Yeah, right, sorry."

Targon half thought the aging guardsman was still dreaming about the attack, though nightmare would be a better word to describe it. "No worries, we have been lying out in the open for the entire morning, so any brigand around could have spotted us, but just the same, if they were close, I'd prefer we don't alert them to our presence. From what I could tell, they had trackers of their own. That is how they found you at the crevice."

Stretching out a bit, the large man suddenly stood, yawning while extending his good arm and flinching halfway through as his injured left arm reflexively tried to stretch out as well. "Ow! That hurts!" He cradled his injured arm in his good one. "Nasty cut. I'll probably need more than just a bandage." He finished talking, then started to wobble on his legs.

Cedric was coming to as well with all the noise, and he jumped up to help the aging guardsman so he didn't fall. "Damn, you're heavy," he exclaimed as Will allowed the weight of his body to rest on Cedric's shoulder, letting his right arm wrap around and use the young man as support.

"I think you've lost too much blood, Will," Targon chimed in. "Best get you to the blind and have that wound looked at."

With that, Targon roused the others, who were none too happy to have had their sleep interrupted after only a few hours, but they knew they were tempting their luck just sitting on a rock along the Rapid River in plain sight, and once rested, they were thinking more clearly now. The group quickly dressed, and Horace helped hold Will steady while Cedric took his turn. With a heave, Targon carried little Karz across the water, stepping on the slightly submerged boulders and then putting him on the dry ground. *No need to get everyone's feet wet again,* he thought to himself. Soon, they were back at the blind, which was dark and quiet.

"Agatha," Targon whispered, first faintly and then louder. He rapped on the door for a second and hissed her name again. "Agatha!"

He could have opened the creaky door himself, but he wasn't sure what state of dress, if any, the ladies inside were currently in, and he called Agatha's name first because he feared her the most of any of the ladies. He did not want to get hit in the head with her black pot. The door did open finally, but it was Marissa, not Agatha.

"Hullo, master scout," she said, a smile on her face. "Is it time to get up?"

"Yes, Will needs help, and we have work to do. Can you rouse the others?" he asked, smiling in return.

"Right away," she responded, and quickly shut the door again. Before he could step a few steps back, there came a nasty retort in Agatha's raspy but distinct voice.

"Time to rouse, he says? I'll rouse him right upside his small little head, I will."

Targon was thankful Marissa had answered his call instead, but it was apparent Marissa had indeed done a fine job of rousing the women. There were murmurs and rumblings, and soon, it seemed the entire blind was alive with chatter as the women inside either complained or made threats of all the things they would do when they saw him again. A short time

later Lady Salina appeared trying to desperately brush her hair with her hands and just ended up making it look worse.

"Is everything all right?" she asked, looking around at the silent group of men and then just realizing how loud they were back in the blind.

"Fine out here, but Will is hurt and most likely in need of a seamstress now. He needs stitches. The bandage is getting too loose, and he has lost a lot of blood," he said, nodding in Will's direction. "Oh, and one more thing, can any of you city folk do or say anything below a roar?"

"Yes, sorry, I'll have them tone it down," she said as she headed back to the shack after looking warily at a very pale Will. The group of men seemed wiser than most as they kept a good distance from the nearly invisible blind.

The noise quickly subsided, and Targon breathed a small sigh of relief before he heard the raspy voice of death again. "Well, why didn't them blockheads say something sooner?" And quickly, Agatha appeared just as sleepy-eyed and disheveled as Lady Salina. With one look at Will, she motioned for them to follow.

"I'm fine," replied Will a bit sheepishly. "Nothing I haven't experienced before."

"I'm pretty sure you haven't experienced death, you old lump of lead," Agatha said as they entered the blind. "Out, all you ladies make room, injured man coming in."

The ladies and young girls scampered out like mice being shooed with a broom. The blind was almost unfurnished, but there were two pieces of a tree log that were moved into the corner and were used as chairs. Pulling them out a bit, Agatha nodded for Cedric to help the injured Will and motioned for them to sit. "Now, let me have a looksee," she said, sitting on the last remaining log and unwrapping the makeshift bandages from his arm. "By Dor Akun's passing!" she exclaimed as the wraps came off and she got a good look at Will's arm. Only Cedric, Targon, and the lady Agatha remained with them in the blind.

"That looks nasty," Cedric said, a sour look on his face.

"Not as nasty as you, you pompous cockatoo," Will fired back, a smile on his face, but Cedric seemed offended anyway.

"Cockatoo, what the heck is a cockatoo?" was all he could mutter.

"Not now, you two," Lady Salina quickly said, jumping in to prevent another outburst from a surly Agatha. "Cedric, go outside and wait with the others. In fact, see to it they stay near the blind and don't stray too far. Keep a close eye on your brother while you're at it."

Cedric looked at his mother and then back to Will, but one look at Agatha and he headed out quickly. Agatha worked in silence, seeming to understand the urgency of the situation now, and Lady Salina started to rip strips of cloth from the remains of a tattered blanket they had used earlier to bind Will's wound. "We are going to need to boil some water, so we are going to need a fire, Kesh scum or no. I'm going to need a needle and some thread as well. You hear me, lad?" she said, looking at Targon.

"The name is Targon, not lad," he responded. "I think a small fire just outside would be acceptable."

"Much appreciated, Targon," Will said, smiling and closing his eyes at the same time as he hunched back against the wall.

Targon left the blind, and Lady Salina followed. The rest of the group was sitting or lying around the ground just east of the blind and away from the Rapid River, which was barely audible in the background. "Cedric, Marissa, Thomas, see if you can find some firewood nearby, but don't stray out of sight of the blind." The three nodded and headed off, looking for dry wood. "Yolanda, you and Emelda help Celeste and Olga with the little ones," Salina said, nodding at the small group of children, including her own Karz. "Horace, can you keep watch? I want a moment alone with Targon."

"Consider it done, my lady," Horace said, standing and moving to a better spot to keep an eye on the surrounding area.

"Good, thank you, sir," she said, nodding in appreciation. "Come, Targon, may I have a word with you?"

Targon nodded and followed Lady Salina around the blind and back toward the river. Before they had reached it, they came near to the riverbank where a tree had fallen. She sat down, motioning for him to follow. Targon nodded, sitting on the same tree log she did, facing the river and looking carefully both upstream and downstream.

"I know you want to find your family much like I would like to find my husband," she started, looking first down at her dirty dress and then back up at the shimmering, fast running water of the river, "but we need help and I fear none of us are up to the task. Will is seriously injured and needs medical attention, and we have eaten the last of our meager food supplies. I don't know what to do, and there are so many of us. Will you not help us first before going after your family?"

Targon pondered her request, knowing full well that with each passing day, the chances for finding his family became less and less. "My heart tells me to go and to go now, but my head tells me my mother would want me to help you first," he concluded.

Salina gently placed her left hand on Targon's right arm. "Your mother sounds like a wonderful person, and she would be proud of you, not for what you are about to do but for what you've already done."

"I fear I've already failed her."

"You have not failed her, and you have not failed us," Salina said, looking him now in the eye. "You are young and I hate to ask so much of you, but we need you now and I fear what will happen to us without your help."

"I will stay one more day, then," Targon responded, sighing a bit as he internally finalized his decision. "Those damn carts can't be that fast: I'm sure I'll catch them on the road. What do you need?"

Salina squeezed his arm. "Thank you, Master Targon, you are a true gentleman. First, we need to help Will. Sepsis will soon set in if we don't

clean out the infection and sew his cut up. The bandages worked to stop the bleeding, but the arm won't heal if left open. I am afraid we have no sewing supplies, but we need something from somewhere. It is a long journey back to Korwell, but perhaps we can scavenge something from nearby?"

"They burned all the homesteads as far as I could tell," Targon sullenly said, hanging his head down and thinking of his own home. "No, wait. I killed the cutthroats at my home just before the attack started. It might be intact, and if so, my mother had a few small needles and some threads she used to mend our clothes. I can't be sure, but it's worth a look." now getting eager to return to his home and see if it was still standing.

"That would be worth a look indeed," she said, smiling at him. "A more pressing need now, too, is food. I'm afraid us city folk aren't accustomed to hunting. These are your lands, no? Is there anything nearby for us to eat?"

"Let me think about this for a minute," he said, holding his chin now in his left arm. "Normally I try for wild rabbits, but they don't usually come out during the middle of the day, fearful of the hawks, I think, and I doubt we'll see any deer with this many of you city folk both yapping too loudly and stinking to high heaven of city smells, so that just leaves scant options for now, but I'll see what I can do."

"Well, I'm sure anything you can come up with will be much appreciated by us city folk," she said with a chuckle, "and I thought you smelled!" With that, the two stood up, Targon taking a good long glance both upriver and down it. Seeing nothing threatening, he and Salina returned to the blind and entered. Will was slumped against the wall in a semi-seated position, eyes closed, labored breathing. *But breathing is good*, thought Targon. Agatha shook her head and returned to cleaning the wound with a damp rag.

Targon headed into the forest, passing the three young wood gatherers as he went, but there were no words exchanged between them. Even

Marissa kept quite as they trundled back with three armfuls of wood. Targon noted they were all hardwoods and dry, which was good because they sent out minimal smoke and would be harder to detect and they didn't smell the way some willow wood and ash did when moist.

Targon was in search of something, a flower called the Arella. The flower itself wasn't special, but the few leaves at its base were. Many years ago, when his mother and brother were sick, his grandfather, Luc, showed him how to find the flower and how to pull it by its root so as to keep the flower and leaves moist. Julia would then put the leaves in a pot of boiling water and use it to wipe their foreheads when they had a fever. She would also put a few leaves in clean water and brew a tea-like drink for them. He knew it had healing properties, and some months later, when Myrtle was attacked by a small cougar from the mountains, Grandfather Luc used the leaves, after boiling them and squashing them in a bowl, on the actual claw marks to save their sole dairy cow.

The flower, however, contrary to popular thought, did not like very wet climates nor extremely hot ones, either, so he wasn't really going to find it near the river or deep in the forest where there was little sunlight. He needed high ground, and his grandfather, Luc, had taken him up into the Border Mountains where they found many of the plant in a high-elevation meadow. Targon knew from experience, however, that in a few places between the Rapid River and Blackthorn Forest, along the old game trail he had used to travel between the blind and home, there were a few locations where the flower thrived. He headed to the closest one and arrived there, north of the blind, in about half an hour. Quickly, he managed to pull a total of seven of the flowers from the forest meadow and returned to the group.

He quickly stopped as he approached and took in the area. He had been gone for only an hour and already the entire area looked different. He first saw both Marissa with an armful of pinecones and Thomas with a large tree branch in his hands, stooped over and swiping it on the

ground from side to side and walking backward toward the blind. Just to the east of the blind, on the forest side, a new ring of fallen tree leaves, tree branches, and grasses were piled high around the entire side of the blind, forming a semicircle.

At first, he was angry, thinking they had ruined the entire camouflage of the blind. The whole purpose of it was to look natural and remain well hidden so any deer or other game animals would approach it. Then he realized he was looking at it from his perspective with a keen eye toward hunting. He was sure any game or deer would steer clear from the area based on smell alone, but now looking at it in the dimness of the forest trees, he realized it would be hard to see that there was some sort of a structure hidden amidst the trees, bushes, and grasses unless one were to specifically look for it.

He could see Cedric approaching him now, and he continued walking to meet him near the blind. "Thought you had left us," Cedric said, smiling and seeming content with himself.

"What is all this?" Targon replied.

"This is our new defense. Not exactly what I would have wanted after living in a castle built hundreds of years ago, but I think it will do."

"What gave you this idea?"

"Well, Mother said we were staying here for a while and that we needed to start a fire, so I decided I'd start work on our defensive fortifications."

"Defensive fortifications? What in Agon are you talking about?" Targon asked, scratching his head with one hand while holding tightly to the Arella flowers with his other.

"Like a castle." Cedric motioned back toward the "fortification."

"That wouldn't stop a blind child! Might as well put out a welcome mat for the brigands to wipe their feet on before they slit all our throats," Targon said as Cedric looked down without responding. Targon caught himself before he said more. He began to see Cedric as if he were a

younger brother right now. "All right, come along now and show me exactly what you were thinking, then, when you organized this little bit of engineering."

Cedric looked up, no smile on his face, but a hint of hope now gleamed in his eyes. "Let me show you," he said, walking over to the blind.

"Halt! Super!" Targon heard a squeaky voice from behind the brush line: if one could call the bastard construct anything, brush line would have to do.

"Jons, is that you?" Targon asked, walking over to the small opening on the north side between the blind and the edge of the brush line.

"Aw, not fair. You're supposed to say the counter to my challenge," Jons whined as he popped up from the cover of the line with one of the Kesh swords in his hands. Targon noted, however, that the sword was being dragged tip-first in the dirt.

"What counter? Is this more city stuff?" Targon asked, looking from Jons to Cedric.

Just then, Targon noticed a large log had been pulled over to the side of the blind, and Horace stood up from where he was sitting. "Let them have some fun," he said, motioning to little Jons. "The last few days have been hard, especially on the wee ones. It will do them some good to have some play."

"Fine," was all Targon said as he looked around and noticed the two crossbows lying across some wood branches, fully loaded and facing outward. "You prepped those, Horace?"

"Yes. Will is still out of it, and I thought we best have something prepared."

Targon nodded in agreement as he took in the scene that was hidden from his view just moments earlier. He could still hear Thomas as he got closer, and he saw the space inside the semicircle was easily twice the size of the blind inside. He noticed Yolanda sitting on a dirty blanket, feeding

her daughter, Amy, probably the last food they had, and Emelda was watching through the brushes, keeping an eye on Marissa and Thomas as they worked. Karz lay sleeping on another small blanket next to her. He assumed Celeste, Olga, and Monique were inside with Lady Salina, Will, and, of course, Agatha. A fire was in the very center of the circle with a crude tripod holding up Agatha's black cast iron pot. Another brigand sword leaned against the blind's vine-covered wall as well as many packs, water flasks, and other gear they had brought there. Will's sword lay against the log very near to Horace's hand, ready at a moment's notice. Jons stood there looking up at Targon expectantly.

"Fine, what is the counter to your challenge, Jons?" Targon asked, but instead, Cedric answered.

"Cedric." He hung his head, looking awkward.

"Who came up with that?" Targon asked, looking around.

"Well, it seemed like a good idea at the time," Cedric said, lifting his head and looking Targon square in the eyes.

"Super Cedric?" Targon said, just shaking his head and looking back to Jons, who was now nodding and grinning from ear to ear.

"Yup, now you can come in, Master Targum." Jons nodded.

"It's Targon, little Jons. I'd think you would know that by now." Targon walked over to the black pot and looked in. Water was steaming a bit, but it had not yet started to boil. Targon made quick work of the flowers, peeling the leaves off of each stem but keeping the flower intact. He then took four leaves and threw the rest into the pot.

"Hey, you'll make Will sick doing that!" Emelda said, coming from the brush line to look into the pot, a look of shock on her face.

"Trust me, Emelda, this will help Will, not hurt him. Let me know when it boils." And with that, he handed her one of the pretty yellow Arella flowers and leafless stem and then quickly handed two to Yolanda as well. "Give one to Marissa," he said, turning and heading into the

blind. Emelda and Yolanda just looked at each other and then down to the flowers and back to each other, speechless. No one noticed as old Horace just rolled his eyes and smiled.

"Oh, good, you're back. I was afraid you'd be gone longer," Lady Salina said, turning to greet Targon as he entered the door. Targon was happy to notice that he was right and Celeste, Olga, and Monique were all sitting on the floor in one corner shucking extremely small nuts from the pinecones they had piled together near them. Even if they picked every nut from every pinecone, it would hardly be enough to feed two or three people, much less sixteen. Monique looked up and smiled at him as she popped open another cone. She was pretty, he saw, and he hadn't really noticed it before, such was his focus. Her face looked recently cleaned as if she had washed it in the river, but her dress remained dirty and tattered around the edges. The hard rocks and country tore it well in only two days.

"Yes, I'm back," he said, "and I have something for Will, but first . . ." He leaned over and gave Monique one of the Arella flowers and a smile. She graciously accepted it and simply smiled in return, a faint blush of red forming on both her cheeks. "Ladies," Targon said, offering them each a flower as well. Both Olga and Celeste accepted and also smiled. Targon stood up and looked at Lady Salina, offering her the last flower.

"That was most thoughtful of you . . ." she said as she looked at him, but before anyone could move, Agatha stood up, walked over to Targon, and snatched the flower from his hand, putting it behind her left ear.

"She's a married woman and a woman of nobility, not deserving of a weedy flower from any peasant such as you! Besides, if we ain't careful with you, we'll find you smooching on one of our ladies here, so if you get the urge to smooch, just come see me, young man, and keep your hands to yourself!" Monique was definitely red in the face now and looked down, doubling her focus and efforts on the pinecones. Targon

wasn't sure to laugh or be angry at the interruption, but then started to laugh once Will chimed in.

"What, no flower for me?" Will said, chuckling and waving Targon over. "The lady tells me you wasted time on me, boy. What did you do, pray tell?"

Targon took the leaves he had saved and popped them in his mouth and started to chew a large wad of leaves in his left cheek as he tried to talk. "Afella, thometimes called sumshimes . . ."

"Take that crap out of your mouth, young man," Agatha scolded him, laying out three strips of cloth to boil and sanitize. "Speak clearly, lad, or don't speak at all."

"You remind me of my grandmother, Agatha . . . only older," Targon said, after taking the lump out of his mouth, and he started to kneed it in his hands.

"Why, you little . . ."

"Enough! Both of you, let's focus on the important things now," Salina chimed in, standing in between the two. "What are you doing, Targon?"

"These are Arella leaves from the Arella flower, sometimes called the sunshine flower due to its yellow appearance," Targon said, continuing to kneed the pulpy leafy mash in his hands. "They have some healing properties and will help Will. We need to mash them up and put it inside his cut and then bandage it. You'll have to trust me on this."

"Putting filthy, saliva-ridden weeds in a man's open wound is not medicine, boy! Who taught you such nonsense?" Agatha asked, her tone mocking.

"Well, since you don't have any *city* medicine, I suggest we use this," Targon replied.

"Let Will decide." Salina looked at Will.

"Fine by me. I've had worse stuffed in me before. After everything the lad's done for us so far, I'll trust him on this one."

That decided it, then, and once fully mashed, Targon laid the mushy pulp into the wicked-looking cut running the length of Will's left arm, from the shoulder down to his elbow, since Agatha refused to do it. She did, however, bandage Will up after asking Monique to take the new cloth strips and soak them well in boiling water. Targon was glad no one told her about the leaves he had placed in the pot, a point of fact best left unsaid for the moment. "Whose idea was it to pluck nuts from the cones?"

"That was Marissa's idea," Lady Salina responded.

"Not one of the city folk, then, eh?" he said, looking at Agatha, his tone mocking, but not daring to tell them just how few nuts they would have for all their efforts. Still, he had to give credit to the young girl for thinking of something. Anything was better than nothing.

"Well, you wood-folk and farmers are shining examples to all of us," Lady Salina said and then smiled at him.

"If you say so," Targon replied, not sure if he had offended Salina while the target of his barb was actually Agatha. He realized using the term "city folk" included the very same people he was starting to like. He left them in the blind and headed to pick up Marissa. *She is turning out to be more of an asset than a liability*, he thought.

"Marissa," he said, walking up to her. She had another armful of cones and was heading to the blind to drop them off for the ladies to shuck. "Did you ever gather wild cabbage?"

"Oh yuck!" she said, making a face with her tongue sticking out like she was going to throw up.

"Okay, so you have gathered and apparently partaken of the foul vegetable. I need you to help me gather some this afternoon before sundown or there won't be anything to eat for anyone. Can you help me?" he asked her.

"Sure," she said, "just let me drop these cones off and then grab my cloak to use to carry them." Targon nodded as she entered the blind.

While waiting for her, Targon saw Thomas approaching from the other side, having finished brushing the many tracks they had made, both to and from the blind. Targon thought the brushing was in and of itself a track, but he didn't have time to argue the point. Besides, it actually looked cleaner than dozens of footprints all over the place. Soon, Marissa came out, and with concerned calls for them to "watch their tracks," they headed back north along the same trail Targon had used earlier.

It took them much longer than he had thought. The cabbages were hard to spot and few and far between so near to the Blackthorn Forest, and as the sun started to set, they quickly returned with a half dozen wild cabbages wrapped in Marissa's cloak. The wild variety of cabbages was much smaller than the domestic version, one being about the size of an apple and not a head of lettuce.

They returned to the blind before the sun set, and quickly, Emelda, Monique, and Olga took the small, rough cabbages to the river to clean them as they were literally crusted in damp dirt. Soon, however, with a new pot of water boiling and the cabbages cleaned and cooking, the group congregated outside the blind in the relative comfort of the brush line Cedric had constructed.

The temperature was already dropping quickly, and Cedric had overseen the gathering of grasses that afternoon so that the entire area around the fireplace was strewn with them. All the blankets had been beaten clean and were now wrapped around various persons. There weren't enough blankets to go around, so they shared and huddled closer to the fire for warmth. It was still early spring, and while the snows had melted, summer had yet to arrive. Targon took a few pinecone nuts that were offered to him by Yolanda while Celeste held her daughter, Amy, for her. He was relieved to see they had been roasted somehow and not boiled. They were not good boiled, and he knew that from experience.

"So do you still intend to leave us?" Cedric asked Targon from across the fire. It was now getting dark, but Targon could not only see but feel

the looks from every one of the fifteen souls sitting around the fire that night.

"Like I told your mother, Cedric, I stayed around today to see to it you were provided for, but if I don't find that slave caravan soon, I may never know where they took my family to, or Marissa's family, either," he said with a nod in her direction.

"What about my grandchildren?" Emelda said, a pleading tone in her voice.

"And my sister?" Yolanda chimed in, looking around at others.

Lady Salina stood up and motioned for everyone to be quiet. "We have all lost," she said, looking around at each person in the circle. "My boys and I have no idea where my husband is. My children don't know if their father is alive or not. Celeste and Olga have lost: both their husbands died or disappeared that day. It is unfair to lay all this at Targon's feet. We are lucky he found us first, and not that filth from Kesh." Several others began nodding in agreement, including Will, who was slumped against the blind wall, freshly bandaged but subdued this night.

"Hey, what about my parents?" asked Thomas, looking a bit left out.

"I understand, Thomas," Salina said gently, looking him in the eye. "You and Jons have suffered greatly as well, and we don't know where either of your parents are, but if they could see you now, they would be happy to know you're safe." After speaking, Lady Salina sat down and looked into the fire while she wrapped her small blanket around herself and her son Karz, whom she held in her lap again.

There was silence again for a bit, and then Agatha used the only wooden bowl they had to scoop out some cabbage soup and passed it to Yolanda to give to Amy. It was clearly understood the young would eat first tonight, and, by the sour look Amy gave, some of the adults weren't too sure if that was a blessing or a curse.

Targon rose and gathered his belongings. He decided to leave the heavy Kesh blade as it was only slowing him down, and at this time, he

needed stealth, not strength. "I will be back within a day or two," he said simply, putting his father's axe in his belt and slinging his bow across his back.

Marissa stood up from next to Cedric, looking Targon in the eye. "Promise me you will, and do it on your father's soul."

Targon met her gaze and responded, "I swear I will, by my father's soul, my grandparent's souls, the dragon's fire, and Agon herself. I will return, Marissa."

"Where are you going, lad?" Celeste asked him meekly.

"I am going hunting," Targon replied, putting his cloak on, and he headed north along the game trail toward his homestead without looking back and was quickly lost to sight.

CHAPTER 11

AMBUSH

Targon found his night vision quickly returned once he left the blind and its little fire. He made good time along the old game trail, all the while hearing the Rapid River with its constant noise to his left. The moons of Tira and Sara soon rose in the east and allowed even more light than that of just the stars, but it wouldn't have mattered anyway. Targon had been using this trail for many years and knew it well.

He had gotten off to a much later start than he had wanted to, and his original plan was now altered. In a bit of bravado, he had promised Marissa he would return, and so his foray could only be for a few days at most. He was not sure where the carts were at the moment, and he feared they would soon, if not already, pass the old bridge on the ancient trade road and head east past the ruined keep and eventually into the Border Mountains where another day's ride would take them to the pass.

Targon had been there once many years ago. His grandfather, Luc, had taken him while they hunted for food. The local game had been spooked, and for weeks, nothing came near the homestead. Hunting was scarce. Some farm animals from across the river had even been killed by a large

predator, and occasionally at night, the family heard noises they could not explain. His grandfather thought it a wild mountain cat or even a bear, and they decided to hunt it once they found its tracks. The tracks confirmed it was a mountain cat, large and willing to roam far from the foothills in search of food. The winter before had been harsh, and it appeared many animals as well as the Ulathans suffered that year.

That was the year after his father had died. Malik was tapped to go with his grandfather, but not knowing how long they would be, Luc allowed Targon to accompany them as a porter, carrying their water bags and some other supplies and provisions. Targon was still young at the time, and Malik was soon to be entering the king's guard. Targon remembered the road and its destruction and just how dangerous it was to traverse the many crags, crevices, and fissures that overtook the ancient path and, in many areas, simply blocked it. It was literally impossible to walk on the road once it climbed into the mountains.

They never found the large cat. Whether it left or was killed by hunger or another predator they did not know, but they did find a large mountain ram, and the three managed to hunt it with Malik making the killing spear throw while Luc had shot and wounded it first. They laboriously carried the carcass back home and managed to make it through that year.

That was the question vexing Targon's thoughts as he made his way home. How in all of Agon did those thieving Kesh manage to bring so many carts, oxen, horses, and men across those mountains? Something was amiss, and the thought of his family making such a dangerous journey motivated him to walk faster with a determined focus, and so quicker than he thought, he soon approached Bony Brook not far from his home.

It was on the southern edges of the brook that the forest and trail all but ended. The brook was not swift and not large, so crossing it wasn't an issue, but the land was. Many decades of logging trees and using the land had made most of the ground from the brook to his home open and exposed. He could just make out the dark form of his domicile far

in the distance across the brook, and though he had a ways yet to go, he was reluctant to leave the trail and the relative safety of the forest's trees.

Even most of the brushes had been cleared from around his home. He had to go around to the east along the brook and then cross after several thousand feet. Farther back, there remained some trees and brushes, and he decided to approach the homestead from the southeast, almost directly opposite of the little trackway to the trade road. He crossed the brook, and after some time, Targon passed the stump of the old oak tree where he had cut wood days earlier and had left his weapons. Using some bushes and a very occasional tree for cover, he crept up to a small bush and wiggled his way through it so he could see his home.

Something did not feel right. It was dark but not pitch. There was enough light, even from the pearl band of milky white stars, to clearly see the area excepting a few shadowy areas of the front porch, and the twin moons were obscured from a few clouds in the night sky. Targon kept his bow on his back and his axe remained tucked in his belt, and he watched and waited. *Dawn will soon approach*, he thought, *if I waste any more time here, and I still want to make it to the road several hours more to the north.*

He crawled out of the bush backward and stood up, turning around, and nearly bumped into a dark, cloaked figure holding a staff. Targon was so surprised that he lost his footing and fell onto his backside, fumbling for his axe. His hand gripped the handle, and just as he was about to pull it out, the figure knelt, leaning toward him, and placed one finger up to his hooded but darkly shadowed face and said, "Shhh . . ."

"By all the passings of Akun!" Targon hissed in a loud whisper. "Who are you?" Targon found his footing again and slowly stood, eyeing the figure in the dark yet keeping his hand on his axe's handle, not yet daring to pull it out but not willing to let it go, either. He could see only the staff in the other man's hand and nothing else, no sign of a sword, mace, or dagger.

"Sorry to frighten you, Master Terrel, but I thought you needed to know you had visitors," the man whispered while he slowly removed the hood of his brown cloak, revealing a white but short beard, bushy eyebrows, and blue, glinting eyes, old eyes but bright and alert. His skin appeared wrinkled, weathered, and old, tanned even, but old. The old man looked intently at Targon eye to eye, seeming to have suddenly become petrified, and didn't move an inch.

Targon wasn't quite sure what to say, much less how to respond. The old man just stood there looking at him. Finally, with the thought that perhaps he wasn't about to get attacked, Targon relaxed his grip on his weapon but left his fingers wrapped around its hilt. "What visitors and how do you know my name?"

The words seemed to release the old man, and he brought his free hand up to his head and scratched it where Targon noticed there was a bald spot forming. "The kind of visitors that aren't very polite and leave your place a mess after visiting," he finally said, "and I've known the Terrel clan for many, many years. This is your place: you live here, so I assumed you were a Terrel."

"Visitors? Clan?" Targon was completely confused. This old man must be from the city and was knocked hard on the head and had wandered out in the wild for a few days until he found himself here. There couldn't be any other answer, except . . . The old, crazy, yes, crazy, man now had surprised Targon, and that wasn't done easily. The stealth that was used was not . . . natural . . . and the glint in the old man's eyes and, well . . . the worn, weathered skin didn't fit in with his hypothesis, either. No matter, "crazy, old city man" it was, then. He'd worry about his observations later. "There is no one there . . . is there?" he asked, nodding back behind him at his home but not daring to take his eyes off the other man.

"There are five of them inside the cabin, two flanking the trackway, just a stone's throw away to the north, and the other two are . . . shall

we say sleeping, just behind that bush," the old man said while pointing behind him to a larger alder bush that was sitting near the brook a hundred paces away.

Targon had not passed far from that bush when he arrived, but finally taking his gaze away from the old man, he looked past him at the bush very closely. He saw nothing. He then took a step to his left, trying to keep the man in his sight but had to take his eyes off of him for a second to look at the homestead. Somehow, he looked and felt comfortable letting his gaze leave the stranger for several seconds. Turning back to the old man, he leaned in, saying, "I don't see anyone anywhere."

The old man leaned closer to Targon and whispered back. "I didn't know you were blind."

"I'm not!" Targon retorted rather louder this time, and again, the old man's finger rose to his mouth. "Don't shush me, old man, and I can see just fine," he said, but whispering again this time.

"Does your bow work?" the old man asked, arching his brows.

"Of course it does. Why?"

"Good, I'll show your visitors to the door. Unless they are close friends of yours, I suggest you shoot anything wearing black that comes out your front door." And with that, the old man turned and started to walk northeast around the back side of the cabin.

"Where are you going!" Targon asked in a highly raised whisper, wanting to yell at the crazy old man but fearing he may be telling the truth.

The old man leaned the staff between his arms and cupped his hands around his mouth and then made a *hoo-hoo* sound, imitating an owl. The call was so realistic that Targon reflexively looked around to see if he could spot the owl, even though he had just seen the old man making the call. Turning back to Targon, the old man arched his bushy eyebrows yet again and whispered, "Make sure when you shoot, its wearing black . . .

NOT brown." Then the old man started to circle the homestead, working his way around it to the right.

Soon, the old man was lost to sight as he rambled his way toward the other side of the cabin. Targon soon came to his senses and pulled his bow off his back and grabbed an arrow, nocking it and moving to the left of the brush where he could just see the front door.

Another hooting owl sound came lofting through the night, and suddenly, Targon saw a large dark shape on all fours charging the rear of the house. There was a loud cracking sound and then a *boom*, followed by the sudden yells and screams of men. The front door flew open, and a darkly clad man came flying out, running so fast that he fell in the dirt just off of the porch. He got up quickly and drew a knife from his belt. As he stood, Targon could clearly see his tall, slender figure. Dressed in black with the wicked-looking dagger in his hand, it could only be a thief from Kesh. He was quickly followed by two more brigands, one bleeding and limping, the other backing away from the door with a large sword in his hand.

Suddenly, the swinging front door crashed off its hinges and lay flat on the ground. The dark shape in the doorway suddenly stood, taller even than the tallest Kesh, huge, stocky, and completely covered in brown fur. The bear roared a challenge and then started to move forward. The Kesh with the sword took a swing with his blade and then lunged at the large bear. The bear seemed to understand and fell to all fours, backing away enough to avoid the lunge. A huge paw tried to swat the large sword, but the Kesh bandit pulled it back quickly and then readied it for another strike.

Targon realized the bear could be killed. Despite the surprise attack, the sword was sharp and the brigand using it was no novice. Pulling the bow back as far as he could, he loosed his first arrow, aiming for the sword-wielding bandit. It struck in the man's sword-wielding arm as the

bandit stood facing the bear. The sword tip dropped, but the bandit held onto it and backed away, looking around for the new attacker.

Targon nocked his second arrow and loosed it just as the knife-wielding bandit spotted him. His second arrow caught the sword-wielding bandit squarely in the chest as the man had turned looking for his attacker. He fell to his knees and gasped his last breath. The third bandit pulled a sling from his belt and fished for a rock in his pocket while glancing sideways at the bear. The knife-wielding bandit charged Targon's location, knife in hand. Targon pulled another arrow, nocking it, but the bandit was close now. Before he could release his arrow, the bandit threw his dagger as hard as he could, forcing Targon to duck and roll for cover.

"Notz so fast, youz little rat!" the charging brigand yelled as he kept coming. "This is all youz fault!"

Targon had dropped his bow and dove behind the bush but somersaulted back up and drew his axe from his belt. The brigand came around the bush, and to Targon's surprise, he found he was armed with another knife. The axe landed right in the brigand's chest where his heart was. The brigand stood facing Targon in the starlight, silent now but staring him in the face. His eyes held hatred, and for a second, Targon pitied the man, to hate so strongly and to not know why. The light quickly left the brigand's eyes, and the body fell to the ground lifeless.

Targon looked at the body but no longer saw the knife. He had only seen it flash briefly in the starlight, and then it was gone. Targon felt something then and moved his hand down to his stomach. There on the very left side of his abdomen, his hand and fingers curled around a hilt. It was buried in his side, and Targon started to feel lightheaded. He was just about to pull it out when he saw the old man come around the bush.

"Oh, dear," the old man said, looking Targon up and down. "This won't do at all."

Just then, the brigand with the sling let loose his missile, and a rock flew across and hit Targon square on his forehead before the bear pounced on him, ending the fight.

Targon slid into the old man's arms as he lost consciousness and darkness took him.

The light filtered into the room, and as his eyelids fluttered, Targon saw a reassuring sight. He saw the dark rafters of his home. He was in his makeshift bed, lying on his back, looking straight up at the rafters. He half expected to hear Ann's voice or see his mother's face as she leaned over to greet him. Instead, he was shocked back from his wonderful dream when the old man's weathered face appeared.

"Hmm, yes, coming around, I see."

"What happened?" Targon asked, trying to sit up and look around. When he did, he wished he hadn't. The room was a mess. There was a large hole in the back wall where the large bear had broken down the door and smashed timbers scattered across the floor. Dried blood was everywhere, but he saw no bodies, and what was left of any furnishings, the table they used to set for dinners, his mother's bed, a small chest, and shelving for cupboards were all destroyed. Only his bed, made with dry straw and wooden framing, and one lone chair the old man sat on seemed to survive.

"It seemed your friend poked you. You didn't lose much blood, but I think the events of the morning, coupled with the sight of the knife sticking out of your belly, must have been too much for you, that and the rock that hit you on your forehead. You simply fainted," said the old man.

Targon looked around and saw it was evening. The sun had already set and light was still in the air but quickly fading. "Well, then, how did I sleep all day if I only fainted?" he asked, looking the old man in the eye.

"Humph, well . . ." And with a bit of squirming in his seat, "I took some liberties with you and gave you some grog." He smiled.

"What is grog and who are you?" Targon said, gingerly touching his wound with his right hand and realizing he was shirtless. He then felt his head and could feel a bump just to the right of the center, and he had a terrible headache.

"Ah, indeed yes, you are right. Pleasantries first. I almost forgot in all the excitement. My name is Elister. We are neighbors."

There was a moment of silence followed by that same awkward pause he experienced just before the attack. The old man, Elister, he had said, just stood there smiling, frozen with that grin on his face. Targon cleared his throat. "We don't have any neighbors. At least, not on this side of the river."

"Why, dear me! All these years and I thought for sure we were neighbors," Elister replied, looking rather flummoxed at the new revelation.

"Well, where do you live, old man?"

"Right here in the Earlstyne Forest," he said, motioning with his arm toward the forest.

"Blackthorn Forest?" Targon asked, looking confused and grimacing in some pain.

"Well, yes, that is what some call it here abouts, though a pitiful name it is for such a fine wood."

"Fine wood? The place is practically haunted. I'm surprised we lived so close to it for so long," Targon replied, now sitting up and putting his feet on the floor, testing his reflexes. "And the grog?"

"Yes, well, a simple concoction of my own making, if I may say so. A bit of honey, warm milk, dab of rum, well, maybe a lot of rum, and, of

course, some fennel seeds. It makes for a wonderful healing effect, but alas, it will make you sleepy. Don't you remember drinking it?"

"Well, no, I don't."

"It seems to be a common problem amongst grog drinkers. You had almost two cups worth: nearly my entire flask is gone. You drank it right after I brought you here to lie down, and then you slept."

"Fine, I don't remember, but if you say I drank your grog, then I guess I drank your grog." Targon looked around again for a moment, noticing the front door was also broken and lying down outside. A pleasant wind was blowing through the house. "Are all the cutthroats dead?"

"Well, the ones you and Core killed, yes," Elister said, standing and walking over to the hole in the back wall and then looking out.

"Who is Core?" Targon asked, looking around again, wondering if he could mean the bear, but bears don't have names.

"This bear does have a name and it's Corrack, but he prefers Core," Elister said, literally reading Targon's mind. "And your other visitors are, well . . . sleeping."

"And just what do you mean by the word *sleeping*," Targon asked, this time arching his own brows.

"Hehe, well, I'm not much for taking life these days. Too violent it is, and life is too precious. Then there are times when we must do what we must do, such as you and Core had to do earlier today. I decided instead to just put the other visitors to sleep."

Targon looked at him closely, trying to see if the old man was serious or not. "And how long will they sleep for?"

"Well, I would think for a decade or two unless someone wakes them before that." Elister walked back and sat down to look at Targon's wound as he gently lifted a small piece of clean cloth where the dagger had entered.

Targon looked down and saw the wound was nearly shut already with no sign of blood or infection. Looking back to Elister, he thought for a second more. "Are we safe with half the brigands sleeping?"

"Oh yes, quite safe. It would take a wizard to wake them, and there aren't but a couple of them in the whole valley and they are quite far away right now."

"There have been no wizards for a hundred years, old man! Make some sense, will you?"

"My, my, a bit testy we are after the grog and all, somewhat dimwitted, too, by most of your comments. Didn't your parents teach you any history? The legend says it was a thousand years, not a hundred, but the legends can be wrong from time to time. I should know." Elister dabbed at the wound a bit and then pulled the cloth away and left the wound open. "Let it breath now a bit, and I'll get your tunic for you, though it has a hole in it. Oh, and again, my name is Elister. E-L-I-S-T-E-R, not *old man*," he said, walking over to the ruined shelving and grabbing Targon's tunic from where it had been hung to dry.

Targon took the tunic and gently dressed himself, but he hadn't needed to worry. There was no pain when he stretched his arms, just a stiffness in his left side and a slight throbbing of his head. He had to admit he was being much too petulant with the old man, since as far as he could tell, the old man hadn't referred to him as son or lad or any one of a number of condescending titles. "Thank you, Elister," Targon said, finishing his task of putting his tunic on. "I guess I should also thank you for saving my life. I'm sure that was a trap for me. How many did you say were waiting for me here?"

"Nine guests," Elister replied as he held up his fingers and started counting. "Two near the trackway, two near the forest, and five inside waiting for you to show up."

"I saw only three here." Targon motioned at his broken interior.

"Well, Core took care of two of them inside and one outside, you took care of the other two outside, and I put four of your guests to sleep, so, yes, nine," Elister finished, delighted to have one extra thumb free from counting.

Targon stepped over some broken timbers and exited the cabin out the front entrance, Elister following. He looked closely and saw some dried blood and drag marks on the ground. He followed them around the north side of the cabin and to the edge of the cabin's cleared ground. There he found five small dirt mounds. "You buried them?"

"Indeed." Elister nodded.

"Where are my weapons?"

"Next to the front door on the porch."

Targon headed back to the west side of the house and noticed the sky getting darker there. Red hews still radiated out from the dragon's setting fire, and a look east showed him the first twinkles of stars coming out to play in the cooling night air. He quickly found his bow and axe and counted nine of his arrows back in their quill. It seemed the old man was not one to waste either. "When was the last time you talked to anyone, Elister?"

"Why, right now. We are talking."

"No, I mean, when was the last time you talked to someone other than me?"

"Not more than an hour ago, I talked to Argyll," Elister responded, cocking his head sideways, apparently not understanding where the conversation was going.

"Where is Argyll now?" Targon asked, looking around to see if anyone else was hiding near his home.

"He flew to your blind to keep an eye on your friends," Elister said, a sincere smile coming to the old man's face.

"Flew?"

"Yes, that is what birds do," Elister retorted matter-of-factly.

"So you talked to a bird?"

"Yes."

"And it talked back?"

"Well, more like screeched, but I understood him," Elister said, the smile being replaced with an expression of confusion.

"Okay, and who did you talk to before that?"

"So many questions. Well, if you must know, since we have time, I had a good chat with Core. I had to convince him to help us."

Targon probably had the same look of confusion on his face the old man had. "The bear? You talked to that large bear?"

"Yes." And again, the nod.

"Where is the bear now?"

"Core is right up the trackway not more than two or three stone throws away keeping watch since Argyll isn't here to do so."

"Wait one second. Let me rephrase the question. When was the last time you talked to a human being, a real person?"

Elister walked over to one of the two tree trunk stumps that were sitting just off the front porch and sat on one, scratching his head. His staff had been sitting next to Targon's weapons, so now he had both hands free. Putting his elbows on his knees, he hunched over and rested his chin in his hands and started to mumble. "Hmm. Let me see . . . hmm . . . how long . . . hmm . . ."

"Fine, who did you talk to last if you can't remember when?"

"Well, that is an easy question. Why didn't you ask that first? I talked to your grandfather, Luc," Elister said, now sitting upright, rather pleased with himself for remembering the answer.

"He's been dead for five years. You mean to tell me you've not talked to a single living soul in five years?" Targon asked, coming over to sit next to the old man on the other stump.

"I speak to living things every day!" Elister responded with a slightly hurt look on his face.

"Understood, sorry. I meant human living being, not animal."

"Ah, yes, well, then, you are correct. It was longer than five years ago. I think the last time we talked he was just a boy."

"Why, that would have been over fifty years ago!" Targon exclaimed, trying to wrap his mind around the information the old man had just given him.

"Yes, seems about right. You are very perceptive."

"So, you two were boys, then? Were you friends?"

"No, not a boy. I was traveling in the area and decided to look in on Mars and Melinda and found young Luc playing just over there, near that brook," he said, pointing to the Bony Brook where Targon often played and bathed.

"How old are you?" Targon asked, his mouth gaping open.

"Not sure. I think I slept a few years here and there, but by last count, I think I am eleven twenty-three, give or take a decade or two."

Targon just looked at the old man in awe. Now he was sure the old man was crazy, and he must have had the wild bear hit him on the head. Over a thousand years old and talking to animals? Yup, crazy was the right word. "Not possible, old man, but let's not argue the details, though one hundred and three I might believe, just the right age for dementia to set in."

"Indeed!" huffed Elister, taking the indignation in stride.

"Really though, old . . . I mean, Elister. I need to get going and see if I can find my family. They were on those Kesh lock carts, and I believe they may have passed the old keep on the trade road nearby sometime today," Targon said as he headed to pick up his weapons and prepare to leave.

"They actually passed by here yesterday," the old man said, still seated but looking intently now at Targon, eyes narrowing a bit. "Don't you have some other guests you are responsible for?"

Targon finished putting his bow and quiver across his back and was tucking his axe into his belt. He had to admit, he felt fairly well for having just been hit in the head with a rock and having had a knife stuck in his abdomen earlier that morning, though it was obvious to himself that the knife missed any vital organs and was nothing more than a deep flesh wound. "You mean the city folk from Korwell?"

"Them and our little neighbor from the old road. What's her name?"

"You must mean Marissa, and you seem to know an awful lot for someone that hasn't talked to anyone alive in over half a century. What about her?"

"Well, she is one of us, not, what did you call them? City folk."

"I'll be back for them soon enough, right after I free my family."

"You'll need more than that bow and axe to free them, I'm afraid." They crossed the mountain pass this afternoon and are now in Kesh. The pass is well guarded."

"But maybe my family is in a different cart, maybe they are still in Ulatha," Targon said pleadingly, almost begging Elister to give him different facts.

"I'm afraid not, again," Elister said, bowing his head in sincere sadness. "Dareen and Ann are already in Kesh."

Targon ran over to the old man and practically shook him till he stood and faced him. "How do you know this and how do you know their names?" Targon practically yelled, still shaking the old man's shoulders.

"Calm down, Targon! As I said, I know your family. Baldric, Dareen, your brother, Malik, your sister, Ann, your grandparents, Luc and Julia, Luc's parents, Mars and Melinda, their parents . . ."

"I get it! You know about me and my family and our history, but HOW do you know about my mother and sister NOW!" Targon had quit shaking the old man and started to feel a tear forming in his eye.

"Argyll told me. He talked to your mother this very day and returned this afternoon. They are doing well, or as well as can be locked in a Kesh slave cart."

"How . . . how could she talk to a bird?"

"Well, a falcon actually, but yes, she has the gift. All the Terrels do, though it lies dormant in most of you, especially the men of the family. Your mother is an initiate of the druid order."

"Nonsense!" Targon retorted, looking about for his black cloak. There is no magic in Agon, just death and suffering." Finally finding his cloak hanging on an old nail against the wall of the cabin, Targon headed north along the trackway at a quick walk.

"Where are you going?" Elister asked, following him up the trackway.

"I'm going to find my mother and my sister," Targon replied without looking back.

"It's not safe, Master Terrel," Elister responded, using the more formal title for Targon. "You forgot your pack too!"

"I don't need it," Targon said.

Targon quickly passed the bear without even seeing him, but Elister stopped on the trackway as the large bear rambled onto it and waited patiently. "Follow him, please, Core. See to it he returns when he learns what I've already told him."

The bear snorted and pawed at the ground.

"I don't care if it's going to rain soon: in fact, it might clean you up a bit from your long hibernation. You could use a good bath," Elister said to the bear. A few more snorts and a growl and the bear still didn't move. "Well, I won't be around much longer, and you will need him soon enough. We just need to save him from himself first." The bear snorted one last time. "I hope you're right, Core. I hope you're right, indeed."

With that, the large brown bear just snorted once and trotted off the trackway, following the young human. He didn't need to see him directly,

as he could smell him and his blood very clearly in the dusk's cooling air. It would be easy to follow the human, and so human and bear traveled north along the trackway for the better part of a few hours at a very quick pace before they arrived at the ancient trade road. The human looked left toward the bridge over the Rapid River for a moment, and then he squatted, looking down at the ground. Finally, he stood and walked along the edge of the road east toward the old ruined keep that could just be seen at the base of the mountain pass. Targon was headed for Kesh.

CHAPTER 12

DESPAIR

The sun set, and like the night before, the small band of refugees huddled around the small fire near the old hunting blind. Salina wasn't happy that some of the children were foraging for food so far from the blind, but she had to admit they didn't have many options. The loosely knit band of refugees fleeing from Korwell was seriously lacking in strong men. It seemed, in hindsight, the Kesh leaders had made a conscientious decision to kill any man or boy old enough to wield a sword. This didn't make much sense to her if they wanted slaves, as a man in his prime would be stronger and more valuable than a young boy, child, or even a much older man.

Salina looked at the group as they talked lightly around her. With the exception of her son Cedric, and, of course, Will Carvel, they really didn't have anyone able to wield a sword. Sure, Horace could fight if pressed, but at sixty-five, he already had one foot in the grave, as the old saying went, and the next oldest to Cedric was Thomas at twelve. Between eighteen and fifty, there were only her son and the injured sergeant of the gate.

Salina grabbed her slender sword from the wall of the blind and pulled it from its leather sheath. She grabbed one of a few old rags she had and

started to clean and wipe her blade from hilt to tip. *No*, she thought, *as wife of the captain of the guard, I will fight, and I am in my prime.* That made three of them.

"Going to kill something?" Will asked her, sitting beside her and looking intently at her sword while gingerly pulling at the bandages on his left arm.

Salina allowed herself a rare smile as she looked back at Will. "Only cutthroating thieves from Kesh . . . and maybe a squirrel or possum if one comes close enough," she said with a small chuckle.

"Aye, food is scarce," Will said solemnly, "but maybe that's a good thing. It keeps everyone's thoughts on eating and not the sorrow and pain that come with loss."

"Did you lose anyone?" Salina asked while returning to her sword polishing.

"Not really. There was, however, a rather nice, big bosomed wench that served ale at that old pub just outside the gate. The Pickled Pig. Did you know it?" Will asked.

Salina laughed louder this time, getting a few looks from the older ladies, especially Celeste and Emelda. "Will, you old coot, the Pickled Pig was no place for a lady. We passed by it all right when heading to the town's market, but I've never stepped foot in the place. What was her name, by the way?"

"Hehe, yeah, I guess I frequented the less savory taverns in town, didn't I? Her name was Inga, and she came from a little town far to the west near the Trovis Mountains before reaching the Western Sea. Far from home she was, but alas, I fear for her and the owners. I'd give mightily for a pint of ale and a word from her right now. Indeed, I would."

"Well, I'd sell my dress for a drink from the Pickled Pig," Salina said, a smile appearing on her pretty face.

Will and Salina sat in silence. Salina kept working on polishing her sword, which was now so shiny and clean that she could eat off of it,

and Will watched the others as they ate pine nuts and wild cabbage. At least Marissa had found a few berry bushes, and her, Monique, Thomas, and Cedric, who said he was standing guard, managed to gather enough berries to eat during the day, so their diet had at least a small variety to it if nothing else that day.

Agatha took Karz from where he lay next to his mother while Yolanda picked Amy up, and the four all went into the blind. The night before, when Targon had left, they had decided the younger children and the ladies would sleep in the blind while the men and boys slept and kept a watch outside. Emelda and Horace got into a serious ruckus when Horace refused to sleep inside the blind. Being her husband and all, she simply wanted him safe, but his refusal had made both Will and Salina chuckle. "I'll not be coddled by an old bat," Horace had said of Agatha. Luckily, Agatha was already in the blind and no doubt heard, but she had the sense to keep it to herself. In the end, Horace stayed with Will outside along with Cedric and Thomas.

"Do you think he will return?" Salina asked Will as she finally finished polishing her sword and put it away.

"You'd know better than I," Will responded. "You had that pretty sit down talk with the lad down by the river. What did he say?"

"Well, he said he would return, of course. You heard him well enough last night. He said his home was just over a half day's walk from here. He'd need an entire day to just get there and return, much less do anything, so it's early yet."

"You sound like you're trying to convince yourself."

"Now, Will, you know how I feel about him. We would have all died back there had he not found us. Nothing personal, Will. You fought bravely and we would have never made it out of the town if not for your bravery and that of our soldiers. We are all thankful, but it would have all been for naught out here in the wild without his help."

"Agreed. I'm fond of the lad meself. Reminds me of, well . . . me when I was his age, but without the frontier skills. I've been thinking just how little we knew about the wilds here until we ran into the young lad. Seems he knows more than any of us about our own lands."

They had become accustomed to at least Cedric and Thomas stepping away from the blind, Marissa too, for that matter, so it was nothing of import when they did, and both Salina and Will assumed they didn't stray too far. In fact, as Will had said, the loss of food kept them distracted from their personal losses, so when a panting Thomas arrived at the south end of the blind, out of breath and sweating profusely, they weren't surprised to see him but rather at his state of arrival.

"Quick! Cedric says you must come and see this!" Thomas said, fear in his voice.

"What is it?" Salina said, pulling her sword out and standing to face him. Will awkwardly stood, using his one good arm to balance himself, and then looked for his sword near the blind's wall.

"Bandits!" Thomas said, his eyes wide with fear and excitement. "You have to come now!"

Will finally found his sword and started for the south opening of the brush line, but stopped when he looked at Salina, who was shaking her head. "What is it, my lady?"

"Not like that, Will. You can barely stand, and you clink loud enough when you walk for the dead to hear you."

Will tugged a bit at his chainmail shirt and looked sheepishly around. "Then who's going?"

"I will." Salina sheathed her sword, which was now getting a workout, and grabbed her cloak and then pointed to Horace. "Stand watch here with Will and get everyone else inside!"

Horace reached for the Kesh blade, and Jons grabbed at one of the crossbows, trying to point it south. "Jons, not tonight, all right?" Salina's

voice came softly now, the fear and edge of panic gone, the voice of a loving, concerned, and kind mother now replacing it.

"Aw, I want to fight!" Jons said, just barely able to lift the bow up, much less point it anywhere. Olga and Celeste were already scurrying around the blind, heading inside, and Monique offered her hand to Marissa.

"I need you to protect the ladies, Jons. Can you do this for me?" Salina asked gently.

With a small pout but head held high, Jons muttered something they all took for a yes, and Salina watched him go inside with Monique and Marissa, taking one of the crossbows with him. "Will, see to it the fire is put out, and stand guard. Don't shoot at anything in the dark until you're sure it's not us," she said with a nod at the lone remaining crossbow.

"I will. Do you think we're safe with Jons and that crossbow?"

"See to it that we are," Lady Salina said, pulling her cloak tightly about her. "Now, Thomas, let's go, but take me to Cedric slowly and keep it quiet."

"Yes, my lady," Thomas replied, scurrying south into the dark, Lady Salina following right behind him.

Will looked over to Horace, who was even now kicking dirt on the fire. "Bloody hell," Horace said as they were plunged into darkness.

Targon traveled until he reached the old keep and then ducked behind a tree just to the north of the road. He stood there for a long while. There was no light and no movement coming from the keep. He knew the crazy old man's bear was following him. At first, he was distracted and didn't hear it, and the bear was trying to be silent. In fact, if the bear was following any one of the numerous city folk, Targon was sure the bear wouldn't be heard. However, Targon wasn't one of the city folk, and, well, despite

all its attempts at being quiet, the bear was a bear. *How could one not hear a half ton bear following you?* Targon thought.

The bear had stopped some distance behind him, and Targon was relieved because he wanted stealth at the moment and the bear's presence worried him. Targon's waiting finally paid off. There, at the base of the keep, was the faintest glimpse of a dark red glow. Someone had lit off a pipe or stick. Targon remembered his grandfather having a long pipe and occasionally smoking some southern Safron weed back in the day. This time, the habit was giving away the location of whoever stood at the old keep. More time passed, and then he saw movement at the top of the broken keep's tower. A figure slowly backed away, and another moved in to take his place.

Some sort of changing of a guard, Targon thought to himself. *What am I doing here wasting time?* His thoughts were almost screaming out loud, and he was upset for wasting so much time. Caution demanded patience, and despite his urgency, he knew he could do no good for his family if he was captured or worse, killed.

Just then, the winds changed direction, and he felt the first pings of rain on his hand and hood. *Oh great, now we have rain. What else can happen?* Targon touched his side and it felt sore and a bit stiff but not much pain, and his headache was slowly subsiding, though he knew it would take a few days for the bump's swelling to die down. Either he should be embarrassed for fainting with such a minor flesh wound or the old man's healing skills were a force to be reckoned with. Either way, he was thankful for the help, and for the first time since this nightmare began, he did not feel he was alone, or at least alone with regards to carrying a large responsibility on his shoulders. Crazy and old, yes, but useful and kind too, so he'd take what he could get. He was just about to make a decision on what to do next when he was startled by the bear coming up behind him.

"By Akun's passing! Don't do that!" Targon said to the bear. It appeared to be much larger when it was right next to Targon. It was on all fours, and its head reached up to Targon's shoulders. He was sure it would tower above him if it stood on its hind legs. The bear just snorted and swung its massive head from side to side. "I don't understand you, crazy bear!" Targon hissed loudly at him, the small fine drops now turning into a heavy rain, loud and pelting.

The bear pawed at the ground and rumbled a low sound yet again. "What?" Targon asked, leaning forward. Nothing. "I must be crazy myself," Targon said, shaking his own head, "having a conversation with a bear in the rain, and a lopsided, one-way conversation it is."

The bear looked at Targon for a moment, and Targon swore he thought the bear was actually trying to think of something to say. Finally, the bear took his huge paw and, with one swipe, put a mark into the bark of the tree next to Targon. The bear just stood there looking at him. Targon was at his wits end, not understanding the bear nor comprehending why the bear was following him. It could only mean the crazy old man must have put the bear up to this, which meant he had to believe the crazy old man could in fact communicate with the bear. Targon wanted to chalk it all up to coincidence back at his home, but here was a wild bear he would have tried to spear had he encountered it a week before, and it was looking at him not more than an arm's length away.

"Druid, my ass!" Targon profaned just a bit, upset with himself for using such language with the bear. "I guess I'm going crazy, old bear," Targon said, finishing his discourse and readying himself to leave, letting the bear do as it pleased. *Indeed, half-ton bears often do as they please,* Targon thought, *so let him be!*

The bear, however, shook its head from side to side as if making a "no" sign as a human would. This struck Targon as odd, and he looked at the bear again. He couldn't understand any of its rumblings, and now

it had stopped grunting and making noises and was using its head to communicate. "Impossible!" he exclaimed, looking incredulously at the massive bear. "Can you understand me?" Targon asked, leaning forward even more.

The bear's head suddenly went up and down, and Targon stood back upright, not wanting to be too close to this particular animal. It had to be a coincidence, but there it was. Shock slowly came and went, and Targon got wetter and wetter from the relentless rain. The bear didn't move, instead it just stood there looking at him expectantly, large raindrops gathering on its brown fur and dropping to the ground beneath him. Finally, Targon pointed to the top of the keep. "Up there bad man. You kill bad man?"

The bear shook its head from side to side. *What good is the bear if it won't help me with the sentry posted on top of the keep?* Targon thought to himself, but before he could answer, the bear put its head down almost to the ground. "You kill bad man at bottom of the keep?" Targon asked, taking his arm and lowering it to the ground level where he had seen the pipe being lit. The bear's head came up and nodded up and down.

"Blimy!" Targon exclaimed out loud, letting out a deep breath at the same time. He couldn't understand the animal, but it could understand him. Targon had an idea. "Okay, bear, you kill bad man on ground, I kill bad man on top of tower." Targon nodded his head, and the bear followed suit.

Targon took his bow off his back and nocked an arrow. He was still too far from the keep to make the shot, but he started darting from tree to tree, trying to stay out of visual sight from the top of the keep with the bear following him. When he got to within about fifty yards, he looked around the large trunk of the tree that was concealing him and saw two silhouettes. They were very faint, and he thought he saw the dark shapes of two tall but slender men. One of them for sure had a pipe and was smoking it while they both had retreated under an arch that was crum-

bling but provided protection from the rain. One stuck his head out and looked up at the offending rain, and in the faint light, Targon saw a brigand of Kesh.

Targon felt anger now rising in him, and he decided to act, bear or no bear. He could just see the top of the tower, so he braced himself and stepped around one tree trunk, taking several steps to clear his line of sight from the canopy of leaves, and pulled back hard on his bow.

Salina quickly caught up to Thomas and laid a hand on his shoulder. "Gently now and quiet. There is no rush," she said in barely a whisper, and Thomas nodded and continued his pace, but a bit slower now, and he started to take deeper but slower breaths as well. Salina had seen her husband many times use some of the same techniques on his soldiers to calm them down, and she was glad she paid attention during her younger days when she oftentimes accompanied them on forays and patrols of the surrounding countryside. That was before she had Cedric, and though her time in the military with her husband was brief, she was using every tool she could to deal with the tasks at hand.

It took longer than she expected, and she was wondering if Thomas had gotten himself lost when finally she could just make out the faint outline of her son Cedric in the dark. He was standing and motioning for them to follow. She could hear the now louder rumblings of the Rapid River as it churned its recently melted snow from the mountains down and along its path all the way to the Western Sea. Cedric put his finger to his lips and motioned for them to lie on the ground. Together, the three of them started to crawl on the small rise toward the river.

As they inched themselves up over the small berm that was blocking the river from view, Salina gasped. There, on the far bank a good thirty yards away but clearly visible, was a large party of Kesh brigands. She saw several small fires and what looked like several small but crude tents

laid out around the area. She could easily see a dozen of the cutthroats standing around the encampment, sentries most likely, and more movement within. There was a snort of a horse she could barely hear above the endless rumbling of the river, but she could not see it. She inched closer to Cedric, who was to her left while Thomas lay to her right. "When did you first see them?" she asked.

"Not long ago," her son responded. "I sent Thomas back to get Will, though I didn't expect Will to stay at the camp and you to be here," he whispered, looking at her as he craned his neck to take another look.

"That was my idea," she responded, somewhat happy he was thinking of her safety but mildly offended he thought her unable to respond. "How many have you counted?" She began thinking he may have seen more than her.

"At least twenty, Mother," he said. It was hard to hear him since he spoke so quietly. "I think I saw two other groups, one headed south, the other north."

"About a half hour ago?" she asked, trying to gauge the time it would take for Thomas to get her and then return.

"Closer to an hour. I had Thomas stay with me for a while as we watched them before I sent him."

Salina had just taken a moment to digest this information when she saw torch brands arriving from the north of the camp. It appeared a patrol was returning or reuniting with the group of bandits they were observing. "Mother, look there!" Cedric hissed, motioning to the south with his hand. There was yet another group making its way north, back toward this main group, but they were farther away. "What should we do?" Cedric asked, his eyes almost as wide as Thomas' eyes were, the glint of fear coming from them.

Salina understood then that Cedric was afraid, as were they all, but in the wild woods, far from the order and security of Korwell, Cedric would be no match for someone like Targon. She started to really miss

the young hunter from the eastern wilds, and despite being younger, he would know what to do, but now that fell to her. Only her husband's military service and discipline, which had rubbed off on her during their early years, kept her from panicking as well.

Salina motioned for them to follow her down the small berm, and she began to crawl backward until she could crouch without fear of being seen from the opposite shore. Her pretty dress was long gone, and the extra mud and dirt caked on it hardly mattered. How much she had changed in just a few days. "Cedric, you keep watch on this group here. Send Thomas as a messenger if anything changes," she whispered to them once they were all together. "I'll return to the cabin"—all the city folk referred to the hunting blind as a cabin—"and warn the others. We can't let them cross the river, if possible. Otherwise we will need to flee into the woods."

She didn't think anything could be worse than the thought of being pursued by Kesh bandits, but once she mentioned fleeing into the forest, both her son and Thomas' eyes got even wider, and she didn't think that was possible. She would have to have a word with Agatha about the stories she had been telling all of them regarding the Blackthorn Forest. "Understood," Cedric answered finally while Thomas nodded.

She started back the way she had arrived, careful to keep the small berm between her and the opposite side of the river. She returned the same way she had arrived, by moving farther into the woods and away from the river before heading back north toward the blind.

She estimated the time at around a half hour in order to travel the distance between the brigand camp and the blind. She wondered just what her son was doing so far from the blind when she almost stumbled upon it in the dark. The only time she had left the blind after dark was the night before to get some water from the "Granite Pool," which was what they called the small eddy of water where the large granite boulder lay that Targon and the men had slept on when they first had arrived.

The adults didn't want the children getting too close to the river proper, and so, being that it was off limits, they all used the pool, which was calmer and safer than the dangerous river itself. When she returned, there was no faint glow of the fire to guide her back. It was very dark under the forest's canopy.

"Halt! Super!" she heard the small raspy voice of Jons challenging her from the dark mass of trees and bushes where the blind was now well hidden in the dark.

"I don't have time for that, Jons, and next time, stay quiet!" she hissed back, walking tentatively for the southern entrance to their small encampment, thinking now it may not have been such a good idea to let him enter the blind with the crossbow fully loaded.

"Put that damn blasted thing down before you kill someone!" Salina heard the crackly voice of Agatha, clearly reprimanding Jons. Salina understood that Targon was right about the city folk and noise in general. Agatha and Jons could be heard for at least a hundred yards, dark or no dark.

"Aw, no one plays by the rules!" Jons whined and then was quickly shushed by at least three different but unrecognizable voices.

Salina entered the encampment and found herself facing a crossbow held by Horace while Will stood with his sword outstretched. "Damn you, woman. You move silently like a thief. We thought you were one of them," Will said, lowering his sword while Horace pointed the bow in another direction.

"Nonsense, Will. Even little Jons could hear me coming, but I don't have time for this. We have trouble."

"What is it?" Horace asked, uncharacteristically speaking. Perhaps the thought of his wife, Emelda, in danger and the children which he was becoming quite fond of motivated him to speak.

"Raiders from Kesh . . . lots of them!" she said, looking from man to man. "We can't let them cross the river, and if they do, we will have to leave quickly."

That was not something either man wanted to hear, and apparently, neither did anyone else in the camp. "We can't leave here: we just got here, and where would we go?" Monique could be heard pleading.

The blind was built with arrow slits on three sides, and the crude door was built in two so that if necessary, the top half could be opened while the bottom was shut. That was the purpose of the hut, to draw game into the area near the calm drinking pool and shoot it, but now the slits were acting as small windows with one of them facing their encampment. Salina could just see the dark shapes of two faces, Monique and someone else by the look of it, probably Emelda keeping watch over her husband. Vines had grown over the blind by design, being planted there long ago even before Targon's grandfather, Luc, had used it. "Well, into the forest, perhaps?" Salina said, not sounding very convincing even to herself.

"No!" Horace said, quietly but firmly. "I'm done running. I'm too old to go traipsing all over these here woods, and I won't have them filthy cutthroats chasing after our kin children." Referring to the orphaned and other children as "kin children" was an Ulathan mark of love and honor. Horace was stating he saw everyone in the group as his family or kin.

"What are you saying!" came a cry from the blind, and they could hear footsteps as Emelda ran out and confronted her husband. *Yes*, thought Salina, *the other figure was indeed Horace's wife.* "You can't throw yourself to your death! What about me?"

Horace looked at her and then placed the crossbow on top of some branches, forming part of the encampment's ring. He walked over to Emelda and hugged her tightly. "You'll be fine. Lady Salina is a fine woman and will see to it you are protected."

"That's not what I meant," Emelda responded. "I can't go on without you!" she started sobbing in his arms. They could hear chatting from the ladies in the blind, and, though they thought Amy was asleep, the little toddler started to cry. Salina thought for a moment that she was going to lose control of the whole damn group.

"Fine! No one is going to go anywhere, then," Salina stated firmly, looking from Horace and Emelda to Will and then to the blind's arrow slit. "If necessary, Yolanda, Monique, Celeste, and Olga will take the children into the forest, but only if we fail. The rest of us then will fight and make those murdering thieves rue the day they ever set foot in Ulatha!"

Will shook his head and slumped back down. The others seemed to take heart and courage from the lady's strong words. They would fight and they would live and they would survive. Order and control quickly returned to the encampment, and preparations were made to settle in for the night. Thunder started to rumble from the north, and the smell of rain was in the air. Hope for now had returned to many in the group. Sadly, Salina wasn't one of them. She had seen the Kesh numbers and knew in a fight, they would all die, every man, woman, and child, and so Lady Salina pulled out her sword and started polishing it . . . again.

Targon let loose his arrow at the dark shape on top of the ruined keep's sole tower. He had been there many times before, even playing in the ruins of the old keep as a boy when his family was in the area picking mushrooms that grew in the deep, dark nooks and crannies of the destroyed structure. This time, he was there for blood and to wipe out the ones responsible for destroying his home and family. Targon could not tell if his arrow struck its target for sure, but he was confident it hit the lump of black mass he was aiming for.

He quickly nocked another arrow and turned both down and slightly to his left, letting loose another missile at the sentry with the pipe. His arrow barely missed, smashing its metal head against the tough granite wall behind the brigand. They were alerted now, but it didn't matter. Before Targon could loose his third arrow, the bear let out an ear-piercing roar and charged the two cutthroats from Kesh. Targon looked for another target but didn't see any, and the bear had stood on its hind legs when it reached the brigands, completely blocking them from sight. All he could see was the shining wet fur of the beast.

Deciding against any more arrows, Targon detached the arrow and quivered it while dropping his bow and drawing his axe. He ran up to the bear and yelled a battle cry, "Ulatha!" while jumping the last few feet and landing next to the bear just inside the archway. There was nothing for him to attack. The crazy bear had killed both bandits, nearly decapitating one of them. Targon wasn't sure if they even knew what hit them.

Quickly with a bound, he ran into the ruined inner courtyard of the small keep and up the very same crumbling stairs the wizards of Kesh had used a few days earlier. When he reached the top, he found his arrow had found its mark and was lodged in the third brigand's shoulder near his heart.

Anger was starting to leave him now, as was his adrenaline, but he didn't want to feel pity for the dying brigand. Walking over to him, he crouched down so the thief could hear him over the pelting rain. "Where are the slave carts?" he asked.

"Burn in hell, Ulathan scum!" the brigand replied defiantly, but then he started to wretch and cough. *The arrow must have pierced his lung,* Targon thought.

Targon was not raised to be mean nor born evil, but he had little time for mercy or compassion, so he gently grabbed his arrow, twisting it just a small bit. The brigand gasped in pain and started to heave blood from his mouth. *Maybe that wasn't the right thing to do,* Targon thought, *but I need to know where my family is.*

"Where are the slave carts? The lock wagons?" Targon asked gently but firmly, no longer twisting the arrow but keeping his fingers wrapped around it.

The brigand coughed again and spat some more blood. "Long gone, scum. They left here yesterday and are deep in our lands now. They belong to us."

Targon realized the slender man was barely older than himself, and now, pity started to well within him. "Why are there so few of you here, then? Where are your other raiders?"

The brigand looked at Targon with scorn, and then softened his visage once the pain returned. Bravado was one thing, pain was another. "You'll find them soon enough. There is an entire company roaming these lands, and they will soon find you and kill you, Ulathan," he said. "We were just a camp guard."

Targon stood and looked at the brigand with a note of interest. This one talked more like he did, more like an Ulathan and not a Kesh, with their uneducated speech and bastardized words. Who was he? No matter, he had no time for this. "Tell your brothers I'll find them first," Targon finally said, pulling out his arrow and walking away as yells of pain came from the Kesh brigand.

Targon wasn't sure if the wounded brigand would live or die, and he didn't care. He just wanted to find his family. He descended the broken stairs and saw the bear waiting for him. He looked at his shattered arrow, the one that had missed and struck the stone wall, and left it. He had to find them, and in the rain, man and bear headed for the road and started running east.

CHAPTER 13

HUNT

Khan was growing angry and frustrated. The pompous Arch-Mage and his own mentor, Ke-Tor, had left earlier to press the attack on Ulatha's southern holdings after the swift surprise attack on its capital. He was being treated as a child and expected to babysit the pillaging troops under his command. Well, actually, they were under Hork's command, or even his lieutenants, but they were supposed to take orders from the mages. They usually followed orders only when it suited them, if they were coerced, or if they were in fear.

The Kesh had suffered heavy losses taking Korwell, and that was expected as it was the only fortified town in the entire realm. The rest would be easy. So it was they had expected little resistance once the little self-proclaimed king was killed and his castle taken. Reality was different, however. First, there was the worrisome fact that the attack, while timed for surprise brilliantly, left a large mounted patrol outside of the castle when it commenced. Their intel on the matter suggested the captain of the king's guard, Bran Moross, was leading it himself. He was one of the few men the Kesh feared, as his counter-raids had killed many a brigand

over the last two decades. Reports had it he was rallying the Ulathans in the South, and that was unacceptable.

Then there were reports that here and there, across the pleasant but simple realm of Ulatha, the inhabitants were not quite as passive as the Kesh were led to believe. "They will fold like a leaf in your hand," he remembered Ke-Tor telling him in the weeks leading up to the assault. Well, some of these leaves were acting more like thorns and fighting back. Nothing major, but many minor incidents and even casualties occurred, and that was not good for Kesh. The Ulathans didn't know it, but the last decade had been particularly hard on Kesh, as what little food and supplies they did have were dwindling, and the population was diminishing. Kesh needed an infusion of food, supplies, and, yes, even slaves to survive. So much had been lost in the last millennia.

A scout had arrived from the surrounding area and informed him a large group of Ulathans had fled and successfully routed one of the many patrols searching the area. Khan had left immediately with a brigand chieftain named Dorsun. They found the patrol, nine dead and three that had deserted. There appeared to be only one Ulathan casualty, though there was blood everywhere, so he wasn't sure if they had wounded anyone else in the attack. Dorsun's men wanted to hang the corpse of the slain Ulathan, but Khan prevented it. Instead, he ordered the deceased Kesh to be buried with rocks as well. No graves were dug that day.

Khan had one tracker who found tracks that they followed east. The first set of tracks were easy to follow. These were harder, but it was impossible to hide well over a dozen tracks in such rough terrain, but then came the real problem. They followed the tracks to the Gregus River where they entered the river at a place where it was impossible to cross. The bank started shallow enough, but in the center of the river, the water was flowing faster than a man could run and it was deep, deeper than what even a horse could safely ford, and the river's current could drown both beast and rider.

Khan ordered scouts both upstream and downstream, but they had to return after searching only a short distance due to the failing light. They had set camp and posted guards to watch.

"Where do you think they went?" Dorsun asked, looking out from the large tent cover that was acting like a porch facing the river. "Surely they couldn't have crossed *that*?" he said, sweeping his arms wide to encompass the huge, roaring river.

"Doubtful," Khan said, bringing his hand up to his chin. It was dark, and thunder rolled across the skies: black clouds formed to the north and were quickly sweeping southward toward them. "Probably walked in the river downstream to prevent us from tracking them. We may have to call for dogs."

"Should have brought them with us," Dorsun said, looking at the younger man intently. "By the time we get them here, it will be too late."

"The hounds would not have mattered. The coming rain will have washed away any scent or tracks as well, and if there is no scent to follow, then the only way to hunt them down is to do so by sight. Wake me at dawn."

"Very well, young master, dawn it shall be," Dorsun said.

Khan turned, entering his tent and closing the cover while contemplating the fate of the unknown refugees, who so far had shown themselves to be very dangerous, most likely soldiers and a leader or two with them. Perhaps warriors of great renown. Little did he know, the group had more women and children in it than men and the group was so close to his own hunting party.

Dorsun walked from the wizard's tent to the center of the encampment where he had a crude map laid out on a large rock. It showed the Gregus River and the Earlstyne Forest, and they had finally reached them both, but he was not happy, either. The map showed only one place to cross the river: far to the north where they had traversed it half a week earlier along with one other bridge much farther to the south in enemy

territory, which was still controlled by Ulathans. Either this group of Ulathans they were tracking was still on the west bank of the Gregus or there was an undisclosed place along the river to cross it. Either way, he was determined he would find out and find them in the process.

Targon ran most of the night in the rain with the large brown bear following him closely. Not far from the old keep, the ancient trade road began to rise and climb the sharp spurs of the Border Mountains. He could see where the road would take him: a cleft in the mass of rock that was looming above him. Even from his home farther in the valley, the mountains appeared large and menacing, but here, on the actual slopes at the base of them, in the rain, they seemed almost frightening.

The rain did not let up, though it did fall in slower sheets and at times almost paused, but then it picked back up and pelted him as he ran. It was darker than normal, as the stars were blotted out by the many dark clouds swirling above his head. Dawn arrived, and the sky lightened only slightly. There would be no rays from the sun reaching Ulatha today.

Targon had long ago stopped running, but continued to walk at a steady pace. Road was a kind word for where he was walking. There were no stones, no paving, just dirt and some rock laid into the crevices where at some places, the original road did show culverts, bricks, and pavers, but most of it had washed away long ago and was lost to memory. Still, he found he could follow the road easily, and while the rain washed away any tracks, he was certain the road could handle the large lock carts the Kesh employed.

Targon took shelter near a large bush not far from the road, trying to press himself against a small rock overhang that was only waist-high. The road had veered southeast from due east as it climbed the shoulder of the mountain. The bear—*What was its name? Carrot or something similar?* thought Targon—had also left the road and seemed to be huddled in a rocky draw between a small tree and a large granite rock. Targon drew his knees tightly up to his chest and tried to sleep briefly. He dozed for a bit, but not long, and continued his climb all day. Soon, the faint light began giving out altogether as the dragon's fire set and Targon started to approach the high mountain pass. His legs burned and ached from the quick journey, and the mountain slopes were merciless to his body.

Finally, he stopped. Just above the tree line, and it was above because even this lower pass was higher than where the coniferous trees could grow, he spotted a fire. Not a wood-burning one, but rather two oil-based fires in towers on a crude wall about fifty yards across covering the entire pass, and two small but covered crude towers with some sort of shallow-looking shiny metallic pans strung below each tower. The pans were both smoking and putting off light and heat. He could see the silhouette of sentries standing guard in dark cloaks. He froze for a second, wondering if he had been spotted, but nothing happened. Targon retreated a dozen yards to the nearest tree and hid behind it, peering out. Nothing. *How did they build something like this without the king knowing?* Targon thought to himself.

The old keep had been used as a base, allowing patrols to foray into the pass and beyond, but there hadn't been a garrison there in decades. There had never been a structure built in the mountain pass, so this took Targon by surprise. It appeared the Kesh weren't worried about just getting into Ulatha, but also keeping anyone out of Kesh appeared to be one of their primary considerations.

Targon snorted in derision and departed back down the road. Obviously the guards were facing inward nearer to the warm fire while he was shivering from the cold rains. It wasn't winter anymore, but neither was it summer, and the rain was cold and the wind even colder. About a half mile down, he veered northeast and started to climb for the mountain meadow he had been to before. He remembered it was also a low spot in the formidable mountains, and he hoped to cross there. It

was actually not far from the pass, but clambering over razor-sharp rocks and slick stones took much longer than using the road. After a couple of hours, he finally reached the old meadow and walked due east with the large bear in tow.

One last climb twenty feet straight up and he stood on a cliff edge looking down into Kesh. It was dark, and he couldn't see anything really, except the ledge and the long plummet over one hundred feet to some rocks and boulders below. When he was here before as a boy, they had stayed on the western end of the meadow, which was over a half mile wide across the peak itself, but the eastern end had another sharp, large ledge where Targon stood. He didn't see any way down and wasn't sure what to do when he heard the bear snort twice and then finally literally growl at him.

"What is it, Carrot?" Targon asked, turning around and looking twenty feet down at the bear. They were both soaking wet, and Targon still managed to shiver, despite his exhaustion and lack of food. Maybe he did need his pack, after all. The bear motioned with his head and swung his entire upper body back and forth to the south. This was frustrating for Targon, and most likely the bear as well. "All right, you big oaf, I'm coming!" Targon practically yelled above the roar of the wind as it whipped up again, and rain kept pelting them and the rocks incessantly.

Targon climbed back down, and the bear took off heading southwest back the way they had come, but about only one hundred yards later, the bear veered south and into a small cleft where there were many bushes, brush trees, and meadow grasses growing. The bear began to eat some wild berries, and Targon grabbed two handfuls and stuffed them into his mouth, one handful at a time. They were delicious, but he was sure they would taste bitter if he had any of his senses left about him. His hunger would make anything taste good at this point. The bear, seemingly done foraging, headed south around a few rocks and into a small draw in the

rock. There, just out of sight, was a dark hole, a cave of some kind barely discernable in the dark.

"Nice smelly, dank hole you found there, Carrot," Targon said, shivering and thinking he would die soon of hypothermia. His cloak and clothes were wet, as were his boots, and he had no means to start a fire and no way to change his clothes. He felt he could have died on that mountain that very day.

The bear entered the cave, and Targon followed, bending over at the waist. The cave was barely as tall as the bear's back just beneath Targon's shoulders, and it was shallow. The cave was really made by a few large boulders that had fallen there from the peak above, and then over a few centuries, dirt followed to fill in the cracks, and grasses and moss had covered the rocks until a small space was all that remained inside the hollow. It smelled feral and animal-like, but Targon didn't care. It was three times as wide as it was high, and so the bear shook his shaggy coat and spun loose as much water as it could and then lay down, curling up with its back to the cave entrance.

Targon took off his boots and cloak and even his tunic and pulled some dry leaves and grasses around near the bear and then lay down. The bear actually moved a bit to get closer to Targon, and he found himself huddled inside the bear's massive four legs, pressed against the bear's abdomen. He felt warmth there, a wet warmth but warmth nonetheless, and he prepared to sleep, hoping he would wake up alive and not dead.

Salina slept poorly that night, worried for her son Cedric. She awoke and found herself sitting where she had dozed off outside with her back against the blind. Horace's light snoring could be heard, and Will was sleeping as she was with his back against the blind in a sitting position. The entire group had finally fallen asleep, and it was quiet again. She

could just barely sense that maybe dawn was in the air, but the first drops of rain started to hit them and she stood up and woke both Horace and Will, and the three of them entered the crowded blind.

Everyone was huddled together around the floor with almost no space for them to sit, much less lie down. The wind whipped through the open arrow slits, and some rain entered with it. It was pretty miserable and not much more comfortable either, but it beat being outside or in the hands of the Kesh. Salina motioned for Horace to sit down near the door, and she whispered to Will, "I'll head out to check on the boys: you stand watch here."

Will just nodded but looked pale. Salina quickly left after gathering her cloak and sword, and headed south. After a bit more than a half hour, she finally reached the place where she had left her son and Thomas the night before, but they were nowhere to be found. She looked around and then lay down on the berm and started to crawl to its crest and peered over.

There she could see the fires burning and the tents of the bandits. Somehow she felt relieved they were still there but scared they were as well. She felt a hand plant firmly on her shoulder, and she stifled a yell. "Who—!"

It was Cedric, and he was drier than she was. He had crawled the berm and lay down next to her. "Shhh," he said, motioning with his finger to his lips. "We are over there," he pointed south a ways, and she could just barely see Thomas smiling at her from inside a large tree. The tree was hollowed out at its base, and the two had taken shelter there when the rain started. "They haven't moved all night." He yawned.

Salina felt so proud of her son, knowing he had stayed up the entire night to keep watch on the bandits. "You did well, my son! Is Thomas all right?"

"Yeah, he slept half the night but just woke up when I spotted you crawling in the mud. You're going to need a new dress, Mother, when this is all over."

"I'll need a good bath as well," she said, smiling. "Is there anything I should know, to tell Will?" she said, thinking her son may be more forthcoming in his answer if she invoked Will's name.

"Well, there wasn't much movement all night, but a small group of them just left and headed back west, though I couldn't tell how many for sure. I just saw a few dark shapes heading up that embankment there." He pointed toward a small rise behind the Kesh camp.

"Fine, well done, my son. Head over to Thomas and tell him to join you, and I want you both to return to the cabin and get some rest. There are a few nuts and some cabbage we left for the two of you. It isn't much, but you'll need something."

"You plan on staying here by yourself?" Cedric asked, not believing what he was hearing.

"Have Thomas send Horace with a sword. We'll watch together."

Cedric looked at her for a long moment before nodding and motioning for Thomas. They soon left and headed back to the cabin. Salina took her place in the hollowed out tree and found it pleasant enough. At least it was dry and, though it faced north, she could sit with her back to the east side, look out, and just see the bandit camp from her vantage point.

Not long after they had left, Salina started to see some movement in the bandit camp, and soon, two large groups of about a dozen or so brigands in each left the camp. One group headed south and away from them, and the other headed north, toward them and the ford. Salina felt her blood run cold. Shortly thereafter, Thomas and Horace appeared.

"Horace, I need you to keep watch here and go back to the cabin if they break camp. Can you do this for me?"

"Yes, my lady, but what's going on? You look pale like you've seen something dangerous."

"I have, about twelve of them dressed in black. Remember, go back only if they break camp. If we have to leave, I'll return to fetch you and we go together from here into the woods, agreed?"

"Agreed." He paused for moment and then reached out tenderly and touched her arm. "Do take care of Emelda for me."

"You can do that yourself. No Ulathan dies today. Not on my watch!" Horace saw her demeanor had changed. Her hollow words from the night before may have calmed the women and children, but Horace knew too well from experience that she had lost hope. Then she was gone, her and Thomas heading back to the cabin, and Horace thought she was much like her husband.

Khan was woken by Dorsun as requested, maybe a tad late, but he had a poor sleep despite the elaborate tent and bedroll. At least he was dry, he noted with a sad look outside as he saw what he had heard earlier . . . rain. "Dorsun, ready two patrols now. One goes north, the other south. Tell them to travel for half a day and then return and report. They'll need to hunt on sight for now."

"Consider it done, young master," Dorsun said with a sour face. His troops would not like the rain much, either, but Khan didn't care. The refugees were either here or they found a way to cross, and if they crossed, his troops would follow, but he needed to know where they were.

The camp stirred as the brigands mobilized and readied for action. Two larger brigands were appointed to lead each group along with a tracker each. Gund took the northern group while Boxer took the southern one. He noticed the heavy rain was making it hard to see even in the daytime, and even their own many tracks were quickly being washed

away by the water, so he didn't hold out much hope to find them today, but he had to make the effort.

The night before, the brigands had felled several trees, using their massive trunks to sit on, and a large mountain rock nearby was rolled over to Khan's tent. He sat on the rock and pulled a finely crafted glass orb from his secondary pack and started to rub it with his hands. He was going to see if he could use a bit of magic to find the Ulathans.

Salina made it back to the cabin almost out of breath. By now, the entire camp was stirring and everyone was awake. Will had not allowed Marissa to take anyone into the forest to forage for food. They were all sitting fairly miserably in the small blind, packed together rather tightly. While not very comfortable, it at least allowed them to conserve body heat for warmth.

"Well?" Will asked, a concerned look on his face.

"Holy mother of Agon," Salina said, getting a much better look at his face this time around. "You look terrible! Agatha, come see this!" motioning for her to come over.

"I've already seen him, and the big lug won't let me down to the pool to wash his dirty bandages. We are out of food and clean cloths, and the wound isn't healing," Agatha said, but this time in a more serious, somber tone.

Salina could see his bandages were almost completely soaked in blood. "Sit down, Will, you can't stand there all day," she said, grabbing his good arm and leading him to the back of the blind toward the corner where Yolanda and Amy were still huddled. "Agatha, go to the pool but stay out of sight of the river. A group of the Kesh thieves are heading this way along the opposite side of the river."

Agatha quickly departed, but the others started to murmur.

"You can't have me back here, lady," said Will, looking weak but firmly pleading his concerns. "I need to be near the door and keep guard."

"No need for that now. I'll return if they come near the cabin. You just get some rest and some sleep, if you can. We will need your strength again before this is all over."

Will just nodded and slumped back in the corner next to Yolanda, who held Amy tighter. Salina saw Cedric finishing the last few leaves of some raw wild cabbages.

"Better if you left me at the thieves' camp, Mother," he said, making a face. "I thought these things tasted bad when they're cooked, but I was wrong!"

"Yeah, I know, better cooked and they are bitter, but they will fill the belly if nothing else. Did you get the handful of nuts I left for you?"

"Yes, Thomas and I split them. Thank you."

"Good, now lie there next to Karz and get some rest."

"Where are you going?"

"To keep an eye on those brigands," Salina said, and then she smiled and grabbed the other crossbow—Jons still clung to his—and wrapped her cloak tightly around her body and headed north toward the pool and the river, passing Agatha as she knelt washing Will's dirty bandages.

She had to protect the ford. She estimated the brigands, who were traveling slowly and following the tracker who was looking for any signs on the ground, should be arriving soon. She had to wait only ten minutes before she saw the group across the river from her vantage spot near the pool. Agatha had just left, and not a moment too soon.

If she thought she was terrified when she first saw them far away from their camp, her fear was doubled at the sight of the grimly armed group of men not more than a few hundred yards away from the blind on the other side of the river. The thought of those cutthroats so close to her own children and her fellow Ulathans made her both afraid and sick.

Luckily, the group of men kept moving north, and Salina started to track them from inside the forest about fifty yards from the river's edge. She moved as silently as she could from tree to tree, but it didn't matter, really. It was dark and overcast, raining hard with a wild wind that blew in gusts and stirred the canopy of leaves in the forest all around her. Add to that the roar of the river's rapids as it churned all that water, and she wasn't sure she could get their attention even if she yelled at them.

The water was indeed rising in the river with all that rain and the newly melted mountain snow. Salina reached the ford located above the many rocks and white water of the river, and the other group halted there as well. This was her biggest fear. This was the ford they had used to cross the wild river. It was still deep and the water was running faster, but she felt a shiver as they stopped and started to look and motion across. Salina readied her crossbow and lay down next to a tree, steadying the bow while aiming at the men on the other side.

There seemed to be some sort of argument as one man motioned and the other shook his head from side to side. After some heated debate and probably yelling, though she heard nothing, the group started again and continued north and eventually out of sight. Salina did not follow. There was nothing north of there, except the main bridge over the old trade road, and that would take a day, if not longer, to reach at the pace they were traveling, especially if she factored in the weather. She just lay there and started to sob.

CHAPTER 14

WOODS

Targon woke before dawn. It was still dark outside, but the faint glow of the rising dragon's fire could barely be seen as he exited the cave and returned to the mountain meadow. The bear had arisen sometime before and was foraging again near the blueberry bushes, seemingly ignoring him. Targon walked to the eastern end of the meadow and scrambled back up the twenty feet of rock and granite to stand once again on a high mountain ledge separating Ulatha from Kesh. The rain had stopped, but it was cloudy and overcast. There wasn't much to see as he looked east into Kesh and stood there shivering, as his clothes were damp, if no longer soaking wet.

He finally saw in the faint light the line of a road from his south looping back up to the north and continuing out of sight east. He saw no movement on the road, and hope left him, while despair replaced it. Slowly, he started to realize his hope of rescuing his family and warning his realm of the danger it was in wasn't going to happen. He was too late with the latter, and his family appeared to be out of his grasp for now. Hungry, cold, somewhat wet, and completely saddened, the young man

took one final look into Kesh and made an important though mature decision.

He scrambled back down the cliff face to the meadow and walked by the bear, who paused to look at him. "Come on, Carrot, let's go home." The bear followed, seeming to snort in agreement, and Targon didn't bother to try to eat anything.

The entire day was overcast and the sun rose, but was never seen, only felt, just beyond the dark grey glooming cloud cover. Targon decided to head due west. Even when he reached the road, he did not stay on it. He felt he was foolish for using the road like a common merchant the day before, and he knew he was lucky no bandit guards spotted him at the mountain pass.

Walking cross country was nothing new for him, and after some time, he felt he should have spotted either his home or the road from it, but instead, he walked right up to the Rapid River as the sun set. This confused him as he looked both up and down the river. His home was just a few hours' walk from the main road, and he was sure he should have been there by now. He kept the dark, glooming Blackthorn Forest to his left, and he could see its northern edge even now, but he didn't recognize where he was at. He started to walk along the riverbank and eventually reached the forest as well.

There, at the edge of the forest, was the huge granite boulder he was familiar with, marking the spot where he often went spearfishing in the river. He was confused because the boulder was located in an open field about a quarter hour's walk northwest of his home, but the forest had somehow reached the rock, which was not possible. Targon scratched his head, deciding to head southeast, entering the forest. It was dark and not easy to keep his bearings without any stars or even the twin moons' light to guide him, but eventually, he came upon a wooded clearing, and there in the middle sat his home. Targon looked around and could not believe the sight.

"Well, hello!" Elister said, exiting the front door of the cabin and walking over to where Targon stood dumbfounded with his jaw half open. "How do you like it?"

Targon looked at the old man, and for a brief moment, he felt fear, fear and power. "What happened here?"

"Come on, I was hoping you'd return sooner, but this will have to do. First, let's get you out of those wet clothes and into something drier, if not warmer, eh?" he said, taking Targon's arm and leading him to the front door.

"Well done, Core, I am glad you looked after Master Terrel." The bear snorted and followed the old man, ending in a growl. "Kesh bandits, indeed! Two of them no less, and Master Targon took care of a third?" The bear swung its massive head and lay down on the porch, curling up into a large ball of brown fur with its head between its massive front paws. "Well, we'll talk more about that later. Argyll told me about the fence, but I'm glad you didn't try to break that down as well." And the old man guided Targon into his house from the front door and offered him a seat at their old table, which was newly repaired.

"Really? You think I believe you're actually talking to Carrot there?" Targon asked as he took off his tunic and boots while the old man went across the room and grabbed something from a large burlap bag. "I mean, he seems like a really smart bear, but not very communicative, if you know what I mean."

"Carrot?" Elister asked, turning around and raising both eyebrows. "Show a little more respect for Core. At least he had the sense to get out of the rain and find something to eat. Animals are a lot smarter than people give them credit for. Here, try these on>" He pulled out a cotton white shirt and black breeches.

"Thanks," Targon said, taking the dry clothes and changing into them. He took his leather tunic and pants off, giving them to Elister, who hung them over a wooden stick hanging by the hearth, which had a roaring

fire burning within it. "Still, you didn't answer my first question. What happened here?"

"Well," the old man said, stoking the fire with a metal rod and grabbing another chair that looked a bit rickety, but he sat on it nonetheless. "I don't like to stray far from the forest, and it seemed we were in need of some type of living quarters other than your old shed by the river, so I invited the forest to your home and made a few repairs."

Targon looked around and noticed the door in the back wall was repaired, though he could clearly see the cracks in between the replaced hinges so it was obvious the old man was no carpenter, but the rest of the place seemed almost the same as he remembered it on his mother's birthday. "Impossible!"

"Maybe it would be better if I showed you? If you're done dressing, let's go outside. Oh, use these boots. They may be a tad small for you, but at least they are dry." And he handed over a set of black leather boots with high shin guards.

"Yuck, these are Kesh boots," he said, making a face as he looked at the old man, who said nothing but frowned back. "Okay, fine, I'll put them on."

Targon finished dressing, departed his home, and passed the bear, now sound asleep on the front porch. He stood and waited for the old man to say something. Elister took one look at Core and shook his head as he walked over next to Targon. "You'd think sleeping all winter would be enough. Anyway, yes, the forest. See how beautiful it is now wrapped protectively around your little cabin?"

"Yes, I see that, but I want to know how that happened," Targon stated.

"Well, the trees were invited to join us, as I said, but let me show you a little of my handiwork over here," Elister said as he took Targon by the arm and guided him to where the trackway should have been. In its place, Targon could clearly see tall meadow grass almost knee high, and the old

man started to walk along it, weaving in and out of the various trees that were getting thicker and thicker as they moved.

"You did this?" Targon asked.

"Yes, a little grass seed, some weed pollen, the rain, and, of course, a little encouragement, and the ugly scars of people have been healed. In fact, the area looks much the same as it did before the first Terrels arrived centuries ago."

Targon was amazed. If the old man hadn't guided him, he would have had no idea the trackway was under his very feet. Any sign of it was gone to the wilds of the forest, grasses, and bushes that seemed to have grown or sprouted right before him in the last two days. Targon stopped moving and pulled away from the old man. "If you can do this, what else can you do?"

The old man looked at Targon for a moment and then seemed to understand. "Yes, of course, this is a bit much for you city folk . . ."

"City folk!" Targon exclaimed, slightly offended.

"Well, fine, then, not city folk, but you still don't understand the ways of nature and Agon, though I must admit the Terrels came closer than most. Come on, then, let's get back to something familiar for you so you don't spook so easily out here in the woods." And he took Targon by the arm again, and they quickly returned to the cabin. "Sit, let me make you some hot tea, and you'll feel better soon enough."

The old man grabbed one of Targon's mother's wooden cups, which were the only ones left that weren't broken. Taking the metal pot he had placed over the hearth sometime before he proceeded to pour hot water from it into the cup, adding a few tea leaves from a small pouch tied to his belt. "Here you go, drink for a moment and relax."

Targon drank and felt calmer but eyed the old man warily. "If you can do this, why can't you kill the Kesh? You could have stopped them or even saved Ulatha from what happened, not to mention my family," he said, looking down and breaking eye contact with the old man.

"Well, yes and no," the old man said, putting his hands on his knees and leaning forward, waiting for Targon to resume eye contact. "I can see your fear, at least your fear of not understanding," the old man resumed, waving off any remarks to the contrary by Targon, "but my situation is, shall we say, delicate, if nothing else. I am Arnen, one of the keepers of Agon. Confusing to you because you have not heard of my kind before, but in the common tongue, we go by the name of druids." He paused to see if Targon understood. "There is power in the Arnen, but the Great Calamity the greed of man initiated left Agon weak and decadent and destroyed the many facets of the Arnen."

"So, you're like some sort of god or demigod?" Targon asked in awe.

Elister chuckled and shook his head. "I was born a wee lad like yourself long ago and raised as one of the Arnen. The Earlstyne Forest was in my care . . . Well, I should say the Blackthorn Forest so you understand me clearly, but it seems a shame to call such a grand old forest with such a noble name something so simple and demeaning as Blackthorn." When there was no comment from a stunned Targon, the old man continued. "Long ago, the forest was much larger, but in the many centuries since then, we are down to the heart of the forest now and this is all I have left to care for. There was once a time when I could walk from the Felsic Mountains to the Great Western Sea and never set foot in the sunlight, always protected by the cool leaves of the Earlstyne, but alas, those days were long ago."

"What about Kesh? Why didn't you stop them?"

"Well, quite frankly I know a lot from my little friends, but it appears all the wizards weren't killed in the Great Calamity, or at least their craft appeared to survive. The attack on Ulatha was directed by them."

"Wizards?" Targon asked, surprised by the news. He had heard from early childhood about the wizards from Kesh but also how they were all destroyed in a fiery mutual destruction of not only them but the dragons as well.

"Yes, even now there is one near your killing shed by the river, and he is searching for your friends."

"Why didn't you say so?" Targon asked as he started to think about Lady Salina and the women and children he left behind, his last thought lingering on Marissa.

"Because he just started trying to use his perversion of our nature and I became aware of him. Besides, a lone wizard is the least of your worries right now. Your friends are cold, wet, and hungry and lost without you, and they face many brigands across the river. Only the heavy rains and some intervention of my own have kept their location a secret. You need to do something!"

Targon thought for a long moment and looked at the old man. He understood now that whatever he was going to do needed to come from him. The old man could be useful, for sure, but it was obvious that either due to social aversion or some ancient code, he would help but not lead. Perhaps it was forbidden for him to help directly? "How much help can you give me?" Targon asked, calmer this time.

Elister looked at Targon intently before answering, as if deciding himself just how much he could help or even disclose to the young man. "My assistance is limited to the forest," he said at last with a sigh. "The power of the Arnen is connected to its heart, and my heart is the heart of this forest. Deep within the forest, I am as one with Agon. Away from the forest, my powers wane and I age faster than normal. Such is the cycle, but soon, my time on Agon will be over, and it's time for a new generation to care for her. You, Targon, are one of many who must decide to protect and serve Agon and her inhabitants or allow evil to grow and fester in the many corners of the world until all of Agon is consumed with it."

"So you hid my home by inviting the forest to surround it, and you hid the trackway by planting . . . grass and bushes?"

Elister smiled. "Something like that. Now you're catching on."

"What of the four Kesh that were 'sleeping'? Where did you *plant* them?" Targon said, placing a strong emphasis on the word plant.

"Well, I couldn't have them sleeping too close to here—the Kesh have spells of finding and crystal balls of seeing—so I made a small raft and put them on it, sending it downriver. Don't worry, the raft is sturdy enough to carry them over the rapids downriver, and with any luck, they won't wake up till they reach the sea. So, what do you intend to do now?"

Targon almost laughed at the thought of the four would-be assassins waking up when they reached the sea many miles from where they started their journey. "Well, if what you said is true, then we need to bring the city folk to safety, and my hunting blind isn't very comfortable nor safe. If I didn't know better, I'd say you did this for them and not me," he said while motioning outside toward the forest and trees.

"Very observant, but they will need food as well. I've sent out a call for assistance, and hopefully by morning, you will have some food to take to them," Elister said while retrieving the hot pot and pouring Targon a bit more hot water into his cup. This was quickly followed by some tea leaves, and Targon took another sip, feeling the tea was more than just an herb—it had certain healing properties—but he didn't want to ask the old man exactly what. He would take what he could get at this point.

"I'll leave just before dawn and take them some food and lead them back here," Targon decided.

"Excellent idea! You see, you will make a great Zashitor, after all."

"What exactly is a Zashitor?" Targon asked.

"Oh, I'm sorry. A great Ranger, Master Targon, you will be a defender of Agon as well as its creatures and inhabitants. One day, you will come to understand what it means to be one of the Zashitor. Alas, it was a few centuries ago since the last of the Zashitor walked upon Agon and guarded their wards. The world has become a much darker and deadlier place without them."

Targon pondered on this for a moment and understood it was going to take time to learn more of what he was being told. It was a bit too much for him at such an early stage of his life. He decided he'd ask more about this from the old man later. Right now, he had something important to do, and he would focus on saving his fellow Ulathans, city folk or not. "Will you stay here, old . . . I mean, Elister?" Targon asked, using the druid's name for a change.

"No. I'm afraid I'm not very social, and I've neglected some other matters for far too long, but I won't be far away. I have a serious matter to attend to in the heart of the forest. I'll leave some things for you and your guests here for when you return, agreed?"

"Sounds fine to me, and is that bear of yours going with you?"

Elister smiled. "Core goes where he wants to go, and I can only ask him or suggest to him a course of action. He has, however, indicated to me that he will accompany you and assist you and your fellow countrymen."

"Well, if he ever wakes up for good, then I'm sure his help will be much appreciated. It's getting late. Will you sleep here?"

"No, as I said, I have work to do and little time to do it. I'll leave some things for you on the table: just don't forget who you are."

"I won't" Targon stated simply, taking off the ugly Kesh boots and moving to the lone bed that his mother sometimes used with Ann to stay warm near the fire. The old man had laid some linen on the wooden bed and prepared a pillow as well. His body ached from sleeping on the ground and his head hurt, but he quickly made his bed and lay down to sleep, holding the Clairton bird carving in his hand while looking at the fire.

He paused for a moment to look over at the old man, who smiled and then walked out the newly repaired front door, closing it from the outside. Targon was alone again, and swiftly sleep took him as he thought of his mother and sister and brother.

CHAPTER 15

RAFTS

Khan was frustrated. For four days, they had been searching for a large group of refugees from Korwell, and he had been camped for over two days on the western bank of the Gregus River in the middle of nowhere. Despite his many attempts to find them, they seemed to have disappeared completely. What was more concerning for him was when he bent his mind and will into the globe of seeing that he possessed, he could see both up and down the river, but as soon as he tried to peer across the river at the forest's edge, his crystal ball would go black. There was a powerful presence blocking his vision past the river, and this was something he had never encountered before.

Boxer and Gund had returned the previous night with little to report. The southern group, led by Boxer, found no tracks and no place to cross the river. The northern group, led by Gund, found a possible ford not far from their camp where the water ran shallower and quicker over a jumble of rocks, but, with the heavy rains recently, the river was swollen and the crossing was deemed too dangerous to attempt at this time.

Currently, his lieutenants were debating whether to build rafts or simply take the one-day journey north to the old stone bridge that

crossed the Gregus and then spend a second day returning along the eastern bank. The issue was that without a way to cross nearby and not knowing what side of the river the refugees were on, his reinforced patrol would be split in two and not be nearly as effective should they encounter resistance.

"Dorsun," Khan called out from his rocky seat overlooking the brigand camp, "what do you and your leaders think?"

Dorsun was stockier than most of his peers but stood just as tall. He walked over to Khan's tent and knelt beside him on one knee where he could speak softly without being overheard. "Well, no one seems interested in walking for two days just to get to the other side of this river, and even less seem inclined to enter the Blackthorn Forest. If we have to, I suggest making some crude rafts today and crossing tomorrow. The rain has almost stopped, and I feel certain any tracks left will have been gone by now. Is it really necessary to track down these particular Ulathans?"

Khan had covered his seeing globe with his robe and deftly replaced it back into its pouch as Dorsun spoke. Khan thought for a second. "Am-Ohkre seems obsessed with them for some reason. Perhaps someone from the Korwell family is with them or they have something he wants, but either way, they have now killed a squad of our troopers and seem to be somewhat organized in such a way as to pose a threat to our operations in the area. If they did enter the Earlstyne . . . or Blackthorn, as you refer to it, then we must go there as well despite its reputation."

"Master Khan," Dorsun whispered almost too softly to be heard, and Khan had to lean in to hear him, "it's been a long time since we raided here, but I remember our raids from years ago. We had many successes along the western banks of the river and even near the Ulathan capital, but most of those who tried to pass through the Blackthorn Forest were never seen again. There is something . . . unnatural within it, and it's not safe."

Khan leaned back with an incredulous look on his face. "You are actually afraid of that wood, are you not, Dorsun?"

"Shhh, not so loudly, please, Master. Most of our troopers are younger and newer to raiding, but the old timers remember well enough. I'm not afraid, Master, but I am no fool, either. Enter the forest at your own risk. I've had my say and will say no more, but I don't advise following them into it. Have you had word from the Arch-Master?"

"Yes, that old Mage is more stubborn than ever. It seems we won the battle near Cree, but took heavy losses. Even now, he and Ke-Tor are returning to Korwell and want us to return as well in order to reinforce the capital, so time is of the essence. We need to cross soon and either find and capture these Ulathans or kill them outright. They would be more valuable alive, but things are moving quickly in the South."

"Your orders, then, Master Khan?" Dorsun asked, standing up and towering over the seated, would-be wizard.

"Build your rafts and do it quickly," Khan said, looking across the river at the tranquil-looking forest. "Tranquil, indeed," Khan said as Dorsun left to order the raft construction and failed to hear Khan's last comment.

Salina had watched the northern group of brigands return at dusk the day before, and she returned to the hunting blind and informed the others. Cedric and Thomas headed south and relieved old man Horace from his watch on the brigand camp. Emelda was happy to see her husband, and he returned to a pretty sad group of refugees.

They had not eaten all day, and Will's condition was pretty much stable. Stably sick. He was pale and weak, and the wound looked infected and red. Agatha had opened it up and tried to clean it out, but the pain was intense and Will almost passed out several times before waving her off, but at least she felt she had gotten rid of most of the festering flesh.

Again, time would tell, but Will pretty much just slept in a corner of the drafty hunting blind, drifting both in and out of consciousness.

So it was that the next day when Horace was preparing to relieve Cedric and Thomas that Thomas appeared yet again out of breath. "Lady Salina!" he said, huffing as he entered the crowded blind.

"Thomas, take your time. What do you need to tell us?" Salina asked calmly.

"Boats!" he said loudly. "They are building some type of boat to cross the river, several of them, in fact!"

The mood in the blind could not have been more depressing, and this news simply added to it. Horace was the first to comment. "I'll go have a looksee."

"I'll come with you," Lady Salina replied, grabbing her cloak and sword and preparing to depart the blind. She turned at the last minute to talk with Agatha. "Keep them in here for now. I'll return as soon as I can, and be prepared to depart. If they are building boats, then we will have to leave right away."

"I'll see to it personally, my lady. You go have a looksee, and I'll get everyone ready soon."

"Thank you, Agatha. Get Will something to drink and make sure his bandages are tight: we may have to travel far today."

Agatha nodded in agreement, and then Horace and Salina took off with Thomas south toward the brigand camp. Soon, they reached the old hollowed-out tree where Cedric was keeping watch. Horace took the crossbow from Cedric, and Salina squatted outside the tree hollow with Thomas.

"There, do you see them lashing those tree trunks together?" Cedric said to his mother, pointing to the north of the main camp just barely visible before the berm blocked the farther shore from sight.

Salina looked carefully, and there, about thirty feet from shore in some tall grass that was trampled, she could make out the construction work on some sort of flat structure. "Are those rafts they are making?"

"Rafts or boats, Mother, I'm not sure which, but they are hauling a lot of tree trunks from the surrounding area." The Blackthorn Forest was on the eastern bank, but there were occasional trees scattered across the land on the western shore. Almost every tree in a quarter mile radius from the brigand camp had been felled, and the entire area looked like a disaster had occurred there with the grasses being trampled and the trees cut. It looked like the area was sick.

"How long have they been at it, son?"

"Since early this morning, and they are making quick progress. Nearly every bandit is either cutting trees or working on the boats. There to the south you can see two more groups of them working on more boats. I think they have three or four in total from what I can see, but the bank over there is higher than here, and I can't see well enough to tell how many they're building for sure."

"But enough for all of them to cross, right?" Salina said.

"I don't know, Mother."

Horace leaned forward, joining the conversation. "I'm tired of running, me lady. Let me stay here and deal with them if they cross. You take the others and get to safety."

Salina was proud at the bravery of the old man but was not ready to give up yet. "We'll fight them together if they try to cross, but we will need to decide who stays and fights and who will lead the others to safety."

"I'll stay, Mother," Cedric replied without hesitation.

"Me, too!" Thomas chimed in, a large grin on his face, though Salina was sure he didn't know what he was getting himself into.

"Thanks, all of you, but someone has to lead the ladies to safety. We have to decide upon a direction as well. Let's all return to the cabin, and we will make our decision there. Everyone will need to have a say in this."

Salina watched as the other three nodded in agreement. "Fine, then. Cedric, you and Thomas head back now and stay out of sight. It will take them a while to build anything, so I don't think we need to rush this decision right now. Horace and I will watch them for a few hours to make sure they stay put, and then we will join you back at the cabin."

"See you there, then, Mother. Be safe!" Cedric replied as he and Thomas left to return and get some rest during what was left of the overcast morning.

Salina watched the brigands as they worked. They had posted a couple of sentries to stand watch, but almost all of them were engrossed in the boat construction. She did notice at one point a young man who was dressed in gold and black, which was different than the red and black attire of the brigands. He looked almost sickly, if not just weak, and walked from site to site, reviewing the work. "Who is that?" she asked Horace, pointing to the man.

"Must be one of their leaders: he isn't doing any work," Horace said with a slight air of disgust. Horace wasn't one for approving of another who shirked their duty.

"If we must fight, I think we should try to take him out first."

"I'll be happy if I can just take out the closest cutthroat to me," Horace said, smiling while he mockingly aimed his crossbow in the brigand's general direction.

After a few hours, Salina motioned for Horace to follow her. Quickly, the two Ulathans entered the forest and headed north, shadowing the river to their left. Soon, Salina had the group assembled in the blind. They were literally packed shoulder to shoulder, and there was no place to walk without stepping on someone.

Salina cleared her throat and looked around at her fellow countrymen. "We need to make a decision now. Some of us have decided to fight the Kesh brigands as they cross the river to buy the others more time. We need to know who will fight and who will lead the others to safety and in what direction. Should we go North away from the brigand camp, south past the camp and hopefully to link up with other Ulathans far to our south or east, deeper into the forest?"

Mostly everyone remained silent: some fidgeted and others looked around. Finally, Emelda broke the silence. "I'll bet my hardheaded husband already told you he will fight?"

"Emelda, let's not go there," Horace replied. "We have scant few men here who can wield a blade, and the few we do are practically boys."

"I don't care, Horace! I won't let you die like Sarson, no matter how bravely. Why can't we all flee? Let us just run into the forest. They can't follow us in there, can they?" Emelda asked, her voice pleading.

"Well, I for one am not for running. I'll ring their bell if they come near me or me ladies' boys!" Agatha said, her tone firm.

"What are you going to do, Lady Salina?" Monique asked, looking up from where she held Karz in her lap.

Salina thought for a moment as she looked fondly at her small son. "I'll be fighting, but I need someone to look after my boys for me."

"Boy!" Cedric said loudly as he toyed with one of his four daggers he had strapped to his chest belt. "I'm fighting, too!"

Salina frowned but knew Cedric, while not trained as a fighter or soldier, was one of the few in the party who could wield a weapon or stand a chance against even a lone brigand from Kesh. "Fine, Cedric joins me, but who will watch after my little Karz?"

"I will keep him safe, my lady," Monique answered as she clutched him tighter to her. Karz smiled, not understanding he would be separated from his mother.

"Right, thank you, Monique. Can I assume, Celeste, that you and Olga will help her watch over my son?" The two older ladies nodded in agreement but said nothing. "Yolanda, you must care for Amy, and Agatha, I need you to care for Will as well."

"Now just wait one minute," Will said, struggling to stand on his feet, almost falling over Yolanda and Amy in the process. "I'll not be babied in this matter, and my sword isn't finished killing Kesh bandits by far."

"Shut up, you old coot!" Agatha screeched at him, stepping over Celeste and Olga and attempting to make Will sit again. "You can hardly stand, much less fight or walk!"

"Now, Will, if you stay and fight, who will protect the women and children? Besides, we need fighters who can run once they get close to crossing the river, and you would die on the riverbank, for sure. I'll not allow it."

Salina was perhaps the only one in the group who could give Will an ultimatum. Will knew he was weak and that she was correct, but the idea of letting others fight while he ran was contrary to everything he was taught as a soldier. With some hesitation, he finally sat down. "Damn, he does have some sense still left in him. At least the fever hasn't affected his thinking," Agatha said, a bit calmer now. "Let me have a look at that arm of yours, Will Carvel."

"Jons," Salina said, looking at the young lad. "I'll need you to help Will protect the women and children. Can you do that?" Salina saw several others smile at the way she worded the request.

"You bet!" Little Jons said, a toothy smile appearing on the young boy's face. "Will and I will kill any of those thieves that try to hurt the ladies!"

Salina smiled back. "I knew I could count on you."

Just when Salina thought things were getting settled, Marissa piped in. "I am not running away. I want to find Targon and my family."

Salina didn't think her manipulations would work on Marissa the way they had on Jons. For one thing, she noted by Targon's behavior that apparently the children of the farmers and wood-folk that lived out in the wilds away from the towns and cities of Ulatha were raised fairly independent, and they didn't take orders very well. She decided to simply be

honest with Marissa and voice her concerns. "Marissa, I don't think that is a good idea. If Targon was going to return, he would have done so by now, and in our current situation, I think he would want you to remain with us, wouldn't you agree?"

Marissa looked at her with a bit of a pout. "All right, but he will return, and if we have to leave, maybe we should go after him."

"Well, we haven't decided which way to go yet. Does anyone have any ideas?" Salina said.

The group remained silent for a moment. "Well, going south will only take us closer to the brigands at first, and while we think we may have some of our friends and family to the south, none of us know the way. We would have to follow the river, and that would expose us too much," Will said with a pensive look across his pale face.

"So east into the forest, Will?" Salina asked.

"No, none of us know the forest very well, and we stayed clear of it when we did patrols many years ago. No one really goes there anymore."

"Surely you don't mean to go north, then, do you?" Salina asked. "The old trade road and bridge are under Kesh control, and they would patrol all along that road. You're not thinking like Marissa, are you?" She pointed to the girl. "You know Targon left that way, don't you?"

"That has nothing to do with it, me lady. I'm thinking of tactics here. The river runs very quickly to the south. If they attempt to cross at the same point as where their camp lies, any boat would naturally want to flow south with the current. If we can disable their rowers or at least distract them, then by the time they get control of their boats, they could be a couple of miles south of here."

"I see your point, Will. So you think north is the way we should go?" Salina asked.

"Yes. Eventually we may have to cross the old northern bridge on the Kesh road to get back on the west side of this river. Even if we went south, the White River would block us from getting to Cree, and we'd either have

to pass through the forest or head far to the east up to the headwaters of the White River in order to cross it and then return west again to reach Cree. It may be better for us to return to the west side of the Rapid River."

"I hate to think that way, Will, but none of us know these lands very well outside of Korwell. At least the river bought us some safety for the time being. I wish Targon was here."

"Hullo!" Targon said, peering through the arrow slit on the east side of the blind. "You called for me, Lady Salina?"

"Targon!" Marissa practically yelled, jumping up and running out the blind and around the corner to give Targon a huge hug. Quickly, the others followed suit, and everyone was outside slapping his back and giving him hugs. Even Agatha hugged him, but Targon turned the brightest shade of red when Monique squeezed him so hard he almost couldn't breathe.

"My, it's good to see you, lad!" said Will after he hobbled outside and sat on a log with his back against the blind's wall.

"It's good to see you, too, Will, but my, you look horrible!" Targon said, grabbing his pack from his back and setting it on the ground, rummaging through it. Quickly, he found what he was looking for and handed it to Agatha. "I know you don't approve, Agatha, but please use these Arella leaves on Will's wound. He'll feel better. Also, I found a sewing needle and some thread to use as well. We'll have to sterilize the needle, but it should do the trick."

"Always trying to poke me." Will laughed.

"I'll use it now, young man, since Will needs help," Agatha said, taking the items and preparing the needle and thread.

"I don't think we have time for a fire," Salina said. "We need to get everyone to safety." Salina then went on to explain to Targon the events from the last few days.

"I understand," Targon said, rummaging in a second bag he carried on his shoulder. He quickly pulled out five fish, four large cabbages, seven carrots, and another bagful of apples.

"Bless you, son!" Olga exclaimed, hugging him again.

"Nicely done!" Yolanda said as she eyed the food. It was small in proportion to the group, but after not eating for two days, it seemed a feast.

Olga and Marissa started to hand out the apples, and Agatha told Monique to put Karz down and grab her cooking pot. "Well, I don't see the harm in eating first if they are still building the boats," Targon said to Salina as she gave an apple to Karz and started to eat one herself.

"Best if we go back and keep an eye on them, but Will is in bad shape. Some food and medicine would do him good," Salina added, biting into her apple again.

"Targon, I'll go back. I've had a couple of hours of sleep, and I've been keeping watch on them all night," Cedric said, his mouth stuffed with an apple as well.

"Do you approve, Salina?" Targon asked her.

"Well, he has been a great help to us there, and he even found a good hiding place where we can observe the brigands. Cedric, I'll take Targon to the brigand camp and keep a watch. We'll have you relieve us once you've had something hot to eat."

"I'm looking forward to it," her son replied.

"Listen, everyone," Targon said, getting their attention. "I have a place for you all to stay. We can leave for there in a couple of hours and arrive just after sundown. For now, stay put and don't stray into the forest. Also . . . don't panic when I show you a new friend. I need everyone to stay calm."

The group almost literally stopped eating, and it became eerily silent. Targon hollered for Core. "Carrot, come on over here now."

The large brown bear came strolling out of the forest brush and approached the blind. Half of the group couldn't see him from over the barricade they had erected since they were sitting or kneeling, but quickly, they all peered over at the bear in shock and awe.

"Bloody hell!" Horace said, finally breaking the group's silence as he raised his crossbow, pointing it at the bear. Targon placed his hand on the bow and pushed it down, lowering it so it was pointing back down to the ground.

"Watch your tongue, Horace!" Emelda scolded him.

"Is that your . . . pet?" Salina asked, turning to look at Targon. The bear slowly approached the blind's north side entrance and lay down, looking at them.

"Well, no, not really. More like a new friend I made in the last few days. Please don't ask, just don't feed him or touch him. He can be grumpy at times."

"At his size, he can be whatever he wants," Agatha said mockingly. "Go on, Monique, fetch my pot. It ain't gonna come walking out here on its own, and Cedric, see if you can start a fire."

Monique quickly retrieved Agatha's iron pot while Cedric grabbed what was left of their wood that they had tucked against the blind's wall. "It will be hard to start one with everything either wet or damp," Cedric said, looking around for some tinder.

"I'll grab something," Marissa said, scampering off into the forest.

"Well? Follow her, Cedric," Salina said, motioning to Marissa.

"No need for that. Carrot, can you follow Marissa there and keep her safe?" The bear rose and started trotting to keep up with Marissa, who was quickly disappearing into the heavy woods.

"Bloody hell!" Horace said, and then Emelda elbowed him in the ribs.

"You said that already," Little Jons piped in.

"Now don't you go teaching the little ones bad words, and all my love, but yes, hell, indeed." Emelda smiled.

"Show me," Targon said to Salina.

"Horace, I will take Targon to the bandit camp and show him what they are doing. You and Will stay here and maintain a watch," Salina stated, her tone firm and authoritative.

Will tried to stand, but Agatha pushed him back down. "Fine by me, but Horace will need to keep watch alone. Just let me know if you spot anything. I have my sword at hand," Will conceded.

Horace grunted his agreement and moved out of the shelter of the barricade and took up a position nearby with his crossbow.

"Let's go," Salina said, walking off to the south. The crossbows were too heavy for her to carry, so she took her lighter sword while Targon had his trusty axe and bow. Soon, they arrived from the east and crawled up the now familiar berm, ignoring the hollowed tree for the moment.

They could see that work was continuing, but clearly now they saw the lip of each construction as an extra layer of tree trunk wood was being added to each edge to make the vessels float worthy. "Those are rafts, not boats," Targon said, observing their work. "You said they started this right at dawn?"

"Yes, well, that is what my son told me, as he was here all night. What does it mean?" Salina looked back at him intently.

"It means a fight," Targon said, his expression turning grim.

CHAPTER 16

CROSSING

Khan watched as night fell and the last of the work was finished on the four rafts. Dorsun and his team had done a good job to complete and lash the four vessels in only one day. He had sent some riders back to Korwell a few days earlier to bring supplies and re-inforcements and they had returned. The skies were starting to clear up a bit, though it was hard to see the stars. Dorsun approached Khan with a faint smile on his face, "Four rafts ready to launch master."

"Good. We rest tonight and cross in the morning. Do you have your teams ready?"

"Yes. Boxer will take the lead boat across with Slim and Burly to tie a rope securely on the closest tree to the riverbank, then we will use long poles and the rope to cross. How do you know they are on the other side master?"

Khan rubbed his glass ball at his side, "Just a hunch Dorsun, just a hunch." Dorsun nodded, then he left returning to the crews to bark more orders for the night shift. Something was preventing him from seeing across the river and he was sure it had something to do with the Ulathans.

Targon and Salina returned just before dark, fairly convinced the brigands would not attempt a night crossing. They noted the faint glow of the fire on the east side of the blind where the blind would, of course, block its light from being seen from across the river. Still, after nearly two nights without a fire, the faint glow of this one seemed unusually bright to them.

The others had made good use of their time. Will had fresh bandages on. Cedric was trying to read his book by the firelight. Agatha's pot had the scaled fish, carrots, and cabbages in it, and Agatha had offered each person a spoonful using one of the two spoons that Targon had brought from his home. There were two apples prominently displayed on a rock by the makeshift fire. The group was thoughtful of Salina and Targon, if nothing else. There was, however, no sign of the bear.

"Anyone seen Carrot?" Targon asked.

"It left right after Marissa returned with some dry leaves and twigs," Horace said. "It never really came close to us."

"All right, let me know if you spot him. He'll most likely be back soon."

Monique motioned for Targon to sit by her and Karz. "Won't you tell us where you've been?" she said, and then she smiled at him.

Targon sat next to her and returned her smile while rubbing Karz's head. "Let's say I found what I needed to find."

"You found your family?" Yolanda asked.

"Did you see my mother or brother?" Marissa followed up, an expectant tone in her voice.

Targon looked around the fire and realized the entire group was outside: no one was in the blind. They were all looking at him intently. "No, Marissa, I'm afraid I didn't find your family and I didn't find my family. Instead, I found my courage."

"Nonsense, lad, you have shown plenty of courage so far," Will said, while many others nodded in agreement.

"Not that kind of courage, Will. I found the courage to do what is right first and then follow my own needs next."

"What do you mean?" Salina asked, sitting next to Targon and placing her hand gently on his arm. Karz leaned against his mother.

"Ever since we were captured and my mother helped free me, I could only think of one thing to do and that was to save them, to free them and run for safety. Now, after much thought, I understand there remains a greater responsibility for me. I am responsible not only for my family but for my fellow Ulathans."

"Well said, young man," Agatha remarked in a rare but kind voice not common for her demeanor.

"So you won't search for them?" Cedric asked from across the small fire, closing his book.

"No, I will never stop searching for them, Master Cedric," Targon said and smiled as he mimicked Elister's tone and mannerism in calling Cedric "master." "But I will do what is right first and what I want to do second."

There was a silence for a long while as everyone contemplated the words of their young woodland savior. Finally, Monique could bear it no longer. "At least tell us what happened to you since you left. You seem so different now, and it's only been three days."

Targon spent the next hour recounting the events of his chase to the Kesh border, including his discovery of the ambush at his home, the fight at the old keep, and his journey to the very border of Kesh itself. They all seemed most interested in hearing about the old druid Elister. Even little Amy who was only three years old appeared to lend an ear at the telling of his news. The kids enjoyed the story of Carrot taking out two bandits and keeping Targon warm in the bear cave, but this part of the story just got raised eyebrows by the elder Ulathans, especially Olga and Celeste.

When he finished, he turned to Salina. "We need to have a plan for tomorrow."

"What do you suggest?" she asked.

"I think it's time we set our own ambush at the river." Targon nodded.

"About bloody time!" Horace said, putting his hand on the crossbow and giving it a pat.

Targon thought old man Horace had gotten too attached to the Kesh weapon, Little Jons as well, for that matter. "Do you and Jons know how to shoot those bows?" Targon asked.

"I've been practicing a bit and used one of these many years ago, but Jons is just a playing with his," Horace replied.

"I can shoot mine, too." Jons jumped up and went for the second crossbow near him where he had laid it earlier.

"I think it would be better, Jons, if you let Cedric use the bow," Targon said.

"And what am I supposed to fight with?" Jons asked in a whiny voice with a pout on his face.

"I'm sure Cedric will loan you one of his daggers. He has four of them, after all."

Now it was time for Cedric to display a pouty face. He wasn't fond of giving one of his nice daggers to a child. "Do I have to?" Cedric looked at Targon.

"No, but I think the more we are armed, the better, even one as small as Jons. If it were up to me, I'd give one of them shiny daggers you got there to anyone else that could wield it."

"Fine, I'll trade a dagger, then, for the crossbow," Cedric said, pulling one of his knives from his chest belt and giving it to Jons, who tucked it into his own belt.

"Seriously, though, do we have a plan?" Will said, bringing Targon back to focus on the situation at hand.

"Well, if they cross the river unmolested, then our chances will diminish for remaining undetected. Then again, we can't win in a fight, either. There has to be nearly fifty of those brigands," Targon said.

"What do you suggest?" Salina asked as she tried to scoop a bit more of the makeshift stew onto the wooden spoon from the pot hanging over the small fire.

"A running fight. We have two crossbows and my own bow. We just need to wound them enough to cover our tracks and buy us time."

"Where will the rest of us go?" asked Celeste, and Olga nodded at her question.

"Well now, Will, don't you object, but I think Will and the rest of you can follow the river north toward my home. There is some safety there, I think, if I can trust the old man, while the rest of us attack the brigands as they try to cross the river, and then we link back up farther upriver," Targon said, finishing his apple.

"I won't object, lad, but running isn't my style," said Will.

"Nor mine," Horace chimed in, patting his crossbow.

"Agreed, but in case any brigands find their way across the river upstream, we will need someone who can fight them off. We all can't be at the river crossing," Targon said.

Salina finished a second scoop of stew. "It sounds like the best plan we could possibly have. I'll take my Cedric, and Horace will join us with his crossbow. Who else will fight with us?"

"I think Thomas is old enough to at least help us load the crossbows?" Targon suggested.

"I've been there with Cedric for two days now," Thomas said, standing up next to him. "Let me fight, too."

"Fight then you will Thomas, but run also. If it looks like they are going to make it across, we have to be prepared to run, so we take only our weapons with us," Targon said. "Marissa should be able to guide everyone else north along the riverbank with Will bringing up the rear. Can you do that, Marissa?"

"Yes, Targon, I will do that for you."

"Good, so it's settled, then. We should leave well before dawn," Targon said, while the others either murmured in agreement or nodded their heads. Soon, Lady Salina had the children and women retire for the night inside the blind while the others spread out their cloaks and blankets and lay down to sleep just outside near the fire.

"We should keep a watch," Will said, his voice sounding tired.

"We already have one," Targon said. "Get some sleep, Will, we wake early and it's over a half day's walk to my home."

Targon awoke the next morning well before dawn. He got a rude awakening from Core, who had returned and seemed to understand what was happening. Quickly, he woke Salina, who woke the others, and he turned to gather his things. Soon, the entire company was huddled around the dead fire with only the reddish glow of the hot embers to illuminate them.

"Marissa, take them north but stay out of sight of the river. Remember when we gathered the wild cabbages before I left?" Marissa nodded her head. "Stay to that game trail and follow the river but don't pass a large granite boulder just at the edge of the forest. I doubt you'll reach it before we catch up to you as it would take you most of the day to find it, but if you do reach it, then stay inside the trees and wait for us there."

"You sure you want to do this, my lady?" Agatha asked, concern in her voice.

"We'll be fine, Agatha. Just take care of the others, and especially my little Karz," Salina responded, hugging Karz tightly and pulling his small cloak tightly around his waist. "All right now, off you all go. Don't wait for us and don't look back."

Soon, the ladies and children, led by Marissa, were lost to sight. Jons was in the front with her and his newly acquired blade. Will did look back

as he wielded his broadsword in one hand and was practically using it as a crutch with Agatha doting after him.

Targon had only been to the brigand camp one time, but he led the way. His eyesight in the dark was superior to any others, and he felt comfortable in the forest. Salina followed, and then came Thomas and Cedric, and Horace led up the rear with Core tracking him just a few yards off to his side. Targon wasn't sure, but he thought he faintly heard Horace exclaim, "Bloody hell," when he realized the bear was near him. Emelda had almost cried as she hugged him good-bye that morning, so Targon was hoping Horace didn't have any more excitement this morning.

Soon, they arrived at the hollowed tree where Cedric had taken cover with Thomas. Core seemed to stay deeper in the forest out of sight while Targon, Salina, and Horace lay flat on the berm and peered over its edge.

It was still dark, but a faint glow was growing in the east and the fires from the brigand camp had not dwindled to embers like their own campfire had, but instead they were fed with a deep black oil. They illuminated the camp, and already it was alive with movement. The rafts were all moved down the small bank and laid up against the shore. They must have done that overnight. Soon, even the crude tents were being taken down and stowed, and other brigands donned leather armor and took cruel-looking blades from their arm's stack and sheathed them to their belts around their waists. The elaborate tent in the center of the camp was taken down last, and Targon clearly saw the young man who was dressed differently standing on the bank and looking across the river.

"Duck!" Targon hissed, feeling stupid for being so casual about the entire ordeal. "That unusual-looking brigand seems to be a leader. We'll need to target him first if he crosses."

Salina and Horace nodded and looked at Targon. "Give the word, lad, and we shoot," Horace finally whispered back. Targon nodded and motioned for them to stay down, and slowly peered over the berm again.

The first raft was being pushed into the river, and at least three brigands were holding onto a rope as it was looped around a lanyard lashed to the raft so it wouldn't quickly flow downstream. Two of the brigands then let go of the rope and grabbed long poles, and they were using them to steady the raft as it slowly started to move against the strong downstream currents, with the third brigand keeping an eye on the rope lashed to the raft itself. Three more brigands stood or squatted in the middle of the raft, trying to keep their balance.

Targon motioned for the others to fall back behind the berm and for Cedric and Thomas to join them. "I see only those six on that first raft. I think they intend to cross slowly at first and then secure the rope on this side of the river. This gives me an idea . . ."

Slowly, the raft moved across the river, and at one point, the third brigand had to grab the last pole and jab it into the riverbed from the north end of the raft, helping his comrades keep the raft from floating downstream. The other two brigands were using their poles from the south end to keep the raft crossing horizontally and not being swept downstream. The three brigands in the middle of the raft actually took a knee and used their hands to balance themselves and not fall.

Finally, after close to ten minutes, the raft reached the eastern bank and the third brigand grabbed the rope, jumping off the raft and moving toward the nearest tree less than ten feet from the water's edge.

The three brigands in the middle of the raft also alighted, leaping into the shallower waters of the eastern bank. One brigand was armed with a crossbow while the other two drew swords. The three brigands then fanned out in a semicircle around the tree where their fellow soldier was securing the rope, and the other two brigands used their poles to stick them deeply in the muddy floor of the river, keeping the raft from moving till the rope was secure.

"Hoi, Chief, all ready here," the rope-securing brigand yelled out, jumping back onto the raft and grabbing the long length of rope now secured to both banks. Both of the other two brigands dropped their poles and grabbed the same rope that now hung across the entire width of the river. In the center of the river, the rope almost sagged into the water. With great effort, the three brigands pulled the raft across the river and back to the west side.

Soon, each of the four rafts were in the water, and at least a dozen brigands stepped onto each raft, pushing off using their roughly hewn poles and grabbing the rope and pulling themselves across. At least four brigands, sometimes five, were heaving on the ropes, while two more had poles at each downstream corner of each raft. When the first raft was almost to the near shore and the last raft was well into the river, there was a blood-curdling roar of a wild beast.

An arrow suddenly appeared in the chest of the brigand standing to the south of the rope where it was tied to a tree on the eastern bank. A crossbow bolt implanted itself in the thigh of the crossbow-wielding brigand on shore, and a third bolt sailed far out over the river, disappearing from view close to the western bank.

"Ambush!" yelled the brigand with the crossbow as he ducked and fell to his stomach in pain, twisting the bolt in his leg to the side as he did so. He let loose his own bolt into the forest, not sure what he was aiming at. The brigand with the arrow in his chest had dropped dead, and his companion, unharmed, quickly took cover behind the tree with the rope, brandishing his wicked-looking curved blade.

Two brigands on the lead raft took up their crossbows and started to fire bolts into the woods behind their companions, while on the second raft, three more did the same. The second raft had the unusually dressed man on it with the staff, and Targon aimed his next arrow at him. The arrow, in an exceptionally unusual shot, lodged itself right into the metallic staff of the strangely dressed man, wedging itself between the metal staff itself and the colorful gem that was set upon its top, saving the man's life. This, however, had the effect of surprising the staff-wielding man and hitting with such force that he stepped backward, tripping over the leg of a brigand and falling to the floor of the raft.

Two sword-wielding brigands from the first raft, which had almost arrived on the near shore, jumped into the river water, which reached their necks. A huge brown shape ran from the forest and, ignoring the brigands near the tree on shore, leapt out in a long fifteen-foot leap, landing with its front paws on the raft but its rear paws in the water.

Core used his rear legs to try to scramble onto the raft, but the impact of the half-ton bear twisted the raft wildly around, unbalancing most of the standing brigands, who quickly fell either on the raft or in the cold, fast running river. When Core managed to bite the leg of the leading brigand holding onto the rope, the brigand released his hold on the guideline and the other brigands backed away, tilting the raft severely, almost capsizing it as it swiftly started to float downstream.

"Horace! Cover me now!" Targon yelled, loosing another arrow and then dropping his bow and pulling his axe from his belt. Targon ran from the cover of the forest toward the lone tree where the brigand rope was tied. Horace was firing from behind the cover of one tree while Cedric shot from another. Thomas and Salina were handing them crossbow bolts as they reloaded as fast as they could.

Targon saw Core finally scramble onto the first raft and take a bolt into his right rear flank. The bear roared so loudly that it could be clearly heard over the roar of the rapids in the river. Quickly, the bear mauled the crossbow-wielding brigand, and almost all the other brigands jumped into the water. Some were lucky and had taken off their swords and heavy belts while others did not expect to be in the water and were dragged into the deep waters by their blades and packs. The brigands only used toughened leather, dyed black for armor, so they didn't sink as fast, but some could not swim, either.

Targon almost reached the tree with the rope when the brigand on his stomach loosed a bolt at his chest. Targon had held his axe forward,

and the bolt hit the axe head, ricocheting off of it. Unfortunately, this threw Targon off balance, and he stumbled, falling just in front of the brigand with the crossbow, who was even now reloading. The axe had fallen from his hand and landed a few feet away. Other crossbow bolts were whizzing over his head.

Targon could see the brigands pulling hard to cross the river as fast as possible, and the second raft was quickly approaching the shoreline. Too late, he saw the brigand on shore with his crossbow, now rearmed and pointed at Targon's head not ten feet away. He would die on the ground and leave his companions to their doom. He had failed them by not being able to cut the rope in time. Perhaps he had underestimated their odds?

"Now, Targon!" he heard Lady Salina scream as suddenly the feathered shaft of a bolt sprouted from the forehead of the brigand nearest to Targon, who dropped the loaded crossbow, dying instantly. Targon scrambled for his axe and looked back as he lay on the ground. He saw Lady Salina running toward him and the tree with her sword in her hand. He could see black bolts flying by her so closely that one even nicked her dress, tearing cloth from it. Targon could feel the anger rise in his heart, and, seeing her in danger, he felt the sudden rush of adrenaline as his mind willed his body into motion. With one fluid motion, he grabbed his axe and sprung back up onto his legs, quickly crossing the ten feet to the tree with the rope tied around it.

The last remaining brigand on shore knew he had to guard the tree and rope but was using it as cover by staying behind it, but now he stepped around the tree and faced Targon, swinging his curved blade in a long, hard stroke designed to separate Targon's head from his body. Targon saw it coming easily, and he felt the battle was so surreal as if the man was moving in slow motion.

Targon quickly ducked the blow and had to use his hands to steady himself on the ground, making the use of his axe nearly impossible, so instead of trying to strike a blow with his weapon, Targon finished his somersault and came out of the roll with a double-legged kick right into the brigand's torso. This arrested Targon's momentum, and the brigand flew onto his back a few feet away. Lady Salina ran by Targon and, with a pointed thrust, skewered the brigand in his heart, killing the Kesh instantly.

"Get down, Mother!" Cedric yelled from the forest line.

Salina looked at Targon. "Cut the rope!" she screamed, and then suddenly two bolts protruded from her body, knocking her to the ground.

"No!" Cedric yelled, and Targon looked back to see him running toward his mother, crossbow in hand. He looked at Lady Salina, seeing she had fallen on her back, an ashen look on her face. She did not move. Targon leaped at the tree and, in one stroke, severed the rope, releasing its secure hold to the tree and from the eastern bank.

Cries could be heard from the brigands as they desperately tried to hang onto the line as they were swiftly being pulled downstream. Targon grabbed the loaded crossbow from the dead brigand's hands and aimed it at the lead raft, lining it up and pulling the trigger at the first brigand he saw who had the rope. The brigand fell dead, losing his hold, and the raft floated downstream quicker.

Cedric knelt next to his mother and took only a quick look at her before he, too, loosed his bolt. He aimed it at the second raft as the first, with Core, was already far downstream and empty. His bolt hit home and another brigand fell. Chaos reigned on the rafts as they twirled in the swiftly running water while brigands tried to secure them to the rope that was still tied to the western shore around a huge boulder near the water's edge. Targon saw Horace arrive with his bow, and he looked to the nearest raft where the strangely dressed man had regained his footing and was kneeling now on one knee, steadying himself with his metal staff.

Horace's bolt headed right at the man, who pointed the staff at them, and a ball of fire left the staff, incinerating Horace's bolt in mid-flight,

turning it instantly into ash. The ball of fire flamed over their heads, hitting the tree behind them, and Targon could feel the intense heat as the tree caught fire. *Magic!* Targon thought to himself suddenly as he looked in awe at the man on the raft and wondered at the power to wield fire. Before he could think to do a thing, the last brigand holding the rope was dropped by another bolt from Cedric, and the second raft quickly twirled in the water, whisking the wizard away as he tried to stand and face them, a look of shock on the man's face.

Thomas had also arrived with Targon's bow. Targon took the bow and pulled arrow after arrow from his quiver as he rained down death from the riverbank. Soon, the third raft was quickly disappearing from sight, as it, too, had lost its handlers and was swept along the river at a rapid pace, several brigands leaping into the water and swimming toward the west bank. Targon noted the last raft had managed to return to the western shore, but it was a good fifty yards south of the crossing area and several brigands had jumped onto the bank, returning missile fire at them.

"Time to leave!" Horace said, tugging on Cedric's tunic.

"We can't leave her here!" Cedric yelled as he tried to load another bolt and fire back at the brigands on the far shore.

Targon quickly shouldered his bow and belted his axe, and he leaned down, ignoring the bolts from the far side of the river, and grabbed Lady Salina in his arms. Her head and legs flopped behind his arms, and he was surprised by how light she was. She was petite and slender, and Targon felt as if he was carrying his sister, Ann, when she had fallen asleep. Quickly, he ran back into the forest, followed by Horace and Cedric, carrying Salina in his powerful arms. Thomas grabbed her sword and ran as well, quicker than all of them, and they soon reached the relative safety of the trees. There were no more bolts flying around them.

"Mother, wake up!" Cedric said as they knelt around her. Her light blue dress was starting to turn a bright crimson color as her blood soaked into it. One bolt had penetrated her abdomen and the second was lodged

in her left shoulder. Cedric started to caress her head while Targon supported it, and he saw that both Horace and Thomas had tears welling in their eyes.

"She's breathing," Horace exclaimed, leaning close to her and placing the side of his face right up to her mouth. "I can feel her breath. It's faint but there." Cedric reached for the nearest bolt, but Horace quickly grabbed his hand with an iron grip. "Don't, boy, she'll bleed to death if you take them out now."

Cedric looked anguished as he wiped away a tear. "We have to do something! We can't just leave them in her."

There was a moment of silence before Targon spoke. "This is all my fault. I do know someone who can help us, but we need to get her to my home first before she dies."

"You mean to carry her half a day's walk, lad?" Horace asked.

"If I must," Targon replied, looking into their faces and seeing nothing but sorrow there, "but it will be best if we all shared the honor. Thomas, I'll need you to carry what's left of our quivers and both crossbows. They will be heavy. Can you do that?"

Thomas nodded as Horace slung one bow across his own back and gave the other to him. Cedric did not protest as his crossbow was given to Thomas. Horace took the lady's sword and also secured it to his belt. "Right, let's go?" Horace asked.

Targon stood with Lady Salina still cradled in his arms. "We go. I'll carry her first, and then when I tire, you and Cedric will help." Targon nodded at Horace.

"Bloody hell of a way to win a fight," Horace said, standing and leading the way north toward the blind.

CHAPTER 17

SORROW

Khan was wet and livid with rage. His entire reinforced patrol was dead, scattered, or missing. Dorsun had either drowned or was missing, and most of their supplies were lost in the river or far downstream. Khan was forced to jump into the river and swim for the eastern shore when several miles downstream his raft jammed against a submerged tree and stuck in the river near the eastern shore. Most of the troopers on his raft were dead or injured, as they took the brunt of the missile assault by the Ulathans. Khan sat on the shore, breathing heavily as he looked around and saw only three others with him. Six were dead on the raft, their blood staining the brown wood in pools as it sloshed back and forth in the river, and three were missing, having fallen into the water.

The first raft had disappeared downstream, and his raft never passed it. That strange bear, having attacked his lead raft, was unnerving to him. It was as if the wild beast attacked his troopers with a purpose. He thought he saw the beast lumbering out of the water a couple of miles upstream, but his raft was twirling so wildly he couldn't be sure of what he saw.

He replayed the attack in his mind. The Ulathans had first attempted to attack his small shore guard and cut the rope, but the second volley of arrows was definitely meant for him. Two of his troopers had fallen immediately, and just when he stood to unleash a fireball into the woods, an arrow had struck his staff, wedging itself between the metal and gemstone that was set at the top. The force of the arrow knocked the staff back into his head, and he fell over one of his own troopers, ruining his spell. Otherwise, he was sure he would have killed several of the ambushers. In fact, had he not fallen, he was sure he could have burned the bear severely and stopped the wild animal's attack. He was grateful he maintained hold of the staff during his swim, as much of the wizard's power was derived from it.

He took no satisfaction in what he remembered next. He couldn't remember such bravery in all his thirty years of life as the lady in the blue dress killed Boxer, one of his lieutenants, with that heart-piercing stab, sacrificing herself so the ambush would succeed. He could still see the ashen look on her face as she toppled backward, crossbow bolts sticking from her torso. He was accustomed to seeing death, but usually it was on a battlefield filled with soldiers. The current campaign of wholesale slaughter against the civilian population filled him with disgust.

"Should we move upstream, Master?" one of his lieutenants, named Gund, asked him, his hair dripping wet, leather coverings a dark black from the moisture.

"Not yet," Khan responded, looking up from where he sat, his hand searching for the glass orb he carried in a pouch firmly attached to his belt. "I need to inform the Arch-Mage first. Set a guard around me until I finish."

Gund nodded, motioning to the other two brigands, and they stood a few paces from Khan in a semicircle facing outward, alert for any sign of the Ulathans, or worse, the wild bear.

Khan pulled the orb from its pouch, uncovering the wet, silky cloth from over it. He placed it on his lap as he sat and closed his legs together to cradle the orb. He rubbed the orb with his free hand and murmured

the sage words to activate its magic. Khan was weak, however, in the arcane arts, and he could not contact the orb of his master, Ke-Tor, directly. He failed to mention this fact to his own trooper, as he didn't want to have to explain the detailed working of the orb. Instead, if his magic worked, it would alert his mentor that he was trying to communicate with him. The constant strain of trying to maintain the link was intense, but he persevered for nearly ten minutes before finally he felt the stress ease and saw the orb start to glow. Soon, he could see the face of Ke-Tor within the orb.

"What is it, Khan?" his mentor asked, looking bothered.

"Bad news, Master," Khan said, his voice quavering ever so slightly. "We have taken some losses in our pursuit of a large group of Ulathans near the Gregus."

Ke-Tor shook his head, a scowl appearing on his face. "What do you mean? This couldn't have come at a worse time, apprentice!"

Khan easily noted the contemptuous use of his title by his mentor, curse him and his ilk. Khan was no longer confident in their cause, but he tried to subdue his feelings. "We were ambushed as we crossed the Gregus by a group of Ulathans. We were scattered, and many of our troopers are either dead or missing. We need reinforcements or permission to return to Korwell and regroup," Khan finished, not sure how he would reach the western shore now.

Ke-Tor's face suddenly contorted into a scowling, leering visage of anger and frustration. "You incompetent fool! You had four patrols to track down a simple group of refugees," he said, pausing as his face turned red and the veins along his neck and forehead started to become pronounced. "What are our losses? How many troopers do you have left?"

Khan sighed, closing his eyes briefly before answering. "Three left here, but I'm sure there are more scattered . . ."

He never got to finish his sentence, as Ke-Tor started screaming at him using all manner of Kesh profanities and colorful metaphors. Finally,

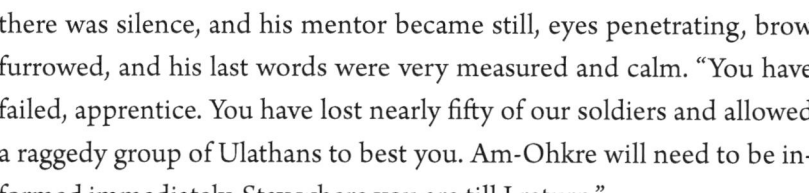
there was silence, and his mentor became still, eyes penetrating, brow furrowed, and his last words were very measured and calm. "You have failed, apprentice. You have lost nearly fifty of our soldiers and allowed a raggedy group of Ulathans to best you. Am-Ohkre will need to be informed immediately. Stay where you are till I return."

Khan didn't want to let his mentor discuss the matter with the Arch-Mage so soon after being informed, especially after seeing his rant, so he quickly improvised. "Master, before you inform the Mage, may I inquire of our attack in the south? How did we fare there?"

Ke-Tor's calm visage again displayed a scornful frown, and he almost literally sneered at his apprentice before answering. "We were successful in routing the last of the armed resistance, but we took heavy losses. Many of our soldiers will not be returning to Kesh. We have returned to Korwell to regroup and were looking forward to your return with half of the Bloody Hand Company. That is a pity now. Am-Ohkre will not be pleased."

Without warning, the orb went dark, and Ke-Tor released Khan's orb. Khan felt a chill run up his spine. He had seen other apprentices killed for less, and he did not relish what was to come next. He thought, however, of the irony of his mentor's displeasure while at the same time informing Khan that they, too, had taken losses. He didn't think much of their success if his masters were counting on the return of only half a company. That meant their losses must have been equally severe, but that would not spare Khan the Arch-Mage's wrath. Khan just hoped he would live to see another day.

Targon felt his arms burning and his legs starting to get heavier and heavier. At first, with the adrenaline of the fight, the lady felt as light as a feather. Now, hours later, the chemicals coursing through his bloodstream had diminished, and the constant pace started to take its toll on Targon's

body. Twice already Horace and Cedric together had helped carry her, giving him a much needed break, but he could see the strain on old man Horace as the punishing pace was sapping his strength, and Cedric, having been born and bred around the books and relative comfort of the city life was weaker and lacked stamina.

Only a half hour after Horace and Cedric took over, their pace fell considerably, and Targon worried Lady Salina was not going to live much longer, so he quickly resumed the burden and pressed onward. Her wounds were beyond anything the Arella plant could heal. At their first stop, they ripped pieces of the lady's dress off at the hemline and used it to bind her chest and abdomen, securing the crossbow bolts and staunching the worst of her bleeding.

Yes, the blood. It stained his hands and white tunic, transforming from a warm red liquid to a nearly black gel. Her light blue dress showed less blue than brown dirt and mud and the reddish black of the congealing blood. Her face was ashen, a hue of pasty white Targon had only seen when his grandparents had died years ago, and looking at her face only urged him to greater effort. One of her boots had fallen off, and Thomas had picked it up and carried it along with a crossbow. Targon could clearly see the game trail now and moved faster hearing both Cedric and Horace's labored breathing behind him.

Finally, when he thought he could go no further, he cleared a tree line into a small meadow, and on the other side not more than fifty yards away, he ran into the other Ulathans and stared into Will's face. He stopped suddenly, almost tripping and dropping the lady as he knelt on his knees, still carrying his burden. There was an anguished scream as Agatha and several others suddenly appeared from the far forest line and ran to meet Targon.

"No, no no!" Agatha exclaimed over and over, arriving and kneeling in front of Targon, taking the lady's head into her arms and cradling it to her.

A shrill shriek of a child shook the air, and Targon looked up, past Will. "Keep Karz away: don't let him see her like this." Targon could see Monique struggling with Karz as the little boy tried to run to his mother. Emelda reached his group and hugged Horace deeply. Targon could only hope there were not brigands around as the group was screaming, crying, yelling, and sobbing loudly all at once.

"What happened?" Will asked as he, too, knelt between Targon and Agatha.

"No time to explain, Will," Targon said, breathing heavily, trying to catch his breath. "We need to keep going. I need to find Elister."

"Who is Elister? The druid you mentioned before?"

"Yes, only he can help. Now, let's go." Will tried to help, but his arm was still bandaged, and while he looked haler, Targon shook his head, refusing his help as he pulled Salina away from Agatha, regaining his feet and continuing along the trail. "About an hour more," he said, looking over his shoulder as he picked back up the pace.

The journey was sorrowful. Karz finally calmed down, and Cedric actually took turns with Monique carrying him. Amy was strapped to Yolanda's chest, and Emelda and Horace almost ran hand in hand. Targon knew this trail well but had to leave it for the last few miles as it stayed alongside the river, and he was heartened to finally see Bony Brook in the near distance. Usually, when he crossed the brook, the terrain would be barren and treeless, with only a few shrubs between it and his home, but now there were brushes and trees scattered all along the brook, and he had to almost literally stumble onto his abode before he could see it.

Will stepped forward and opened the cabin door with his good arm, allowing Targon to enter the main room and lay Lady Salina onto the makeshift bed he had used earlier. To Targon's astonishment, the room was clean, if not still rustic, and a healthy fire was burning in the hearth. "Agatha, can you do anything for her?" Targon asked as Agatha entered and knelt at the bedside.

"I don't know, young man. I've done more than a little healing in my time, but not when someone was so close to death as our lady here," she said, taking off her cloak and wrapping it around the bolts sticking from the lady's body. "Will, hand me your cloak as well."

Will took off his cloak, and Agatha folded it, putting it under Salina's head. "Is there anything we can do?" Will asked meekly, a look of concern easily visible across his brow.

"Send Emelda in here with Celeste," Agatha commanded without looking at them.

Cedric entered the room. "Can I bring Karz in to see our mother?"

"Send him in, then, but keep everyone out for the time being," Agatha responded.

Soon, Karz and Cedric were at their mother's bedside. Karz draped his arms around his mother's neck while Cedric took her left hand in both of his. Agatha barked some quick orders, and Celeste took off running with her flask toward the Bony Brook, taking Yolanda with her. Targon wasn't sure where Yolanda put her daughter, Amy, but he was sure someone would be watching over the small child. Karz started to weep silently, and Cedric looked like he was about to do the same. Having done everything he could, Targon stood up and stepped a few feet away to allow Agatha room to work and Lady Salina's sons space to grieve.

"What in all of Agon happened out there?" Will asked in a hushed whisper, stepping over to stand near Targon, his eyes wide, a look of sorrow across his countenance.

Targon proceeded then to relate the events that had happened to them since Will had left with the group. He took care to keep his voice low and mentioned more than once how things had started to go wrong but were corrected when the lady demonstrated her extreme bravery. "It was my fault." Targon ended his tale as he looked to Will for some sign of emotion.

Will shook his head in disbelief for a moment before responding. "Don't take it so hard, lad. The lady knew what she was doing, and we all knew this would be risky. You did your best, and, to be honest with you, I hadn't hoped to see any of you at all again. Ten-to-one odds are not something that inspire hope, son. All of you did well out there, and we have lasted much longer than I could have ever expected."

Just then, before he could respond, Yolanda returned with two flasks full of water. Agatha took them and looked around for something. "Targon, do you have any linen?" she asked, looking him hard in the eye.

"One moment," he replied, walking to one of the back rooms. The nice blankets they had were gone, but there were a few items still left, and he grabbed a rough woolen sheet from a corner in the room and took it to her.

"Now, go on, out with you all. I need privacy for the lady. There is nothing more you can do here," Agatha said. "You, too, Cedric. Take your brother outside and let us work."

Targon followed Will outside, who in turn had followed Cedric and Karz. Karz didn't protest and was led hand in hand by his brother to the front porch where Targon noticed Amy sitting with Olga, and the rest of the group was all lined up along the porch edge, sitting with solemn, gloomy faces. Targon sat next to Will at the very end of the porch.

"So this is your place, eh?" Will asked, looking around the wooded area, taking it all in. "Seems cozy enough."

"Well, it is, but the area was cleared until just recently."

"What do you mean by cleared?" Will asked, arching his brows.

"You wouldn't believe me if I told you . . ."

"Look!" Monique almost yelled, pointing to the edge of the small clearing where the cabin stood. Targon looked in the direction she pointed to, and there, standing at the clearing edge between two tall cedars, was none other than Elister himself.

"Am I glad to see you!" Targon said, standing and quickly walking to the old man. "What are you doing just standing here? Have you been here long?"

Elister seemed to be looking at the porch and counting the group. "You seem to be missing three of your guests."

Targon took a moment to understand, and then realization dawning on him, he motioned inside. "They are in the cabin. One of our party is hurt seriously, and we need your help." Targon started to walk toward the cabin, but the old man stood still. "Well, what is it? Come on, let me show you," Targon said in exasperation.

"So many people. I could smell them from a mile away." He looked worried. "Oh, but yes, Argyll told me of the battle, though I could not find Core anywhere. I do hope he is all right."

Targon realized the old man was just as concerned for the bear as he was for his fellow countrymen, but he felt impatient and it came out in his voice. "We don't have time for this. Can you help her or not?"

Elister seemed to come out of his daze. "Of course I can, Master Terrel, I was already here preparing things for you and your guests when Argyll brought me the sad news. I had to return to my abode to obtain something for her." And with that, he started off toward the cabin door side by side with Targon in step.

"Did you bring some grog for her?" Targon asked.

"I do have some grog left in my flask here," Elister said, patting the second of two flasks at his side lovingly, "but grog won't be enough. I had to retrieve something a bit more potent."

Targon reached the door and opened it, peeking inside. "Holy mother of Claire herself, boy! Didn't I tell you the lady needed privacy? She is not fit to be seen like this!" Agatha's voice screeched from inside.

Before Targon could respond, the old man elbowed his way inside and came right up to the makeshift bed where Agatha knelt next to Salina while Celeste was patting the lady's head with a dry rag, soaking up some sweat from her brow. "We don't have time for pleasantries, madam. Now, if you please, I must administer something to your patient. Step aside."

Agatha wasn't used to being ordered about, but there was something in the old man's bearing and the tone of his voice that was polite but much more compelling than Targon had heard before. Agatha seemed to take this in as well because she stood and stepped back, but only a step, keeping an eye on Elister and occasionally glancing back at Salina, as she seemed hesitant at the new guest's arrival.

Elister stepped forward, looking at Lady Salina. Targon saw most of her dress was now ripped open from top to bottom but still covered her where modesty would suggest. Her skin was a pale white. Shallow puffs of labored breathing came with long pauses between breaths. Targon could sense himself willing her to breathe again after each pause. Elister looked at him. "Fetch me that chair," he said, and Targon grabbed the nearest chair and brought it to him.

The old man took the chair and placed it at the head of the bed and then sat. He pulled out several rolls of cloth and took two of them, putting the rest back in a pocket of his cloak. He then removed three small vials of a dark-purple-looking liquid that were tied together, and slipped one loose of its cradle, returning the other two to his tunic pocket.

Picking up two rolls of cloth, he poured a small amount of liquid from the vial onto the ends of each cloth that were rolled much the way a cigarette would be. He sat these down on the pillow and then took the vial and pressed it to the lady's lips, slowly pouring the remaining contents into her mouth. There was a slight involuntary gag as Salina coughed, and the old man took her head in his hands and elevated it ever so slightly. He then laid her head back down and turned to his pack, which he had dropped on the floor next to the chair, rummaging into it and then removing a light tan cotton sheet and a dark brown and green striped wool blanket. He handed them to Celeste, who now stood to his right. Looking

at Agatha, he spoke softly but firmly. "Remove this blanket and her dress: they will infect the wound."

Agatha stared at him for a moment and then up at Celeste and finally at Targon before stepping forward and removing the blanket and depositing it on the floor. With a final look at Targon, she quickly pulled the dress away from the lady, gently lifting her back and then her shoulders. Targon quickly looked away, not prepared to see the lady in such a state of undress, and then quickly, the old man motioned for Agatha to remove the crossbow bolts. "Take them out now?" Agatha asked, a frown on her face but concern masked there as well.

"Do it quickly, both of them," came the druid's reply.

Leaning over Salina's body, Agatha grabbed the bolt sticking from the lady's abdomen, pulling it free, and then she pulled out the bolt sticking from her shoulder. Suddenly, the old man stood and, quick as lightning, inserted the soaked purple cloths into each wound, stopping the flow of blood. The old man sat back down and motioned for Celeste. Celeste laid out the soft, clean tan sheet, covering the lady's body, and followed it with the equally clean wool blanket. He then laid his right hand on her forehead and closed his eyes. "Leave me till dark. Don't disturb her healing," he said without looking up or opening his eyes.

With a slight pause, Celeste and Agatha stepped outside, and Targon followed, bolting the door shut against the wind. He saw the entire group was seated in various positions along his front porch, and they were all looking at him now, even Celeste and Agatha, who remained standing, had turned to face him. Targon took a long moment to take in each look, returning each gaze, eye to eye. He saw sorrow, despair, depression, anguish, and deep sadness. Indeed, the entire group was melancholy and quiet, but he thought he also saw relief as if a great burden and stress had been removed. Finally, sure that he had communicated silently with each of the refugees, he stepped back, placing his spine against the door,

and crossed his arms, looking forward. He would stand until he learned Lady Salina's fate.

Khan sat waiting to hear from his angry mentor as he placed his arms in his hands and his elbows on his knees, facing the river, which was still swollen with the recent rains and additional spring snow melt. The roaring of the river as it flowed past the shore and rocks and boulders barely submerged was like a large, never-ending droning sound that threatened to drive the young apprentice crazy.

Finally, he felt the pull of the orb, and, grabbing it from his pouch, he laid it on his lap, replacing his elbows with it as he pulled it clear of its covering. There was Ke-Tor, looking rather satisfied considering the news, and he also had an odd gleam in his eye, one Khan was not pleased with. "Is Gund with you?"

"Yes, Master. Do you wish to speak with him?"

"I do," Ke-Tor replied too quickly. Khan was sure he was suspect and thought perhaps his mentor wanted to hear Gund's version of events, which, of course, was humiliating at the thought that he would not be trusted in front of the very troops he was supposed to be commanding. He called Gund over and stood up, holding the orb out toward the lieutenant, trying hard to catch a glimpse or sound of what his mentor was about to say.

There was some nodding but no talking until finally, the orb went dark, and Gund, who had been leaning forward more and more, had finally been released by the gaze of the wizard, blinking his eyes as if awakening from a dream. Khan took the orb and looked into it, turning it to face him, but it was dark. He shook it once and was upset his mentor had broken the connection without talking to him when he heard Gund speak. "New plan, boys."

Khan looked up to see Gund turning toward him, drawing his weapon, and then suddenly the man kicked Khan's staff out of his hands, swinging with his short sword. Khan dropped the orb and fell back, startled by the attack. A quick lunge and Khan turned to his right, exposing his arm, and the sword penetrated it, sending a piercing, stabbing jolt of pain into it. Just as Gund pulled the blade out, they heard a roar followed by a scream from one of the other brigand guards. Gund stopped long enough to look around, and Khan saw the large brown bear charging the other two brigands, quickly killing one with a swipe of its massive claws and trampling the other with a large cracking of bones, clearly heard even above the bear's roar and the raging water of the river.

Khan scrambled to his feet. He had a split second to decide what to do: mauling by bear or drowning by water. Khan was never a good swimmer, though he had to cross a lake once before several times and practically dog paddled his way across, each time terrified the inky dark waters would suck him under. His hesitation only lasted for a split second, as the bear continued the charge right toward him and Gund. Khan didn't even wait to see what happened next as he turned and jumped into the water, wading out quickly into the swiftest and deepest part of it, leaving his staff, orb, and pack on the shore.

There was another roar as the bear seemed to be in pain. Perhaps the short sword struck the bear somewhere tender, but the ear-piercing scream that came from Gund was one Khan had only heard before from men in the midst of dying. As the rapidly flowing waters of the Gregus sucked Khan out and down, Khan had no doubt Gund was now dead, and soon, when the air in his lungs gave out, he, too, would join Gund in the underworld. Khan's last thought as the river swept him under was how dearly he had wanted to be a wizard. Now he would never know.

CHAPTER 18

HEALING

Ke-Tor was somewhat pleased with himself. The High-Mage, Am-Sultain, had been most displeased by the news in Ulatha. Ke-Tor had seen to it the failure in the South was neatly and cleanly laid at the feet of the imperious and aloof leader of the mission, Am-Ohkre. Am-Ohkre was too powerful, however, for Ke-Tor to handle by himself. Indeed, Ke-Tor knew he only needed to make arrangements for his own master, at the moment, to be removed from power. He didn't need to see to it Am-Ohkre met the same fate as his apprentice Khan. No, a simple disfavor by the High-Mage of Kesh would do the trick, and, from what he could gleam from the communications between the two, the High-Mage had personally tasked the Arch-Mage with the success of the mission.

The situation was much more complicated. What his apprentice Khan did not know was that the remainder of the Bloody Hand Company had all but perished in Korwell. The Iron Chain Company had returned to Kesh with over thirty lock carts filled with prisoners and slaves, leaving only the Black Hand Company to maintain control over the newly conquered capital of Korwell.

After the mutually devastating Battle of Cree in the South, the remnants of the Kesh invaders returned north to Korwell only to find the castle itself was being contested by rogue Ulathans that knew a secret way into the structure. They had nearly taken the castle and had even killed the lone stone troll that was there before Ke-Tor and his surviving troops finally secured Korwell a second time. Only eight soldiers of the Bloody Hand Company survived, and Am-Ohkre was furious. "Where is that little rat of a wizard?" he had screamed when the tally was complete.

Ke-Tor had learned of Khan's fate along with the losses of the other half of the Bloody Hand Company before his apprentice had informed him of the fact. He had put on a show of anger to distract his apprentice from the real danger.

Wanted the glory for himself, no doubt, thought Ke-Tor angrily. Then the arrogant fool had the nerve to ask how their battle fared! Ke-Tor did not know the extent of his apprentice's mastery of the orb, but he suspected now that Khan held much back and perhaps saw their defeat at Cree prior to asking. *Gloat, he wanted to,* Ke-Tor thought again to himself, rubbing his hands together for warmth along the parapet of the tower's walls. Even now, he was imagining Gund's sword taking the pompous fool's head clean off.

Khan was not the first nor would he be the last apprentice Ke-Tor found cause to eliminate in his lifetime. He would have to summon his newest apprentice, Zorcross, from the Onyx Tower. It would most likely take a fortnight for Zorcross to arrive, but the way things had progressed, Ke-Tor no longer saw a speedy end to the Ulatha campaign.

Speaking of which, he gleefully gloated over the news he had received earlier that day from Am-Ohkre that only Am-Shee survived the Rockton raids. Both the wizard Ke-Urns, his biggest rival, and his apprentice Sigture had met unseemly demises in Rockton. It appeared there was a Rockton spy in Kesh, and they were alerted before the Kesh assault. Casualties there had been high. Too bad Am-Shee didn't perish as well. Ke-Tor could almost feel his ascendance to the ranks of the Arch-Mages, if only there was a position available, but Ke-Urns was a much greater danger to Ke-Tor, so the situation was one that met with his approval for the time being.

Ke-Tor took a moment to look around the destroyed ruins of Korwell. Am-Ohkre had ordered every building within bow range of the castle to be torn down and destroyed after the fiasco that had occurred the prior day. The razing of Korwell was slow going, and they had to use fire on most of the buildings, as they had few hands and only one stone troll remaining from the initial five that had started the campaign.

The Iron Chain Company had yet to return and weren't due for another week. After securing the first load of slaves and prisoners, the two companies that had returned from the South, the Red Throat and the Iron Hand, were at half strength. Normally a company consisted of ten patrols of twelve Kesh each, ten soldiers, one leader, and one tracker.

For the Rockton and Ulatha campaigns, each company was reinforced with an additional two patrols increasing the company from ten patrols to twelve or one hundred and twenty swords to one hundred and forty-four. With four companies, that made it five hundred and seventy-six swords in all. Add the five stone trolls for specialized tasks, the three wizards, plus eight assassins and spies, and the entire composition of the Ulathan raiding force should have been enough to bring them victory. This, of course, assumed the element of surprise remained in Kesh's favor.

Ke-Tor remembered the Ulathan reprisal raid of one thousand soldiers seven years ago. He remembered how hard it was to allow them as far as the first Kesh village of Ulsthor without responding, but Am-Sultain ordered the Ulathans be given free reign of the village. The battle was bloody, and many Ulathans perished, as well as most of the Kesh in the village. The few remaining survivors were prisoners or slaves, and the Ulathans freed them and then returned content to Korwell and disbanded. Most of the Ulathan forces were farmers, peasants, and

tradesmen, soft in the art of killing and undisciplined but loyal. Korwell normally only maintained a garrison of just under two hundred soldiers, with half of them confined to the tower and castle itself. The other half was scattered across the far flung and sparsely populated land. There were not enough Ulathan soldiers to man all of their old fortifications, and the last two decades saw them quickly fall into disrepair.

This was Am-Sultain's plan all along, Ke-Tor now observed, impressed. The many yearly raids were tapered off over the last few decades until the realms surrounding Kesh were lulled into a sense of false security. Spies were sent to many lands where they infiltrated those realms. Kesh wizards were known for their patience and long life. Fifty years was nothing for an Arch-Mage but represented a generation in other lesser men. *Indeed, Sultain had thought this through nearly a century earlier,* Ke-Tor thought. *Very clever, indeed.*

Ke-Tor heard the slight creak of the door and sensed immediately Am-Ohkre's presence. A soldier was like a dark to Ke-Tor's arcane senses, but when Am-Ohkre entered his presence, it was like a radiant source of heat and light to his nervous system. A wizard as skilled as Ke-Tor didn't miss the aura surrounding an Arch-Mage, and indeed, from what most others had said, even a common Kesh could feel it, too.

"News so soon again?" Ke-Tor asked without looking, making sure Am-Ohkre would know his entrance did not go unnoticed.

Am-Ohkre did not respond immediately: instead, he walked over to stand next to Ke-Tor. *Perhaps a bit too close,* Ke-Tor thought. Indeed, he could now see the Arch-Mage with his peripheral vision, and there was no movement and nothing said.

Finally, Ke-Tor turned to face the Arch-Mage, but the Mage spoke first. "News indeed, wizard. Sultain is agitated at our lack of progress and our excessive losses." Ke-Tor noticed the difference in speech between the plural form Am-Ohkre used when describing failure and the singular form he often used when successful.

"Only agitated?" Ke-Tor asked, masking as best he could his sarcasm in his tone, if not his words.

"Yes, agitated. We have new orders."

"We?" Ke-Tor asked, now dropping all pretenses of smugness.

"Yes, you will accompany me to the Gregus due east of here and help me retrieve what remains of the Bloody Hand Company," Am-Ohkre said matter-of-factly. "We need every sword now that we can get."

"The Bloody Hand is all but destroyed or routed. It will take a week if not longer to find any survivors near the Earlstyne," Ke-Tor said, alarm in his voice.

"Sultain appears to agree with you but demands the action. He thinks one of the Arnen may be involved and may have a bearing on what has transpired."

"This would explain much if true," Ke-Tor replied, pondering on the revelation, forgetting for the moment that he was going to have to accompany Am-Ohkre, "but then again, the Arnen are extinct. None survived the Great War."

"The very same is said across Claire Agon of wizards and magic, but yet here we stand, no?" Am-Ohkre said, an arch of one brow and a telling look crossing his face.

The irony of the statement was not lost on Ke-Tor. "Yes, indeed, it would again explain much of what has happened in and around the Earlstyne, but we investigated it thoroughly three decades ago and found nothing there. Not even a presence of the Arnen."

"Was it thorough?" Am-Ohkre asked, maintaining the arching brow of his left eye as he looked sideways at Ke-Tor, making Ke-Tor suddenly feel as if he was the last to be in on a bad joke. Ke-Tor had been part of that foray, and now he wasn't sure how to answer the Arch-Mage.

"Am-Sunsi, Ke-Urns, and I searched the forest thoroughly after all the reports by our raiders. I am certain there was nothing to be found," Ke-Tor now said, suddenly changing tact and dismissing any rumor of

a surviving member of the Arnen. Ke-Tor would not allow Am-Ohkre to lure him into the possibility that his mission many decades ago had resulted in failure and was only conveniently becoming noticeable just now, thirty years later.

Am-Ohkre dropped his brow and looked down at what was left of the burned and cindered town of Korwell. "What news of your apprentice?"

Ke-Tor tensed for the moment he had expected. It was long a Kesh tradition that an apprentice of any wizard was fully under the care and discipline of his mentor. However, when an Arch-Mage was involved, a prudent wizard would at least tactfully inform, if not obtain the consent of, the Arch-Mage before meting out any unusual punishment. "Well"— Ke-Tor sighed—"Khan was released from my tutorship early."

Am-Ohkre did not need to ask. No apprentice was ever released once mentored unless they had achieved the rank of wizard and were granted the title and its honors at a ceremony within the Onyx Tower. Am-Ohkre implicitly understood this to mean Khan was executed. The only question, really, was how. "By your hand?"

"No, I had Gund release my student," Ke-Tor said, now realizing Am-Ohkre would mark Gund as one of his servants and not one committed to Kesh only or the Mage specifically.

"Such a shame. Your pupil had showed promise and skill," Am-Ohkre said, shaking his head in disapproval.

"Unfortunately, he was very insubordinate as well, talked poorly of your designs, and openly criticized Am-Sultain's war," Ke-Tor said, trying to stay the Arch-Mage's disapproval.

"Yes, he had a very unscrupulous tongue and a serious attitude that needed adjusting, but I thought him ready soon of the Onyx Ceremony," Am-Ohkre said, stopping his head shaking and absorbing the revealing information. "I take it you called on a new apprentice?"

"Zorcross will replace Khan," Ke-Tor said simply.

"That will take weeks," Am-Ohkre said, raising his hand to silence Ke-Tor's protest. "In the meantime, we must rally the survivors at the Gregus and collect your friend Gund and his soldiers. We leave immediately."

"But we are weak and understaffed!" Ke-Tor said, shocked at the speed and magnitude of the decision. Whatever was out there, Ke-Tor felt it would be better if he could remain within the high stone walls of Korwell. "One of us should stay in Korwell to maintain its defense, especially after what happened here yesterday. We almost lost the castle again."

"We will only take two patrols, one each from the Bloody Hand and the Red Throat, and the last stone troll stays here," Am-Ohkre said with a final nod.

Ke-Tor preferred to have a troll near him when he traveled. The creatures were dumb but in awe of the Kesh wizards, and this gave him the leverage to manipulate and order a stone troll to do his bidding. Unfortunately, the awe was limited to the wizard caste, and it was not unknown for a stone troll to kill a Kesh brigand or two from time to time in an argument. For this reason, the trolls, unlike their immensely chaotic and uncontrollable hill brethren and their equally independent mountain cousins, were used commonly as personal bodyguards by the Mage class. "Would it not be better to take Grinder with us?"

"No," Am-Ohkre replied simply. "As you noted, the security of Korwell is key here, and Grinder will do well as the last of his kind to guard the gate. We collapsed the secret tunnel the Ulathans used to infiltrate the castle and detached the chains to the gate portcullis. Grinder is now the only way to open the gate. He stays."

Ke-Tor understood the Arch-Mage's words were final and, indeed, most likely wise, but in the interest of self-preservation, Ke-Tor wanted the stone troll, Grinder, to accompany him personally. Ke-Tor would have to watch his back. "Anything else?"

"No, gather your things and meet me in the courtyard. The patrols are ready to go, and we go mounted for speed."

"As you wish," Ke-Tor said with an ever so slight bow, just enough to prevent the Arch-Mage from accusing him of disrespect but as little as possible to show his contempt, if not disagreement. Ke-Tor did not jump from the parapet wall this time, instead electing to use the stairs and retrieve his pack on the way down. He didn't trust the magic of floating so close to the Arch-Mage, especially after such news. Magic accidents were known to occur more often in the presence of Arch-Mages and resulted in the high mortality rate amongst the common wizard. No, indeed, Ke-Tor would walk the three hundred and thirty-three steps to the courtyard below.

Targon had stood for a couple of hours at his front door, waiting patiently. He told Marissa to take Thomas, Jons, and Monique around back to his mother's garden and see what they could find. He didn't have the heart to say anything to Cedric or Karz, as Cedric just held his little brother in his lap and leaned against the cabin wall while stretching his legs out on the uneven and worn planks of the front porch.

Agatha took the time to change Will's bandage, and Yolanda was walking nearby with her daughter, Amy, barefoot, enjoying the lush green grass around the cabin. That was so odd for Targon to comprehend, as he was so used to the ground being trampled by their many boots as well as Myrtle's daily walks around the cabin, that the ground was always bare as he remembered it.

Horace had grabbed a crossbow and sat it on his lap as he and Emelda sat watching over Yolanda and her little girl. Celeste stood nervously near Targon by the door, and he half thought she was going to try to open it and run inside. Olga was sitting by herself near the Moross boys, wringing her hands and generally looking worried.

Finally, after some time, the door bolt swung to the side, and Targon stepped away from the door to see the old man Elister as he exited. He could hear Celeste gasp as she, too, viewed the old man. He looked aged beyond what they had just seen hours before. His peppered short cropped beard was now fully white, no longer grey, and his balding head seemed to have lost more of its hair. Wrinkles furrowed his brow, and he showed crow eyes near the edges of his eyelids. Targon looked inside and saw Lady Salina sleeping on the makeshift bed, breathing shallowly but firmly. He grabbed a chair, placing it next to the old man, and, taking his elbow, gently guided him to a seated position on the chair.

Word must have gone around as the younger refugees came back around the front of the cabin loaded with various foods from the garden. Yolanda and Amy ran over as well, and everyone perked up when Elister opened his mouth. "She will live," he said with a sigh and some finality. Karz and Cedric almost shouted in glee at the news, but the older ladies just started to sob in relief. No one could feel more relief than Targon. He didn't think he could bear the guilt if she had died. He felt as responsible for this group of his fellow countrymen as he did for his mother, Dareen, and his sister, Ann.

Finally, Celeste spoke. "Can we see her?"

"Yes, yes," Elister replied, bending over but waving his hand in the air. The boys didn't wait and ran into the room first, followed by Celeste and the others, everyone except Agatha and Will, who remained as she changed Will's bandage.

"Well, go on, boy. See to the lady," Will said, motioning with his good hand. Targon waved him off and knelt by Elister, ignoring the other two.

"Are you all right?" he asked tenderly.

Elister seemed to not hear him at first, but then finally, he lifted his head and looked Targon in the eyes. "Yes, I'm fine. Thank you for asking, young master Terrel." There was a pause as the old man looked around

and then back to Targon again. "Let the weight go, son. You have done well for a Zashitor."

Targon nodded, not saying anything nor protesting the title bestowed on him by the wizened old man. After a few moments, he stood, and, with a final touch to the old man's shoulder, he walked into his home.

The makeshift bed had been moved nearer to the hearth, and Targon wondered if the old man did that or if his fellow companions had. Karz and Cedric were each holding one of their mother's hands, and each knelt on opposite sides of the bed. The head of the bed was just against the wall nearer to the front door, and then the back door and the hearth was in the exact middle. Everyone stood around the cot and looked at Lady Salina in silence. She was still pale, but a tiny bit of pink stood out in her cheeks and brow. The last rays of sunset were peeking into the room, giving it the brightest glow he was used to seeing, and a warm reddish glow emanated from the fireplace. It was calm and peaceful for the moment, and Targon allowed the moment to fill him with hope. Hope not only for Lady Salina and her group of refugees, but for Marissa's family and his family. He would never allow the Kesh to destroy that hope, and he locked away the memory to serve him at a later time.

"Well, son. This is your home, and we are your guests," Horace said, standing with the crossbow perched on his right shoulder. "What would you have us do?"

Targon looked around and saw several of his companions nodding at him. Taking a deep breath, he motioned to the lone pot sitting near the hearth. "Take my mother's kettle and fetch some water to boil. If Agatha lets us, then we use her pot to make a stew for everyone. Lord knows it's large enough." Several of his companions chuckled at that comment, as the pot was indeed large, and more than one brigand had been on the receiving end of it.

"Well, you heard the man," Olga chimed in. "Come on, children, show us what you gathered from the young man's garden."

Monique and Thomas ran to the front porch where they had deposited their armful of vegetables and brought them inside. They had gathered some cabbages, not the wild bitter kind but the large, round sweeter domestic ones that were commonly farmed in the valley, as well as a few potatoes and some carrots. Marissa had a better understanding of gardening and recognized more of the leaf tops, managing to collect some sage and thyme for seasoning, as well as two beets. The older ladies used the table to organize the produce, and Emelda took the Terrel pot down to the nearby brook, followed protectively by Horace with his crossbow.

"Do you have any other seasonings?" Olga asked, now excited to contribute to the group's provisions. Targon gathered by the small talk during the many marches and time at the blind, that Olga was one of the cooks at the Pickled Pig Tavern and knew how to cook, along with Agatha, who was the master of the royal kitchen.

"Let me look," Targon said, moving over to the crude shelving standing next to the wooden basin that acted as a kitchen along the side wall of the cabin. There had been a burlap bag of salt, but when the brigands took it, some of it spilled on the shelf second from the top, and there was a small handful there. "Just a little salt is all," Targon said, frowning.

"Bless you, my boy, a little salt will do!" Olga said gleefully, scuttling around the table and over to the shelf, grabbing a small, crudely made wooden plate deftly as she passed. The others took note to get out of her way, and Targon did the same, watching as she swept each grain of salt onto the small plate. Targon wasn't sure what else was being swept along with the salt, but Olga seemed eager to gather every grain. Content that she had all the salt that she could gather, she returned to the table, grabbing the knife Jons had tucked into his belt and holding her hand up to silence him.

Shortly, all the cabbage, carrots, potatoes, and both beets were added to the pot Emelda had brought back, half full of water, and grabbing a nearby rag that was discarded by the brigands, Olga hefted the pot onto

the cooking bar hanging above the hearth and then hung the Terrel pot also with water next to it.

Thomas and Jons were already in the loft, having climbed the crude horizontal ladder alongside the west wall of the cabin with Monique admonishing them to be careful and telling them the loft was not a play place. *Whatever that means*, thought Targon. Soon, everyone joined them inside. It was cramped, but not nearly so much as the blind. Elister remained outside, and no one disturbed him for over an hour.

Targon directed the ladies to the rooms in the back while he and Cedric moved Lady Salina, bed and all, to a back room. Agatha knelt by the lady's bedside and stroked Salina's hair as he had watched her do earlier. Targon left the two in the back room that had belonged to his mother and Ann and returned to the common room of his cabin. Olga tended to the cooking, the children were playing, and there was small talk amongst the adults. Will used a chair to lean his good arm on the table and rested near the fire. Content that his "guests" were comfortable, and, indeed, they made themselves at home in short order, Targon exited and sat next to Elister on the front porch.

The sun had just set, darkening the dragon's fire till morning, and Targon sat in silence next to the old man for several moments, watching the western sky fade from bright oranges and light reddish hues to the deeper, darker violet blues and purples that marked the onset of night. "What did you do to her to save her?" Targon asked sincerely.

The old man didn't hesitate this time and turned his neck to look at Targon in the eye. "Another hour more and she would have been beyond healing. It's a good thing you arrived when you did. To answer your question, Master Terrel, I simply tended to her in Agon's way."

"So you're a healer, too?" asked Targon in mild surprise.

"Too? What else would I be?" the old man asked, slightly amused.

"Well, it's obvious you're a wizard," Targon replied, shrugging his shoulders and looking west at the fading sunset. "You command powerful magic to be able to move trees and make grass grow in a day."

"Nonsense," Elister replied with a chuckle as he, too, admired the fading glow of the dragon's fire. "I simply channeled the power of our mother, Clair Agon, into the young lady and allowed nature to take its course."

Targon smiled as he thought of Lady Salina, who was twice his age with a grown boy for a son, being referred to as a young lady. Only someone such as Elister could say such a thing. It made him fonder of the old man, strange though he was. "I can't say I understand, but my mother often referred to Agon as the mother of all of us. Besides, I don't care what you say, I think you're a powerful wizard just the same."

Elister chuckled, seeming to regain some of his strength the last hour he had sat in silence and solitude. "Then you would really be surprised to see a real wizard. Quite a site when you catch one at work. Mostly death and destruction they wreak on those near them, but at times, the actions they perform are quite spectacular. They, however, draw their power from Akun and the dragon's fire, not from our mother, Claire Agon."

Targon turned from his seat to cross his legs and face the old man, who remained seated on the rickety chair he had brought to him earlier. There weren't enough chairs inside for everyone, so Targon made due with his rear. "I wouldn't have believed you until today . . ." he began, and then recounted the battle that occurred, ending with the huge fireball he saw the oddly dressed man with the brigands hurl at them.

"Then you have witnessed a wizard of Kesh in person and lived to tell the tale. Impressive, indeed," Elister said, and then smiled.

"Well, he was so frail looking, almost sickly and thin as well, but tall like the brigands, but dressed differently. We took him at first to be a

leader or chieftain of the Kesh until he hurled that ball of fire at us. I swear it came from the tip of his staff," Targon concluded.

"Well, he was a chieftain. Didn't you know the wizards rule the Kesh? This is part of their society."

"Before today, I had no idea they even existed . . . The wizards, I mean, not the brigands."

Elister chuckled again, smiling at Targon, amused but fond of the young man. "That is part of their plan to lull what's left of Agon's realms into a false sense of security. They have been weakened, however, since the Wizard-Dragon War more than a millennium ago, but it now appears their chief wizard has been slowly rebuilding their ranks, and now they have made their move at last."

"Move for what?" Targon asked with a quizzical look on his face. Wizards were, after all, just a tale to scare the children of a magical age that was lost long ago . . . or so he thought.

"Why, for the one thing most men crave, Master Terrel. Power. Men do terrible things to obtain it, and even worse things to maintain it. It is addicting. It makes men drunk in the head, so to speak. Always remember this, my young Zashitor. Never succumb to its enticing enchantments. Seek to use what power you have wisely, and share what you do not need with others. Empowering others with free will is the key to true power. Never forget."

"Drunk like what your grog does?" Targon asked intently, shifting his cross-legged stance to lean closer to the old man.

Elister let loose with a large, hearty laugh and slapped his knees with his hands. "Oh my," he started, barely controlling himself, "grog simply heals, though I can't deny some certain intoxicating properties of the beverage," he said, leaning forward now and lowering his voice to a whisper, "but there is nothing quite like honey ale. Sweet and invigorating it is in moderate doses, though I prefer my own 'beaver brew' that I make from time to time. That one will put hair on your chest, young man!" Elister smiled a broad, toothy grin.

"Agon knows I don't need any more hair on my chest, but I didn't know you imbibed," Targon countered with a conspiratorial whisper and a look at the door to make sure no one could hear him from inside the cabin.

"More so in my younger days." Elister leaned back now, looking out at the night sky, and then sat back upright again, speaking louder but softly. "These days I don't have the time for making a good brew, and I spent far too long sleeping and not enough time drinking. Ah, if only I was a few centuries younger . . ." he finished, letting the thought linger between them.

"So what do we do now?" Targon asked, liking the old man even more now that he seemed more like an Ulathan and not a powerful wizard from the deep past.

"Tonight, you and your guests rest. You must let Lady Salina sleep and regain her strength."

"What will you do? Will you stay with us?"

The old man looked over his shoulder at the door, and the sound of children playing and voices talking intermixed with light laughter could just be heard. "No, I think your guests can finally spend a night in relative peace, comfort, and security. No need for a stranger to add to their anxiety. Besides, I have work to attend to. I sense there are more of them magical types about. They keep poking and prodding me here in the forest, and I am forced to repel their intrusions. It would not do for them to find you and your friends so soon after what has transpired. I need to discuss this with the guardian of the forest."

Targon furrowed his brow as he took in what the old man was saying. "Guardian? I thought you were the guardian of the Blackthorn."

"Earlstyne!" Elister shot back, but he was smiling, not in the least offended by the use of the old forest's common moniker. "I am not exactly the forest's guardian. I abhor fighting, don't you know? No, I am more like a caretaker. Call me a gardener, if you will. I care for the forest and its inhabitants. Of course, I can defend the creatures that live here if need be, but the real guardian I am not."

Targon nodded his head but spoke the opposite. "I don't understand. Are there two of you? Two "Arnen," I think you called yourself, no?"

"Well, yes, two of us, but Arnen, no. The guardian of the forest sleeps, as do I, most of the time, but I do digress. I am the only Arnen here: however, there are many inhabitants and they, too, protect the forest. You met one of them, don't you remember? Large furry brown fellow with a nasty temper from time to time?" Elister asked with a nod and a wink.

It was Targon's turn to chuckle now. "Yes, I do remember the bear, though I have no idea where he is. The last I saw of him, he had taken out an entire raft of brigands and was chasing more of them, I think. We left too quickly and never saw the bear again."

"Well, I am worried for my old grumpy friend, as he is long overdue. I was hoping to see him before sunset, but I'll have to wait till morning now. If he doesn't return by then, I'll send Argyll to look for him."

"You mean that bird you told me about when we first met?"

"I mean falcon, young man. Argyll will eat a bird for dinner," Elister said, motioning to the carving of the Clairton bird that hung on a leather strap around Targon's neck.

"Back to the talking animals?" Targon sighed.

"All creatures talk, young master Terrel. The problem is most folks don't stop to listen or bother to hear what is being said."

"Well, I couldn't hear a word that bear said, though I must concede it seemed to understand me well enough, though I don't know how."

"Of course he understood you. He is from the Earlstyne. He is not a wild bear from the barbarian-infested wastelands of the North, nor is

he a cute and cuddly bear from the far south jungles of Lunde. He is one of Agon's own children, and that makes him special unlike his cousins in the wild."

"Is Argyll also one of Agon's own?" Targon asked.

"Yes," Elister responded.

"So he is like your pet?" Targon tilted his head inquiringly.

Elister sighed, lowering his shoulders, hands on his knees as he leaned forward. "Argyll is his own master. He helps me because I asked and he agreed to. He is no pet and is not caged. Did you not hear a word I said about power and its abuses, Master Terrel?"

"I did. I was just confused about how you interact with these . . . creatures," Targon concluded humbly, lowering his voice as he spoke.

The old man placed a hand on Targon's shoulder. "You have been through much and in such a short period of time. You have experienced loss, and I need to be a bit more patient with you. Just remember what I said about power and understand that the world is much more than you have imagined and you will do fine."

Targon smiled at the old man and then suddenly remembered what he wanted to ask him. "I almost forgot, what did you mean by 'magical types' and something about them 'poking and prodding' you here in the forest."

"Ah, yes, the intrusions . . ." Elister began, lowering his voice and looking around again as if he was being watched. "Most suspicious these magical types are, always poking and prodding and peering around where they are not welcome. They use blasphemous orbs of glass to peer into faraway places and some places not so far away."

"You mean that young wizard I saw today was trying to find us using magic?" Targon asked in a loud whisper, eyes wide open in astonishment.

"Well, yes, though he is just a sapling. The real test came from the mighty oak deep in Kesh. I can't be certain all was hidden from them. We must prepare for the worst, just in case. I fear my time on Agon is coming to an end."

"You can't mean that! We just met. What are you talking about?" Targon asked, slightly panicked.

"Now, now, don't worry yourself over someone such as myself. I am old. Old and tired, Master Terrel, and I feel it in my bones. Soon, I feel I must rest the eternal sleep of my ancestors and return to our mother. Now don't you go making sad faces at my remark. I still have some life left in these old bones," Elister said, standing, and Targon stood to face him. "I must leave now. I feel I've rested enough to travel. I'll either return or send word . . . Well, I'll return personally, then, seeing as how I don't think you, much less the city folk inside, will understand the messenger I send. I should be back by tomorrow evening. Remember my words, and do allow the young lady her rest. She should be awake in the morning if you don't disturb her."

Targon nodded, not saying anything at first, and then hesitantly, he embraced the old man and pulled back. "She will rest, I promise. Thank you for your help . . . Elister. You are a good man."

"Thank you for saying." Elister smiled and grabbed his staff from where it was leaning against the cabin wall. "Rest easy tonight. You are protected at least for this evening." And clutching his robe tightly around his waist to ward off the chill that was growing as the night progressed, Targon watched the old man walk south and disappear into the forest, and then he turned, opened the door, and entered his home.

CHAPTER 19

ENEMY

Khan saw the twin sister moons, Sara and Tira, as they rose and chased the dragon's fire across the sky. It was dark and not long after sunset, but the moons and band of milky white illuminated the ground where he was lying. He couldn't believe he was alive. Unfortunately, he was still on the eastern shore of the Gregus at the edge of the Earlstyne forest, only much farther downstream. How much farther he did not know and did not care. He was only elated to be alive. *What a miracle it is*, he thought to himself.

Khan remembered the pull of the river and the intense pain from Gund's stabbing wound in his left arm. He only knew how to dog paddle, and even that he was unable to do as his arm would not follow his commands. He blacked out several times, if he remembered correctly, and after a long time was somehow able to grab onto a tree limb that was hanging in the water. He could not pull himself out and several times almost let go. Only when he found the primordial strength that one obtained when facing certain death was he able to loop his legs around the branch and ever so slowly, half in and half out of the raging water, he

edged himself to the shore until he could drop his feet and trudge out of the clutches of the Gregus.

He remembered he passed out again for who knows how long. When he came to, he was shivering with cold. His strength was sapped, and he couldn't stand. He thought one or more of his ribs was cracked, and his left arm was not only lacerated with a deep, open, gashing wound but he was sure it was fractured as well. Death was waiting to take the young man to the underworld.

With great effort, he pulled his good arm up to his necklace chain made of pure gold where there were three small but dense porcelain balls with the same sheen and size as a pearl. The larger one was red, and it was flanked on either side by two smaller blue ones. His staff, his pack, his orb, and all his supplies were lost, except for the lifesaving magic in the small pearl-sized balls. He had no choice. This was the exact reason he had the magic necklace. He would have preferred to use one of the two blue healing balls, but he knew he was beyond the power they had to heal. No, if he was to survive the day, he needed to use his one and only healing Talaman. He took the small red globe and yanked it from the necklace and then placed it in his mouth and swallowed before he blacked out again.

Now he was alive. He knew he had awoken in Agon and not the underworld because he saw the twin sisters in the night sky. Mages didn't normally have healing magic. They required the administrations of a powerful cleric or shaman from a nurturing civilization. Kesh was not known for nurturing, but rather for destruction. It had cost Khan more than he cared to remember to obtain his Talaman, and he had hoped to never have to use them, but today showed that hope to be in vain. Khan sat up and realized he must have crawled from the river's edge to the base of a tree that had a pile of wet leaves around it from last year's fall season. The leaves clung to his wet robe and were stuck to his skin and in his hair. He should have died from hypothermia, but he felt hot. His body was

burning intently, and he gingerly stood and removed his robe, throwing it over a low hung branch to dry with both arms.

Yes, both arms. His wounded arm bore a nasty gash where Gund's short sword had penetrated all the way to the bone and fractured it. Now it was sore, but he swung it around his shoulder and stretched it, feeling his blood coursing through the arm, heat coming off of his body in huge waves. It was dark and there was a chill in the air, but Khan did not notice. His Talaman was working and would do so for a full day. Khan quickly stripped out of his wet clothes and returned to the river to drink. He was thirsty: the heat was so intense he was sweating and had lost a lot of fluids, not to mention blood. He drank in long swigs until he felt the intense thirst finally relent and his skin felt warm and not so hot. He returned to the tree and sat at its base, removing his boots and leaning them upside down against the tree. He was now dressed only in his breeches. His trousers, tunic, cloak, socks, and boots were all off and either hanging on the tree or set on the ground. He doubted they would be completely dry by morning, but when his Talaman wore off, he didn't want to be wearing cold wet clothes, if he could help it.

He felt no hunger, however. Thirst seemed to be his only discomfort outside of some soreness where he had suffered the worst wounds. He felt his chest and gingerly touched his ribs where he thought they had broken on his right side. He felt the customary soreness one felt after healing quickly, but no pain. All seemed intact.

Anger. Now that he could think past his own survival, he found himself mulling over the reasons for his ex-mentor's actions. He could not fathom the reason behind them. Certainly there were losses, but he was sure there had to be more troopers in and around the area. It would be a simple matter to regroup. No, something else must have happened adding to their prior history to cause the attempt on Khan's life. Khan was no fool. He knew full well the dangers of being associated with certain wizards, and indeed with this one in particular. He felt rage as hot as his

own body, which was under the influence of the Talaman. He would seek and obtain his retribution one way or the other, but how?

He looked around in the dark, listening to the river's roar nearby. He could hear an owl hoot and the faint dull sound of insects chirping in the dark. He could not go south downstream: that would only take him closer to the last remaining lands of the Ulathans, and he was pretty sure they would kill him on sight. He could not cross the river west: it was impassable. East was the Earlstyne forest, and the thought of walking in there unarmed was as close to suicide as he dared to imagine. No, despite the attempted assassination on his life, he could only hope to return north and see if he could regroup, perhaps find a way to discuss the situation with Am-Ohkre. Better yet, return to Kesh ahead of his rival Ke-Tor and plot to have him eliminated upon his return. He had some resources in Kesh stockpiled for just such an occasion, but the immediate need was to remain alive.

He was on the wrong side of the Gregus River. He was alone and without provisions or his staff, which he needed to work his magic. There was that wild, enraged bear loose on this side of the shore, and finally, he had to deal with the fact that there was an armed and deadly group of Ulathan rebels also in the vicinity. He thought for a moment of his odds to survive and gave himself a one in three, if not a one in four, chance. He wanted to better those odds, so he determinedly decided his first course of action when dawn broke was to head north and seek out his staff. Gund had kicked it away, but the bear intervened, and if the Ulathans didn't discover it, he could retrieve it as well as his orb and provisions. That was his plan.

He folded his arms then and noticed across the river on top of a lone tree was a bird. It looked like an eagle, and it was looking intently at him or near him. After some time, the bird took flight and disappeared northeast over the river and forest. Khan suddenly felt a shiver come over his

otherwise raging hot body, and he was filled with dread. Something was watching him.

The night was quickly over. Dawn broke over the Border Mountains, and Targon woke from his makeshift bed on the floor near the hearth. He could hear the early morning birds tweeting outside as Agon warmed and came to life. He saw Marissa, already awake, sitting near the fire, stoking it with the poker. It looked like she had added a couple of logs that were stored near the hearth by either side. When the brigands raided their home, they took mainly provisions, animals, and foodstuffs. Targon realized, despite the hearty meatless stew they all ate last night, there was scant food left for today, much less this morning.

Targon rubbed his eyes and walked over to Marissa by the hearth, who was still stoking if not playing with the fire embers. "Good morning," Targon said, stifling a yawn.

"Morning," Marissa replied sadly.

"Something wrong, Marissa?" Targon asked, now concerned.

"I miss my family," she replied simply.

Targon realized suddenly that the fire in the hearth reminded him of the night he had met her: her house had burned down before their very eyes. The thought of the fire and solace in the early morning must have led her to thoughts of her family. He knew it would do the same to him. "I do, too," he said, kneeling by her and putting his arm around her tenderly.

Targon gave her a moment and then decided to do something for the group. Quietly, he left the cabin after grabbing his axe and bow where he had left them by his bedside. He didn't want to disturb Lady Salina's sleep where she lay all night, along with Agatha, who was now tending to her. Monique, Olga, and Celeste were also in the same small room his mother and Ann had used. Horace and Emelda shared his room with Yolanda

and her daughter, Amy. Cedric, Karz, and little Jons were all up in the loft. Targon could hear Cedric's breathing, though he couldn't really see them from his vantage point. He'd have to half climb up the crude ladder against the wall or step all the way back to the doors to the rear rooms to be able to see any part of them. Will, Thomas, and Targon had slept in the main room on the floor. Cedric had insisted on sleeping with his brother, and Thomas complained quickly that the loft was too hot for him and had come down shortly after everyone retired for the evening.

The cool air of dawn slapped Targon in the face, but it felt good. He loved the outdoors. Despite the warmth of his home, it had felt a bit stuffy with so many people crammed inside. Quickly, he ran out to Bony Brook, running alongside it to the southeast, heading a bit deeper into the forest. Soon, he found what he was looking for: The latest warren of rabbits near the area a couple of stone throws away from the brook. With sixteen mouths to feed, he was going to either have to be very lucky or hunt all day. Targon drew an arrow and strung his bow and took aim.

Ke-Tor couldn't believe their luck, or lack of it, to be more precise. They lost another half dozen soldiers to a group of Ulathans that were hiding in one of the castle's storehouse sheds, even though they were supposedly searched well. Am-Ohkre delayed their departure by two more days to make sure the castle was secure. He had used his critir orb to magically search the castle grounds, and he ordered Ke-Tor himself to set several defensive spells on key doors and corridors. By the time they had finished, three more Ulathans were found and executed, and both sorcerers had to rest to recoup from the exhaustion their magic use had caused them.

They were finally rested and ready to depart early the next day. Ke-Tor had tried several times to use his own critir to contact his apprentice's orb. The call would be very compelling for Khan to ignore, such was the

way the orbs worked. The weaker-willed individual would eventually succumb to its call, unless he was either dead or a good distance away from the orb. Ke-Tor had actually connected with Khan's orb and peered through it but saw only dirt and grass. Why Gund would not bring the orb back to him as ordered troubled the conniving wizard. Ke-Tor felt fairly confident that Khan was dead, but the lack of information from Gund was most bothersome.

"Problem, Master?" Hork asked as he approached the tower.

Ke-Tor looked over at their brigand leader and appraised the man, taking his measure. Was he with Am-Ohkre or another? Could he be trusted with a task? Ke-Tor decided to roll the die. Fortune, after all, favored the bold. "Take two of your swiftest scouts on our fastest steeds and send them due east to the Gregus River. Look for either Gund or my apprentice Khan. Have the scouts watch them only. One watches and the other returns to report. We will be leaving shortly, so your men will have to go now. Tell no one about this," Ke-Tor finished, with an unspoken threat hanging in the air.

Hork looked around for a second to see if they were truly alone. Hork knew Ke-Tor to be one of the most ruthless wizards in all of Kesh. Seeing no sign of Am-Ohkre, the brigand chieftain nodded and walked away, ready to order the scouts to leave. He wasn't sure what was going on, but he'd find out in good time. He always did.

Ke-Tor watched the approaching dawn and waited for Am-Ohkre to make his appearance. He'd make the Arch-Mage climb the stairs first, however. One way or the other, he would see to it this fiasco was laid at the old man's feet. Let him disrespect the High-Mage personally and see what follows.

Am-Sultain rose before dawn and ascended to the High Chamber of Seeing within the Onyx Tower. His old apprentice Ke-Grenson was waiting for him.

"Ready for Ulatha today, Master?" Ke-Grenson asked cordially. The two had spent most of the prior day observing their raids in Rockton using the high critir permanently set within the Chamber of Seeing. The high critir was, as legend goes, said to have been the first critir ever made by the wizards of Kesh. It was the master orb, the most powerful of all divination devices the Kesh used. It was three times the size of a normal portable critir and set into a basin of clear water penetrated only by three large iron prongs, which held the critir tightly suspended above the clear water. The orb worked best when one wizard could activate it and maintain the activation and the other wizard could guide the orb to see things happening as desired by the user.

"Most ready, my old friend. Am-Ohkre has made a mess of the Ulathan campaign, almost as much as Am-Shee has the Rockton. Time to see if they can turn things around or if I need to send you there to take over."

Ke-Grenson nodded and approached the high critir and started his spell of activation, murmuring the arcane words and using his hand to charge the orb to life. Am-Sultain waited for the large critir to glow, and he approached it with his arms outstretched, willing the vision within to bend to his will and direction. The orb showed flashes of battles past as he started to control the direction in which he wished to view. The orb at first moved in accordance with his wishes nearer to Korwell. He could see the crenellated towers and darkly dressed figures moving along its walls, but before he could slow the vision or move it in closer, the Ulathan castle was gone and the orb's vision was dragged violently back to the east. Am-Sultain looked up from the orb at Grenson to see if he was doing something, but instead saw the elder wizard's face contort in effort and even pain as he fought to maintain the orb's power of seeing. Suddenly, the blurred landscape that was flying by was replaced by a face.

Am-Sultain looked back at the orb and into a set of sparkling blue eyes. The man's head was bald with a ring of white hair along its edges, but short, not flowing past the neckline. There was a white beard, short but well-trimmed. A brown cloak with a hood hung about the man's shoulders, and the tip of a gnarled deep brown staff was in the man's right hand. It was adorned with what looked like a simple piece of grey granite, flecked with specks of white and black. This was no wizard of Kesh: indeed, the staff alone gave that away. The Kesh used metallic staves as straight as an arrow adorned with expensive and wildly powerful gems at the top. It was the signature accouterment of a wizard.

A sudden feeling of dread accompanied the vision of the old man. He was stocky and robust, much like an Ulathan. The man's eyes pierced the High-Mage's defenses. Am-Sultain cried out, "No!" Ke-Grenson opened his eyes as he started to lose control of the orb. Suddenly, in a flash of blinding white light, the orb cracked and a wave of air pressure flattened the two sorcerers as they landed on their backsides.

Am-Sultain came to within the dark chamber. His friend and old apprentice Grenson was slowly moving, moans of pain coming from his lips. With great effort, the High-Mage crossed the room, almost stumbling, and lent a hand to his friend. Grenson stood, wiping his mouth, as blood coursed down his chin, staining his beard, from having bitten his tongue so hard.

"What was that?" Grenson asked feebly, shaking the disorientation from his head.

Sultain looked him in the eye until he was sure Grenson would understand him clearly. "That, my dear friend, was one of the Arnen."

The sun was finally rising in the sky, and its warmth shook off the chill of the forest air. Khan was walking not far from the Gregus, upriver, looking hesitantly and sometimes expectantly at the forest just to his right. He refused to walk within the trees, though occasionally he had to cross several that reached to the very riverbank itself. He stayed close to the shore and watched his step gingerly. As predicted, his clothes were damp, but not wet, and with the Talaman only starting to wane, he was still warm and bundled his cloak around his waist, preferring to walk in his trousers and tunic only.

He could not shake the feeling that he was being watched. It was unnerving to him, and he oftentimes looked across the river, behind him, or into the trees to his right, but always he kept moving north. It was during one of his scans that he noticed the first Kesh body all the way across the river. The body, dressed in black leathers, was floating face down near the far shore, apparently stuck on something as it twirled and bobbed around a central point. Not that he knew every brigand in his old company, but even if he did, there was no way to make out who it was lying facedown.

About another mile upstream, he came across some packs and gear that had washed ashore. He rummaged about and managed to secure some dry beef and an empty canteen. The pack stayed afloat as it carried a few empty flasks that gave it some buoyancy. He moved on further with apprehension, not knowing what he was likely to find. Much to his surprise, he happened finally onto a small group of brigands. Three in total, two quite dead and the third barely breathing, but this one he recognized. It was Dorsun, who was on the lead raft when they had crossed, but now he was sitting with his back to a boulder facing the river. The other two lay near the water, one face up, the other facedown, arrows and bolts sticking from their torsos. Dorsun had a nasty arrow still sticking from his abdomen and several bloody cuts and bruises along his knuckles and hands as if they were sliced while trying to claw his way out of the raging river. Suddenly, the chieftain's eyelids fluttered open.

"Master?" he said, barely audible as he gasped for air and then was taken by a fit of coughing.

"I am here, Dorsun. Can you hear me?" Khan asked, as Dorsun's eyelids had just as quickly fluttered shut again.

"You live," Dorsun gasped, spitting blood onto his lips. "Did you kill them?"

Khan was surprised to find anyone alive, but also elated that he was not alone. Quickly, that feeling left him as it dawned on him Ke-Tor had marked him for elimination. He didn't think Dorsun could know anything of the matter that had transpired after Dorsun was injured, but he also felt suspicion creep into his mind. Dorsun was a lieutenant of the Bloody Hand Company, and the actual leader of half the patrols he had led to, what appeared to be, their doom at the hands of a wild bear and Ulathan rebels. Khan thought carefully before speaking. "No, Dorsun. Most of the Ulathans escaped, and we lost most of our company. We are scattered and lost. Whom do you serve?" Khan asked the last question quite pointedly.

Dorsun appeared to be more alive than Khan first thought as the brigand's eyes opened wide and a frown came across his face, followed by a grimace of pain, before the man finally spoke. "I serve Kesh, Master . . . and you."

Khan thought for a moment and then stood and took a stride over to the dead corpse of one of the other brigands, pulling a dagger from his belt as he did so. Turning to face Dorsun, he squatted next to the large brigand who was wheezing laboriously. Khan held the dagger across the other man's throat. It would be a mercy to kill him now, to relieve the man from his pain. To Dorsun's credit, the man held still, and despite his weakened state, he looked Khan right in the eyes. "If you had to make a choice, Dorsun, between serving Kesh or serving me, what would you decide?" Khan didn't think this was a very fair question considering the other man's circumstances, but he needed to make a decision soon.

"I serve you both," Dorsun finally said softly, trying hard not to start another spasm of coughing, which was no doubt painful. "I serve you, Master, and you serve Kesh."

Khan steeled himself for what was to come next. "I no longer serve Kesh, Dorsun. Do you understand me? I serve only myself." Khan paused to allow his comments to sink in and give Dorsun the dignity to respond. He fully expected the man to reject this notion of a rogue wizard repudiating his own order, the most powerful order in all of Agon. No, better to be dead than to be a renegade hunted by wizards and Arch-Mages.

Dorsun attempted to look around at his surroundings. Khan thought that maybe the man saw the questioning as a trap. When he did answer, Khan was slightly surprised. "Do with me as you will, Master, but if allowed, I will serve Khan, not Kesh."

Khan looked intently at the man for any signs of sarcasm or deceit. He remembered the man's concerns about raiding in the Earlstyne Forest, and he knew Dorsun was a veteran of many campaigns and raids and had managed to survive them all. Dorsun's life hung in the balance, and it could teeter in either direction. Finally, and mostly due in large part to the merciful side of Khan, the blade was tucked into the wizard's belt and Khan pulled one of his blue orbs from his necklace, leaving a lone Talaman hanging there. He gently placed the small pearl-like pill to Dorsun's lips. "Swallow this, quickly!" Khan ordered.

Dorsun took the small orb and swallowed it, which brought on another fit of coughing, and Khan saw the man grimace in pain. Khan did not know how far gone Dorsun was, but he hoped the Talaman would save his life. Khan stood for a long while and waited patiently but alertly as his eyes darted to and fro, spending most of their time on the forest and keeping a watch on Dorsun. Soon, Dorsun began to respond, moving a bit, and the fits of coughing died off. Khan saw the color start to return to the man's face. "This is going to hurt. Try not to scream," Khan stated, leaning over and grabbing the arrow shaft in his right hand while pushing on the man's abdomen with his left.

"Argh." Dorsun stifled the words as he brought his leather-clad arm up to his mouth. The arrow came out with a pulse of bright red blood, and Khan quickly grabbed a strip of cloth from his cloak's hem and placed it over the brigand's wound.

"Hold this," Khan said, and Dorsun put pressure on his own wound to staunch the bleeding. Khan left the man where he lay and proceeded to drag the bodies of the other two brigands over to the flattest spot he could find near the river. Khan wasn't overly joyed at his task, but he searched the bodies of the two, and, retrieving what he could that was beneficial, he started to collect large rocks and lay them over the bodies, creating a cairn.

When he had finished, he started to feel the exertion of his efforts. It would be midday soon, and his Talaman was quickly wearing off. Before the effects left him completely, he wanted to finish the most strenuous of his work. He gathered what wood he could, though nothing was completely dry, and started a small fire at the edge of the forest not far from where Dorsun rested. He used a small amount of black oil and one of the brigand's flint sticks to ignite it. Sure that it would not go out, Khan walked over to where Dorsun sat almost in a state of sleep except for the fact that the man opened his eyes without moving any part of his body and just looked at Khan.

"Come on, man. Up you go," Khan said, offering a hand.

Dorsun took Khan's arm, hands grasping each other's elbows, and Khan hefted the man onto his feet, escorting him over to the small fire and setting him back-first against the nearest tree to the fire. Dorsun looked up at Khan, weak but obviously feeling better from the smaller dose of the Talaman that had been given to him. "Thank you, Master."

"Please, from now on I go by my name only. Agreed?" Khan replied, wrapping his own cloak around Dorsun's shoulders.

"Agreed . . . Khan," Dorsun said unfamiliarly, trying the moniker on for size, so to speak. "Why did you help me?"

Khan looked at the freshly made cairn where two of his brigands lay never to see the dragon's fire again. Finally, Khan looked back to Dorsun intently and sighed before speaking. "Frankly, it was still a selfish act. I am alone, and my own mentor turned on me." This got a look of surprise from Dorsun's face as the news sunk in to the brigand lieutenant. "We have somewhat of a history together, and I personally chose you to lead my half company as I trusted your expertise and loyalty. Now loyalty can be not only a virtue but a vice as well to me. The only way for me to be accepted back into Kesh society is to kill my master, Ke-Tor. Do you understand my situation?"

Dorsun nodded and looked into the fire. "So the dagger finally came for you . . . Khan."

"Yes, but it was actually a sword. The damn coward couldn't do the deed himself."

"Who?" Dorsun asked, looking at Khan intently.

"He had Gund do it, though for all I know it could have been you. Gund just so happened to be one of the few swords around," Khan stated, looking suspiciously back at Dorsun.

"No, Master . . . uh . . . Khan. I would never do such a deed, though many of us would relish the act. Not for him and not for you. On my word I tell you this. Gund was one of your master's servants, not a true servant of Kesh."

"I believe you," Khan replied, at last the look on his face softening as he looked around the forest, "but nonetheless, a wizard is most vulnerable when alone and unprepared. I now find myself in just such a situation. I need your help, and you can't help me if you die here on the riverbank as your companions did."

Dorsun allowed the words to linger a bit before answering, as if mulling over how to respond. "Khan. You saved my life where most others would have left me to my fate. You know our order best, and the life of a single Kesh is not valued much. I am sure it cost you dearly to use your powers on preserving my life, and for that, I am grateful. I will serve Kesh by serving you."

Khan looked at him intently. "You understand what that means? We are both likely to die soon, anyway, but before we do, I plan on doing as much as I can to make Ke-Tor pay for his betrayal. Things must change. We are too weak to continue this way. Kesh will perish eventually, despite the High-Mage's machinations and plotting against the other realms. I do not know the way, but the events of the last few years, and especially yesterday, have shown me our society and my own order in a new light. I intend to do something about this and am glad to have you with me."

The two men sat in silence and thought upon the events leading to their predicament. Khan had made a fateful decision to save Dorsun, and little did he know, it would change the course of his life forever.

CHAPTER 20

GATHERING

Targon returned much later than he had wanted to. The sun was waning in the west, and he labored under burden. He had managed to kill a buck, and carried it over his shoulders back to his home. He had to travel far, almost to the shadow of the mountains, to find it. He knew a few conies wouldn't feed so many mouths. Finally, after much effort, he arrived through the strange new trees to see the rear of his house. Marissa looked up from the garden area where she was planting something and waved him over.

"Good afternoon, Marissa," Targon said, walking over and setting the buck down on the ground, stretching his arms and rotating his shoulders for good measure.

"Hoi, Master Targon," she said, her mood much alleviated from the morning. "Looks like a mighty fine deer you have there. Is that for us?"

"Of course. Do you know how to skin and butcher an animal?" he asked.

"Not really. My father and brother could skin, and mother oftentimes cut the meat, but I spent more of my time drying the pieces she gave me in our smoke shed."

"Sounds like you know how to preserve the meat, then, and jerk it. I am not sure we will have much left after long, but it's a good skill to have nevertheless. Here, help me carry it 'round to the front, and let's see what the others are up to."

"Yes, and you can talk to Lady Salina, too!" Marissa replied, smiling.

"Is she better, then?" Targon asked.

"Much! She even managed to come out to the porch earlier for some fresh air. She asked about you, you know."

"Really? Well, that is great news. Yes, indeed, let's see how she's doing," Targon replied, thinking he understood the young girl's mood change now that Lady Salina's condition was explained to him.

Soon, they had come around the front, and Targon couldn't say he was surprised to see both little Jons and Horace pointing crossbows at him. Olga and Agatha came out and admired the catch and started at once to hang the buck and get started on the butchering. Targon was invited inside, and everyone was abuzz about the news of Lady Salina's recovery. Targon heard Agatha barking orders to have someone help grab some wood and make poles of them to hang the buck on as he entered the cabin.

"It is good to see you, my lady!" Targon exclaimed, looking her over and seeing Monique was brushing her hair with his mother's crude brush. Apparently, someone had found one of his mother's simple dresses for Salina to wear. The contrast was remarkable compared to her more elegant blue dress she had worn previously. Her garb now was a simple light brown, almost khaki in color, with small, light-colored flowering embroidered here and there on the dress.

Karz sat at his mother's feet and looked up at Targon as he entered the room. Salina did not respond at first, instead standing on her feet, surprising everyone in the room. Celeste rushed to her side, and Monique grabbed the lady's arm to steady her. Salina took a few steps toward

Targon and then embraced him in a long, deep hug. "I heard what you did for me," she practically whispered in his ear.

Targon embraced her in return but released the deep embrace to grab her by her shoulders and lean back so he could see her face clearly. "I did nothing nearly as brave as what you did for us, my lady."

Salina smiled, as she was flanked still by Monique and Celeste, and also held Targon now by his shoulders. "What I did was necessary. My boys were involved, but they both told me how you carried me for nearly half a day and saved my life, and for that, I am most grateful."

Targon somewhat blushed. "In truth, the old man of the forest, Elister is his name, did more for you than I did."

"There would have been nothing for the kind gentleman to do if you hadn't have gotten me here in time. Again, thank you, Targon."

Targon was about to reply when that screeching cat voice was heard from the doorway. "By the daughter's moons of Agon, what are you doing standing there?" Agatha screeched at Salina. "And you, Master Targon, making an ill woman stand to greet you! How rude! Put her down this instant and quit smooching on all the ladies you meet!"

Targon stuttered, seeking a response, and turned a brighter shade of red, but Salina interjected. "Now, Agatha, I stood on my own and embraced my hero. The decision was mine and mine alone, and we were only embracing, no smooching . . . I am a married woman, so how dare you accuse me of smooching!" Salina winked at Targon in mock offense, turning to replace the wink and smile with a scowl as she looked at Agatha intently.

Agatha tried to wave her off as she approached and took Salina's arm, replacing Monique and shooing her back. "Now, my lady, you know I didn't mean you no offense. I was directing my comments at young master Terrel, as he is called around here, and didn't want him smooching and making you stand and all, seeing as you're sick, and were near death not long ago when . . ."

"Enough!" Celeste practically screamed. "Give the lady's ear a rest, will you!" And she started to guide Salina back to her chair. Monique was now smiling and holding her hand across her mouth to hide her giggles while Karz simply didn't care but was beaming from ear to ear just happy to see his mother up and about. Agatha harrumphed and took a deep breath but said nothing and just helped the lady to sit.

"It's good to see you up and about," Targon finally said.

"Good to see you, too," Salina responded. "Again, thank you, and not only for what you did for me, but for allowing all us . . . city folk into your home. We must be a terrible burden for you, especially with your family missing."

Assured that Salina was comfortable and sitting, Agatha gave Targon a swift glance and exited the room to oversee the butchering of the buck. Celeste hesitantly stepped back and sat on a chair near the table while Karz sat at his mother's feet.

"May I continue, my lady?" Monique asked with the brush held over Salina's head.

"Please do, and thanks, I felt like a bird had made a nest in my hair." Salina chuckled. Monique continued to brush her hair, and Celeste spoke softly from her seat. "Yes, Mister Targon. Thank you for taking us in, and I am sure the lady and I speak on everyone's behalf."

Targon waved them off. "This is the least I can do. I wouldn't have it any other way. Speaking of which, has anyone seen the old man? Elister is his name."

"I woke not long after you left, but no, I'm afraid there has been no sign of him yet. I do hope he returns soon, though. I'd like to thank him personally as well, for his aid and kindness in my time of need," Salina said.

"Well, he said it would be a while, so I won't worry till morning, but I agree with you that it would be nice to see him again. I have a few questions of my own to ask him."

"I'm sure you do. We all do," Salina responded with a gleam in her eye. Targon smiled and left the room to wait for the old man's return. *At least we are eating,* he thought to himself. *Oh, and no one has died yet. Not since Sarson in the old crevice.* They may actually live longer than he had hoped. Hope. The one thing he wanted and the one thing they needed. Targon desperately missed his family.

Ke-Tor was tired of riding. Am-Ohkre led them at a blistering pace after losing nearly two days in Korwell, and they had traveled cross country almost due east from the capital. They came across no survivors and were debating on whether to stop and camp for the night or continue on in the darkness. One horse was already limping, having cut its leg on a sharp rock when they had crossed a small brook in haste earlier in the day. Occasionally, Am-Ohkre would stop to peer into his Orb of Seeing, or critir, and adjust their course accordingly.

This was frustrating to know the Arch-Mage could so easily manipulate the orb. It took Ke-Tor considerable effort and time to direct the orb to show him what he wanted to see, and now the Arch-Mage was peering into his critir as if it were some picture window and not a powerful tool of magic. Such was the ease of which Am-Ohkre mastered the orb. Finally, at a suitable place, the Mage ordered them to prepare their camp.

Within an hour, all the tents were set up and the appropriate sentries posted. Ke-Tor was summoned from his own small tent to the larger tent of Am-Ohkre. *Another slight,* thought the wizard.

"Well?" Ke-Tor asked not so kindly after he had entered.

"News . . . or, to be more precise, the lack of news," Am-Ohkre responded, looking up from a small portable table with his critir placed on it, and motioned for Ke-Tor to seat himself on the other only chair opposite the Mage.

"What do you mean?" Ke-Tor asked, sitting and looking suspiciously at Am-Ohkre.

"I mean I have been unable to reach Sultain. It is as if the master orb is not there."

"That is impossible. Am-Sultain is simply ignoring you," Ke-Tor shot back.

Am-Ohkre paused a moment, placing his left hand on the critir and looking piercingly into the other wizard's eyes. "No, not impossible, only implausible. Even if the High-Mage ignored my call, I would be able to see the Chamber of Seeing. Did you not know this?" the Mage asked with an arch of his brows.

Ke-Tor did not like being surprised. He did not know the Mage could actually connect with the master orb. Indeed, what few times Ke-Tor had needed to contact the High-Mage personally, he could never connect on his own, but rather had to wait for a response from the Chamber of Seeing. Either Am-Ohkre was being facetious with him or he was letting slip some key information on his own capabilities, at least as far as they related to manipulating a critir. Ke-Tor decided discretion was the better course. "Of course I knew," Ke-Tor replied, "but I still think Am-Sultain is ignoring you."

"You have not been listening to what I have been saying. I cannot reach the Chamber of Seeing in the Onyx Tower. Either the tower is not there or the master critir is not there. Either way, this does not bode well for Sultain. I am worried."

"You, worried!" Ke-Tor replied, his face showing utter surprise and incredulity. "I find that hard to believe."

Am-Ohkre sighed, much like a parent would to a wayward child. "I am not worried for the High-Mage personally. He can take care of himself. I am, however, worried for what this means for Kesh and our order. This does not bode well for us."

Ke-Tor's eyes narrowed. "What are you suggesting . . . Am-Ohkre?"

"Nothing specific as of yet, but this does show that something is happening in the Onyx Tower, and whether it is benevolent or benign I do not know, and I do not like not knowing," Am-Ohkre finished matter-of-factly.

"So we stay on plan?" Ke-Tor asked expectantly.

"For now, yes. We need to regroup and eliminate any resistance in Ulatha. We can ill afford any more frivolous losses. Any news from your . . . ex-apprentice?"

"No, why? Should there be?" Ke-Tor now asked, more annoyed, as the question itself was disturbing to him. Did the Mage know something about Khan that he did not?

"Just asking. I always thought the young man rather resourceful, if not just disrespectful. Cheeky sort of chap, but still a shame . . . his fate, I mean."

Ke-Tor disliked, and even distrusted, the emotions and even the sympathies the Mage was giving to his apprentice. Ex-apprentice, he had to remind himself. "He failed me and he failed Kesh. Lost the better part of the Bloody Hand Company and almost lost Korwell, if not for our intervention. He was incompetent, insubordinate, and . . . and . . ." Ke-Tor's face contorted, anger crossing his brow as he attempted to spit out his next words. "And yes . . . too cheeky for one of our order. He did not know his place. Zorcross will replace him and do a better job . . . I am sure of it."

Am-Ohkre sat back in his rickety portable chair, taking his hand off of the critir where it had lay. He rubbed his beard on his chin and placed his hands in his lap. Ke-Tor could see the faint outline of a smile barely visible dancing across his mouth, and it was most disturbing. Finally, Am-Ohkre spoke. "I am sure Zorcross will do fine, but it will take some time for him to arrive, and that is a shame. Very well, we are done here. Return to your tent and prepare. We leave early tomorrow. There is something odd happening in the Earlstyne, and we must be rested and ready."

Ke-Tor stood, staring at the Mage, not concealing very well his contempt. To be summoned and then dismissed like a mere apprentice was humiliating to him. He said nothing and returned to his lodging and prepared to sleep. He set a spell around his tent first, however, never trusting one of his fellow Kesh to protect him, and slept fitfully for the remainder of the night.

Targon was happy to see the old man when he finally showed up after dark. The butchering of the buck was done, and most of the meat was being cooked as they had no plans to preserve it for later. The garden was large and ignored by the brigands. They took what was already harvested or stored, and it was obvious they were pillagers, not gardeners. They would not crawl on their hands and knees to pull roots from the ground, and for that, Targon was thankful.

Agatha had resumed her charge of the others as she organized them into a self-contained group. Each was assigned with a task, and any laziness or slothfulness was not tolerated and was quickly remarked on by her sharp tongue and acidic remarks. Only Targon, who had permitted them to stay in his home and who had provided the buck after hunting all day, and Lady Salina were spared her barbs and criticisms. Even Will was called an "old loaf" when she caught him lounging around too much, despite the fact that his arm wasn't healed fully.

The meeting between Elister and Lady Salina was brief and cordial but warm. She embraced him and thanked him profusely, but Elister just seemed to be more embarrassed at all the attention he was receiving and was quite taken aback when Karz hugged his legs and almost started to cry. Elister simply waved them off and said it was the least he could do, and very quickly, he exited the cabin after the formalities were finished.

The others remained inside, bundled against the cool air of the evening, and Elister preferred to sit on the front porch now with Targon,

but this time, Cedric joined them as well after the impromptu meeting that had been arranged. Horace had returned to his perch at the end of the porch with his crossbow. He remained away a short distance from the three companions and resumed his silent vigil on the small home-stead and cabin.

"You seem upset," Targon remarked when they had all seated them-selves on the porch using old tree stumps as stools. Elister had pulled a leather bag from his robe and lit up a long wooden pipe using some tobacco from the pouch. His pipe glowed red, and deep dark puffs of grey smoke blew out from his lips as he settled in.

"There is nothing like Southern Safron in one's pipe. Good and hearty, gives a man's senses a kick, you know?" the old man said in reference to his weed.

"I didn't know you smoked," Targon said, smiling at the druid.

"Well, the weed I had was all dried out and stale. You know, several decades of storage will do that, so I was fortunate to find this little stash."

Where did you get it from?" Cedric chimed in, seemingly happy to be taking in on the adult conversation and happy to be away from the women and ladies, especially Agatha.

"Took it from one of the brigands, you know?" Elister responded with a look over at Cedric. "I didn't steal it, if that is what your look means. The poor man was asleep and wasn't going to need it for a very long time, so I sort of borrowed it. He can stop by anytime, and I'll happily replace it for him if he so desires."

"Sleep?" Cedric asked, a look of confusion on his face.

"It's a long story, Cedric," Targon said. "I'll explain later. I need to know if we're safe here or not. I mean, I appreciate all your help and what you did for Lady Salina"—at this Cedric nodded vigorously in agree-ment—"but we need to plan for the near future."

"Well, I think not," Elister finally said after a good long pull on his pipe. "I'm afraid I went and did something rather rash."

Targon felt uneasy but had to ask. "What exactly do you mean by rash? Are we in danger?"

"Well, with the Kesh nearby, you are always in danger, but I fear I have alerted their pesky leader to my presence."

"And how does that affect us?" Targon asked hesitantly.

"Well, I broke their little peeping glass, nasty intrusive device that it was, but they will probably repair it in time. Till then, however, I fear they have a better understanding of the forest and most likely will come here sooner or later," Elister said, pausing to take another drag on his pipe.

"Is there anything we can do?" Targon asked.

"Well, there are many things one can do, but not all things are good to do. Doing the wrong thing, or even the right thing hastily, can turn out all wrong for the doer. I must give this some thought first. Oh, I learned Core is alive and doing well, but he was hurt a bit."

"You mean that big bear?" Cedric asked in awe.

"Yes, the bear, young man. It seems he was hurt by the Kesh, and that really upset him. He won't return till his anger subsides, and he appears to be killing any of the poor brigands he comes across."

"How did you learn this?" Targon asked, amazed at how the old man seemed to know more about the happenings in and around the forest than he did or more than any human should have known.

"Well, I was fortunate this afternoon and Argyll showed up to tell me. He spotted Core as well as a few brigand survivors on both shores of the Gregus . . . er, I mean the Rapid River. I sent him to keep a watch for us and on Core." Another drag and puff and the slowly stirring night air whisked the smoke away and down the porch toward Horace, who was waving his hand around, dissipating the offending smoke.

Targon thought for a moment and pondered the news. It appeared, if the old man and his crazy animal friends were correct, that the Kesh were all either dead or routed. He was sure there were survivors, as he re-

membered seeing at least one raft make it back to shore, but he couldn't know for sure how many were there.

Cedric ran into the cabin for a moment and returned with his red leather-bound book and a candle. "Hold this," he asked Targon, giving him the candle and opening his book, looking for something. Finally, he held the book near the candle and started reading:

"The Magocracy always took the form of a triumvirate, the Mage, the wizard, and the apprentice, and the three were always bound by three to form the nine, which formed the basis for Kesh society."

Cedric cleared his throat and tilted the book to glean a bit more light.

"Always, the nine were led by the one. The one formed the ultimate representation of Kesh power and authority. To kill the one was to destroy the nine."

"What in the blazes are you reading?" Targon asked, admiring the book, though it looked old and fragile and Cedric always kept it covered in a black cloth, wrapped and tied securely when he wasn't using it.

"This is one of the few books of history that I could find in the old library. It was written by the ancient historian Diamedes a long time ago, but I'm not sure when. It says much about Kesh, and, of course, Ulatha, but more about how it was than now. I'm sorry, but I find it quite interesting."

"Excellent, young man!" Elister said, smiling, removing his pipe to speak. "It is most refreshing to see one remember his elders. Have you read the whole book?"

Cedric smiled at the praise from the old man. "Yes, twice at least, but the pages are starting to rot, and I fear the book won't last much more use. I'd like to transcribe it to preserve its history."

"What does *transcribe* mean?" asked Targon, somewhat embarrassed at his lack of vocabulary in front of Elister.

"He means to copy the book, Master Terrel. He is a scholarly man and a gentleman. Very good, indeed! Can you read, Master Terrel?"

Targon felt the looks from Cedric and Elister, and even imagined old man Horace may have perked up at the question. "Well, yes, my mother taught me to read, but perhaps, not so well as Cedric."

"Good for you! You'll make a fine Zashitor if you're educated in your letters as well," Elister said, putting the pipe back in his mouth, clapping his hands together in delight.

Just then, Horace whirled and aimed the crossbow into the dark. There was a flurry of noise as a large bird flew in, flapping its wings violently and arresting its dive from the sky, finally coming to perch on the crude tripod of wooden poles that had been constructed nearby to hang the buck Targon had hunted. The bird gave them no notice and started to peck at the meat of a hind leg that remained hanging as remains to be discarded.

"Argyll, my friend," Elister said, standing and walking over to the bird. "So good to see you again so soon."

The bird finished picking at some meat and started to screech, bringing a feeling of dread and suspense to Targon, who also walked over with Elister but stayed behind the old man. He was joined by Cedric while Horace remained on the porch, and the door opened with Will standing there holding his broadsword menacingly.

"What did you say?" Elister asked, cocking his head and waving his hand behind him to keep his companions hushed so he could hear. "Where were they? Ah, yes, I know the place. How many were there? Hmm, not so many as last time, yes." At this, the old man gently started to stroke the bird's head and neck. "Go on . . . yes, I see. Good. You will? Thank you, Argyll. We will meet you at the killing shed near the river come the morrow. You, too, thank you." And gently, the man pulled his hand from the bird, and it departed, taking flight just as quickly as it arrived. There was, for a moment, utter silence broken only by two words from Horace.

"Bloody hell!"

The night quickly came, and Khan looked over at Dorsun as he seemed to finally stir a bit, opening his eyes. They had spent most of the day allowing the injured man to rest and the weaker Talaman to make its effects felt. During the day, his own Talaman faded away, and the chill of the air was almost welcome. Khan felt the burning subside and his body return somewhat to normal, if not sore. The only real thing he saw halfway through the dull, boring day was another body of one of the Kesh brigands facedown as it floated down the river and out of sight. He thought it must have gotten caught on something upstream and finally dislodged, though he did not see any arrows or bolts sticking from it.

The entire day was filled with dread for Khan. He imagined more than once the rustling of the bear as it approached the campsite. Khan wasn't stupid, however, and sat cross-legged facing the forest while Dorsun's back was against the tree he was facing and much closer to the bear should it arrive from that direction. Always, Khan kept the river in his mind. It had nearly killed him once but had saved him twice. "How do you feel?" Khan asked his companion when the man finally looked at him.

Dorsun winced but nodded. "Better, Mas—Khan. What was it you gave me?"

Khan touched the last remaining blue Talaman around his neck. "Do you recognize this?" he asked, and Dorsun nodded in the affirmative. "I gave you one of my weaker Talamans. I had to use the greater one on myself as I was at death's door not long ago."

"Those are very expensive and very rare, Master," Dorsun said, forgetting to call Khan by his name, habit being much too powerful for the elder brigand. "They are not lightly wasted on a lone soldier of Kesh."

"Just Khan, please, and, yes, they are a bit pricey even when you can obtain them. Unfortunately, I only had three of them, two lesser and one more potent. The important thing is they worked. We both live, if not pleasantly, and we still breath, and any breath for a dead man is a good breath. I had hoped it would do more for you, but you still seem to be in some pain. Can you fight?"

Dorsun suddenly stood up and attempted to suppress a grimace of pain. He kept one hand on his abdomen as if supporting himself, and he took a few steps over to the small pile of items Khan had scavenged from the other two dead brigands. Dorsun had lost his spear in the river, but he took a nicely sized rapier and hefted it in his right hand, swinging it back and forth and making two quick thrusts into the air at the river. Finally, he lowered the blade point end into the ground and lightly leaned on it. "This old dog still has some bite left in him, Master."

Khan stood, partly happy Dorsun showed some major signs of life despite the pain, and partly because, well . . . Dorsun was showing signs of life and he was now armed. Khan thought for a moment that putting the blade to the veteran's throat may have been a bit too melodramatic, but Dorsun seemed to have forgotten the act.

"Good. You seem more than capable, Dorsun," Khan said as the moonlights reflected off the long slender metal of the blade. "More rest, however, is needed. We will head north at dawn and see what remains of our company. I need my staff, however, and we must retrieve what we can from my pack. There are items in it that are necessary for our future." Khan was glad to have Dorsun with him and not against, as the Kesh chieftain looked rather wicked and most deadly swinging the rapier a few more times. The firelight cast illumination on his mostly black-clad frame, and the blade twinkled between the light of the fire and the light illuminated by the twin moons overhead.

Dorsun walked over to the tree and planted the blade deep into the grassy soil so that it stood upright on its own, and with some effort, he sat down with his back against the tree, gingerly touching his abdomen. "I feel pain still, but nothing I can't handle. I think I will be fine by morning

to travel, but what then? What do you plan to do when you have your staff, Master?"

Khan gave up trying to get Dorsun to call him by his familiar name. Perhaps better to let the man continue to know his place by using the moniker of respect. "I do not know yet, but if I can obtain my critir . . . you know, the Orb of Seeing my kind uses?" Dorsun nodded affirmatively. "Well, if I can secure that, then I will use it to plan our next actions. We lost an entire day today, and I worry another brigand, or worse, an Ulathan, will stumble across them if Gund did not carry them off already."

"Do you think he did that?"

"Doubtful. I did not see his demise, but I heard the bear and I heard his scream. I do not think Gund survived nor his other two companions. I can only hope, however, that my possessions do not draw the attention of any of our enemies."

"I feel warm," Dorsun said.

"It's the Talaman. It will do that for a day while you heal," Khan said, folding his arms.

Dorsun stood and took off Khan's cloak that he had worn all day, draping it over Khan's shoulders, surprising him. He then walked over to the supplies, which included the cloaks of the dead brigands, and grabbed both and then hung them over the nearest branch. Dorsun then rummaged through a pack and found some dry beef and split it in half, offering one piece to Khan, who took it and started to eat. Dorsun took a bite and sat back down. "Leave the provisioning to me, Master. You took watch all day, so I will watch tonight. Get some rest, and I'll wake you before dawn."

It was getting late and Khan yawned, agreeing with a nod of his head. He curled the cloak around him and laid his head on his makeshift pack that he had taken earlier in the day, and used his arm to cushion his head like a pillow. "The bear is still loose, Dorsun. I seriously doubt that blade of yours would do much more than anger it, so if you even think you hear it, wake me and we run for the river."

Dorsun smiled and nodded in agreement and then looked around before grabbing the rapier and laying it across his lap as he took another chew on the dry beef. Khan closed his eyes and listened intently for any sound that the brigand chieftain would stand and try to kill him. The image of Gund leering as he stabbed at him with his short sword filled his mind, and he chilled at the thought of how simple it would be to kill someone such as himself.

He realized there was a greater need for trust and loyalty if one were to survive, a lesson he did not truly understand before now. Finally, thinking on this, he let his guard down and decided that one way or the other, he had to trust Dorsun with his life. Either tonight or in a future battle or situation, the time would come sooner or later where the man he had just saved could turn on him. Better to find out now and let it happen then to worry every night and at every encounter for Dorsun's rapier to pierce his body. Having made the decision, Khan quickly fell asleep.

CHAPTER 21

REGROUP

Many of the refugees gathered outside to discuss the old man's strange behavior, while a few of the ladies stayed indoors out of the chill night air as the sister moons wheeled and danced overhead.

"Talk, I said. The man was having a talk with that bird!" Horace was relating to several of his companions in astonishment.

"Falcon, actually," Elister chimed in from a short distance away while he waited patiently for the group to come to some type of a conclusion.

"I saw it happening, I did!" Will added, nodding in agreement with Horace.

Agatha was with the group and eying both men with a healthy dose of skepticism, and then scrutinized Elister. "Sounds like more of that magical mischief, if you ask me. He even looks like one of them there sorcerers with his staff and hood and all."

"Come on, I'm not even sure you would know what a sorcerer would look like," Olga chirped back, drying her wet hands on a rag she was carrying.

"Quiet! All of you," Targon exclaimed loudly, holding up both his hands to the small group that had gathered around him. Once sure that he had their attention, he cleared his throat and spoke somewhat formally. "I think it best to allow Elister a chance to explain what is happening right now. Elister, if you don't mind, please," Targon said, stepping back a bit and motioning with one of his hands for the old man to join them.

Elister sighed and then took a big drag on his pipe before walking over and removing it from his mouth. "Now calm down, everyone. I find it hard to believe I am the cause of all this commotion. There is nothing to worry about. Argyll . . . theeee biiiiiird . . ."—he said this with a long tone rather creepily as if accentuating the vowels of each word—"has simply informed us of another group of guests that appear to be not so kind, if I may say so myself. They will be at the edge of the Gregus . . . Rapid River by evening tomorrow." There was a long pause of silence as everyone waited for Elister to finish. Not seeing any questions forthcoming, he continued. "There appears to be two of those sooorceeeereers with them," he said, again stretching out the word for emphasis so the city folk could understand.

After a pause, there was much discussion between the various companions until finally Agatha hushed everyone and looked at Elister. "So what does this mean for us, Mister Elister? Are we in danger? Must we leave?" There were more murmurings about this and many comments made about having just arrived from their long trek in the wilderness, and quite frankly, Targon felt it all a bit melodramatic, but then Elister answered.

"Well, I think most of you will be fine, but I don't think it wise to allow them to cross the river. One of them I know, and he is most unpleasant and would simply make a mess of our fine forest. I'll need some help, however, if we are to deter them from being our guests."

"Why is the old man always referring to the brigands as guests?" Marissa asked, tugging on Targon's tunic to get his attention.

"It's a long story, Marissa," Targon said to her, and then he turned to Elister. "What kind of help do you need?"

"Well, there are less than two dozen of them, and I need to keep them away so I can have a nice chat with this unpleasant fellow, perhaps even a bit of privacy?"

"Fine, I'll see to it. When do we need to go?" Targon asked.

"Tomorrow morning before noon would be fine," Elister responded. "They have an entire day to travel yet, and we have only a half day. If they stay on course, they should actually arrive at the same camp where the other brigands set up on holiday. We can meet them there."

"Holiday!" Horace asked, looking incredulous.

"Not now, my love," Emelda said, pulling on Horace's arm. "Come with me, sit, and let me fetch you some tea."

Horace wanted to wave her off but allowed himself to be guided back to the porch, and sat down while Emelda went into the cabin to fetch some tea. Horace kept the crossbow, however, at the ready in his right hand, leaning it against his shoulder for good measure.

"Elister, we will leave with you just before noon, then. We will discuss who we want to go and let you know. Will you stay with us?" Targon asked, his tone sincere.

Elister took a long breath on his pipe and then nodded. "Yes, I think I will, but I'll stay here on the porch tonight. It is a fine evening for the pipe, and the air is clean and fresh, brisk but not too cold."

"Good, then, it's settled. All right, everyone, let's get inside and discuss who will accompany the old man . . . Elister tomorrow," Targon said, motioning for everyone to enter the cabin. Even Horace joined them despite the crossbow and lack of tea, leaving Elister alone on the front porch.

Once everyone was in the common room of the cabin with Jons, Karz, and even Thomas up in the loft, Targon relayed everything to Salina,

Celeste, and the others that had remained inside. Emelda had brought tea to Horace and was offering to make some for anyone else that wanted it, but most seemed uninterested, as if a great burden was back on their shoulders again.

"Is this another fight, then?" Will asked after plopping down on a chair at the lone table in the room, sighing as he finished his sentence.

"It certainly sounds like one," Agatha piped in. "I don't think the lady has the strength to wield a blade again."

This brought many conversations again, with Cedric the loudest, insisting his mother stay at the cabin. Targon hushed them before speaking. "I think no one decides for another. We all decide for ourselves. Agreed?" Everyone nodded in the affirmative. "All right then, I will be the first to decide and declare that I will go with the old man."

There were several nods of approving and murmurings of agreement. Targon now appeared to the refugee group as the most capable, strongest fighter and defender they had. It seemed almost taken for granted he would go.

"I will go as well," Lady Salina said from her seat near the hearth, and looked around. This was immediately followed by more yelling and shouts, but this time of disapproval. There was some arguing amongst each other, but Agatha's voice, as usual, rose above the din.

"Holy mother of Agon, my lady! It's the fever, I tell you! The fever is making you delirious. You don't know your own mind! Once is enough, my lady, please, I beg of you!" And with that, Agatha took a knee and grabbed Salina's hand in her own and gave her an imploring look.

Cedric also walked over and squatted beside her. "Mother, you can't. Who will look after Karz?" There were several nods of agreement before Will silenced everyone.

"Quiet now! Let the lady choose for herself, as Targon said." Will motioned around at everyone. "Take a seat!"

Several of the group sat back down, Will's booming voice commanding respect, and then Salina spoke again. "All right, everyone. I didn't know you all felt so deeply about my safety, and for that, I am most grateful. If it will appease everyone, then, I will stay and help look after the children, for in this they do not have a choice, but rather must stay here. That I think we can agree upon?"

"Yes!" Agatha said, standing and looking around. "Karz, Amy, Jons, and where is that girl . . . there, Marissa, and yes, you, too, Monique, you all stay safe here. Much too young to be outdoors this time of year anyway!"

"I'll go if I want to!" Marissa shot back, standing from her seated position. "You can't tell me what to do, old lady!"

There was a gasp and a few chuckles as Agatha's face contorted and turned a bright shade of red. "Who are you calling—"

Salina cut her off. "Now, now, both of you, please! This is neither the time nor place for bickering. Now, come, child," Salina said, waving for Marissa to step over to her. "Tell us why you wish to fight. Would you not feel safer here, with us?"

Targon was impressed with how calmly Lady Salina conducted herself. He thought he saw real leadership there, not like the kind they thought he had. *I have a lot to learn*, he thought to himself as he listened to Marissa's reply. "I want to find my family. They killed my papa and took my mother and brother."

"That is a very noble idea, Marissa, and I can understand you completely. What would I tell your family, however, if they returned and you weren't there? Can you understand the situation from their point of view? It's your decision and none of us will stop you, but you've been such a great help to us city folk, and we are so thankful to have you and your help. Will you not stay to help us further? I will stay if you stay."

Everyone fell silent for a moment, and Targon thought he saw Marissa's lips just ever so faintly curl up into the beginnings of a smile. "Agreed, Lady Salina. I will stay if you stay, then."

Targon sighed, as did several others. The room was quiet for only a second before Emelda spoke. "Oh no, not again, Horace! You just stay there in that seat and quit thinking you're thirty years younger!"

"Ah, your old coot has a death wish, Emelda. Best to just let 'em be! Besides, he is one of the only few men we have, anyway, so better if he went."

"You're damn right, Agatha," Horace piped in, hefting his bow in his arm for emphasis. "Master Targon, count me in."

"Me, too. I can't let a grandfather outfight me, and I've done enough sitting and running as it is for a soldier." Will smiled.

Emelda frowned at Agatha and then sighed and continued to pour hot water into several cups that remained. Cedric stood from his squat where he had been looking at his mother and listening to their conversation. "Well, I will represent my family," he said.

"That makes four of us: that should be enough," Targon remarked quickly, hoping to silence anyone else who thought of volunteering. He had quickly changed his mind about this idea of volunteering after having Marissa declare her intent. *Again*, he thought, *I wasn't thinking well about the words I said.* A real leader would have grasped that. It seemed a good idea when he said it, but now he was regretting it.

"The rest of us shall stay here, then, by your leave, Master Targon," Salina said, pulling Marissa to sit on her lap and stroking her hair. "We will wait for you."

Targon nodded, wondering if Salina was thinking much the same as he was. He was glad Thomas and Jons had kept quiet. Perhaps the sight of Lady Salina, all bloodied, pale, and close to death, may have tempered

their rambunctious spirits, as they wisely remained silent in the loft, though he was sure they were listening. "Fine, then, we are in agreement. Will, Cedric, Horace, and I will accompany the old man tomorrow and see what we can do to keep those brigands at bay."

Everyone nodded in agreement, and they broke up into smaller groups, interacting and discussing things with one another and preparing for sleep. Targon looked around at his home a moment longer and sighed heavily before exiting the room to inform Elister. It looked like the bloodletting would never end.

Morning rose quickly after the twin sisters had set, and the brigand camp was alive with activity. Ke-Tor fumed, as usual, astride his mount as he waited for Am-Ohkre to finish discussing minor details with Arkhale, the lieutenant who had accompanied them from Korwell since Hork had been assigned to oversee the defenses of Korwell in their absence.

Soon, they were mounted and riding quickly overland, passing several copses of trees that gave Ke-Tor a creepy feeling. *No doubt the remnants of that accursed Earlstyne Forest,* he thought to himself. At one point, their scout and tracker dismounted to check some tracks and found some blood on the ground and on a few leaves.

"Fresh?" Arkhale asked.

"No, more than a day old," replied the tracker, looking up at his leader.

Am-Ohkre nodded but said nothing, and Arkhale motioned for the scout to remount and continue on. They stopped once for lunch, nothing extravagant. There was a small pond that had collected rainwater, and they allowed their mounts to drink. Finally, as the day drew to a close but before sunset, they could hear the Gregus River's roar in the near distance. Am-Ohkre had only used his critir twice that day and didn't pull it out yet.

Ke-Tor was somewhat jealous at the silent rapport Am-Ohkre had with the brigands. He spent entirely too much time with them and was much too comfortable around them. Ke-Tor had to watch as silently, the Arch-Mage motioned with his hands and the brigands moved out single file with weapons pulled or drawn.

"What are we doing?" Ke-Tor hissed at Am-Ohkre as they moved toward the river spread out like a skirmish line armed and ready for battle.

Am-Ohkre frowned at the man. "You spend too much time in your books and scrolls, Ke-Tor. Have you not been paying attention?" When Ke-Tor just looked more confused and said nothing, the Arch-Mage continued. "The scout heard voices up ahead near the river. We approach to engage in case they are the Ulathans."

Ke-Tor nodded but wondered at how he was supposed to have gleaned all that just by the hand signals they were passing with one another. *Yet another reason*, he thought to himself, *to hate the Arch-Mage more intently.*

Within minutes, the lead scout put his hand up in a fist and then lowered it. "Hoi, all clear!" he shouted back, and then he disappeared over the crest of a small ridge. Soon, they had all gathered along the shore of the Gregus River, and Ke-Tor noticed, with some ill contempt, they had literally approached the old brigand camp from exactly behind it. Another slight? Another way to show Am-Ohkre's superiority over his junior? Ke-Tor fumed but was impressed nonetheless.

"Well met," Arkhale said to a slightly taller and leaner brigand who had blood stains on his leathers and looked tired and more than slightly disheveled.

"I am Ropes," said the lean man, taking Arkhale's arm hand to elbow in the traditional Kesh greeting.

Arkhale released the man and looked around. A few small tents were set up in an area that was much larger and could have handled many

more, though there were no signs of other Kesh. A quick count showed seven other Kesh in black leathers besides Ropes. "What news, Ropes? Where is Dorsun?"

There were looks around, especially amongst the Kesh survivors they had stumbled upon. It was understood that in the presence of a wizard, one did not ask for a Kesh lieutenant or even a chieftain like Dorsun. Though they did not know it, they understood implicitly that something unpleasant had happened to the young wizard. "We were ambushed, we were, by those Ulathan scum." And with this, Ropes spat on the ground, a bit of blood mixed in with his spittle. "We lost three of our four patrols either to their arrows or the river or . . ." At this, the man hesitated and looked around as if seeking some sort of approval or confirmation from his comrades and then finally said, "The bear."

Ke-Tor looked at Am-Ohkre and then at their men. The other seven troopers were nodding in agreement while most of the newcomers seemed to be shaking their heads in disapproval or even disbelief, but it was Am-Ohkre's response that was the strangest. "A large wild bear that acted less wild and more purposeful?"

There was a pause, and no one spoke till Arkhale nudged Ropes, who seemed entranced at the Mage's words. "Yes, Master, exactly, but how could you know?"

"About the wild animal I know nothing, but about the Arnen I know much. It is just as I feared. Sultain may be correct in his assessment. Arkhale, set up camp here and post double sentries and send scouts both upriver and down. Tell your men to stay armed and alert. The Arnen and his ilk are not so far off. I can . . . sense them near."

The words of the Mage quickly took effect and, falling in with their new masters, the brigand group went about setting up camp in the rays of the setting sun. Ke-Tor waited impatiently for his tent to be set second, again behind the Mage's tent, and then watched as Arkhale and Am-Ohkre listened to a full accounting of the events of the past several days.

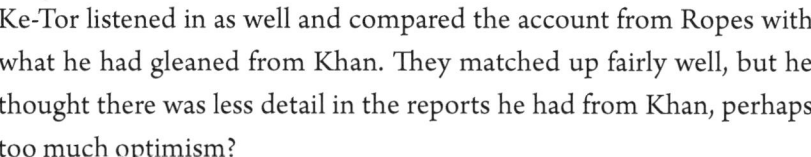
Ke-Tor listened in as well and compared the account from Ropes with what he had gleaned from Khan. They matched up fairly well, but he thought there was less detail in the reports he had from Khan, perhaps too much optimism?

Ke-Tor looked around at the entire area. The Earlstyne was clearly visible across the river, and it now took a much more sinister visage to his eyes as he looked at it warily. From everything he had heard, they were dealing with much more than simple Ulathan farmers and peasants. Someone had clearly underestimated the enemy, and he was sure there was going to be hell to pay.

Khan had woken well before dawn and was relieved to see Dorsun sitting silently, looking out over the river and keeping watch, rapier in his hands sitting across his lap. Dorsun had commented on just how alert he was feeling, and Khan attributed that to the Talaman he had taken.

Soon, when dawn had come, they broke their small camp and headed north. The terrain was not familiar to either of them. "The river is powerful, Master. It must have taken us far downstream," Dorsun said as they picked their step amongst the roots near the riverbank.

Dorsun had complained once about walking so close to the river, but after a detailed telling of the wild bear and how it had attacked them, Dorsun now seemed amenable to going slower if it kept the forest a bit farther away from them.

After several hours and a small provision break, Khan saw the area looked vaguely familiar and motioned for Dorsun to stop. "I think the bear attacked us just past those trees ahead." And he motioned to where he was looking. Dorsun nodded, drawing his sword from his belt and walking forward slowly, listening intently for any sign of noise.

It took them nearly ten more minutes to reach the trees and pass through them when they came upon a small clearing on a jut of land and

rock that had sprawled out into the river. The deep black pools of dried blood and parts of rotting human flesh demonstrated that this was the same place Khan had come ashore earlier. Khan felt the hope leave his body, however, as he ran over to the exact same place where he last saw his orb and staff. There was nothing near other than a large mass of dried blood where Gund had stood not more than two days earlier.

"What is it, Master?" Dorsun asked, looking around in apprehension.

"My possessions are gone. They were last here, but now I don't see them. I am defenseless without them." Khan slumped to the ground and covered his eyes with his arms and hands. He felt hopeless and vulnerable without his staff, and it would take months to fashion a new one, if that was even possible. A wizard put a lot of his soul into his staff when it was made.

"Come, let us leave this area. It smells of death and danger. It is not safe to stay here," Dorsun said, tugging at Khan's cloak, urging him to stand and leave.

"What difference does it make?" Khan barked back. "Go on, Dorsun! Leave me and return to Kesh: rejoin your companions there," Khan said, despair filling his voice.

There were several moments of silence, and Khan sat, much as he had two days before with his elbows on his knees and his chin in his hands. Finally, Dorsun spoke. "Where are the bodies, Master?"

Khan looked over at the man and saw him searching around near the forest. He wanted to shout to Dorsun not to enter the forest, but it was too late. Dorsun was looking down intently, following something, and Khan stood and moved to where he had been, looking at the ground as well. Dorsun had disappeared into the same brush where the bear had come from, and Khan was almost paralyzed with fright, but he forced himself to keep moving. There, on the ground very clearly visible, were several small lines of dry blood as if they had been laid there on purpose.

Khan heard the bushes moving about almost violently at one point, but dared not call out. He peered into the heavy brush under a heavy canopy of oak trees and finally saw Dorsun come out, moving branches with his arms and dragging something. When he finally cleared the brush line, Khan saw two packs being dragged with his critir orb in one of Dorsun's arms, cradled there like a baby no less, and his staff was laid across the hooks of both packs, securing them together. Dorsun stopped, handing the orb to Khan, and then reached back and hefted the metal staff from the packs and offered it as well.

Khan couldn't believe his eyes. "I thought all was lost!" he finally said, surprised.

"There was a blood trail, Master. It was good of you not to follow. What was left of Gund is back there, deep in the brush, along with most of their gear and your possessions," Dorsun said, almost scowling.

"Bless you, Dorsun!" Khan exclaimed, holding the staff in his hands again and swinging it from side to side, feeling its weight. "Quickly now, open my pack and grab my scarf."

Dorsun did as he was told, and Khan wrapped the orb in his scarf and had Dorsun secure it in his pack without taking the pack off. It would be harder to reach for it without taking the pack off. "You are pleased, Master?"

"Most pleased, Mister Dorsun! I feel fate has for once turned for us and not only against us. Remember," he said, tightening his pack straps to his chest, "I only need you to buy me some time. No need for you to kill anyone, just keep them off of me till I can engage them, agreed?"

"Yes, of course, Master. Do you think we will find anyone alive?"

"We will, Dorsun, we will. Perhaps not right away, but we will. Lead on and stay near the river." He motioned with his hand to proceed.

The two men then moved away from the killing ground and continued the river upstream. For a long while, they saw nothing, before Dorsun,

who was in the lead, pointed across the river again. This time the body looked like Boxer, one of the leaders of the patrols. The brigand had made it to shore only to die there with one bolt and one arrow protruding from his abdomen. His body was just starting to bloat in the sun, but luckily it was still springtime and not too hot in Ulatha yet.

Dorsun nodded and motioned for Khan to follow. After a few more hours, Khan started to think on their plans for the night. "How much further do you want to travel?"

Dorsun stopped, looking around and then back to Khan. "It will get dark in a couple of hours. We don't really have a tent to set up, nor camp to make, so I think we can safely proceed until dusk. What do you think?"

"Unfortunately, we are on the wrong side of the river," Khan said with disgust, observing the area as well.

"Wrong side for whom, Master?" And Khan swore Dorsun winked at him.

"What do you mean?" Khan asked.

"Well, you said Gund turned on you after talking to Master Ke-Tor, no?" Khan just nodded. "Then it stands to reason that if we cross any of our company, we may want to discuss the situation with them first so we can understand their frame of mind in this matter. In fact, like the Ulathans before us, we may indeed have good use of the river being placed between them and us. Do you understand me, Master?"

"What does it matter? We are isolated and alone. The river only reinforces that notion."

"Not as alone as you think, Master."

"What is that supposed to mean?" Khan asked.

"Time will tell, Master. Some of my soldiers may be happy to see me, and you are more appealing to the soldiers than Ke-Tor."

Khan nodded. "If I did not know better, I would say you are with me and not Ke-Tor. I did not expect your loyalty so easily, Dorsun."

"Do not be surprised, Master. When it comes to a wizard's quarrel, we Kesh try to stay out of the way. I would be little use to you against Ke-Tor, but my motivations are done in my own self-interest. Do not mistake my loyalty for weakness. By serving you now, I serve myself and even Kesh."

Khan was intrigued by where their conversation was going, so he decided to make camp right where they were at. They actually moved another two hundred yards to the north, where there were a few boulders and a small berm or bank that kept them somewhat sheltered and out of sight from the forest and to either side of the shore. They could only be easily spotted from someone on the river or across it.

After breaking out some rations from the packs and taking long swills on their flasks, Khan resumed his conversation with Dorsun. "Tell me again, Dorsun, how you serve yourself by serving me. I already told you that swearing allegiance to me would most likely mean your doom. I am a wizard apprentice with no stature in the Arcane Order, an outcast from Kesh, if you will."

"For now, Master, maybe yes. Yesterday, however, I was prepared for my death. I was only waiting for Father Akun to take me to his abode into the black. I walked amongst my ancestors and felt them ready to embrace me. I was ready for death but did not want it. Then you arrived. You saved me, and as you know, it is our custom to owe a debt to one who has saved our life. I now will repay that debt."

"Very eloquent for a brigand." Khan winked as Dorsun looked up in confusion at first. "But answer me my question. What good is your debt if you die in the process?"

Dorsun did smile then, a large toothy smile that belied his many years as a soldier. "Good question . . . wizard." Now it was his turn to wink back at Khan, who wondered if he was being mocked. "Ke-Tor is one of the most ruthless magicians Kesh has ever encountered. While no wizard is entirely pleasing to deal with, it is doubly the opposite with that one.

I would see you succeed in your quest and take Ke-Tor's place by the Mage's side. I think you can do this, and I would not be here now to tell you this if not for your magic and . . . well, compassion."

Khan thought for a moment before responding. "I agree with your assessment of my mentor. Ex-mentor, actually now: however, he is adept at the arcane arts, and his own suspicious nature makes him alert and cautious. There is, however, a weak point in his façade, and his armor is not foolproof. Hubris will be his downfall. I simply need to find a way to take advantage of that fact."

"You are very wise for one so young," Dorsun said. Khan looked at the man intently. His face was middle aged, maybe forty-five to fifty at the most, and weathered, as if he had spent most of his adult life outdoors. His eyes gave off a gleam Khan was used to seeing in the brigands of Kesh. A gleam of death and greed, but also there was a faint light of wisdom as well. One did not see Kesh soldiers reach these ages so easily, and the fact he was acting as a lieutenant of a Kesh company spoke volumes to the man's intelligence and resourcefulness. At least as far as this compared to his fellow Kesh.

"You are surprisingly thoughtful and articulate for a Kesh brigand," Khan fired back, smiling.

Dorsun chuckled as the sun started to set, and asked, "Do we leave early tomorrow before dawn? Do you have a specific plan, Master?"

Khan looked at the sky as the sun's rays disappeared from the ground but remained touching the tall oaks and pines of the Earlstyne, giving it a more regal hue than what Khan was thinking of earlier in the day. "We accomplished our two most important tasks." At this, Dorsun perked up and actually stopped chewing on the dried beef in his mouth for a second to give Khan his undivided attention. "First, we retrieved my possessions from the bear attack and the betrayal by Gund. The man got what he deserved, though I must say that is a terrible way to depart this world. In

hindsight, I wonder if he knew he would be giving his life to save mine. I digress, however: the second task was that we survived another day."

Dorsun looked across the river and back to Khan with his eyes opened wide. "The day isn't over yet, Master, not over yet."

CHAPTER 22

TITANS

Targon informed Elister the night before, and the old man just nodded, sitting on the porch till late into the night, puffing on his pipe and listening to Targon tell him more about the refugees and their sojourn to his home. When Targon tired of speaking, he decided to sleep on the hay in the small barn instead of inside his own home. Besides, feeling that it was crowded and stuffy, he also disliked the loud snores from old man Horace and the occasional nightmare murmuring of Will, who was still dealing with the initial assault, or at least he was doing so in his dreams . . . though nightmares may have been a better choice of words. Marissa had come out once to inform him that they were all retiring for the night, and he had thanked her and remained with Elister.

Upon waking just before dawn and coming out into the cold, brisk air, Targon was surprised to see Elister exactly where he had left him, only now the pipe was put away and the old man was stretching and looking around, occasionally whistling back to the birds that were darting hither and thither in the trees.

"Good morning, Master Terrel," Elister said with a grin. "Fine morning for a wonderful breakfast, but alas, I fear we will have no rest with our guests so close."

Targon walked over, stretching as well and moving his arms wildly about to circulate his blood and warm up a bit. He could just see his breath in the morning air. "Agreed, Elister. My mother would have been awake already and had eggs cooking on the pan with a dab of bacon grease and potatoes in another skillet while my sister, Ann, would have had fresh milk on the table by now." Targon smiled back.

Soon, the others started to awaken, and several moved down to Bony Brook to wash their hands and faces, while others used water from the night before in the lone basin inside the cabin. Breakfast consisted of some boiled potatoes and cabbage, ever so lightly seasoned with sage and salt. *Olga must be conserving our meager supply*, thought Targon.

Finally, as the sun was getting much higher, the need to depart grew more urgent. There was quite the commotion they had come to expect as Emelda wept and sobbed and hugged poor Horace, who said he thought he'd die first from his wife's grief before he had even shot a single bolt.

Lady Salina and her son Cedric had stepped down to the end of the porch, and unheard words were passed between mother and son. Karz also ran up and hugged Cedric intensely as the family said their good-byes.

Monique approached Targon, holding out his Clairton bird carving he had given her the day before when she had asked him for it. She had taken off her small amulet charm and used her silver necklace to attach the carving to it, and Targon lowered his head as she adorned it around his neck. "For luck, and to remember us and your mother," she said, a rare smile appearing on her face.

Targon held the carving out in his hand as far as the chain would allow. "I am honored," he said, admiring her handiwork. A silver neck-

lace was nothing to trifle with, and he knew it meant a lot, not only being valuable but sentimental to Monique. "I will return it to you when we come back."

"Keep it till you are reunited with your mother, and let it always remind you of why you fight," Monique said, blushing and then, just as quickly, she embraced him and kissed him on the cheek and then stepped back with her head down and her face red.

"What did I tell ya? Too much smooching going on around here! Now you just make sure you return, young man, and bring them others with you," Agatha said, mocking the gesture but not too harshly.

"Oh, let them be, you old hag!" Will said, scorning as he did so.

"How dare you talk to me that way, Master Will, especially after all that tending I had done for you and your poor arm."

"Now, Agatha, Will is just saying let them be. 'Tis natural for the young folk to feel passionate one toward the other," Horace said, half chuckling.

"Well, you can show a bit more passion this way, my dear!" Emelda said, grabbing Horace and wiping her tears on his tunic while burying her head in his chest again.

Horace embraced her as best he could one-handed while he kept the crossbow pointed up. Targon swore the weapon and the man's arm had most likely become one, fused together by sheer will. "Elister, you ready to go, sir?"

Elister walked over from the porch where he had remained seated all morning and stood amongst the group outside in the clearing off the front of the cabin. Salina, Karz, and Cedric had all walked over from the south end of the porch, and they stood together looking at Targon. "Ready as ever, Master Terrel."

The group said their final good-byes. Targon followed Elister, who started out at a brisk pace for an old man, and the others hurried to keep up. Elister led, and then came Targon, Cedric, and Horace while Will

Carvel brought up the rear. They could still hear Emelda sobbing as they walked out of sight.

They took only one break in order to drink and had only a few apples to eat that Elister had brought with him. They walked mainly in silence, but after some time when Targon had reckoned they were nearing his family's hunting blind, they stopped and he heard Elister hoot like an owl. The sound was odd because it was full day and most owls were resting in the hollows of the forest's trees. After a few minutes of everyone looking around to see if an owl would actually hoot back or fly over, they were not so surprised to see Elister's falcon wing down from above and land on Elister's outright arm.

"Can you believe that!" Horace said, shaking his head, and Will nodded in agreement.

"Where did you say they were? Ah hah, I see, Argyll, very good. Yes, thank you, I will most certainly take care of the situation. Yes. Of course, if you don't mind, and do tell that stubborn ursine he can rejoin us at any time: he needn't do all the protecting himself. Most appreciated, my winged friend, and fair flight to you and yours, then. Yes, I'll be there waiting for you." Then suddenly, the bird took flight and disappeared to the south while Horace murmured under his breath and shook his head.

"It appears the smaller party of unwelcome guests has taken up camp about a half hour's walk south of here on the other side of the river in the same location as your original group, Master Targon," Elister said.

"Do we engage?" Targon asked apprehensively.

"Most certainly. A Mage is not welcome in the Earlstyne and could wake the guardian before his time."

"That would be bad?" Targon ventured, letting the last word linger.

"Yes, mostly for the Kesh, but bad for us as well." When Elister saw a confused look on Targon's face, he added, "The guardian needs managing is all, and that is what I have been doing for centuries. It won't do now to have him woken prematurely and without purpose."

"I'm afraid to ask," Targon said sheepishly.

"No matter now: let's move on and approach this group from the forest." Elister took off at a brisk pace deeper into the forest, heading south. After the better part of an hour, the group slowly started walking from tree to tree until they heard and, shortly thereafter, saw the Rapid River just beyond the forest's edge. Targon instantly recognized the place and looked for the hollow tree near the river's edge where they had taken shelter before.

On the far side, clearly visible, was a Kesh camp, and its sentries were observing the area and river as well. Elister closed his eyes and pressed his hand upon the bark of the large oak tree he was leaning on, and Targon watched intently as the old man seemed to sway to and fro with the effort. Then they heard a loud, booming voice, clear and gentle yet strangely amplified in a mystical sort of way. "I know you are there, Arnen, so you may as well come out and face me. You may be able to thwart the High-Mage of Kesh, but your powers pale when compared to my mastery of the critir. Do not hide behind the poor citizens of Ulatha or your mighty oak trees. Come out and let us discuss your surrender."

Targon, Cedric, Horace, and Will looked at each other, mouths wide open, but Elister remained attached to the oak tree, continuing to sway. Finally, after a moment of silence and swaying, Elister spoke. Softly and musically, his voice carried on the wind and soothed the companions as they heard it. "Indeed, Master Ohkre, Arch-Mage of Kesh. Welcome at long last to the Earlstyne. So good of you to have come in person instead of sending your minions. Perhaps a discussion of your surrender in these lands, which do not belong to you, would be appropriate."

"Tsk, tsk." They all heard the disapproval of the other voice as it boomed across the field, artificially loud, and while lulling in its pleasant tone, it seemed more abrasive after hearing Elister speak. "These lands are not for the Arnen either, but enough bickering. Come out and show yourself . . . druid."

Elister opened his eyes and then turned to his companions. "Be prepared for the second wizard and keep the Kesh occupied. I'll deal with the Arch-Mage personally."

"You can't be serious, old man!" Will said, reaching out and grabbing Elister by the arm before the druid could turn and walk toward the riverbank. "It'll be suicide to go out there!"

"The Earlstyne is my ward, and I've slept enough. Time to deal with this threat once and for all." And Elister turned to Targon, placing a hand on his shoulder. "Dareen would be proud. Remember to care for the Earlstyne and your companions." Suddenly, the old man released his hold on Targon, and, using his staff to navigate the tree roots and mossy dark ground, he quickly moved toward the river.

The companions hurried forward while Targon motioned for Will to stay behind him and for Horace and Cedric to take up positions on either flank with their crossbows. Once in position, they hurried to catch up to the old man as they marched in a line across the forest floor, finally stopping at its edge and watching as Elister stood alone with his staff in one hand and his other raised head high, palm out, as if in greeting.

"Hail, Mage, and well met," Elister said simply, his voice no longer carrying as it once was, but still he spoke loudly to be heard over the roar of the river and from across the wide expanse.

"At last, the Arnen shows himself! See there, Ke-Tor, that was not so difficult to flush out the Earlstyne interloper. Now come, Arnen, and let me release you from your service. Return to your ancestors and rest in peace."

Targon had taken his bow off his back while he walked and had pulled his first arrow, nocking it. He could see clearly now the man that was speaking. He was tall, even for a Kesh, and had a bright blue robe on that glittered in the noonday sun. His head was covered with a pointed hat with a strange golden tassel on it, and he had a strange orb set up on a tripod in front of the chair he sat on. His right hand was on the orb,

and in his left, he had a long slim staff made from some kind of dull grey metal that gleamed in the sunlight despite its dull color. The staff was adorned with a large diamond-like stone. In fact, it looked like it might be a diamond, if Targon remembered his mother's tales of the jewels and gems Sir Baldwyn had thrown into the night sky to distract his princess's evil red dragon, but he couldn't be sure as he had never seen a diamond before.

There was another man equally dressed and garbed with another me-tallic staff and ornamented with a similar but smaller stone, red in hue and color this time. The brigands were scattered along the riverbanks, and Targon quickly counted a dozen crossbowmen on the other side. He realized they were outnumbered six to one, or four to one if he in-cluded himself and his bow. Many of the other brigands had spears, and a couple had wicked-looking javelins. He did not fear the spears really, as they were too heavy to reach across the river, but the javelins looked just as lethal as the bolt bearers. Targon knelt to make himself into a smaller target and used his tree as cover for over half his body. He was satisfied to see Horace and Cedric had done the same, and he felt Will's hand on his shoulder as the man stood directly behind him but behind the tree.

Elister lowered his arm and responded. "Now is not the time for hubris, Master Ohkre. Return to Kesh and leave these lands, and your life will be spared."

The familiar use of the Mage's name twice now seemed to anger him, and he took his hand off the orb. Using his own staff to lean on, he approached, standing from his seated position to the river's edge, and looked menacingly at Elister before responding. "Enough, Arnen. You are not the first, but you will be the last!" And suddenly, the Mage pointed his staff at Elister, moving his lips and saying something that could not be heard, but its effects were seen immediately.

A giant ball of fire, much like the one Targon saw days earlier at the same spot, flew across the river, but this fireball was much bigger and flew

faster. Targon cringed, thinking the old man would be incinerated before his very eyes, but just as quickly as the ball of flames flew across the river, he saw Elister raise both his hands as if in chorus, staff clenched tightly in his left, and a huge wave of water leaped from the river, intercepting the fireball in midflight.

The result was a spectacular hiss as untold volumes of the water was instantly transformed into steam, clouding the area above the river instantly with a semitransparent glaze of water vapor. The brigands did not hesitate and launched spears and bolts at the old man. Targon screamed, letting loose his first arrow, aiming at the brigand closest to the enemy Mage, and he was satisfied to see his arrow hit the mark squarely in the man's chest, causing him to fall.

Quickly, the air was filled with various missiles as the two parties unleashed on each other. Several bolts seemed to hit the old man, but Targon saw no discernable wounds, and at least two of the bolts snapped and broke upon impact. A second fireball crossed over the river and was, in turn, repelled much like the first. Elister started to whistle a call into the air while continuing to hold his ground. The second wizard wasn't fighting at all, but rather watching intently his companion, occasionally flicking off a bolt in midair from Cedric or Horace that came too near.

A spear landed close to Targon's feet, and he could feel Will's hand steadying him on his shoulder. "Can you hit that spell caster?" Will asked.

Targon aimed his next arrow directly at the blue-robed man with his white hair and bushy white beard, and pulled back as far as he could on the bowstring. His arrow went true to his mark, and the other man looked like he was about to do something again with his staff when he waved it downward, and Targon watched his arrow change direction in midflight, landing in the dirt by the shoreline a good twenty paces short of his target.

"Akun, take the man!" Targon exclaimed in dismay as he watched his arrow fall short. "He is protected by some sort of foul sorcery, Will."

A huge flock of various birds filled the air, flying from the forest in all directions. They were composed mainly of large black crows flying chaotically as if a large black velvet curtain descended from the skies. They swarmed many of the brigands, and Targon saw there were many other birds intermixed with the crows. He saw owls, finches, hummingbirds, and ravens, as well as a few of the milder Clairtons his mother favored so much. Many of the birds fell to bolts and spears as they were cut down, but they continued to harass the brigands, pecking at their eyes and clawing at their faces when they could.

Targon took hope and changed his next target to a larger brigand, who was cutting down large numbers of the avians with his slender but wicked-looking scimitars that he held in each hand. His arrow flew but dropped and hit the brigand in his chin, causing the man to drop to one knee and look around. Suddenly, the air around the brigands crackled, and a large blue light flashed across the sky as if lighting was suddenly brought down from the partly clouded sky. Many of the birds dropped as if struck dead in that instant, and soon, Targon could smell the stench of burned flesh and feathers waft across the river.

"I can't see anything!" Cedric called from his place of concealment a dozen yards south of where Targon was located. Targon looked over and saw that Cedric had dropped his bow and was dabbing at his forehead with some sort of rag he had in his hands. Blood was dripping from across his brow where a nasty head wound bled profusely from the near miss of a crossbow bolt.

"Will, can you help Cedric?" Targon asked, turning this time to face the veteran warrior.

Will looked at Cedric, who was slumped down, back against the tree, somewhat sheltered from the river, though several bolts and a spear were lodged in his tree on the riverside. "I'll take care of it. Keep shooting those scum!" Will responded, running as fast as he could to Cedric's aid, dodging a couple of bolts as he ran.

Targon returned his gaze to the battle that was raging across the river. The returning fire from the bolts had lessened, as at least half the brigands with the crossbows had been killed or maimed, either from return fire or from the huge flock of birds that had suddenly appeared. The birds were seriously depleted, and what remained of the flock continued to harass the brigands sporadically.

"How are you doing over there?" Targon cried out to Horace, who he could not see on his right somewhere amongst a denser copse of trees.

"Damnest thing I've ever seen!" Horace cried from his place of cover. "I guess we can dine on poultry tonight, young master Targon, eh?"

Targon chuckled despite the chaos and bloodshed going on around him. He had to give Horace credit for seeing right to the heart of any matter in any circumstance. Targon loosed one more arrow, which went long this time at the same brigand that was down on one knee. "Can you hit those two boltmen on the far right?" Targon shouted over the din of battle. "They are crouched in those alder brushes near the riverbank."

Horace didn't respond initially, but Targon was gratified to see three bolts fly from where he thought Horace was concealed in the bushes. "I think I got one of them bastards, though his mother won't be missing him," Horace yelled out triumphantly.

There was a sudden flash of light, and then *BOOM!* Targon felt his ears pop, and the loud cracking sound rolled over him. Targon looked at Elister and saw the ground falling back down to the riverbank where he stood. Something had hit the ground and flung it into the air. Again, but this time Targon witnessed it, a bolt of lightning flew from the Mage's staff impossibly fast, but just as quickly, the ground in front of Elister rose up in a solid mass, several yards thick, and grounded the electrical bolt in a fury of flying dirt and dust. Elister was momentarily clouded by the debris, and Targon could barely make him out as he stood there facing west across the river. The sound of dirt, pebbles, and loose rock

pattered down across the ground, landing near him and in the canopy of tree leaves overhead.

Targon was in shock. This could have been his fate had he crossed into Kesh and met with one of the sorcerers there that were not supposed to exist. Obviously, Elister was much more than a crazy old man, well, still crazy, but powerful beyond what Targon could have imagined, especially after meeting the man. He had to help him, but how?

"Enemy! Our side!" Targon heard Will's shout, and Targon turned, looking south past Will and Cedric, whose face was streaked red with blood. There, across a small clearing, stood two men, both Kesh in features, but one was armed with a slender sword dressed in black leathers, looking fierce and dangerous, while the other man . . . he knew! It was the very same who had hurled his own fire magic across the river from the raft days earlier. Things just kept getting worse.

Khan and Dorsun had traveled most of the day and found themselves resting not far from their old camp, but on the eastern shores of the river instead. They had just finished eating a poor meal of dry meat, overly salted, along with a pear each that was the last of their fruit, when loud voices began to come from the north. The two men could not make out what was being said, but Khan instantly recognized the distinct artificial sound that a critir orb made when used to vocalize one's voice across a distance. He could almost fancy the voice belonging to Am-Ohkre.

Then the voices subsided and soon were replaced with faint screams and shouts. Dorsun grabbed their packs and pulled out his rapier while Khan followed, gripping his staff tightly. Soon, the sounds became clearer, and Khan shuddered as he heard the death screams of Kesh brigands. There was something else, too, a loud rambunctious cawing of birds and the beating of many feathers. Smoke and water vapor drifted down-

wind on the false currents provided by the rapidly flowing river alongside them.

"Battle, Master!" Dorsun said, wide eyed, turning to look at Khan as they moved quickly, almost at a trot, through the sparse trees, trying to keep near to the river's banks.

A loud sonic boom rattled both men, and again, Khan winced as he recognized the effects of a lightning bolt hurled from an Arch-Mage of Am-Ohkre's stature. Khan knew the air was almost literally split asunder from the intense heat of the bolt. Again the boom, and the men ran faster but paused more often at various trees, looking around them to see who was involved in the battle.

Finally, after the sky was almost blotted out by a dust cloud, the two men came into a small clearing and could just make out their former companions on the far shore Khan recognized as being their former camp. The air was littered with dust, debris, and a small flock of ravens and a few other birds that seemed to be attacking the Kesh. Khan saw a young Ulathan slumped against a tree with his back to it, and the tree had many bolts and even a spear in it, while another older Ulathan man was on one knee tending to him. It looked like the younger man had a nasty head wound that was bleeding profusely. The other man stood, seeing them. His reaction was immediate, and Khan heard him shout as he looked back and then drew his broadsword. Khan was impressed, as the sword looked nearly as long as a man was tall, or at least as tall as an Ulathan, and the blade of the sword was the thickest he had ever seen on a blade.

"Master, look!" Dorsun said, pointing across the river at Ke-Tor, who was standing near Am-Ohkre. Khan saw his old mentor standing and watching the battle between another oddly dressed man on his side of the shore and Am-Ohkre. It seemed the old man had a very weathered look, even a tired look, about him, but it was the Arch-Mage's face that told the story. Khan had never seen Am-Ohkre that upset before. His

face was contorted in rage, and the diamond on the tip of his staff glowed a bright white, a sure sign that immense amounts of magic had poured forth from it at the Mage's command.

Khan didn't care anymore for the two men that battled across the river one against the other. Now his eyes narrowed, and he focused on Ke-Tor. "Dorsun, guard my back!" Khan shouted, ignoring the Ulathans and turning to face the river while raising his staff and murmuring the words of his most powerful spell.

Targon watched as Will ran to the Kesh that had suddenly appeared on their side of the river. The man with the rapier was as tall as Will was, and, while stocky for a Kesh, he was more slender than the Korwell sergeant. His blade was slender, though just as long as Will's, and with quick movements, the brigand dodged Will's first blow while lunging his own blade at Will's chest.

"Watch out!" Targon cried, almost helpless to do or say any more. Only one bolt flew out at Will as he ran, missing him by falling behind. Once engaged with the Kesh, the two men circled and parried blow after blow with the Kesh man yielding ground to the heavier Ulathan. No more crossbow bolts came from the river at Will. Obviously too dangerous as they could just as easily hit their companion from such a long range.

Targon looked at Elister and saw the man bend over slightly at the waist, leaning on his staff. Obviously the last two magical blasts of electricity had drained something from the old man. Targon saw the surviving Kesh being waved over toward the wizard who had engaged Elister. Once near him, the birds flew around the Kesh group but could not penetrate the area around the man with the staff. The other wizard looked at Targon and then farther south at Will. Targon was too far away to be sure, but he swore he saw the other man's expression change to one of utter surprise. Then the man's face started to glow as it reflected light, and Targon realized a ball of fire was hurled at the man from his side of the river.

The ball of fire almost reached the man when he knelt and wrapped his cloak around his body, lowering his head inside of it. Only the tip of his spear protruded as the ball of fire engulfed him. The man disappeared for a moment until the flames sputtered out, and Targon saw the ground burned black around the man. His cloak was no longer blue but now sooty black, with only a smudge of blue to tell what color it was before the attack. Smoke stirred from the cloak and staff tip and wafted up into the air. Several birds were also incinerated in the attack, as they were too near to get clear of the blast.

Targon looked back to Will and saw the Kesh fighter was sparing with Will, keeping him away from the younger wizard who stood a few paces behind him downriver. The younger wizard's face contorted, and he pointed his staff again at his fellow wizard across the river while another slightly smaller ball of flame was flung from the tip of his staff and crossed the river.

"I'm almost out!" Targon heard Horace yell, seeing another brigand near the Arch-Mage fall dead with a bolt sticking from his neck.

Targon winced, wondering how they were going to make it out of there alive when he nocked another arrow and took aim at Will's opponent. He was much closer than the brigands from across the river, but still Targon hesitated as the men circled and danced around an invisible central point with the clanging of steel on steel as blades met.

The other man seemed much older for a brigand, and he must have spotted Targon as his circling stopped and he suddenly shuffled from side to side, keeping Will between himself and Targon. Targon admired the skill of the man as he fought a seasoned Ulathan soldier, and not just any soldier, a sergeant of the gate, and at the same time kept Targon at bay with his bow.

Targon was just about to yell to Will to either duck or hold still when out of his peripheral vision he saw the water in the river rise as if floating, yet still streaming as fast a man could run. Targon lowered his bow and turned to watch as the entire river floated at least ten feet off the riverbed, creating what looked like a circular tunnel along the bottom of the river. The Mage motioned for the remaining brigands to follow him, and they started to walk under the roaring river and into the riverbed itself, leaving only the other wizard, wrapped in his smoking cloak, on the far shore.

After the second ball of fire petered out, the crouched man stood quickly and pointed his staff at Will, or more specifically, the man behind Will and his enemy and shouted, "Khan, you insolent fool! Die!" A bolt of electricity, much like what Targon witnessed earlier but not nearly as potent, crackled across the river faster than the balls of fire. The young wizard held his staff out in front of him, and the bolt hit his staff, rebounding high into the air and out of sight but knocking the younger man onto his back, and he dropped the staff, his hand blackened and burned.

The younger wizard cried out in pain and attempted to crawl over to his staff when Targon saw the older man across the river level his staff again, pointing it in their general direction. The man's hair and beard were blackened and falling from his head, while smoke continued to waft from his cloak and body. Targon suddenly shifted his stance and took aim at the lone remaining wizard with his staff leveled and released his arrow with all his might. He never saw what happened to it.

As the Mage and brigands crossed under the raging river, Elister had stepped up to the riverbank itself, right where the water had risen up and flowed over an invisible tunnel. Above the roar and din of the electrical bolt, yelling brigands, and raging water, he heard a distinct voice come from the Kesh Mage. "NO!"

As they exited from the tunnel and attempted to step onto the dry shore of the nearside riverbank, the Mage reached out with his staff, trying to hit or poke Elister, who in turn used the end of his granite-tipped staff and smote the Mage's staff. A brilliant flash of white light erupted, blinding everyone within range of sight. Targon raised his free hand after releasing his arrow, and used it to block his eyes. Before he lost consciousness and before his hearing was fully bloated out by the loud blast of noise that deafened his ears, he half fancied he heard the soft words of Horace from nearby. "Bloody hell!" Then darkness took him.

CHAPTER 23

AFTERMATH

Targon slowly felt the light returning to his closed eyes. He felt something on his chest and noticed he couldn't really hear anything. The river seemed to be muffled as the sounds slowly came back to him. He struggled to open his eyes and was looking at the sky peeking through the sparse canopy of tree leaves where he had fallen near the mighty oak that had been protecting him from the Kesh bowmen. The light hurt his eyes, and he squinted them shut again in pain. Slowly, he remembered what had happened. He tried one more time to open his eyes and was greeted by the blurred image of a Clairton that was chirping on his chest as it pecked at something around his neck.

Instinctively, Targon reached up and felt his mother's gift, the carving he had made still connected by Monique to her silver chain. It felt oddly comforting in his grasp, and he allowed his head to rest again and closed his eyes, resting and not caring what was happening around him. After a long time, he started to feel not just a sense of urgency but a sense of curiosity. What was so powerful that it had knocked him out? The bird chirped and sang a few notes and then gently flew away into the trees.

Targon struggled to stand. The entire area looked familiar, and indeed much as it had before, except near the shoreline where he had last seen Elister. The entire area was devoid of anything: it was scoured black and sooty from some sort of apocalyptic blast. No, there still standing was Elister, but not moving. Targon struggled to stand and held his hand above his brow to block the afternoon sun as it streamed into his eyes. Things were blurry, but he was sure he spotted the druid, staff in hand, standing still at the water's edge, which had resumed its normal and natural course.

Turning his attention farther north, he couldn't see Horace anywhere, but he wasn't that concerned, as he hadn't seen the elder Ulathan for the entire battle, and he was one tough old buzzard. Targon had dropped his bow, and it lay on the ground with its string broken and the entire bow limp and impotent. He drew his trusty axe and walked over to Cedric lying prone, facedown in the dirt amidst the roots of a gnarled old tree. He gently turned the young man over and was relieved to see he was still breathing. The blood from his head wound had finally congealed and stopped.

Standing, he left Cedric where he lay and walked over toward Will and his opponent. Before he had gotten more than a few steps, he heard the rustling of leaves and brushes, and his heart almost stopped. He held his axe out blade forward and prepared for battle, but just as quickly, he saw Core, the large brown bear, come trotting out from the brush line near a tree not far from Will and the Kesh. The poor bear was bleeding from his left rear flank and was making faintly heard moaning sounds with his muzzle. "Don't do that, Carrot! You scared the spirits out of me, for sure!" But secretly he was happy to see the bear, as he felt very alone despite the prone bodies.

Bear and man walked toward each other and met near where Will lay face up, and again a sigh of thanks as Targon saw the man taking shallow

breaths. Targon knelt by the bear and allowed the bear to nuzzle his massive head along Targon's shoulders. Ever so faintly, Targon startled as the bear growled softly, and in his head, he thought he heard a word, but one that made no sense to him. There it was again: *Elly.*

Targon rubbed the large bear's head. *It feels like a furry anvil the blacksmith used in Korwell,* he thought to himself, looking around for the sound of the voice. Again came the voice: *Elly.* Targon looked around, startled, but realized the voice was inside his head, though it sounded much like external noise. He was sure whatever blast had occurred had rattled his brain, and he was hearing things. He took one last look around and left Core and stepped over to the Kesh fighter.

Yes, fighter, Targon thought, *not brigand.* The man deserved at least that much as his skill and bravery had impressed Targon. It wasn't any man that could stand and face down Will Carvel and his broadsword. Agon herself knew Targon would be loath to face Will in battle. Better to hit someone of Will's size and strength from afar with a pointy arrow.

Targon knelt and flipped the Kesh over onto his backside. Again, labored breathing. Well, at least the blast hadn't killed everyone. Targon opened the man's black cloak and found two knives of Kesh design tucked into his belt. Targon took both of them and stuck them into his own belt, blades down. Remembering the night his family was taken captive, he moved down to the man's boots and found another dagger, a very slender one, tucked and even strapped into his right boot. Targon removed it and finished his search.

Targon saw the man's rapier lying nearby. He walked over to it and, lifting it onto his boot, he kicked it into the nearby brush and out of sight. Feeling better about the situation, he moved to the last prone man lying nearby in his blue robe, burned hand clutching the metallic staff. The ruby gemstone on top of the staff still glowed a dull red, and Targon almost touched it but didn't as he could feel heat coming off of it. The man was lying on his side with his bottom arm outstretched and clutching the staff. Targon moved around, squatting in front of the young man without touching him. He saw his face pale and clean shaven except for the faint stubble of a beard on his chin that had yet to really grow. He looked unarmed, but Targon feared touching him. He was very pale, and if he was breathing, it was not noticeable.

Targon decided to take no chances, and, using his booted foot, he tried to kick the staff free, but the other man's grip was too tight. In the end, he had to bite his lip and pry the staff from the young Kesh man's fingers. It felt surprisingly light to hold, and the metal was dull grey but warm. Targon didn't fancy holding the Kesh instrument and very quickly walked over to their hollowed tree near the river and dropped the staff inside of it where it would remain hidden till he could think what to do.

Elly . . . Elly dead.

Targon spun around and looked for the voice again sounding so real, yet it had to resonate from inside his head, as there was no one there to speak the words. Only the bear. Targon paused, looking intently at Core, who had walked over to him looking forlorn and sad, if that could be said of a bear, and Targon knelt, looking into his eyes as the bear shuffled its massive paws in the dirt and hung his head.

"Carrot, was that you?" Targon asked, looking at the bear intensely for any sign of intelligence.

The bear looked into Targon's eyes, growling softly, and immediately Targon heard the strange voice. *Elly.*

Targon fell to his knees, dropping his axe. No, the bear wasn't speaking in the common tongue. There was nothing but the coarse animal growl of a member of the ursine family, specifically a brown bear, but it *was* Core speaking to him. *How odd,* Targon thought to himself. Both odd and amazing as the voice sounded much like a small child speaking inside his head.

"Carrot, who is Elly?" Targon asked, looking intently again at the brown bear.

Elly, do-ed. Elly, friend, came the response as the bear shook its head from side to side and shuffled its front paws even more, finally lying down to rest with its massive head between its front legs.

Targon felt a chill run over his spine, and he picked his axe up and ran over to the river's edge where he saw Elister standing. There was no sign of any Kesh, but there was something wrong with the old man. Targon stopped, squinting at Elister's form. He could see no flesh. He slowly approached the old man from the side, and as he got closer, he realized the entire figure was a flat grey, as if the same color as stone or dull mountain granite. He reached Elister and put out his hand, touching the figure of the old man.

The body felt cold and coarse to the touch, much like a rock would feel that wasn't fully weathered. The staff, the man's features, and even his clothes and wisps of hair, all were a dull, flat grey. The man had petrified? Targon didn't understand, but there it was. Elister the man was no more, and instead a stone-like statue stood there as if guarding the Rapid River, staff erect in his right hand and his left arm out as if blocking something. Targon walked completely around the figure before he was startled again.

"Bloody hell!" It was Horace, and the man approached, a bit wobbly on his feet. His eyes were wide open as he took in the same sight. He was bleeding from one of his ears, and the left side of his face looked burned, a bright shade of red.

"You seem to say that a lot, Horace. Didn't your mother teach you how to utter damnations in any other way?" Targon asked, trying to be light-spirited with the old man, but Horace wasn't having any of it.

"By Agon's lover, Akun, lad, what happened to your friend?"

"All right, I've not heard that one before, but in all honesty, I have no idea, Horace. He stands as I found him only just now. Are you hurt?"

Horace reached up, touching his ear and wiping away some dried blood, but he was otherwise unarmed. Targon did not see the crossbow he wielded earlier anywhere nearby. "No. I seem to be intact, and unless

we are both dead and in Agon's bosom, then alive would be the word I would use."

Targon looked from Horace back to Elister, or at least, the statue of Elister, and then scratched his head. "Did you hear any voices in the last several minutes?"

"Voices?" Horace asked, puzzled, and then he looked like he might understand. "No, no voices, but bells and whispers from angels, yes."

Seeing that Horace's mood had lightened, Targon looked over to where Cedric and Will were still lying on the ground. "Can you see to the others?" he asked Horace, motioning to them with his free hand. Horace nodded and started walking toward Cedric. "Wait a second, take this," Targon said, reaching into his belt and pulling out a dagger, offering it to the elder Ulathan.

"Not necessary," Horace replied. "I used up all my bolts. I'll grab the youngsters bow and use that, but I will take your flask. I seem to have lost mine."

Targon put the dagger back in his belt and offered him the flask that was still attached by a leather cord. "Be careful, the Kesh are still alive, both of them."

"Kesh, eh?" Horace said, looking surprised, arching his eyebrows. "I didn't know there were Kesh on this side of the river. I was too busy with the spectacle them two old men put on for us, but don't you worry, lad, I'll see to them Kesh if they are alive."

"Don't kill them, Horace, not if they don't threaten us," Targon said, hesitation in his voice.

"Understood, lad, I'll see to it they can do no mischief, then."

Targon watched as Horace quickly covered the ground to where Cedric's feet were visible, sticking out from the old tree, and he gave a sidelong look at the bear deciding he had to know for sure. He walked over to the bear and knelt beside the massive form and stroked the bear's head, feeling pity for the animal.

"Elister is dead. Do you understand me, Carrot?"

The bear instantly raised its head and let out a long mourning call that wasn't a growl, but was more like a long howling sound.

"You do understand me, I see. I need your help, Carrot. Can you help me?" Targon asked, stroking the massive anvil-shaped forehead of the bear.

Core help Tar, came the response, and despite preparing for it, Targon still felt a tinge of surprise and awe. Had something happened to him during the battle? He continued to stroke the animal's fur and was glad to have come to some sort of understanding with the animal at last. The gentle moment was broken by Horace's yell.

"Lad! Come quick, they are moving!"

Targon stood and saw the men starting to stir but were still disoriented, including Will. Targon gripped his axe and ran toward the men, calling for Core to follow.

Horace had gotten there first and stood over the Kesh fighter with Cedric's loaded crossbow aimed squarely at the brigand's head. Will had sat up and was rubbing his eyes while the Kesh brigand looked around, blinking frequently as if looking for something, grabbing at his belt.

"You won't find them nasty blades there, Kesh," Targon said, and then the man reached to his boot, but Targon spoke faster. "Your boot blade is gone, too. Don't do anything . . . foolish," Targon finished, hefting his axe.

"Master?" the man said, looking around and seeing his companion. "Master, you live?"

The man ignored Horace's instructions to stay still, and he literally crawled the few feet over to his companion, who was just stirring and coming to. Targon felt a hand on his leg.

"What hit us?" Will asked, blinking a few times and grabbing his sword, which had been under him.

"I think the two older men killed each other," Targon responded sadly.

"You mean that likeable old Elister fellow is dead?" Will asked, standing and bracing himself against Targon.

"I'm afraid so," Targon replied, and once he was sure Will wasn't going to fall, he let the man loose and walked over to where the two Kesh were on the ground, the older man helping the younger man to sit up.

"I'll be fine, Dorsun, thank you. Can you see Ke-Tor from here?" Khan sat up with help from the brigand called Dorsun. "Where is my staff?" he suddenly asked, a note of panic in his voice as he looked around.

Targon kept his axe at his side but visible, and stepped over near the man. "Your staff is in my keeping, wizard. What is your name?"

"Don't get too close to him, lad, he'll fry you for sure with that sorcery of his!" Horace exclaimed, slightly adjusting his crossbow to aim it at the younger Kesh and stepping a tad closer.

Both brigand and wizard looked at Targon with an expression of surprise on their faces. "Could it be the same—"

"Quiet, Dorsun," Khan said, his eyes never leaving Targon's face. "Let me do the talking."

"I can hear you, you know. I'm standing right here. I'll ask only one more time, wizard, what is your name?"

"My name is Khan. This is Dorsun. Obviously we are from Kesh, and I'd like my staff back, if you don't mind."

"Can you imagine the arrogance?" Will said, leveling his sword at the younger man's head. Dorsun pushed the blade to the side and pulled Khan closer to him, away from the blade and bow.

"I'd say he's rather more used to giving orders than taking them," Horace chimed in, still holding his crossbow aimed at the younger man.

"Carrot! Come on over here. I need your help!" Targon yelled behind him. Soon, the bear trotted over, and both the Kesh scrambled backward several feet, fear obvious in their eyes. "Keep an eye on these guests for us, please, and don't hurt them unless they do something rude."

"Mother Agon!" exclaimed Dorsun, holding very still, not taking his eyes off of the bear, who now stood head down, occasionally growling softly.

Targon motioned the others to him and stepped a few feet away, out of hearing range of the Kesh. Horace and Will gathered around him. "We lost Elister, and Cedric is pretty banged up. I'm not for killing these Kesh outright, and something isn't right with them. I saw both those Kesh sorcerers try to kill each other. What do you think?"

Will spoke first, as Horace kept glancing over at the Kesh, not trusting even the bear to keep them behaved. "The only good Kesh is a dead one. If you can't do it, let me take care of it."

"Now, Will, maybe the lad is right. It may be good to learn something from them, and they can't do us much harm now, not really with that animal of Mister Elister's watching over them," Horace responded.

"I know how you feel, Will, but while my heart agrees with you, my head tells me they may have information we can use. I'd like to know why they are in Ulatha, how many of them are here, and what their plans are. Don't you agree some questioning might be in order?"

"Perhaps," Will responded, a bit softer in his tone, "but I still wouldn't trust a Kesh to tell the truth. All bloodthirsty cutthroats and assassins they are!" He rubbed his left arm.

"You feeling all right, Will? Arm doing better?" Targon asked.

Will held his sword, tip into the ground, with his right hand and flexed his left arm in a circular motion. "Yeah, I'll live. I think I pulled a stitch or two and it's sore as hell, but I'll manage."

"Good," Targon replied, and then looked where Cedric lay. "Can you and Horace see to our friend? He has a nasty head wound and doesn't look too well."

"Aye, he is still sleeping, that one. Tough as his mother, though. He'll be all right, lad, we'll see to that. Come on, Will, we have work to do," Horace said, walking toward Cedric.

Will started to follow but looked back at Targon and then eyed the Kesh and motioned with his head before turning back and walking after Horace. Targon returned to the bear and the two Kesh men. He noticed they had stumbled to their feet and had moved slightly to stand with their backs against a lone tree, watching the bear intently.

"My companion says we should kill you both." Targon looked at both men seriously.

Dorsun was about to speak when Khan took a step in front, placing his right arm across the man's chest, hushing him. "Death would be deserved at this point, Ulathan, though you do not appear to be like your fellows. May I at least ask of your name before sentence is passed?"

Targon placed a hand on Core's massive head, soothing the bear, who was growling, becoming more active at the sight of Khan stepping forward. "My name is Targon, and no one has judged you yet, much less decided to execute you, though you stand now in Ulathan lands and not Kesh lands." At this, Core growled again, his head swaying from side to side as he showed his canines peeking through his lips, making the animal appear even more menacing than previously. "I'd like to ask why you attacked your fellow Kesh?"

Khan appeared to sigh a bit, and Targon noticed that despite the bear and Khan's restraining hand on his chest, the veteran Kesh fighter seemed tense, as if ready to leap. He seemed to have somewhat regained his courage, and courage was not a trait well known nor attributed often to Kesh brigands.

"Ah, yes, you saw that, then?" Khan asked rhetorically. "That was Ke-Tor, my old master and mentor, and I seriously doubt as an Ulathan that you can appreciate the level to which we Kesh go when it comes to betrayal and deceit. Quite frankly, after that battle of ours, my master found me lacking and connived to have me executed for my failure. Failure that came at your hands."

Targon gripped his axe tighter. "That failure would not have occurred had you not invaded our lands."

"Quite right," Khan said, letting out his breath. "We should not be here, but those are not the decisions made by myself or even some of my companions. You still have not told me who you are. You look Ulathan, yet different."

Targon relaxed a moment but kept an eye on the Kesh fighter with his peripheral vision. "I am Ulathan, but not from the city nor a farmer near the capital. I reside in the wild parts of Ulatha," Targon said, and then finally making up his mind about what to do with them, he finished. "You both will come with me, then, until we decide what to do with you."

"Did you see Ke-Tor, I mean, the other man from across the river? Did he survive?" Khan asked somewhat excitedly, pointing across the river where his old mentor had stood before the massive blast had knocked them all unconscious.

"I saw no one when I came to. Either he left before I awoke or he was consumed in the blast," Targon said, motioning for Will to come over.

"Cedric will be fine. We splashed some water on his face and he is coming to, but he is weak from blood loss and battle stress," Will said matter-of-factly.

"Do we have any rope?"

Will patted his belt and then looked back toward where they had deposited their packs when the battle started. "I have a length or two in my pack from when we made the crossing."

"Fetch two pieces large enough to bind their hands. We are taking them with us."

"You sure that's a good idea?"

"No, not really, but I'll not kill them in cold blood. Kesh we are not. Besides, we have Carrot here to keep an eye on them."

"Who will keep an eye on that bear, then?"

Targon chuckled. "We'll be fine. There is more going on here than we know."

Will quickly fetched the rope, and reluctantly, the two Kesh allowed themselves to have their hands bound in front of them. Cedric had regained his footing, and Horace had retrieved his own crossbow and slung it across his back on top of the pack while keeping Cedric's crossbow in his hands pointed at the Kesh. Before they had started, Will asked to have the men blindfolded as well, but Targon told them they would be returning to his home by a different route, the one the old man Elister had used.

"How will we find it?" Will asked. "I don't fancy getting lost in these woods."

"Carrot will lead the way," Targon responded.

The party departed into the forest, and Targon took a last long look at the stone figure of Elister, standing there to forever guard the river and clearing, and soon the group was lost deep in the Blackthorn Forest. Core led them at a leisurely pace with the Kesh following the bear and then Horace right behind them with his bow. "Stay behind me," he had told them when they started. "I want to have a clear line of sight in case I have to shoot one of them."

Will followed Horace closely with his broadsword unsheathed and in his good right hand while the blade rested backward on his right shoulder. Targon followed, taking up the rear, occasionally stopping to listen in case they were being followed and then, just as quickly, catching up to his companions. The sun set, and the darkness of the forest was much deeper than they had thought. Luckily, the twin sisters rose quickly and shed some small illuminating light beyond the canopy of leaves, and, though they occasionally stumbled, they finally made their way back to Targon's homestead, tired and sore from the day's events.

The homecoming was intense as Emelda ran to Horace and Lady Salina greeted her son affectionately. Agatha came and administered to

Cedric, who quickly started to have a fever as they laid him on the lone makeshift bed in the common room near the fire. Olga had prepared a nice cabbage stew with plenty of meat from the buck, and Marissa had led the efforts to smoke and dry what meat remained so that it would keep. Targon blushed somewhat as Monique also gave him a heartwarming hug, and Salina had hushed Agatha before she could comment on "all that smooching."

Khan and Dorsun were released from their bonds against the will of most of the refugees, but the presence of Core was undeniably reassuring. "Make one move and I'll skewer you to that porch," was all Horace said as he sat on a log stump in the front clearing, leveling his crossbow at the two men, and Core lay down, head facing the Kesh, eyes open.

"Olga," Targon called as the group of Ulathans came from inside the cabin to the porch to somewhat gawk at their prisoners. "Bring two cups of stew for these men when you get a chance, will you?"

"I'd rather they go hungry, Master Targon!" Agatha screeched from the doorway, looking most scornfully at the Kesh.

"Humor me," Targon said, also standing watch, sitting on a tree stump log, but much closer to the Kesh than was Horace.

"Thomas, get away from them!" Celeste had to say to keep the curious boy at a healthy distance.

Targon looked around and agreed. "Salina, can we keep the children indoors? It's getting late, and for their safety, it's best if they weren't outdoors at this time of night."

Thomas groaned in complaint and Karz didn't want to leave his mother, so Salina took them indoors with Agatha coming to admonish both Marissa and Monique as well as they stood gawking at their prisoners. Soon, two large cups were brought from inside, and Olga told them they'd have to sip it as spoons were in short supply.

"I almost didn't recognize the place," Khan spoke, looking at Targon and thanking Olga and then taking his cup gingerly, as it steamed in the cooler night air.

"No, Master," Dorsun said, refusing his cup. "It may be poisoned." A look of concern crossed his face.

"Nonsense, you filthy cutthroat! Be glad you are given anything at all!" Agatha screeched from out of sight but obviously not out of earshot.

"Olga, shut the door on your way in, please," Targon asked. Olga complied, placing Dorsun's cup next to him on the rickety wooden porch. Will also sat on the porch but leaned against the wall, seeming to not tire of holding his broadsword, or at the very least, stoically maintaining his silent vigil.

"Eat, Dorsun, we may not get another chance with some of these Ulathans, and poison would be fitting, anyway," Khan said, resigned, blowing on his stew to cool it, gingerly putting his lips to the cup and tasting it. Dorsun hesitated for a moment, but it was obvious Khan was famished and had already made up his mind, so the brigand chieftain picked up his cup after rubbing his wrists where the rope had bit into his flesh and started to eat.

Targon allowed the men time to eat. He, Horace, and Will had eaten earlier, and the Kesh did not complain, sitting in silence. Finally, somewhat sure the men had finished or were close to finishing, Targon spoke. "Khan, is it?" Khan nodded. "Why are you in Ulatha?"

Khan cleared his throat and went to wipe his mouth with his sleeve, hesitating for only a second before determining it was soiled, anyway, and any excess stew wouldn't matter. "Our High-Mage demanded it. He said it was for slaves and provisions, but I know he seeks something, and the knowledge for what he seeks was rumored to be in Korwell where . . ."

He was quickly interrupted by Dorsun. "Master, no! Do not tell them—"

"It's all right, Dorsun." Khan quickly silenced his protector. "There is no harm in explaining our actions. Besides, we may need to gain their trust if we are to fulfill my mission."

"You mean Ke-Tor?" Dorsun asked, eyes wide open. "He is dead most likely, Master, you have nothing to fear from him."

"He was still a good distance away from Am-Ohkre when the Mage's spell backfired, though I am unsure of how that old Ulathan man could do such a thing to him, but, anyway, I looked carefully and did not see his body across the river. I fear he lives still, and we now have a blood feud that can only end when one of us is dead."

"Then we must seek him out," Dorsun began, taking a long last swig of his stew, tipping the cup as far back as it would go and downing the last he could get. "But first we must find your staff, and I must have a blade."

Targon looked at Will, who just shrugged, and then back to the Kesh men as they held their own private conversation, oblivious to the Ulathans. "Excuse me, Khan, but I think you're getting ahead of yourself."

Khan looked at Targon and then back to Dorsun and then back to Targon again, seemingly understanding his current predicament. "Understood, Ulathan Targon, however, I have a blood feud with my old mentor, and as long as I live, I am honor-bound to complete it. That is our way, the Kesh way, though I doubt you to understand."

Targon was about to speak when Marissa came out the door. "Targon! Come quick!" she exclaimed. "Cedric is getting worse. We need some of those Arella leaves to help him."

"Get inside this minute, child!" Agatha's grating voice yelled over everyone, and Targon noticed that even the Kesh grimaced when she spoke.

Lady Salina appeared at the doorway and motioned for Targon to come inside. "Master Targon, my son is ill. We need your help."

Targon looked warily at the Kesh and then asked Horace and Will to keep an eye on them as he entered the room. "What is it?" he said after Monique had closed the door behind them.

Salina knelt at Cedric's bedside while Agatha wiped the young man's brow with a wet cloth, and Olga was trying unsuccessfully to get him to eat some stew. "Clear away. Give the man some room," Celeste said as the others scurried away.

Targon bent over and felt Cedric's forehead. It was hot to the touch, and it appeared he had quickly become ill for no apparent reason. "Did one of those cutthroats do something to young Master Cedric?" Celeste asked, concerned.

"I don't know, but I don't think so. Cedric was in a bad way before we left. Perhaps the stress and exertion was too much for him.

Targon hadn't heard the door open, so he was surprised to hear Khan's voice. "It's not a natural fever: it's poison."

"Get that filth out of here!" Agatha said scornfully as she attended to Cedric's forehead again with her cloth, only glancing up to scowl at Khan, who stood in the doorway not moving, Will standing next to him protectively.

Targon didn't think Khan was capable of hurting them. He was frail and lean, even for a Kesh, who were normally tall and slender, anyway, though he couldn't be sure the Kesh sorcerer didn't have some sort of dark magic at his disposal. "How do you know that, Khan?" Targon asked, standing back up to face him.

"The Red Throat Company uses poisoned bolts from time to time, and half those soldiers you fought today bore the sigil of that company. It would have killed him sooner, but it appears only a small amount of the toxin managed to enter the young man's body."

"Why, those no good, brigand, cutthroating . . ." Emelda chimed in, shaking her head, speaking before Agatha could grate them with her coarse voice.

"Targon, quickly, can you find more of those Arella leaves for my son?" Salina pleaded with him.

Khan spoke before Targon could answer. "They won't help him. He will die soon before they can take effect. The toxin is too powerful for the Arella."

"You know of the Arella?" Targon asked, looking skeptically at Khan as he fingered the blade on his axe stuck in his belt.

"Of course. It is a basic part of our herbal and potion studies in Keshtor."

"Well, effective or not, we have to do something. I can't let the lady's son die," Targon said.

"Perhaps I can assist?" Khan responded, stepping into the room toward Cedric. This brought an instant commotion, as the ladies grabbed the children protectively and pulled them behind themselves and Will took two large strides to grab Khan by his shoulder and stop him from moving further. Targon could hear Horace and Dorsun start to argue while Core was clearly audible as a deep bass growl permeated the entire cabin, even from outside.

"Stop!" Targon yelled, releasing his axe and holding both hands up, waving them from side to side. "What are you proposing, Khan?"

The room was eerily silent until Cedric vomited what little he had eaten back into the cup Olga had held to his lips. "Mother Agon, help us before the father takes him!" Olga exclaimed, taking the damp cloth from Agatha's hand and wiping Cedric's chin, cleaning him up.

"I have something . . . something that can help . . . the only thing that can help him," Khan said hesitantly, looking around at the room of scowling Ulathans.

"What? Do tell, and no games," Salina asked, a look of concern across her face as her brow furrowed, and she looked sternly at Khan.

Khan cleared his throat and raised his hand to touch his last remaining Talaman and took a long moment in deciding his next words. "I have magic . . ."—he allowed the words to linger, and indeed, they had the

desired effect as looks of both awe and revulsion crossed the faces of the Ulathans—"magic that can cure your friend."

"Don't let him touch your boy, my lady," Celeste whispered, while Olga, Agatha, and Monique nodded their heads in agreement.

Salina never looked at them. "Do you have honor in Kesh?" She spoke softly but sternly.

"We are not all alike, much the same as most Ulathans differ one from another," Khan replied firmly, still holding his Talaman.

"Then undo what your companions have inflicted upon my son, and by our father Akun, I will slit your throat if you harm one hair on my son's head. Am I clear, sorcerer?"

Targon exhaled deeply, shocked by the sternness of Salina's words, and no one had any doubt she would carry through on her threat. "Understood," Khan replied simply, but not moving.

"Release him, Will. Let him attend to my son," Salina commanded. Even Agatha knew to keep her mouth shut, and Will released his hold on the wizard, who quietly crossed over to Cedric's bedside as Agatha and Olga drew back in fear from the Kesh man. Khan knelt at Cedric's side, and under the careful watch of everyone in the room, he pulled his last Talaman from his chain and held it to Cedric's lips as Cedric's eyes fluttered open.

"Take this and do not spit it out," Khan said rather hastily and crudely. "Get him some water. The . . . magic is rather chalky-like, and he must consume it all."

Olga quickly grabbed a cup of water, and Khan inserted the orb into Cedric's mouth. Cedric must have understood, as he chewed feebly and coughed once, trying hard to keep his mouth shut till Olga could bring the cup of water to his lips for him to drink. Confident he had consumed the Talaman, Khan stood and faced Salina.

"His fever will rage all night, but it won't affect him nor hurt him. He will be fine by morning," Khan said with some finality.

Salina's words were soft but chilling. "I hope so for your sake, Sorcerer. If my son dies, so do you."

Khan was grabbed rather harshly and led out of the room by Will. The fate of Khan now was tied to Cedric, and morning would tell whether the two men lived or died.

CHAPTER 24

DISCOVERY

Ke-Tor stumbled yet again as he walked across the rocky fields of eastern Ulatha toward Korwell. He still had his staff and had retrieved his pack with his critir in it. He had tried to use it once to contact Am-Sultain, but his mastery wasn't near the level of that of Am-Ohkre's, and not only could he not communicate with the High-Mage of Kesh but he didn't receive any communications, either. The orb would alert him if it was being accessed.

Curse that arrogant Mage, Ke-Tor thought to himself, remembering Am-Ohkre's demise, which nearly killed him as well. He was fortunate he had his protective cloak, his most powerful magic item, on him. It had turned both blade and spell several times in the past. It was made of pure silver, hammered down to a thinness that made the material flexible, like a sort of foil the bakers used in their ovens when making food for the High-Mage. The metallic cloak was covered in arcane symbols and warding glyphs and then nicely disguised within a cloth cloak of blue fabric, hiding the odd metallic cloak from any visual inspection.

Ke-Tor spun around, grabbing a piece of his cloak and looking at it. The entire bottom end was burned and charred from the fireballs his

ex-apprentice Khan had hurled at him, and he'd need a new covering for his arcane metallic cloak if he were to repair it back to its original condition.

Damn that Khan to Akun's embrace as well, Ke-Tor thought again, almost speaking the words out loud. What in all the arcane arts was he doing alive and on the other side of the river, and who was that with him? It looked like Dorsun, if not Gund, as both were large brigands and adept with any weapon. So either Gund had failed him or he betrayed him. Either way, Gund was a dead man in Ke-Tor's eyes. Failure was just as bad as betrayal. Didn't Khan know when to stop fighting his fate and just accept his demise? He knew now that if the magical blast that emanated from Am-Ohkre in his death throes didn't kill Khan, then he'd have to do it personally. The code and blood demanded it. If he did not kill Khan, then Khan would kill him, if Am-Sultain didn't beat him to it.

Ke-Tor had rested most of the night huddled like a poor Kesh beggar in the streets of Keshtor, trying to keep the chill from him. Luckily, his cloak was still functioning and it radiated warmth throughout the night, and he had wrapped it around himself tightly, sleeping fitfully till dawn. Now he arose and continued walking . . . walking of all things! Him! The most experienced and skilled wizard in all of Kesh, destined to be an Arch-Mage himself, and he was reduced to the mere act of walking. Curse them. Curse them all.

There was no escort present. As far as he could tell, they had rallied around Am-Ohkre and were following him under the river when disaster struck, disintegrating them all. Even the few wounded and dead on the shoreline nearby were immediately transformed into a pile of ash and vapor. He was much closer to the Mage than those Ulathans, and curse him, Khan, across the river, all except the bane of Ohkre, the Arden.

There would be hell to pay if Am-Sultain found out an Arden had eluded detection by Ke-Tor himself. Perhaps it was for the best that there were no survivors in that epic battle between Mage and druid. Ancient avatars from an age of greatness and power reduced to some sort of mutual destruction, such a waste. Even the Arden had died, though he found it extremely odd that his body, which had transformed into a pile of ash, had somehow held its form. He saw the body standing there, ash a pale grey instead of black.

Time! Ke-Tor needed time to think, plan, and regroup after yet another fiasco in Ulatha. The Kesh didn't need any enemies. They were doing a fine job of failure on their own without much need for any interference. Yes, time was what Ke-Tor needed. He would return to Korwell and regroup, forming an impenetrable fortress of defense that would fortify their gains until his new apprentice, Zorcross, arrived and until Am-Sultain or Am-Shee contacted him. He'd find an excuse, and the blame and debt would be laid at Ohkre's feet. No need for respect and formalities now when referring to the former Mage. Ohkre had met his match and doom in Ulatha, and Ke-Tor would fill the vacuum and void created by it.

Perhaps indeed this was the most successful outcome for Ke-Tor personally, if not Kesh in general. Ke-Tor smiled to himself and picked up his pace. He wanted to be safely behind the high walls of the ancient Korwell castle before nightfall, if he could manage it.

Targon had relieved Will on watch. The Kesh were put in the barn, and the door was blocked with a thick plank of wood across two metal latches with Core sleeping just outside the doors keeping watch. Despite the massive guard, the Ulathans decided to take turns keeping watch, with Horace and his crossbow taking first shift, followed by Will. Now the sky in the east started that all too familiar glow as the twin sisters had ran

from the dragon's fire and set in the west and the birds starting singing their songs of morning and lightness from nearby.

"Good morning, Targon!" Marissa said as she quietly came out the front door of the cabin.

"Morning, Marissa. You're up early today," Targon responded.

"Too much snoring between Horace and Will. Hard to sleep, you know?"

Targon stood and stretched as he looked back at the cabin while Marissa came and stood next to him. "I thought Horace and Emelda were in that back bedroom next to the ladies?"

"They are, along with Yolanda and Amy, but I can hear the old man snoring from the next room, and Agatha curses in her sleep."

"She does what?" Targon asked, wiping his eyes and having a good stretch.

"She mumbles in her sleep, mostly bad words, ones my papa never approved of, and sometimes she cries, too."

"I had no idea," Targon said, surprised.

"Well, don't tell her. She'll scold me for sure if you do. Did you want to talk to Lady Salina?"

"What now? Isn't she still asleep?" Targon asked, stretching his arms out and moving wildly about, trying to get the sleep out and the circulation up.

"No, silly, she's been at Cedric's bedside near the hearth all night. You'd have known that if you didn't insist on sleeping on the porch, especially since this is your own house. You know some of the older ladies think you're upset that we're here. 'A burden' I think they said we were to you."

"Nonsense," Targon replied, stifling a yawn and moving about in a circle. "You are all most welcome here. 'Tis only my preference being a woodsman to enjoy the fresh night air is all," he finished with his most convincing voice that he could muster for such a time in the morning.

"If you say so, Targon."

Targon looked at her sideways and then back to the barn and then back to her again. "Do me a favor for five minutes and keep a watch on the barn. Holler if anything is amiss."

Marissa nodded and sat down on the log seat he had just vacated, so he turned and entered the cabin. Sure enough, Will was lying against the far wall on a bed of spare cloths and a blanket, snoring loud enough to fill the room. Cedric was on Targon's old makeshift bed near the hearth, and Lady Salina had kept the fire stoked well all night, as the common room was unusually warm for so early in the morning. He walked over to where Salina sat and pulled up one of the chairs to sit across from her, Cedric between them on the bed. "How is he doing?" Targon asked.

"The Kesh man saved his life," Salina responded without looking up as she gazed at her son intently.

"Really?" he asked, surprised but pleased. "Will you not rest now?"

"Not yet. His fever burns but not as bright as his entire body is warm, so I am keeping him cool with cloth and water," she said softly.

"Very well. I'll inform the sorcerer that he has avoided your wrath for now."

Salina then did look up at him and smiled. "He will be happy to hear that, though there is much to pay for what they have done."

"Agreed, my lady. Care for your son and I will return shortly."

Salina nodded in agreement and continued with her care of wiping her son's body down with a cloth dampened with cool stream water from Bony Brook. Targon looked around and then left his home, relieving Marissa, who ran around back to start collecting some potatoes for breakfast. Targon walked over to his small shed that acted as a barn and unbolted the door, lifting the wood plank from the two latches secured on either side of the door. Core stood on all fours with a grunt and moved away from the door. Targon realized he was starting to get too comfortable around this wild animal, but the feeling just came naturally to him.

"Rise and shine, gentlemen," Targon said politely, viewing the two men who were just now stirring from the noise made by his efforts to open the door. "It appears, Mister Khan from Kesh, that your life has been spared today by Lady Salina. Her son lives."

Khan brushed some straw from his cloak and clothing and gingerly brushed his burned hand that had yet to receive any kind of treatment. "That is good to hear. I trust we have some kind of understanding, then?" he asked.

"We do have an understanding, but trust we do not. That would have to be earned, though I can say I never thought a brigand from Kesh would use magic to heal an Ulathan."

"Normally, you would be correct in your assumption, Master Targon, but I am no brigand and helping the young man seemed the right thing to do knowing he would die if I didn't. Don't mistake my actions for too much altruism, however, as things would have gone worse for my companion and I had the young man died. Saving him assisted my cause."

Targon eyed the young sorcerer carefully. He was pale and almost seemed fragile, if not actually harmless, but with his own eyes he had seen fire magically called forth from the man's staff, so he knew better. "What exactly is your cause now if not to imprison me and my fellow Ulathans?"

"I have no desire to subjugate your fellow citizens," Khan replied. "That is for another, *sorcerer,* as you call one of us. I was doing my duty to my own realm and order: however, the equation has changed since we first met on the river and you almost killed me with one of your arrows. Do you remember?"

"Hard not to. You almost killed me with one of your magical fire orbs. I just ducked in the nick of time."

"May we step out into the fresh air?" Khan asked, motioning past the door.

Targon stepped outside. "Carrot, let them outside. If they try to run, kill them."

"That is most reassuring in the most disturbed way you could imagine," Khan replied as he and Dorsun stepped outside and took deep breaths of morning air while looking to the east, awaiting the sunrise that was soon to come.

"You need to take care of your hand, Master," Dorsun said, looking down at Khan's hand where it was burned almost black from wrist to knuckles across the backside.

"Well, for this burn the Arella leaf would help, if our benevolent captor will allow for it," Khan said, lifting his hand for inspection, turning it to and fro, frowning at the color of the skin.

"You seem well spoken and educated for a Kesh. Not what I was used to seeing from a brigand," Targon said warily.

Khan put his hand down. "I have mentioned this before. I am no brigand. I am of the wizard caste, rulers of Kesh and defenders of the order. Dorsun here, is a Kesh chieftain, a leader of a Kesh tribe and commander of troops. Indeed, some of our fellow Kesh are . . . shall we say . . . less than educated and less in stature, but we tolerate them for expediency sake, if not morally."

"You lost me there, Mister Khan, but I get your gist." Khan frowned at this but remained silent, if not a tad indignant. "There still remains the matter of what to do with you and your chieftain. In Ulatha, it is not considered wise to allow a brigand to sleep near you. One may never awake after having his throat cut."

"A wise philosophy to follow, but I would prefer something more genial from those whom I helped to save a friend's life," Khan countered.

"We'll see. Have a seat on the porch and I'll try to get you both something to drink and eat and some salve made from Arella." Targon motioned to the porch, and Core followed them over.

Soon, the group arose early, and Horace came out to resume his guard with Emelda by his side, while Agatha complained of having to eat potatoes and cabbage all the time. Most of the others couldn't understand

her distaste, but Salina explained that Agatha was the court cook and prepared meals for King Korwell and his family, retainers, and courtiers, and she was used to having a much broader range of produce to choose from. "Let her eat dirt," Horace had remarked once upon overhearing this, and the others chuckled at the grumpy old man.

It was not long before Monique came out and asked for Targon and Salina. She had found a crude letter folded and sealed with what looked like a dab of candle wax. It was a letter, all right, and they opened it, as it was addressed to Targon Terrel. Salina read the letter aloud.

Master Terrel,

If you are in receipt of my missive, then I fear grave danger awaits you and your companions in the near future. I cannot describe in a mere few words what you must imbed into your soul in order to prevail against the forces that have arrayed themselves against you, your companions, and our beloved mother, Claire Agon. I have done what I could over the centuries and have prepared recently to the best of my limited abilities in order to assist you, but I fear it will be too little too late.

The most important mission for you, my young Zashitor, is to keep the guardian of the forest asleep, at least until the time of arrival of our father, Dor Akun. I have left a scroll with instructions for you in my humble abode. I know you will have the urge to satisfy your curiosity in this matter, but it may be for the best if you restrain yourself from looking upon the guardian, at least until such time, as you have the necessary tools to assist you in this matter. Time is short, despite the many centuries that have marked its passage, and I bid you luck and success in protecting our Agon.

Yours in friendship despite the brevity,
    Elister

P.S. Core will be able to guide you.

Several others had gathered around Targon and Salina as they read the letter, and stared at one another in silence for a long moment before Will spoke aloud. "What does it mean guardian of the forest?"

Targon took the letter, looking at it intently again before handing it back to Salina. "He spoke of this before, but I thought him a bit senile if not mad and just assumed he was referring to himself. Certainly he was the guardian, no?" Targon asked, looking around for reassurance.

Several others nodded or shrugged their shoulders in ignorance. "He was certainly our savior with what he did and all at the river yesterday," Horace finally said.

"I'll need to take the bear with me, so we'll have to double the guard on our Kesh guests," Targon said, motioning to the barn where the two men stood.

"Why do you keep calling them guests?" Marissa asked innocently.

Targon chuckled for a second. "It's something the old man Elister always said when referring to them. No matter that now. Elister is gone and these men are our guests, for better or for worse. I saw that sickly evil-looking fellow over there hurl a ball of magic at his Kesh companion across the river. Had I not seen it with my own eyes, I wouldn't have believed it."

"He also saved my son's life, did he not?" Salina said.

"Aye, he did, my lady, cutthroat that he is," Horace responded. "Don't you worry, lad, we'll take care of them for you. Who will you choose to go with you to Master Elister's abode?"

Targon thought for a moment before responding. "I think it best if I go alone with the bear." He was thinking, however, that the warning about whatever lurked in Elister's home was best encountered without the frailer and easily frightened city folk.

No one protested, and soon, the group was preparing for the day with the additional responsibility of guard duty being thrown into the mix. Targon prepared his pack and weapons and was ready to leave after having a bit of morning potatoes fried over his hearth by Olga. When

he looked for the Kesh and didn't see them, he asked Marissa, who was walking with him, "Where are our guests?"

"Around back. Want to see them?" she said, a smile on her face.

Targon nodded and went around to the back of the cabin and found Horace with his feet kicked up on a rock as he sat leaned back against the cabin wall, crossbow in hand aimed rather closely at the garden patch where he saw both the sorcerer Khan, and his bodyguard, Dorsun, tilling and weeding the ground. "What's this?"

"We gots to eat, so Agatha put them to work the same as the rest of us," Horace said.

Targon nodded in agreement, not envying the Kesh their time with Agatha overseeing their job duties, and walked up to Khan, who seemed to be doing a mediocre job at creating a furrow in the ground for seed planting. "Hoi, Khan of Kesh. I have to leave for a day and will be taking our protector with us, but don't underestimate these people. They will kill you if either of you try to leave or harm them." And he looked sideways at Dorsun, who had stood from his kneeling position where he was putting pumpkin seeds into the ground. "And if for any reason you are successful in harming my companions or escaping, the bear and I will track you down personally and see to it that your miserable lives are terminated and your bodies left to rot on top of Agon's bosom."

"No need for bluster, Ulathan. We will respect the situation as it is for now, though I fear I am wasting my time when there is need to pursue my feud," Khan said.

Targon looked him in the eye and then put his hand out in a gesture of greeting. Khan looked at it for a long moment and then grabbed Targon's elbow in his palm and returned the gesture in true Kesh fashion. "I thank you for saving the lady's son Cedric. For that, you have my gratitude. Now help us to rebuild and you will have my respect," Targon finished, withdrawing and nodding. Khan simply nodded in return and then, without another word, turned back to his task at hand. Dorsun eyed Targon warily and, with one last look at his master, knelt back down and continued his work as well watching Targon walk away.

"He looks very much like his brother," Dorsun whispered, continuing his work. "Do you think he knows?"

"You mean about his brother? If they are the same Terrels, and they very much look alike, then I would say he still does not know," Khan said, looking to see if they could be overheard amidst their duties.

"He won't be happy when he learns that his brother is a traitor," Dorsun said, his tone serious.

"Indeed he will not, and I am not sure his brother will be pleased to learn that we took his family either. Not if he survived," Khan whispered back.

"Best not to be at that family reunion," said Dorsun.

"Agreed," Khan answered, renewing his work in the garden without saying more.

Targon waved farewell to his companions and promised to return within two or three days, not being real sure how far he had to travel, but he knew it couldn't be outside the forest, which meant not more than that amount of time to make his journey and retrieve what Elister had left for him. Marissa accompanied him as far as Bony Brook before she turned back, and Targon found himself passing his old oak tree he had used for firewood, and it brought back memories of his family.

Core led the way, often looking back to make sure he was following closely because the trees soon got dense, and Core headed straight into the heart of the forest.

They took no breaks, and Targon didn't complain. Nightfall came, and the bear stopped to allow Targon to sleep. Core curled up between the roots of two large cedar trees, nestling himself amongst the pines on the ground. Targon ate an apple and some dried veal from his earlier success and drank plenty from one of his two flasks before he lay out his blanket and, using his pack for a pillow, fell soundly asleep.

Core had awakened well before dawn and had roused Targon from his slumber. Targon was used to getting up early on the homestead, but he swore it was more like the middle of the night, but he didn't complain and gathered his pack and only drank from his flask before continuing on.

They only traveled till about noon when Core seemed to stop and smell the air. Certain he was near, they continued into a forest meadow where before there had been nothing but dense trees. The meadow had yellow Arella flowers along with equally bright yellow sunflowers and tall green meadow grasses that grew abundantly in the soft sunlight. In the middle of the meadow, Targon saw a huge hill, like a large mound a few hundred feet high, and the top and sides of the hill were covered in trees. Oaks, pines, cedars, and adler brushes grew all around it like a woodland crown on the head of a forest king.

Core never stopped and headed right to the hill's base. At first, it wasn't visible, but as they were almost to the base of the hillside, Targon's sharp eyesight saw the stone arch made of grey and black granite over a set of double doors made of ancient dry petrified wood and bound with iron hinges and latches. The huge doors were closed, but there was a latch that was made of a hoop of iron, and it was sticking outward invitingly.

The bear grumbled and swayed its head at the door. *Open.* Targon heard again the child's voice he had heard the day before. He looked intently at Core and just nodded, understanding somehow the communication but not wanting to question the details of why he was hearing this wild animal use human words within his own head. It wasn't just the fact that this was happening but that if he were to imagine any human voice associated with the extremely large ursine, he had imagined it to be a deep voice like that of Will or a captain of the king's guard, not the voice of an innocent young child. The spectacle humbled him in ways he had never imagined.

Targon took grasp of the iron ring and pulled. The door swung outward much more easily than he had expected, considering its size.

He peered inside as Core stood motionless. He took this to mean the bear would not enter further, and so reluctantly, Targon entered the short corridor alone.

The corridor ended at a large room which was illuminated by natural sunlight coming through small stone shafts set at angles against the hillside. The room was spartanly furnished: a couple of wooden chairs sat around a small table. A cupboard stood against one wall with wooden crockery and utensils scattered on it. A painted picture of a woman sitting on a rock near a waterfall surrounded by trees hung from over a stone hearth. Targon marveled at the painting, which was very lifelike, and he had only heard of such things residing in the large cities to the south. It seemed almost out of place within Elister's cave home.

In the middle of the table lay another piece of parchment similar to the letter he had read the day before. It was laid out at the corners by tiny knickknacks the old man had lying around: a small vial of ink stoppered with cork at the end, a cup stained with tea inside its rim, a small book, and a piece of pottery shaped like a horse rearing on its hind legs. Targon took the items and moved them away so he could pull the paper closer to him, and began to read.

Oh dear. You're reading this, so things have indeed gone poorly for me as I much feared. We have no time for pleasantries, so I'll be quick about this, Master Terrel. The people who took your family you call Kesh, but they are more than brigands and outlaws. They were once a civilized society that ruled many lands and traded as a cultured and well-mannered people. If not for a bit of pride and an occasional tad of envy, we could have always called them neighbors, but that was long ago and things have changed.

You'll be wanting to free your family, and I understand that anything I could ask of you would not have the same sense of urgency nor priority as this one desire you hold dear to you. After you free your

family, I have need of your services most likely for the rest of your life, but if you don't complete your first desire, there will be no room for mine.

Therefore, I have decided to assist you with your first desire. In order to face the Mages of Kesh, you must be better prepared and with more than just your courage, bow, or axe. I urge you first to seek the Shield of Ulatha that once belonged to Uthor, the rightful Duke of Ulatha, ruler of its capital, Ulan Utandra, Defender of the North, when he ruled kindly and justly under the good king Roarwell of Tyniria in the realm also known once as Akula.

The shield was enchanted with the ruins and hieroglyphs of the ancients, and was proof against offensive magic and dragon's fire. It is priceless but has been lost to our knowledge. The duke was rumored to have given it to his nephew, Andrew, before the great cataclysm of Dor Akun after the Great War.

The historian Diamedes may have learned where Andrew took it, and it may be found in his book of Ulathan history that was located in Korwell. The book had a red binding gilded with copper and decorated on its cover with the sygil of Diamedes. Your young friend Cedric may have seen it if it survived after all these years. Search there first and recover the shield. Without it, you will be vulnerable to the sorcery of the Kesh and unable to secure the release of your family. Find it and free them.

Finally, for my task. The guardian sleeps, and my spell will allow her to sleep for another summer and into winter, but she must be managed and this can only be done by securing the ancient Draconian Rod of Agon. I have left a small book on this table, and it contains my notes on where this is located. Do not wake the guardian and do not tell anyone else of her presence. With the rod and her proper name, you can command her. Her true name is secret, ageless it was, and yet deadly. Utter it not without the rod, for she will hear it in her sleep and it will command her to awake. Destroy my letter after you memorize it and again, utter it naught without the rod. Her name is Ariella Zaloynaya Drakona. Now, waste not time and save your family. I am with you in spirit if not body, young master Terrel.

Your friend, however brief that was,
    Elister.

P.S. Sorry I referred to her as a he, but you'll understand soon enough.

Targon looked at the note in the smooth flowing script Elister scribed and felt a pang of guilt at all that had transpired so far. He wondered at the events and understood the world was a much bigger place than he had imagined, and what of this guardian Elister wrote of so sinisterly? Targon put the letter down and proceeded to the back of the room and the lone door there, opening it. There was a tunnel that delved down deeper into the hillside but was darker than night. No shafts illuminated it from above. He grabbed a brand from the hearth, and it burned faintly as he proceeded down the tunnel as quietly as he could. Soon, he sensed the tunnel ended with a large boulder almost blocking the exit.

He edged by the side of the huge rock and entered into a large cavern that must have been hollowed out right under the hillside, but it was pitch black except for the faint illumination of his brand that just barely lit the area but enough for Targon to gasp at what he saw. There, lying in the middle of the cavern, eyes closed, head between its massive front legs, wings tucked into its side, was an enormous sleeping green dragon.

Targon gasped for air, the sound echoing in the dark chamber, and he cringed at the loudness of his own breathing. In shock, he was only able to mutter two words. "Bloody hell."

EPILOGUE

SCHEMING

Sultain skulked as he reviewed the situation at hand. He had no word from even the messenger birds on events happening in Ulatha, and Am-Shee seemed mired down in a fierce battle of attrition with the Rockton partisans. He had waited too long to be thwarted now by these rag-tag fiefdoms bordering Kesh. No, when Father Death, Dor Akun, arrived, he would be ready to retrieve the Staff of Alore and with it, he could dominate all of Agon. The ancient artifact wasn't created for that purpose, but as the High-Mage had learned many years ago, it could be bent to the will of a powerful wizard, and Sultain imagined himself to be that individual.

First, however, he had to have the necessary magical tools to make the leap from Agon to Akun when the two planets were closest. It was still risky, and more than one Arch-Mage had made the attempt and failed, but where they had met nothing but defeat, the great Sultain would succeed. He was sure of it. He needed the scrolls and information they contained within, however, and those were either located in Ulatha and Rockton or the information to obtain them was located within those two realms.

Decades ago, the Kesh were too weak to launch any assault more than just a pillaging raid or a hit-and-run attack, but Sultain had seen to it that the wizard ranks had grown. Less of his order met with untimely fates and accidents, and the ranks of the brigand caste was swollen with captured slaves and orphaned children of all races of Agon.

Sultain would recruit the barbarians of the North, as well as having already signed a pact with the master assassin of Balaria and his guild to work toward this one common goal. The stone trolls were proving useful if hard to tame, and he would soon have the aid of the clerics of Akun, death worshipers and fanatics of destruction.

Indeed, the worst was yet to come for the haughty realms of Ulatha, Rockton, and the rest of the miserable fiefdoms littering the once proud lands around and near Kesh.

Sultain smiled.

CONTACT THE AUTHOR

MAILING LIST

If you liked this book, please feel free to sign up for Salvador Mercer's mailing list to receive news on new releases with special discounts, as well as information about the world of Claire Agon. Sign up in one of three ways:

1. Click here if your reader allows the hyperlink.
2. Go to my website: www.salvadormercer.com/ in your web browser, and then click on the red link near the bottom to sign up.
3. Finally, put the following MailChimp link into your browser, and because it is cAsE sEnSiTiVe, make sure to use lowercase letters: eepurl.com/benueb.

As always, your email address will never be shared with any other entity and MailChimp makes it easy to unsubscribe at any time. I hate spam mail too, so my use of the mail list will be both relevant and judicial in nature.

REVIEWS

This book is an independent work, and because honest reviews are critical to the success of an independent book, I'd be grateful if you would consider leaving one on Amazon, Goodreads, or wherever you picked it up from. Thanks in advance for your honest feedback and critique.

CONTACTS

If you'd like to contact this author for any reason, and I'd love to hear from you, then you can reach me by the following means:

By email: salvador@salvadormercer.com
On Facebook: facebook.com/salvadormercerauthor
On Twitter: @Salvador_Mercer
On Goodreads: Salvador Mercer

ABOUT THE AUTHOR

Salvador Mercer loves to read. Having read the works from Tolkien, McCaffrey, Donaldson, Asimov, Burroughs, Crichton, and many others, the desire to write took over the once sane man and now he finds himself immersed in telling tall tales and intricate fables from this world, and across the stars to many others.

His stories are inspired by past author greats, but written and moved forward by Mercer who sincerely hopes that the stories delight and entertain the reader. He invites you to enter the worlds and realms of his books, and hopes you share with him your experiences there.

Salvador Mercer is fluent in English, Russian and Spanish, having served in the US Army, 750th Military Intelligence Brigade as a Russian Voice Intercept Operator, works in the field of Public Transit, loves languages, history, reading, boating, traveling, and science. He lives in Ohio with his three boys, a baby (elf), toddler (hobbit), teenager (orc), and wife, Masha.

APPENDIX A

THE "SCIENCE" OF CLAIRE AGON

Claire Agon is the second planet orbiting Tau Ceti, located just less than twelve light years from our own planet Earth. It circles its star in the habitable zone, just over two-thirds of one AU, or astronomical unit, which is the distance of Earth from the sun. This places it in orbit about the same distance around Tau Ceti as Venus is to Sol. It has an atmosphere similar to Earth's, but it is different in composition, because the inhabitants of Claire Agon are silicon-based life forms, not carbon-based as on our planet.

Claire Agon has two companion moons about half the size of Earth's moon, but circling the planet much closer, four times closer, in fact. The two moons are tidally locked to Claire Agon, each showing the same face to the planet. The two moons in the common tongue are called Tira and Sara, in that order. Tira rises first, followed a few hours later by Sara. Both moons are named for Claire Agon's daughters in Agonian mythos. Lunar eclipses are not uncommon due to the close orbits of the two moons to the planet, and a full lunar cycle occurs approximately every nine days. Both moons are much like small Agonian worlds, and their blue, green,

and white cloud-tipped atmospheres can clearly be seen from the surface of Agon.

Claire Agon, or simply Agon in the common tongue, isn't the only planet circling Tau Ceti. Recently on Earth, astronomers have detected up to five planets circling the class G star, which is similar in type to our own Sol, but it masses only four-fifths that of our own sun. The astronomers are almost correct insomuch as the system actually has six planets. One planet, however, they could not have imagined; it circles Tau Ceti in an elliptical and eccentric orbit, tilted at thirty degrees above the solar plane. That planet is the size of our own Neptune, but instead of being a gaseous planet, it is a rocky planet, with a huge mass relative to Earth and an atmosphere and magnetosphere in a class unto itself. Agonians call this planet "Dor Akun," or "Death World," though the term "Father of Death" is also used, depending on the culture.

Dor Akun orbits Tau Ceti once every two hundred years, and when it approaches perihelion, or its closest approach to the star, it actually comes *within* the orbit of Claire Agon. In addition to this, Claire Agon is also pulled by the gravitational force of Dor Akun, to the point that it, too, reaches perihelion and does so at the same time as its bigger mate, Dor Akun. During this time Dor Akun is a mere million miles from Claire Agon, and it reaches perihelion exactly on the solar plane where Agon orbits Tau Ceti, thus eclipsing Agon as it transits from perihelion and begins its slow, arduous journey up and back to its aphelion, to begin the cycle all over again.

The eclipse lasts an entire Agonian month, and its tidal forces pull mercilessly on the smaller Agon, flexing its crust and creating huge tides and displacements of waters both great and small. Agon is cast into a cold, dark, month-long isolation, suffering immense damage to life there.

Fortunately for those who live on Agon, the event occurs only once every two hundred orbits of Agon and once every orbit of Dor Akun. Where the two planets actually cross orbits, the larger planet, Dor Akun,

is inclined by several million miles, and so the paths of the two planets never cross.

Some Earth-based scientists, if they could witness the odd but regular orbits of Agon and Akun, might conclude that the event will eventually decay the Agonian orbit to the point where it either degrades into Tau Ceti, in a spectacular but deadly spectacle of death, or, more likely, on one pass, it will be captured by Dor Akun and her orbit will take her into the deeper regions of Tau Ceti space, where it is cold and dark and eventually even silicon-based life would freeze to death.

This, however, isn't the only thing that occurs during the transit event. On Earth, we are protected from radioactive particles by its magnetosphere. In Agon the sphere is weaker and charged particles rain down from Tau Ceti yearly, but during the transit event the great magnetosphere of Dor Akun acts much like a wing does on a modern-day airplane as it slices through the air; it funnels a steady stream of highly charged particles from the local star around itself and onto the surface of Claire Agon every two centuries. The phenomenon causes mutations in the silicon-based life forms of Claire Agon, and so evolution there takes place at a much more rapid pace than it does on Earth.

Such are the science of Claire Agon and its dance of death and change with its bigger mate, Dor Akun, all around a nondescript class G spectral star located not very far from our own sun. Thus magic is created and dragons are born.

APPENDIX B

RANGER RISING GLOSSARY

A   Agatha, Elderly woman, Ulathan refugee, lead domestic cook of King Korwell

Agon, Short common name for Claire-Agon

Alar Thorton, Father of Marissa

Am-Ohkre, Kesh Arch Mage, leads attack on Realm of Ulatha

Am-Shee, Kesh Arch Mage, leads attack on Realm of Rockton

Am-Sultain, High Mage of Kesh

Am-Sunsi, Arch Mage of Kesh, deceased

Amy, Daughter of Yolanda, Ulathan refugee, 3 years old

Ann Terrel, Targon's sister, 8 years old

Arella, Flower with leaves that have healing properties

Argyll, Falcon, friend of Elister

Arkhale, Kesh Lieutenant to Hork

Arnen, Ancient Order of Druids

B   Balaria, Island realm, known for its thieves and assassins

Baldric Terrel, Targon's father

Bandit War, Kesh raids into Ulatha seven years earlier

Blackthorn Forest, Common name for the Earlstyne Forest

Bony Brook, Small brook near the Terrel homestead

Border Mountains, Common name for the Felsic Mountain range separating Kesh from Ulatha

Boxer, Kesh brigand scout

Bran Moross, Captain of the King's Guard, married to Salina Moross

C Cedric Moross, Son of Salina, 18 years old

Celeste, Elderly Ulathan woman, Ulathan refugee

Claire-Agon, The planet/world

Clairton, A small forest bird, favorite of Dareen Terrel

Company Bloody Hand, Kesh brigand group

Company Iron Chain, Kesh brigand group

Company Iron Hand, Kesh brigand group

Company Red Throat, Kesh brigand group

Core, Nickname for Corrack, the brown bear

Corrack, Brown bear, friend of Elister

Craylyn, Balarian assassin

Cree, Ulathan town south of Korwell

Critir, Magic Orb used for communication and divination

Cutter, Kesh brigand

D Dareen Terrel, Targon's mother

Diamedes, Ancient Ulathan historian, deceased

Dor Akun, Sixth and largest planet in 200 year orbit around Tau Ceti

Dorsun, Kesh brigand chieftain

E Earlstyne Forest, Ancient name for the Blackthorn Forest

Elister, Druid of the Arnen

Emelda, Elderly woman, Ulathan refugee, Horace's wife

F Felsic Mountains, Ancient name for the Border Mountains

G Gregus River, Ancient name for the Rapid River
Grinder, Stone troll, in the service of Kesh
Gund, Kesh brigand lieutenant

H Hans, Soldier of Korwell
Horace, Old man, Ulathan refugee, husband of Emelda
Hork, Kesh brigand chief, leader of the brigand armies into
   Ulatha

I Inga, Server at the Pickled Pig Tavern in Korwell

J Jons, orphaned boy, Ulathan refugee, 9 years old (Jonathan)
Julia Terrel, Grandmother of Targon

K Karz Moross, Son of Salina, Ulathan refugee, 5 years old
Ke-Grenson, Kesh Wizard, Assistant to High Mage Am-Sultain
Kendral, Balarian assassin, employed by Kesh
Kesh, Wizard/Brigand land east of Ulatha
Keshtor, Capital of Kesh
Ke-Tor, Kesh wizard, mentor to Khan
Ke-Torra, Arch-Mage of Kesh, lived 1000 years ago, started the
   Dragon-Wizard War
Ke-Urns, Kesh wizard perished in Rockton campaign
Khan, Apprentice wizard of Kesh/Ke-Tor
King Korwell, Ruler of Ulatha
Kovar, Soldier of Korwell
Kritor, Kesh Lieutenant to Hork

L   Luc Terrel, Grandfather of Targon
Lunde, Jungle of the South

M   Malik Terrel, Targon's brother
Marc Thorton, Brother of Marissa, 6 years old
Marissa, Young frontier girl, Ulathan refugee, 12 years old
Mary Thorton, Mother of Marissa
Monique, Teen girl, Ulathan refugee, 17 years old
Myrtle, The Terrel's dairy cow

O   Olga, Elderly woman, Ulathan refugee
Onyx Tower, Seat of government for Kesh, seat of the High Mage

P   Pickled Pig, Tavern near the main gate of Korwell Castle

R   Roarwell, King of Tyniria, Ancient Realm South of Ulatha
Rockton, Realm south of Kesh
Ropes, Kesh brigand

S   Safron, Realm to the south of Ulatha known for its fine tobacco
and weed
Salina Moross, Wife of the king's guard captain, mother to Cedric
& Karz
Sara, Moon of Agon, first to rise
Sarson, Old man, Ulathan refugee
Sigture, Apprentice wizard of Ke-Urns
Staff of Alore, First magical staff of Agon

T   Talaman, Healing globe
Targon Terrel, Ranger, Zashitor, Defender of the Arnen,
Protector of Ulatha

Thomas, Orphan boy, Ulathan refugee, 12 years old

Tira, Moon of Agon, second to rise

Traps, Kesh brigand

Trovis Mountains, Mountain range in the West of Ulatha

Tyniria, Ancient kingdom south of Ulatha

U Ulan Utandra, Ancient name for capital of Ulatha (Korwell)

Ulatha: Valley Realm where Targon lives, West of Kesh

Ulsthor, Western town of Kesh, closest to Ulatha

Uthor, Ancient Duke and founder of Ulatha

W Western Sea, Sea to the west of Ulatha

Will Carvel, Soldier of Korwell, sergeant of the gate guard

Y Yolanda, Middle aged woman, Ulathan refugee, mother of Amy

Z Zashitor, Ancient name for a Ranger

Zorcross, Newest apprentice wizard of Ke-Tor

15910360R00208

Printed in Great Britain
by Amazon